But

by

First For Love

TRACY STERN

SIMON & SCHUSTER

New York London Toronto Sydney Tokyo Singapore

SIMON & SCHUSTER
Simon & Schuster Building
Rockefeller Center
1230 Avenue of the Americas
New York, New York 10020

SIMON & SCHUSTER and colophon are registered
trademarks of Simon & Schuster Inc.

Designed by Laurie Jewell
Manufactured in the United States of America

1   3   5   7   9   10   8   6   4   2

Library of Congress Cataloging in Publication Data
Stern, Tracy.
But first for love/Tracy Stern.
p.   cm.
I. Title.
PS3569.T415B88   1991
813'.54–dc20   90-26755
CIP
ISBN 0-671-70079-0

For B. B., naturally.

ACKNOWLEDGMENTS

A SINCERE THANK YOU to my treasured Turkish friends who gave of their time and knowledge so generously while I was researching this book. They include Çağrı Erimtan Aker, Leyla Alaton, Yankı Erimtan, Ömer and Claudette Gabriel Karabey, Mrs. Nurettin Koçak, Zeynep Özker, Barbara Pensoy, Müberra Volkan, Haluk and Zuhal Yorgancioğlu. Mustafa and Cevahir Özkan graciously opened the historic doors of their outstanding yalı, one of the most glorious homes on the entire Bosphorus. And to Faruk Yorgancioğlu, who, over the years, has had the enduring patience to give me insight and understanding about a fascinating country and its people.

CHAPTER

1

*I*T WAS IN MAY OF 1940. There was so little time left. Even so, Cyrielle packed slowly, carefully folding and refolding each specially chosen item she would take with her. It hadn't been easy, painstakingly selecting from among all the beautiful things that hung in her spacious, well-ordered closets. The pretty party dresses and blouses, many of the cuffs and collars edged with lace or embroidered in brightly colored threads; the skirts, pleated precisely and made from the best fabrics; the collection of exquisite Hermès silk scarves, a gift left to her by her mother. As she stood before the overwhelming array, hands planted firmly on her hips, reviewing her choices, she still felt uncertain whether or not she had made the right decisions, for she really had no idea what to expect. Istanbul. The ancient Constantinople. The place that was the crossroads between the Occident and the Orient. What city could be more different from Paris? If it had been London, or Rome, or any of the other European capitals, making the choices would have been much easier. But those cities were also at great risk of being torn apart by the war, just as Paris was expected to be within weeks. The Germans had invaded the Low Countries a few days ago, and soon they would be in Paris. So Cyrielle Lazare was being sent off to Istanbul to stay with the Turans, longtime friends and clients of her family.

"You will stay there until this ghastly war is over. Just until then, Cyrielle," Maurice Lazare had assured his favorite daughter.

At first she had been vehemently opposed to the idea. "But when will that be?" she had insisted. "Why can't I go and stay with Nathalie? At least then I would be nearby. Please, Papa," she had begged. "I don't want to leave France. And what if Turkey becomes involved in the war?"

"So many questions, my darling," her father replied. "Cyrielle, I don't know how long the war will last, no one does, but the one thing I am sure of is that the Germans will be in Paris before month's end. After that, I hope it won't be long before it's finally over. But who knows what will happen? And when. As for Turkey's involvement, I feel certain that they will not become a player. They've signed declarations of mutual assistance with France, as well as with Great Britain, but right now they are maintaining a strict policy of neutrality. Their President, Ismet Inönü, has said repeatedly that Turkey would only enter the war under two conditions: if the security of the Straits, which lead to the eastern oil fields, is threatened; and two: if Bulgaria or the Greek region of Salonika is invaded. Right now, neither of those things seems likely, so I feel secure in saying that Constantinople is a safe place for you to be. Your brother and I will stay here, and if it gets too risky, if things become too difficult, then we will go to stay with Nathalie.

"No, Cyrielle, I know you would like to stay close by, but I think you had better go on to Istanbul and stay with Omer Turan and his sister for the time being. He reminds me of his father a great deal— he is a delightful young man, stable, serious, and also very interested in paintings. In fact, he already has a very nice collection of his own. Mostly Impressionists, and you certainly can't go wrong with those. He will take his father's place in the business one of these days. You know what a charming man Mustafa Turan is; he has been one of our best clients for a long, long time, and has become a very dear friend to us over the years. You will be in good hands. They are one of Turkey's premier families, and they are welcoming you into their home with open arms. From all that I've heard it is a beautiful house, situated directly on the Bosphorus. Boats are docked beneath the house itself! Like Venice. It sounds wonderful," he continued, trying to paint a rosy picture for the young girl. But inside, his heart was breaking. He loved his younger daughter, the one who reminded him so much of his late wife. "They will treat you just as they would their own daughter. You'll only have to stay until the armistice is signed and it is safe to come back, I promise you. Besides, you can continue your studies there. Where else to better learn about the porcelains you love so much? And you will be there when the collection of paintings and sculptures arrives. You can safeguard it for us until the war is over and we can bring it back to Paris and open the gallery again. You'll see, my darling, everything will be just fine," he repeated, reaching out for her and comforting her in his arms. He prayed that she would not pull away before he was able to stop the tears that threatened to fall from his troubled, weary eyes.

In the week following their conversation, Cyrielle had found little time to think of anything but wrapping up her work at the gallery and saying good-bye to her closest friends. She resigned herself to the plan, and slowly turned the prospect of travel to the exotic country into an adventure. Now that she would be leaving in the morning, her excitement was building, and she was eagerly looking forward to the trip. She was only eighteen, and she hated having her life torn apart by the war. She ached for the people whose lives had been turned upside down by the events of the past year, and she had longed to help in some way—doing volunteer work or whatever was needed—but the outbreak of war had taken all able-bodied men from the gallery, and she had been forced to spend all of her free time there. Now restrictions, worry, and an overwhelming sense of despair had taken over the streets and permeated every aspect of her old way of life. She lived with her family in a beautiful apartment on the Faubourg St. Honoré, she had masses of pretty clothes, she went to the finest private school where she had good friends, and during her spare time she did what she really liked, she worked alongside her father in his gallery. But now that the war was escalating all around them, she was looking forward to departing for such an exotic place as Turkey. She had always been fascinated by the country, and had studied its culture and heritage extensively in school. Each time Mustafa Turan came to Paris to buy another Picasso or Braque or a Giacometti sculpture from her father, she would beg Maurice to include her in the dinner plans so she could question the kind man about life in his country. She had hoped to continue studying at the École des Beaux Arts, and to specialize in the study of the famous Iznik porcelains. Now she was going to be in the country where it had all begun. Just a hundred miles or so from the very spot where so much of history was created. That was something to be thrilled about!

Of course she would miss her family, but everyone had scattered during the last year. Her older brother Alexandre had joined the resistance forces, her sister Nathalie and her husband had moved to the town of Pau in southwestern France, and Jacques, her younger brother, was always out with his friends, so she rarely saw him these days.

She had never met Omer Turan. He had been in the gallery once, stopping by to pick up a transparency of a painting his father had bought. She had been out on an errand at the time, and when she returned the secretary had raved about how handsome he was. Now she would see for herself. Tomorrow she would be driven to the station with her new passport, issued under a false name, a safe name that would guarantee her passage out of the country and on her way to the faraway shores of Ottoman civilization. She wrapped her favorite silk scarf around her head and danced about her room, her mind filled with wild imaginings of whirling dervishes and elegant palaces.

She folded the last sweater and made room for it in the small valise she was going to carry with her. Nothing too big or bulky that might attract the attention of the border guards, just a simple brown leather case that contained enough things for her to get by with until she could purchase new ones in Istanbul. She loved to shop and she fantasized about the new clothes she would find—billowy harem pants, brightly colored shawls and the loveliest blouses made from gauzy fabrics.

There was still one more thing she had to put into the case. She knew she shouldn't; if it was discovered it might place her in more danger than even the largest and fanciest of suitcases, and if her father learned that she had taken it there would be trouble, but she just couldn't leave without it. She turned slowly and walked the distance from the canopied bed to her dressing table. She would leave behind all of her mother's silver monogrammed hairbrushes, combs and mirrors, but she just couldn't leave without the drawing. She reached up and removed it from the wall beside the mahogany table. It was her most prized possession, a gift from her mother on her sixteenth birthday, just months before Dominique Lazare had died.

"A real Rembrandt?" she had squealed when she tore the wrapping paper away and the magnificent self-portrait was revealed. It was only a small work, five or six inches square, but the hand of the master was evident in every line. She treasured it more than anything she had ever owned.

"Of course it's a real one!" Dominique had countered. "Would I consider giving my lovely daughter a *copy?*" She had sounded as if it hurt her even to mention the word.

Cyrielle had run to her mother's arms. By that time the ravages of disease had reduced her once glorious face and figure to those of an old woman, although she was barely forty. Cyrielle had hugged her tightly, feeling only bones beneath the silk bed jacket.

"Thank you, thank you, Maman," she had cried. "I will treasure it forever."

"Do," her mother had said. "It is a lovely thing. Truly a work of art. Remember me when you look at it." Three months later she was dead.

Now as Cyrielle stood holding the small object, recalling the day it had been given to her, she was even more convinced that taking it along with her was the right thing to do. Hurriedly, as if at any moment she might be caught, she rushed back to her bedside, rummaged through the neatly packed bag, and pulled out a soft nightgown. Carefully she wound the silken fabric around the drawing, being sure to cover its frame completely. Then she placed the gown back inside the lingerie pouch. She felt safe; surely the customs officials would not dare to examine a lady's nightclothes. A naive young girl, she had always traveled first class, and never in wartime. Still, for the moment, she felt her drawing was secure.

Locking the valise and placing it on top of the dresser, Cyrielle went out in search of her father. He had promised to take her to her favorite restaurant that night, and in turn she had promised to stop by the gallery one last time to make absolutely certain that everything she had been working on was in order. Ever since the age of twelve, Cyrielle had worked by her father's side in the venerable Galerie Lazare. Located in the fashionable eighth arrondissement, on the narrow, charming rue de Miromesnil, it was only a five-minute walk from the Lazare apartment on the Faubourg St. Honoré. Its gracious marble facade, discreet but elegant, had welcomed the cream of the world's art collectors for over one hundred years. The gallery was always stocked with valuable works, and the warehouse in Orléans contained even more treasures. Maurice Lazare, and his father and grandfather before him, had earned their place in the top echelon of Paris art dealers. Along with having an impressive eye for spotting masterworks, Maurice was a shrewd businessman. He had secured his spot in Paris' haute society when he married the glorious Dominique Saujet, a woman considered by many to be the most beautiful mannequin the French couture had ever sent down a runway. After their marriage, Maurice and Dominique had quickly become the toast of Paris; they were fixtures at all the very best parties, they took their winter vacations in Gstaad or Saint-Moritz, and they spent summers in Provence. They were blessed with four beautiful and talented children—Alexandre, Nathalie, Cyrielle, and Jacques. It was Cyrielle who had inherited her mother's fine bone structure, her sense of grace and ease of movement. It was Cyrielle who made men's heads turn in the streets; those old enough to remember were convinced they had seen the ghost of Dominique Saujet; others merely stared at her self-assured, magnetic beauty. The remarkable resemblance was one of the reasons Maurice had become so close to his daughter since her mother's death. He had allowed Cyrielle to cut back on her course load at school in order to spend more time in the gallery. She was innately talented in the business of selling art, it came as naturally to her as a sport might have come to another child. She had a keen eye for spotting works that would sell, and she was possessed of a sweet yet effective manner when dealing with clients. He would miss her greatly now that he had made the hard decision to send her off to stay in safety until the end of the war, but he knew he had no real choice. Not if he wanted to ensure her survival. The Nazis had left him very little say in the matter.

Cyrielle entered the gallery with her key. She swung the tall doors open and paced quickly across the marble foyer to the door of her father's office.

"It's me, Papa," she announced when she heard his voice from the other side of the door.

"Come in, my darling."

Maurice Lazare sat at his desk, and, as always, his face lit up when he saw her. For a time right after Dominique died, he could not bear to look at Cyrielle, the pain of remembrance was too great. But over time, he had come to realize that his daughter was the most precious gift Dominique had left him, and he treasured her more than life itself. That was why it was so painful, as the hours grew short, to know that he would be sending her off, knowing that when he would see her again was anyone's guess.

"Cyrielle, *ma petite,* how are you? Have you finished your packing? You are all set to go in the morning?"

"Yes, Papa, but not without having a lovely dinner with you first. Are we still going to go?"

"I wouldn't miss it for anything," he said, never having spoken a truer word. "I just have to finish up some paperwork here, and then I'll be ready. Why don't I come by the apartment and pick you up at eight-thirty?"

"I'll be ready."

He was still smiling, a bittersweet smile full of hope mixed with a tremendous apprehension about the future, long after she had pulled the door shut behind her.

Their dinner was a great success. The waiters at Le Pré Catalan, the elegant restaurant in the Bois de Boulogne, hovered over the young Cyrielle as they had over her mother for so many years. Cyrielle felt like a princess, out with the most handsome and gallant of men, her father. She had promised herself, as she dressed in the outfit she knew her father liked best, and waited to hear the announcement that the driver was downstairs, that she would make this evening the most pleasant experience ever, full of laughter and lightness. There was no point in dwelling on the imminent parting. Tomorrow she would leave and the future was out of her hands. For the time being, that was. But as soon as the war was over, the very minute the armistice was signed, she would return to take her place at the Galerie Lazare. Her wonderful papa had promised her.

Things happened so quickly once they reached the train station there was little time left for a long good-bye. As soon as the man who would be responsible for ensuring her safe passage across the border into Switzerland spotted her, she was whisked away into the first compartment on the train.

"Wait a minute, please," she begged the man, but he had already taken her bag with her precious contraband and was headed toward the platform.

"No, mademoiselle, please, we have very little time. You must hurry, and you must not create any disturbance, or call attention to yourself, by going back to the car. Please, come with me at once, or the whole plan may be in jeopardy."

So Cyrielle, instead of going back for one last hug, had to be content to wave to her father, who sat in the car struggling once again to hold back his tears of uncertainty and fear.

"Good-bye, Papa, *je t'aime*. I will see you soon," she yelled from the top of the steps, over the heads of the other passengers. The man was once again at her side, and he quickly grabbed her hand, urging her to follow him. She turned back for one last glance as she boarded the train, but the car had already pulled out of sight, leaving only a sea of unfamiliar faces.

CHAPTER

2

WHEN SHE STEPPED onto the platform at the train station in Istanbul, Cyrielle was dead tired. She had finally arrived at Sirkeci Station, the terminus of the fabled Orient Express, which had first come to the city in 1888. They had faced delay after interminable delay, and what was supposed to have been a two-day trip had taken nearly five. She hadn't had a proper bath since she'd left Paris, and she vowed to soak for hours the very minute she was able to.

The first part of the trip had passed without incident, and for a few hours she was even lulled to sleep by the clatter of the wheels as they made their way southeast from Switzerland to Venice. From Venice they had traveled through Yugoslavia, making stops in Zagreb and Belgrade. At each city they were made to wait much longer than they had anticipated. A stopover of one hour often turned into a wait of six or seven hours. Each time she held her breath as the gruff border officials checked her false passport. She kept her art books on her lap, hoping that if she had to explain herself to them she could simply hold up one of the textbooks to confirm that she was only a student off to continue her studies in Istanbul. As the train passed into Bulgaria, they were again delayed, but the checks at both Sofia and Plovdiv were tense yet uneventful. But as they crossed the Turkish border at Edirne, their last checkpoint before arriving in Istanbul, a troop of soldiers boarded the train and demanded that all passengers disembark. Her hands shook uncontrollably as she handed the dark-skinned, unsmiling man her papers. She could feel the beads of perspiration dripping down the back of her blouse as he questioned her about her journey to Istanbul. She tried to remain calm, but the man's broken attempts to speak French made her even more nervous. She held back her tears, for now she was not only frightened, but exhausted as well. They had come so far, only to be held up almost within sight of the safety of Istanbul. After what seemed like hours, the man returned with her papers and pushed them toward her. She took them and held on to them for dear life. Even then they were not allowed to board again; they were forced to sit on hard wooden benches for nearly five hours while the men continued to check every piece of luggage, every box, and every parcel on the train. She hid her little valise underneath the bench and was eternally grateful that it escaped scrutiny.

Now she still clutched her suitcase tightly. It had traveled all the way without discovery, the precious drawing remaining undetected, and for that she was thankful. She had kept the case right by her side during the entire ordeal, and even now she pulled it close to her chest as a porter approached.

Her spirits brightened slightly when, immediately upon leaving the passport-control desk, she was greeted by an attractive woman whom she guessed to be in her mid-twenties.

"You are Cyrielle, I hope?" the woman asked in perfect French.

"Yes, yes . . . I am. And you?"

"My name is Semra. Semra Turan. I'm Omer's sister. I'm here to meet you and take you to our home. In fact, this is the third time we've been here. The train information is so unreliable these days, and we certainly didn't want to miss you. So we just kept driving out each time they promised that a train from Bulgaria was arriving. I'm so glad to finally see you. I was beginning to worry that perhaps you would never get out. You must be exhausted. Here, let me take that for you."

"No, no, I'm all right. I'll keep it, thank you," Cyrielle responded, pulling the case back toward her.

The woman looked hurt, and immediately Cyrielle felt bad, for she knew that Semra meant well and was only trying to help. Nothing in her voice gave the slightest hint that she was annoyed or perturbed at having made so many extra trips out to the station. She seemed genuinely concerned and happy finally to see her, and now Cyrielle had refused her sincere offer of help.

"I . . . I didn't mean to be so sharp," Cyrielle apologized. "It's just . . . yes, I am tired. The trip was much longer than I had anticipated. And I'm terribly sorry you have had to come here so many times. I feel terrible. I hope it's not a very long trip."

Semra laughed. "It's no problem at all. I was pleased to do it. As for the length of the trip, one of the first things you'll learn about this country is that nothing gets done very quickly here. *Yavaş* is the Turkish word we use to describe it. It means 'slow,' and it applies to many things. Turkey moves at its own special pace, which I'm convinced is several beats behind most other countries. Istanbul is faster than the rest of the country, but it's still not at all what you're used to. I spent a year in London, before this awful war, of course, so I know how other countries move; they have a sense of urgency about things, and it was a big adjustment to come back here. Frustrating beyond all belief," she continued, throwing her hands up in the air. "Makes you want to scream and yell, neither of which will do you any good. Anyway, I'm lucky, we have a driver, and a nice comfortable car. I usually just throw a book in the back seat so that at least I can read when I get tired of looking at the stalled traffic. And now we have each other to talk to. If you can stay awake in the car, that is. Come," she urged, taking Cyrielle's arm, but not trying for the suitcase again, "the car is waiting right out here for us."

Safely in the back of the large Bentley, Cyrielle at last let go of her suitcase. Her hand ached from carrying it, and even through her gloves, she felt the beginning of a blister.

They rode in silence for a few minutes, Cyrielle grateful for Semra's presence and concern. She had liked Omer's sister immediately. She had a warm, caring face, and bright eyes that sparkled with enthusiasm when she spoke. She was a little older than Cyrielle, and certainly shorter, but then most women everywhere were. At five feet ten inches, Cyrielle towered over most of her friends. Dominique had been even taller, but Cyrielle was thankful that she had stopped just short of six feet.

Semra had long dark hair, nearly the same length as her own, which she wore pulled back tightly into a ponytail. Their hair was practically the same color, but Semra's skin tone was much more Mediterranean. The contrast between Cyrielle's fair skin, the color of crème fraîche, and her raven hair was one of the first things that drew people's attention to her startling beauty.

"We're awfully glad to have you here," Semra said.

Cyrielle snapped out of her daydream and turned to the woman who was trying so hard to welcome her.

"I'm . . . I'm happy to be here," Cyrielle offered weakly.

"Well, I'm sure that's an exaggeration, but let's just say that we're going to do everything we can to make your time here pass in the most pleasant way possible."

Cyrielle began to relax and was suddenly very glad that it had been Semra who was at the gate as she arrived. She knew at once that she could tell her the truth about what she was feeling, and about how hard her trip had been.

"Thank you, that's really very kind. You're right, of course, leaving was awfully difficult. There is so much uncertainty in France right now. The only thing people talk about is when the Nazis will march down the Champs-Élysées. Soon, it seems. So, as hard as it was to leave my father and my brothers and sister, in a way I am really looking forward to being here. I want to study while I'm here, the famous Iznik porcelains."

"Yes, Omer mentioned that to me. It sounds wonderful. You'll certainly know more about them than I do. I never really studied them, I should have, though, they are an important part of our culture. Iznik is a fascinating place, steeped in history, as they say. So you'll just have to teach me everything you discover. In the meantime, I'll teach you other things about my country. It's really a very fascinating place."

"I know. I can't wait."

"Oh, by the way, you're probably wondering why I'm alone.

Well, there's a good, and predictable, explanation. Omer and my father have gone off on yet another business trip. They're in Ankara for the week. They'll be back on Saturday. So in the meantime you'll have a chance to catch up on your sleep and get back on your feet before the rest of the Turan clan arrives. That, I promise, is your first big break here. They can be a formidable group."

"I've met your father two or three times. I think he's a wonderful man."

"He is, indeed, he's really very special. He thinks the same of yours. You'll have the chance to spend some time with him. He's promised to stay with us for the weekend and then return to Ankara on Monday."

Cyrielle looked puzzled. Immediately Semra read her mind.

"Oh, you don't know what the setup is here. No wonder you look confused. My parents live in Ankara, where it is dark and polluted most of the time. The rest of the time it's raining. I'm exaggerating, but only a tiny bit. It is a dark, depressing place. Still, it is the capital of the country, and we do a great deal of business there. Omer is in charge of the operation in Istanbul." She laughed a warm, full laugh. "I'm the family renegade, and refuse to settle down right away, so I run the house here in Istanbul for my darling brother. And we're going to have the most wonderful time. We're going to be housemates, I guess you'd say. But don't worry for a second, you'll have your own room and private quarters. You'll only have to see us when you feel like it. We have a big house, with lots of servants, right on the water. I hope you'll like it."

With this, Cyrielle relaxed. Everything sounded as if it was going to be just fine, especially since she was becoming so fond of Semra. She was relieved that she would not have to meet the rest of the family right away. She needed a little time to rest before they returned.

Darkness settled in, and through the heavy rain that had begun just as they were leaving the airport, it was impossible to make out any of the minarets or the domes of the great mosques. She lay her head back against the soft seat, and confident in the knowledge that her mother's precious gift was now safe, for the first time since leaving her homeland she felt all of her worries drift away.

"Cyrielle . . ." She heard a voice in the distance, accompanied by a soft nudge on her shoulder. "Cyrielle, we're home."

She was startled and for a moment completely disoriented. Was she still on the train? Which border were they crossing? Then her sleepy eyes focused and she recognized Semra's sweet face. The car had stopped in front of a large house, and the door on her side of the car was open. The suitcase was no longer at her feet. She reached down into the empty space, and suddenly panic overcame her.

"Don't worry," Semra assured her. "The driver, his name is Murat, has taken your luggage upstairs to your room. It's waiting for you there. Come on, let's get you up and into a hot bath."

"I must have fallen asleep." She rubbed her eyes and breathed deeply. The rain had stopped and the atmosphere was heavy with the smell of salty air.

Semra helped her out of the car; she was so tired she was a little shaky on her feet. "Yes, I think that's a fair statement. You didn't even make a move when the car pulled into the driveway and the dogs were barking like mad."

"I'm sorry, I must really be tired."

"No apologies necessary. You've had a long journey. I'd think there was something wrong with you if you weren't exhausted. Come, follow me, and I'll show you your new digs."

Semra led Cyrielle into the house and up a grand marble staircase to the landing on the second floor. From there they walked down a long hallway at the end of which Semra stopped and motioned her to enter.

"Right in here, sleepy one. Welcome to your new quarters."

Cyrielle stepped through a narrow doorway into a bedroom that was surely twice as large as the one she had left in her apartment on the Faubourg. Beautiful peach silk curtains lined the far wall from floor to ceiling, up to a height that she quickly estimated to be four-teen feet or more. An enormous bed was covered in pretty white sheets with many pillows piled up at the headboard. It was the most luxurious thing Cyrielle had ever laid eyes on, and she would have been content at that very moment simply to strip off her soiled clothes and dive straight under the covers, there to remain for a day or two.

Just as she was contemplating this move, a door on one side of the room opened and a small woman emerged. She was not even five feet tall, and she wore a simple black skirt with a white blouse. Her head was covered with a scarf and on her feet she was wearing clogs that made a shuffling sound when she walked. She came toward Cyrielle, her head bent down, but with a shy smile on her face. She offered Cyrielle a lush white terry-cloth robe that had been neatly folded, its belt tied around it snugly.

"Cyrielle, this is Melek, she will be your personal maid. Her name means 'angel' in Turkish, and I know you'll come to think of her as one. She is very sweet and kind, and anxious to make you feel at home. Right now, I've told her to run a nice hot bath for you, and to help you unpack your things. She doesn't speak any English or French, although I know we once had a Japanese guest who taught her a word or two. But I'm not worried; I'm going to leave you two alone for a while and let you work things out. She's been with our family for a long time, and I know you'll get along just fine."

Cyrielle took the robe from the tiny woman's hands and offered her a smile accompanied by a friendly thank-you. The woman stared at Cyrielle, she seemed to be amazed at how tall she was; perhaps most of the women she had seen were Semra's height. Soon a smile replaced her look of wonder, and she returned to the bathroom to shut off the tap.

Cyrielle scrubbed every inch of her skin and washed her hair vigorously, trying to erase the scent of musty train compartments and smoke-filled stations. Then she perfumed herself and wrapped the lush robe tightly around her slim waist. Walking back into the bed-room, she heard a light knock on the door and Semra entered. Behind her followed another woman, dressed in much the same manner as

Melek, bearing a tray with a teapot, a cup and saucer and some cookies.

"Thought you might want a nice cup of tea before you turn in," Semra said, motioning the woman to place the tray on the side table by the chaise at the other end of the enormous room.

"How kind of you," Cyrielle said, walking toward her as she rubbed her hair dry with another lush towel that had been laid out before Melek left the room. "Oh, I can't tell you how much better I feel. The bath was exactly what I needed."

"And a good night's sleep. Unless you've had a sudden burst of energy and want to stay up talking all night, I'm going to leave you alone to have your tea. I'll see you in the morning, or in the afternoon, whenever you feel like getting up. In the meantime, if you need Melek for anything, just press this button by your bedside." She pointed to a small brass button located in the wall at the side of the headboard. "Otherwise, I've told her not to disturb you until she hears from you."

"That's wonderful, Semra, I can't thank you enough."

"It's nothing, Cyrielle. Welcome to the Turan house. We're glad to have you. Now get some rest and I'll see you tomorrow." She kissed her lightly on both cheeks before leaving the room.

It was only a matter of minutes before Cyrielle, after taking her first taste of the aromatic Turkish tea, which was served in clear tulip-shaped glasses, and downing two almond cookies, had slid under the covers of her new bed.

Her sleep was deep and peaceful, and she awoke to the soft sounds of gentle breezes wafting in from behind the long peach draperies.

CHAPTER

3

*I*STANBUL was not at all what Cyrielle had expected even in her wildest dreams. Formerly called Constantinople, it had served as the capital of the Eastern Roman, or Byzantine, Empire for almost eleven centuries, and had then been the seat of the Ottoman Empire until 1922. Once a city that had competed with Athens, Rome, and Jerusalem in determining the course of human events, it was today a city in chaos. The streets were crowded and hectic, the narrow passageways overflowed with people. There were no wide, manicured boulevards to stroll down leisurely, and the shop windows were filled with clothing from an earlier time, not at all similar to the latest fashions that were stocked in the many trend-setting boutiques in Paris.

Thousands of Istanbulis pushed their way through the gridlocked streets on their way to work or to do their daily shopping. All the faces were dark and foreign, and the men took on the silhouettes of pack animals as they walked hunched over, carting enormous burdens on their backs. Copper pots and pans dangled from the sides of overstuffed burlap bags filled with grain. Monstrous piles of curled rope and wooden crates stuffed full with merchandise—all were delivered by human transport. Nearly every man had a pannier strapped to his back. Shoeshine boys sat patiently in dark doorways waiting for customers, each boy with an ornate brass *sandık* poised between his gangly, skinny legs. Not more than ten or eleven years old at the most, they smiled sweetly at Cyrielle and Semra as they walked past. Murat and the car were never out of sight.

Spice vendors, fruit merchants and fishermen proudly displayed their wares in open kiosks jammed together along the sides of the already crowded streets. The women, dressed mainly in black with a long *çarşaf* or scarf draped across their faces, carefully examined the tomatoes and cucumbers, discarding the bruised ones and digging deeper into the carefully created displays in search of the perfect specimen. The city was alive with people in motion, living and shopping and conversing in the streets. For all of these reasons and more, Cyrielle was enchanted and mesmerized by Istanbul. She fell madly under its spell and couldn't seem to get enough of it.

Even the smells and the sounds of the city were totally different from any she had ever experienced. Twice a day, once at mid-morning and again just before late-afternoon teatime, the freshly baked *simit,* the doughnut-shaped breads covered with lightly browned sesame seeds, appeared at every corner. Men brought them out stacked high on large rectangular trays. As soon as a vendor set up his makeshift stand he was open for business, handing the fresh treats to waiting customers. Cyrielle was entranced by the ritual, and after her first taste of the delicious, still warm, crunchy bread, she wanted to have one every day.

The scent of meat cooking on the grills in the open *lokantas,* or restaurants, wafted out into the streets, luring passersby inside. Dark-faced men sat at small wooden tables in the glass-fronted teahouses, sipping a glass of strong *çay* or a brew of thick, mudlike *kahve.* With looks of fierce concentration on their faces, they played a game of *pişti* or dominoes or their beloved *tavla.* The sound of the dice as they ricocheted off the hard surface echoed through the smoke-filled rooms. Those who weren't playing smoked their *narghile,* the water pipe that held a thick clump of tobacco. To most visitors, the teahouses were dusty and decrepit places. To Cyrielle they were exotic and intriguing.

Outside, the fishing boats pulled in with their catch each afternoon and the strong odor of fish permeated the banks of the Bosphorus. Five times each day the haunting, repetitive chant of the *müezzin* broke through the usual cacophony of the city as he called the people to prayer from high atop the minaret. The high-pitched, monotonous wailing reminded her once again how far from home she had come. Still, she did not long for the Paris she had left, there was too much here before her very eyes, so many new and fascinating things to experience.

"Cyrielle, come on, we really have to get going," Semra urged, although she hated to tear her visitor away from the museum so soon. This was the second day in a row they had visited the mammoth Topkapı Museum. It was so filled with treasures that they were able to cover only a small area during each visit. She watched Cyrielle's eyes dance as she strolled slowly through the galleries, stopping at each showcase to savor the artifacts of the rich, ancient civilization. Every day they went out on a different excursion, and Cyrielle drank in the sights, asking question after question, never satiating her appetite for knowledge. Semra loved sharing the city with her new friend, but now it was time to go home. "I'm sorry, but Omer will be here tonight, and Seta is preparing a special welcome-home meal for all of us."

"I know, I know, I'm coming," Cyrielle said, closing her sketch pad and hurrying along.

As much as she enjoyed the monuments and the sounds of the fascinating city, Cyrielle was always glad to return to the Turan home. Since the outbreak of war in Europe the entire city was darkened at night, and behind the blackout curtains the spacious house provided a wonderful, safe retreat from events of the outside world. Her father had been right about the luxurious surroundings, and once she had had the chance to explore the enormous house, she loved it even more. It was a large wooden structure, called a *yalı*. In the era following the Ottoman conquest, these houses, among the most grand in all of Istanbul, were built along the shores of the Bosphorus, the Golden Horn, and the Marmara Sea. At the beginning of the nineteenth century it was estimated that nearly one thousand waterfront mansions lined the Bosphorus. After the First World War, many of the historical buildings were used as tobacco- or coal storehouses. Others were burned or torn down. Now less than half the original number remained. They ranged in size from small fishermen's houses trimmed with gingerbread cutouts, to magnificent mansions like the Turans'. Some, like the one belonging to them, were very special, historically significant homes and had once belonged to the sultans and other members of the royal family. Many held great secrets and stories that became the basis for Turkish fairy tales. The *yalıs* represented the lifelong efforts of powerful men and their passions, beautiful women and their loves. Over the centuries many had been the scene of lavish entertaining, visits by royalty, and critical political plannings; some even guarded the secrets of murders and other heinous crimes. The *yalıs* were mysterious buildings, practically invisible from the street. Most were hidden behind high-security gates and dense shrubbery. Once inside the private enclave, in the courtyard, there was usually a garden. The foundations of the buildings were adjacent to the waterfront, often the house itself rested on piles that had been driven into the water. Many, including the Turans', had private boat houses tucked underneath the structure, practically allowing the sea inside the house. The main orientation of the *yalı* was toward the water. They were puzzling, enigmatic buildings, shrouded in the intrigue of generations. Cyrielle was curious; she felt compelled to lift the veil and reveal the mysteries that might lurk behind the walls of the Turans' old house.

She loved her new surroundings, and she took time out each afternoon to write her father and her best friend Marie-France, anxious to tell them about all that was happening to her, hoping that they would respond with their own news about developments at home.

Her favorite place for this activity was a small room on the main floor of the *yalı,* a square-shaped, intimate room lined with banquettes on three sides that were covered in brightly colored kilims. Pillows of traditional Turkish patterns dotted the divans. The room's long windows, duplicates of the ones in Cyrielle's room upstairs, opened directly out onto the fierce waters of the Bosphorus. She loved to sit on the comfortable divans, her legs tucked up underneath her, and look out at the activity on the busy waterway. She could hear the cry of the sea gulls outside and the shrill whistle of the ferryboats. Tankers from surrounding nations plodded by. A smattering of private yachts snaked their courses bravely around them. She would squint her eyes against the blinding sun as she looked across the shimmering waterway to the Asian side of the city. She reminded herself that Istanbul was the only city in the world to stand upon two continents: to the west, Europe; to the east, Asia. Two continents that represented two totally different views of the world. For now, she was anxious to explore and learn all she could about this new one, the one that was so foreign to her. It was here, with her thoughts wandering wildly, stationery on her lap and pen in her hand, that her host, returning home, found her.

"Hello, Cyrielle," he said softly, not wanting to startle her.

She turned quickly, and saw the face of a man she knew instantly had to be Omer Turan. He was very handsome, bearing a close family resemblance to his sister. The wide features and strong jawline were better suited to a man, she decided at once. A dark crop of wavy hair was swept back, revealing an open, sincere face. He smiled warmly at her, white teeth glistening. But by far his most mesmerizing feature was his intense brown eyes. Rimmed by thick long eyelashes, they seemed to reach out with a personality of their own, shining with kindness and genuine warmth. He had a mischievous look, and if Cyrielle had not known that he was thirty-two, she would have guessed that he was in his mid-twenties. Suddenly she smiled, remembering the fuss the secretary had made when he had visited the gallery; now she knew what all the excitement had been about.

"I hope I didn't frighten you," he said, entering the room and extending his hand in greeting. His French was as flawless as his sister's. "I'm Omer."

"No, not at all," she said, putting aside the tools of her letter writing and getting up to take his hand. She was happy to see that Omer stood a good three inches taller than she. It was a nice surprise; somehow she had expected him to be much shorter. She was afraid her thoughts, meant only for herself, showed through clearly, and she chuckled nervously.

"Why are you giggling?" he asked. "Were you thinking funny thoughts just now?"

"Oh, not at all," she replied, embarrassed at her inability to control her laughter. "I was just remembering something someone said to me before I left Paris, that's all."

"Well, I'm glad it was a pleasant thought."

"Yes, it was," she said, lowering her head and trying with all her might to be serious. "Anyway, welcome home. How was your trip?"

"Oh, just another tedious business trip, I'm afraid. I should be the one asking you. You've had the far more difficult journey. Semra told me you were delayed for three days."

"Yes, it was not very pleasant, I must say. In fact, right at the Turkish border, it was downright terrifying. But it's all behind me now. And ever since I landed on Turkish soil, I've been treated like a princess. Your sister is so charming, so nice, and she has been very generous with her time. We've been all over the city, and I'm afraid I've been dragging her around far too much. But I'm just so fascinated with everything, I can't help myself. She's really spoiling me, and I hope that someday I will be able to repay the kindness."

"We're glad to have you here, Cyrielle. Your father has been a wonderful friend to my father for many years. In fact, he'll be here shortly and is anxious to see you. He says that it has been some time since he last saw you in Paris. Anyway, we're happy to show you our country. Istanbul is a big city, Turkey a big country, with many varied cultures and climates. Perhaps now that I'll be home for a while, I can relieve Semra of her duties and take you around myself."

Cyrielle smiled back at him, thinking that he had suddenly become even more attractive. "I would like that very much."

"Me too," he replied, staring back at her with his deep brown eyes.

Cyrielle felt a shiver travel down her spine. She was grateful that at that very moment Semra appeared and announced that dinner was served.

It was a mild night, and the table had been set for the evening meal out on the terrace. Cyrielle followed Omer and Semra as they joined their waiting parents.

"Welcome, Cyrielle! *Hoş geldiniz,* as we say here. It is lovely to see you again," the patriarch of the Turan clan greeted her. He rose, kissed her on both cheeks, and introduced her to his wife, Sibel, the formidable mother of Omer and Semra. She spoke only Turkish, but made herself understood with a large smile and hand gestures that assured Cyrielle she was welcome in their son's home.

Warm breezes came in off the Bosphorus and the waves lapped up against the front of the house. It was a comforting, peaceful noise that rose and then subsided as the boat traffic increased or decreased on the waterway. They sat at the round table, which had been beautifully set and graced with a colorful bouquet of spring flowers from the expansive front garden. Two servants presented them with an array of traditional Turkish hors d'oeuvres—the part of the meal called the *meze.* Lightly baked *börek,* a delicious treat made of puff pastry as thin as tissue paper and filled with feta cheese and parsley, eggplant pureed with onions, and dolmas made from grape leaves and stuffed with a tasty mixture of rice and zucchini.

"Cyrielle, would you like to try some *rakı?*" offered Mustafa. "It's practically our national drink. Here, let me pour you a glass. But remember, we do not call it 'lion's milk' for nothing. It's very potent. And also, unlike wine, your national beverage, which can be drunk alone, we never drink *rakı* without having food. It's strictly to be taken at meals. Here's how it's done," he demonstrated. "You pour a little into a glass, then you add some water. When the water mixes with the liquor, it becomes cloudy and it looks like milk, giving it its nickname."

Cyrielle smiled and gratefully accepted the drink. She liked the anisette flavor and sipped from her glass slowly throughout the dinner.

The tasty appetizers were followed by a refreshing cold yogurt soup, prepared with bits of diced cucumber and dill, and topped with a sprig of freshly picked mint. As her soup dish was removed, a sizzling skewer of delicious lamb shish kebab was placed before her. She even took a second portion when offered, a move that did not escape Omer's attention.

She felt his eyes on her and raised her face to meet his gaze. Once again, she broke into a giggle.

"I'm afraid I must apologize again," she said, trying to keep the conversation just between the two of them.

"For what? For eating so ravenously?" he teased.

"Yes. I've just been gobbling up everything in sight, don't you agree? I've been quite rude. I can't help it, it's the most delicious food I've ever tasted. I can't seem to control my appetite."

"That's quite a compliment, coming from someone with a sophisticated French palate. I'm pleased to see that the food suits you. Are you aware that Turkish cuisine, along with Chinese, and, of course, French, is supposed to be one of the three best cuisines in the world?"

"Really?" she replied, putting yet another fork laden with the delicious lamb into her mouth. She was self-conscious now and tried to slow down and be more the lady her mother had raised.

"Yes, it's true. But more important, Seta will certainly be glad to hear that you are enjoying her cooking. She has been with the family for over twenty years. My grandmother actually gave her to Semra and me as a gift when we moved here."

"What good luck for me."

"Yes," he agreed, "not everything about this house turned out as it was meant to be, but she has certainly been a blessing."

"What do you mean by that?" she asked after this ominous comment.

"Oh, nothing. Well, not really nothing. I'll tell you later."

Cyrielle tried to be content with that. "All right, at the same time I'll tell you why I started to laugh when you came into the room tonight."

"You have a deal," he said, turning his mesmerizing eyes back to his parents and sister.

They spent the rest of the evening discussing Istanbul and its history. While the servants presented them with thick aromatic coffee served in delicate hand-painted porcelain cups, accompanied by a large tray laden with peaches, figs, and grapes, plus a wide array of rich pastries, Cyrielle impressed the Turans with her extensive, detailed knowledge of the city, its buildings and history. She knew more than any of them about the porcelains and ceramics for which the country was famous.

"I had no idea you were such a student of my homeland," Omer commented.

"I told you I was enchanted by her vast knowledge of the subject. In Paris I was floored with her understanding of not only the history, but the culture and art of our civilization as well. This is a young lady who can teach you a thing or two," Mustafa Turan said. Cyrielle thought she caught the slightest hint of a mischievous smile. "Now that you're here, you can go directly to the very place where all of this began. To Iznik. Although I haven't been there for many years, the roads must be better by now. Omer, can't you find some time to go down with Cyrielle soon? She really should visit before her classes begin."

"Oh, that's all right," Cyrielle began. "I'm sure that we'll be going during the course."

"No, I'd love to go," Omer insisted, "I haven't been there myself since it was required of us in school. I've been meaning to plan a trip anyway. It's in that area where the new chrome deposits have been discovered. Yes," he said decisively, "we'll go next weekend. Would you like that?" He turned his attention to her. Those eyes. That magical smile again.

First she melted, then she beamed. She hoped that no one else at the table noticed the flush of her cheeks. "Yes, I would love it. But I don't want to be any trouble. Surely you have other plans for the weekend."

"None that I can think of. No, I don't. So, if you agree, it's all set. Next Saturday morning we'll take off bright and early so we can arrive before it gets too hot."

"Wonderful," Cyrielle said, secretly ecstatic that he had offered to take her. She looked forward to going on an adventure with this charming man to a place she had read and dreamed about for so long. Trying in vain to come back down to earth, she reminded herself that he had some business in the area, that the trip was not just for her. Still, she found it impossible to keep a very silly smile from her face.

The elder Turans retired soon after dinner; Mustafa was drained from the endless meetings and grueling schedule of their long week on the road. Semra begged off also, claiming she was right in the middle of the best book she had read in ages and was anxious to finish it. "I can't believe how caught up I am in it. It's called *Gone With the Wind,* and it's about the American South and the Civil War. Each time I put it down I can't wait to get back to it," she said, dashing off to her room before they had a chance to say a word. This left Omer and Cyrielle alone in the living room, with only the faint sounds of the servants cleaning up in the distance.

"Would you like another cup of coffee?" he offered.

"No, no, thank you." She knew that she too should probably go to bed, she was due at Robert College early the next day to register for her classes. But she wanted to stay longer and talk with him, and his next words canceled out any inclination to climb the stairs to her room.

"Come and sit with me in the library for a while then. I'm anxious to find out more about what you've seen and done so far."

She followed him into a room she had only seen in passing. It was his private room, a combination office and formal library. Except for the Turkish rugs, it was the only room in the house that was not decorated in traditional Ottoman style. It was an exact copy of an English library, complete with cherry-wood-paneled walls and brass desk lamps with green glass shades. Typical English hunt prints, framed in traditional burled woods, adorned the fabric-covered walls. Dark colors enhanced the masculine tone of the room; a mahogany coffee table was piled high with books and current magazines from Europe and America.

"I like this room very much," Cyrielle said as he beckoned her to sit on the red leather chesterfield.

"Me, too, it's really my favorite. Except for being outside on the terrace, I'd rather be in here than in any other place in the house. It suits me, and I feel very much at home here. It must remind you more of the surroundings you're used to."

At his words, Cyrielle realized that for the past three hours or so she had, for the first time since her arrival, completely blocked out all thoughts of her own family, so engrossed had she been with the Turans. The euphoric feeling she had experienced all evening suddenly left her. Her expression switched from happiness to concern, and she wore a faraway look. Omer noticed the change at once. Quickly he was by her side on the tufted sofa.

"What is it, Cyrielle? I hope I didn't say something to upset you?"

His concern was appreciated, and she managed a smile. "No, no, it's not anything you said. It's just that, well, I am of course terribly worried about my family, most of all about my father and brother. Alexandre is off with the Resistance, so there is rarely news of him. I can only hope that he is safe. And my father insisted on staying in Paris. I worry so about him. I pray every day that this horrible war will end. Have you read anything, or heard anything more about what's going on? Semra has been buying the foreign papers for me, but by the time they arrive here, the news is already two weeks old. I read yesterday about things that had happened even before I left."

"I can understand your frustration," he said sympathetically. "The news is a little slow getting here. And no, I don't have anything new to report. All I know is that here in Turkey Inönü is maintaining his policy of neutrality. There's not much more to say right now.

Even so, Turkey is trying to increase the strength of its army. At the present, it's still equipped with bayonets, which wouldn't be much of a contest against the modern aircraft and artillery, I'm afraid. What you must remember is that Turkey has no real reason to become involved. We don't have any colonial territories to protect, and we certainly don't have any desire to increase our boundaries. I know all of that doesn't do you much good when your main concern is about France. I'm sorry. Oh, Cyrielle, it must be so hard for you. I think you're being very brave about the whole thing. We've just got to keep your spirits up and your hope alive. We're all praying that the end is near."

Even as he said this he knew he was avoiding the truth. The end of the war was nowhere in sight. In fact, it was escalating at a rate beyond anyone's control. He had heard only yesterday that the German forces were moving swiftly toward Paris. The fate of this lovely girl's homeland, the most beautiful and charming girl he had ever met, seemed more in jeopardy than ever before in its long and difficult history.

"We just have to keep praying," he repeated.

Talk of her father and the war put a damper on her previously buoyant spirits, and even with the mention of their upcoming adventure, he was unable to bring back her joyous smile of earlier that evening.

Suddenly she looked as if she carried the weight of the world on her shoulders. Her eyes misted, but she held back her tears. "Please excuse me," she said, her voice weary and so different from the tone he had thrilled to just moments before. "All of a sudden I'm very tired." A glimmer of the smile returned. "Omer, I had a lovely evening. I want to thank you for all that your family is doing for me. I am so very grateful."

"Not at all," he said, rising to stand beside her. "It will be the first of many lovely evenings, I predict."

She felt that familiar shiver that seemed to pass through her every time he was near her.

"Thank you, Omer. Thank you for everything."

"Sleep well, Cyrielle. If you are not up before I go to the office tomorrow, I'll see you tomorrow night for dinner."

"Good night."

When she returned to her room, the small Rembrandt she had guarded so protectively and unpacked so carefully after its long journey was waiting for her. It held a place of honor on top of her dresser, and she had asked Semra to give Melek strict instructions not to touch it, or dust it when she cleaned the room.

Once in bed, thoughts of Omer Turan kept her awake. Her last vision was of his kind face, looking into hers with his lovely eyes. She shivered again, pulled the covers high up around her neck and drifted off into a fitful slumber.

CHAPTER

4

THE WARM BREEZE whipped through Cyrielle's long hair as they made their way southward. They drove out a little after seven in the morning from Istanbul on uneven, barely paved roads populated by donkeys and pedestrians, as well as a few cars. They made their way cautiously on the bumpy, inadequate route. Cyrielle looked out the window, fascinated by the small villages they passed. Children played outside their humble one-story adobe homes, accompanied by dogs, goats, sheep, and an assortment of chickens. Women hung the laundry out to dry. Men busied themselves with weekend chores.

The going was slow, and as they traveled on, Omer occasionally turned to her, a look of happiness on his face.

Cyrielle smiled at him. She was dressed in a pretty floral-patterned sundress that exposed her shoulders and the creamy texture of her smooth skin, which remained untouched by the sun. Her thick raven hair was held back with one of her brightly colored scarves, away from the face Omer never tired of looking at.

"Semra warned me about this dress," she had told him that morning when he came downstairs to meet her. "But I have a little jacket that covers my arms," she reassured him, "so when we visit the museums and mosques I won't have any problem. I asked her if I should change it, but she said that as long as I didn't have bare arms, it would be okay. I certainly hope she's right. I wouldn't want to offend anyone. I'm thankful that I have Semra to point out all these things. It's so different from Paris."

He thought even more of her for her considerate nature. She was determined to learn all she could about this new world into which she had been thrown. And he was just as determined to help in every way possible.

"That's good, Cyrielle. We're still a bit backward, I'm afraid. Over the last two decades, since Kemal Atatürk switched from the Arabic to the Roman alphabet, adopted the Western calendar, and prohibited the wearing of the fez, the changes have been phenomenal. Only since 1930 has the name of the city been officially changed from Constantinople to Istanbul. It's a great deal of upheaval for any group of people to handle, and particularly difficult for an unsophisticated majority like we have here. Atatürk turned this entire country into a classroom. Imagine the enormity of the task of converting people to a totally new language when all they had known for generations was the ancient Arabic. It has been an incredible undertaking. Even though women can now vote, and their testimony counts equally against a man's, instead of the old Islamic law that required the word of two women to be the same as one man's, we are still a conservative nation. The old rules die hard. People are not yet fully into the twentieth century. So I'm glad you'll be covering your lovely shoulders."

She blushed, and as he continued to stare at her he felt the same stirrings he had experienced that first moment he saw her as she sat quietly writing letters in the small room in his house. Even as she ate one of the sandwiches Seta had packed for them, he found her irresistible.

"I can't wait to get to Iznik. I've read about this place for so long now, I feel as if I know exactly what it will be like. This is really the heart of the area where it all began. Do you realize that in the sixteenth century there were over three hundred and seventy-five kilns producing tile for all of the great Ottoman mosques? Just think of it, all those magnificent blue-and-white porcelains," she said, dreaming of the beautiful objects. "Oh, Omer, thank you so much for taking me there."

"There's no place else I would rather be."

"Me neither," she replied, and the look in her eyes left no doubt in his mind that the stirrings he felt were not his alone.

When they finally reached the ancient city, after seven hours of arduous driving, Cyrielle's face held an expression of childlike amazement. Omer had arranged for a curator from the porcelain museum to meet them there. He was an old family friend who spoke excellent French, and he took them to places in the old city that were strictly forbidden to anyone other than serious scholars or those, such as Omer's family, who had connections in the upper echelons of the government.

Omer left her with the professor for an hour while he went to investigate the mines he was interested in buying.

When they stopped for an early dinner at a small local restaurant, Cyrielle showered him with her appreciation.

"Omer, that was truly spectacular! I thought I knew so much about this place, but I found out things I never even heard of before. In the thirteenth century Iznik, which was then called Nicaea, was the capital of the Byzantine Empire. That's just one of the important details I had never known.

"I know you went to a great deal of effort to get Professor Kolsal to meet us here, and I want you to know what a help he's been. Now I have a head start on my class."

"Well, I'm glad you enjoyed it. When does school begin?"

"On Monday, and I am really looking forward to it. Besides the porcelain and art classes, I have six hours of language classes a week, and one conversational practice session. Thank heavens that all the courses are given in English, although French would be even better! I'm so frustrated not being able to understand a bloody thing anyone says. I can't wait until I learn enough so that I will at least be able to follow a conversation."

"That will take no time at all, I'm certain. You seem to have a gift for languages. And you're going to enjoy the faculty at Robert College. It is the best in the country."

Robert College, where Cyrielle would be taking her classes, was the American school that had been founded in 1863 by Cyrus Hamlin, an American missionary who had worked at the Florence Nightingale Hospital in Üsküdar, across the Bosphorus in Asia. The college was named for Christopher Robert, a nineteenth-century American philanthropist who had provided the funds to construct and operate this fine institution. It was the first modern lycée of its kind in Turkey, and had deservedly won its reputation as an outstanding educational facility. Cyrielle looked forward to exploring the library, which contained an important and extensive collection of books about the country. The college had also produced some of Turkey's most important women, like the writer Halide Edip Adıvar, who had become an outspoken supporter of Atatürk's fight for independence. She had joined his forces in Anatolia and had recorded her experiences in her rich novels. It was because of brave women like her that, after the founding of the republic in 1923, Turkish women had become emancipated.

"Yes, I've heard such good things about the school, and I'm certainly looking forward to it. But right now, I'm starving. Would you mind translating the menu for me?" She smiled, leaning toward him, anxious to hear about the specialties.

She liked his kind, gentle manner. He seemed to enjoy teaching her all about his culture and his language. He never once acted as if it was an imposition to translate a sentence, or to explain what a sign along the highway meant. He was always so concerned about her, whether she was happy, always asking her if she was having a good time, and if she wanted anything at all. She was learning very quickly what a truly remarkable man she had found in Omer Turan.

As Omer had predicted, Cyrielle triumphed in both areas—her art studies as well as in the mastery of the difficult and complex Turkish language. Every night she would wait patiently for him to return from the office so she could practice what she had learned that day. By the end of the first month she could follow a conversation and was capable of holding her own with waiters and shopkeepers. Semra had taught her some slang and colloquial expressions that she used to surprise, and sometimes to shock, Omer.

On hearing one of these phrases, Omer's disdainful gaze would immediately turn to Semra, who would respond with an unconvincing "Not me!" look on her face, and a shrug of her shoulders. Then they would all break into laughter, knowing full well who had added some spice to Cyrielle's vocabulary.

On Wednesdays her first class was at eleven, and she allowed herself the luxury of sleeping a little later than usual. She and Omer had stayed up late the previous night talking and laughing, and she looked forward to her extra hour or two of slumber. But a racket from the courtyard awakened her even earlier than on other days. She rose from her bed and went to look out the window in her dressing room. A large truck had pulled into the courtyard and three men were unloading crates of various shapes and sizes. Her breath quickened and she breathed a sigh of long pent-up relief. Her father's collection had arrived safely! Weeks of worry about the fate of the masterpieces were swept from her mind. She had agonized over the paintings and sculptures, certain they would either be lost or diverted, and that she would never see any of them again. Omer Turan, she thought, what a powerful man he must be to have so quickly and so successfully arranged their transport out of France. And now they were here, safe and sound, being unloaded right in front of her eyes. Suddenly she felt that the future was bright. The war would end. Everything in the world would be right and normal and sane again. She would be able to be with her family once more. And the legacy of the Galerie Lazare would live on.

She was so anxious to go downstairs to find out more about the arrival of the precious collection that she only threw her robe around her and dashed from her room, running the length of the hallway toward the main staircase. She was traveling at a fairly fast clip when she bumped straight into Omer.

"Oh, good morning, I'm . . . oh . . . I'm sorry," she said, clutching her robe tightly around her and reminding herself that she should never have left her room in such a state. Her hands rushed to straighten her hair, but it was far too late to make any improvements in her appearance now.

"I certainly didn't expect to run into you," she continued. He was usually long gone by this hour. Even on her early days, when she had to be at school by eight, she was still in bed when she heard the crunch of the gravel as the driver pulled the car out of the courtyard.

"I know, I'm a little late today. The men arrived a few days earlier than expected, and I wanted to stick around until they finished unloading."

"Yes, I saw them. I'm so excited. The collection is finally here. I couldn't wait to get downstairs and have a look. That's why I ran out looking like this." She glanced at him, embarrassed. There he stood, towering even higher over her now that she was in her bare feet. As always, he was dressed elegantly in a finely tailored English suit, with a crisp striped shirt and lovely silk tie. She had a sudden urge to go into his arms, to have him hold her tightly, this wonderful, handsome man who was doing so much for her, who, she suspected and hoped, was being so generous because he truly cared for her, not simply because he had made a promise to her father.

He looked back at her closely, at her still sleepy face, untouched by a trace of makeup. His eyes examined her perfect skin, her sweet smile. She looked much younger than her eighteen years. Her mussed hair, twisted into soft tangles by her pillow, made him long for her with a desire more powerful than any he had ever known. He wanted to pull her toward him, to hold her, and then to sweep her into his arms and carry her right back to the bed from which she had come. It took all of his willpower to keep from doing so. He made his hands into tight fists to help fight back the overwhelming desire he had to touch her.

"Yes, it appears they're all here. Isn't it wonderful? Even I didn't expect them to arrive so soon. But I'm certainly glad to see them, too. It's comforting to know they are safe now. Shall we go down and have a look?"

"Yes, I'd like that, but I suppose I should go back and change into something a little more appropriate. I'll just be a minute."

"Don't be silly. You come just as you are. Anyway, you look lovely to me," he couldn't help but add. "Let's go and see, and then we'll have breakfast together." He could stand it no longer. He took her hand in his and led her down the stairs.

Cyrielle warmed to his touch, and she curled her delicate fingers around his. The shivers returned, and when their eyes met, she felt an intimacy with which she was completely unfamiliar.

He loved to see her smile. She watched the men as they carefully unloaded the crates and placed them in the main salon, to be opened later.

"Do you think you can wait until tonight to open all of them?" he asked her as they sat at the breakfast table eating a traditional Mediterranean breakfast of fresh bread, olives, tomatoes, cucumbers, and creamy white cheese. They were alone, as Semra had left early to catch a plane to Ankara. She would return the next night.

"It will be a long day, but I think so."

"Good. I've got to dash off now, I'm already late. But I'll be back around eight. We'll look at the paintings and then have a late dinner."

Cyrielle spent the remainder of the day thinking about Omer. Even when she was in school, where she was usually totally immersed in her studies, she found her mind wandering to thoughts of him. When the teacher called on her she was in another world, and was painfully embarrassed that she could not even attempt an answer. Instead of spending a few hours in the library after classes had ended, she rushed straight back to the house. There she carefully planned what she would wear that evening, and then she headed directly for the kitchen and Seta.

By the time Omer arrived home, an elegantly laid table had been set out on the terrace, and Cyrielle had showered and perfumed herself and changed into a beautiful summer dress. It was a midnight-blue silk, the color of the waters of the Bosphorus at night. Its style was simple, and it accentuated her long trim figure, the figure of the perfect mannequin, just like her mother's. She had pulled her hair back and tied it with a matching ribbon. She had a single blossom tucked into the ribbon, a fragrant rose that she had picked from the garden. She had taken extra care with her appearance, carefully applying only the softest touch of rouge to accentuate her high cheekbones, and rimming her eyes with eyeliner, just enough to make them even more prominent in her already glorious face.

His breath quickened when he saw her. She was sitting in one of the large white chairs that surrounded the edge of the water, reading a book. From his vantage point he could only see her profile. To his eyes, it was perfectly formed. Just the right-length forehead, an elegant nose, and sweet, full lips. He stood watching her for a moment, his presence undetected. He would have been content to stay there all evening if she had not felt his eyes on her.

"I thought someone was there," she said, turning toward him to reveal her full beauty.

"I didn't mean to startle you."

"You're always doing that. Remember the first night when you came home and I was in the little room? I kind of think you like it."

"You're right, I do like looking at you," he said, walking to her. He kissed her once on each cheek, inhaling the sweet scent of her perfume. "And tonight you look especially lovely."

"Thank you. It's a special night," she said softly, putting her book down and walking with him into the house.

They changed the plan and ate dinner first. As Omer tasted each of the dishes served to him, Cyrielle watched his face carefully.

"Good, isn't it?" she asked as he took another serving of an eggplant dish made with chopped beef.

"Delicious. This is one of my favorites. Tonight it tastes especially good. I must remember to compliment Seta. It is one of the hardest dishes to make because if you add just a touch too much olive oil, the whole thing turns into a soggy mess."

"Oh, I would never do that," Cyrielle said.

"Well, it sounds easier than it is. It's really quite difficult. You'll have to try it sometime."

"I already did."

He looked at her quizzically. "What is that supposed to mean?"

"I cooked everything you have eaten so far, and more that is to come, all by myself. You see, I've been watching Seta carefully, and I thought that tonight, since we were just going to be the two of us, well, I thought that tonight might be a good time to try my hand at this delicious Turkish cooking. So I went straight to the kitchen after school, kicked Seta out, and took over. I spent the entire afternoon in there. I'm glad you like it."

That smile again. A slight tilt of her head, raven hair falling gently over one shoulder. That glorious smile. Suddenly he was jolted by the depths of his feelings for her.

"Cyrielle, if you're kidding me, I'll never forgive you."

"Why would I kid about something like that? I'm telling you the absolute truth. Why don't you ask Seta to come out here and see how she liked having the afternoon off? It's true; I did all of this by myself."

Seta appeared and confirmed Cyrielle's story, telling Omer that in addition to the main dishes and the vegetables, Cyrielle had also prepared the desserts Seta was about to serve.

"She says you chose very complicated desserts, too," Omer said. He looked into the face he knew he was falling in love with. "You are really something special, Cyrielle. Forget how talented you are; it was just wonderful of you to think of doing this at all."

"It's a small effort to thank you for all you are doing for me. Especially all the trouble you have gone through to get the collection here."

"It's nothing. I'm just glad everything seems to have arrived in one piece. Are you ready to go in and look?"

As the two housemen carted the packing materials away, one by one the treasures of the Galerie Lazare were revealed. Masterpiece after masterpiece, each one selected with love by her grandfather's or father's unerring eye for greatness. Many of the paintings had been in the family for two generations.

"This is truly exquisite," Omer said as a new drawing was revealed.

"Oh, yes, that's one of my favorites," she agreed.

During the next few hours they discovered that they shared similar tastes in art. Omer loved the luminosity and mysterious encrusted surfaces of the late Monets, the simple, elegant lines of the Matisse drawings, the revolutionary Picasso still lifes—all the qualities that appealed to her, he liked too.

As the last piece was uncrated, an exquisite Monet grain-stack painting, with the sun coming through the mist at dawn, Cyrielle's expression changed. In one instant she turned from a happy, smiling young girl to a very troubled woman.

"Please, bring that one over here," she asked Omer.

Aware of the dramatic change in her mood, he said, "Of course, Cyrielle. I'll be happy to."

She got up from the sofa and moved closer to the canvas, then sat down on the floor in front of its large frame. She remained perfectly still as she studied the soft hues of the work. Suddenly she was overcome with a longing to be home, to see her father's comforting smile, to smell the welcoming scents of the Parisian bakeries, to sleep in her own bed. Tears ran down her cheeks.

From the other side of the room Omer could see her shoulders rise and fall with uncontrollable sobs. At once he rushed to her side.

"Oh, Cyrielle, please don't cry. I know how hard this must be for you, seeing all these familiar things. I'm so sorry we did this. Perhaps it would have been better just to have them put away in storage until after the war has ended."

"No, no, it's all right," she managed between sobs. "It's just that this painting is so special. Of all the paintings in the gallery, this was my father's favorite. He always loved it best. It must have been so hard for him to send it away. It was the one work that he swore he would never sell. Never. Not at any price or for any reason. He couldn't bear to leave it in the gallery, so he had it brought to the apartment. It hung in our living room, and often when he came home at night he would just sit and look at it for a long time. Oh, it's so beautiful. . . ."

Her tears began again, but this time they were much softer, a reflection of her profound sadness about all that had changed.

It broke his heart to see her so unhappy. He went to her and took her in his arms. She melted into his embrace, pressing her face against his chest, and wrapping her arms tightly around him.

"Oh Cyrielle, no more tears. Everything is going to be just fine. I promise." He kissed the top of her head, suddenly aware of the sweet scent of her hair. He continued to stroke her hair, slowly, gently, until her crying ceased and her breathing returned to normal. "Cyrielle," he said again. "Oh, my darling . . ." Lifting her face up to his, he kissed her forehead, the bridge of her nose, and finally her lips . . . softly at first . . . until she responded to him. "Cyrielle, I love you so. Stay with me. Nothing terrible will ever happen to you if you are here with me."

Gazing back into his eyes, she told him what he had longed to hear. "Yes, Omer, I love you too. I have since the day I first met you. The very first day . . ."

He covered her mouth with his and gently parted her lips. He was thrilled beyond his wildest imaginings with her declaration of love for him, and now he wanted to envelop her, to touch, to explore, to possess every inch of her delicious being. Cyrielle, too, was anxious to show him, beyond words, how much she felt for him. She opened her mouth to him, and their tongues met. Slowly they explored the intimate reaches of each other, and with every stroke their urgency for each other grew.

"Oh, my love . . ." Cyrielle began, but he silenced her again as his hands reached up to caress her cheeks. Their eyes locked, and they looked at each other for a very long time, their feelings revealed in the joy on their faces.

Kissing replaced words, and their desire for each other grew to a frenzied pitch as Cyrielle's soft fingertips traced the outline of Omer's face. As if she were blind, and the tips of her fingers were her only memory, she touched him carefully and thoughtfully. It became almost a game, a secret lovers' game, to be shared only by two. She would stroke his face, and when he could no longer endure it he would reach up and cover her hand with his. Then he would return the affection, running his hands once again along her nose, across her lips and down her neck. Cyrielle would throw her head back in anticipation of his sweet kisses, and Omer responded by showering every inch of her ivory skin with tiny bursts of adoration.

At one point Cyrielle was certain she would explode if she did not pull away from him for just a moment. She wanted him so, she yearned for him to make love to her at that very instant. Gladly she would have allowed him to touch her as no other man before, to explore the most intimate, private areas of her body, but she knew that they must wait. She pulled her head back and moved slightly away from him. She caught her breath, waited for her pulse to slow, and then, with a smile that conveyed to him the happiness she felt, she returned to his waiting arms.

They remained on the floor of the living room in front of the painting caressing and fondling until the pale light of dawn, the same light Monet had captured in his masterpiece, swept across the Bosphorus.

CHAPTER

5

SEMRA NOTICED the change right away. When she returned from her trip, there was an unmistakable aura of happiness in the house. She had arrived home from Ankara to find a new Cyrielle, a livelier, lovelier, glowing Cyrielle. At first she thought that maybe her friend had received a letter filled with good news from her father, or that she had simply had an especially good day. But then Omer came home whistling and acting happier than she had seen him in years, and when she saw his eyes light up the moment Cyrielle entered a room, it was the only confirmation she needed. She immediately concluded that the two of them had fallen madly in love with each other.

"It seems as if you and Omer are getting on famously," Semra said to Cyrielle one afternoon when they were shopping. She didn't in any way want to pry, but her curiosity was killing her.

"Your brother is the most wonderful person in the world," Cyrielle said without a moment's hesitation.

"It seems he's quite crazy about you, too," Semra replied. Sensing that maybe she had opened up a subject that for the time being was better left alone, she added, "Please don't misunderstand me, Cyrielle, I'm delighted to see you both looking so happy. Omer deserves his happiness more than anyone in the world. He's been so down for the past two years, ever since . . ." She stopped, convinced that if Cyrielle didn't already know the unfortunate story, then she certainly should not be the one to tell her.

But it was too late. "Since what?"

"Oh, it's really not for me to discuss. I'm sorry, I thought by now you two would have talked about it."

"Semra, whatever are you talking about? I don't have any idea, and you can't just bring up a subject, especially one so important to me, and then drop it like that. Now come on, tell me."

"Oh, I knew I was headed for trouble, but I just want Omer to be happy more than anything in the world. You see, two years ago he was engaged to a wonderful Turkish girl. He bought the yalı for her, for them to live in after they married."

"The one we are all living in now?" Cyrielle asked, unable to stop herself from interrupting.

"Yes, the one we live in now. Well, he bought it and restored it completely. You have no idea how much work went into it. The house has quite a history. It was built in the eighteenth century for a Russian princess. Over the years it has been an embassy, and then finally a private home. After the last family moved out, it was allowed to run down, and when Omer finally bought it, it was in almost complete ruin. Anyway, that is not the point of the story. The point is that right after they announced their engagement, his fiancée became ill. She was diagnosed as having a rare form of cancer, a cancer that could only be treated in Switzerland. She went away for treatments, which at first seemed to help. When she was finally well enough, she returned to Istanbul. But as the date of the wedding drew near, she became sick again. She died on the very day they were to have been married."

What a horrible story, what an awful agony for him to have endured. Cyrielle's heart ached for Omer.

"He was devastated, and after that he threw himself completely into his work. He would travel and stay away just so he could escape the reminders of her. For a time he couldn't even stay in the house. He turned totally to his work and to his collection. He would travel anywhere to see a painting. Of course the war curtailed all of that. And then you arrived. Since that day he's been a new man, he's his old self again. The brother I thought I had lost forever. Yes, I have you to thank for bringing him back to life. Oh, Cyrielle, I hope that you two will marry. You would make him so very happy."

Cyrielle smiled. "I would like that more than anything in the world. Of course, he hasn't asked me, and I'm not certain if he's even thinking about it, but oh, wouldn't it be wonderful?"

"Yes, my dear, it would be the best thing for all of us. I'm being selfish, of course, for I would get you as a sister-in-law, and my brother would get a perfect wife."

" 'Perfect' is overstating it by miles, but I would do anything to make him happy."

"As he would for you, I know."

On June 14, 1940, German troops marched through the streets of Paris and claimed the city as their own. Cyrielle read about it in the Turkish papers the following morning. She spent the remainder of the day downstairs in the library, her ear pressed against the radio, desperately trying to tune in the BBC news broadcast. It was hopeless. The reception was so poor that through the crackles and interruptions she could only pick out an occasional word or two. Finally she grew so frustrated that she switched the instrument off in disgust, breaking off the knob she had been so frantically turning all afternoon.

Omer came home early that evening to find Cyrielle still sitting on the sofa in his library. The pained look on her face told him of her despair, and even though she attempted a smile when she saw him enter the room, neither of them was fooled.

"I don't suppose the radio has been of much help," he sighed as he took her in his arms and tried to comfort her.

"No, not at all. In fact, I'm afraid I've broken the dial. I got so frustrated, not being able to hear anything clearly, that I pulled it too hard when I was only trying to turn the bloody thing off."

"Don't worry about it for a minute, love. Here, I've brought the evening newspapers." He put them on the table in front of the chesterfield. "They may have some more-updated information than the ones you got this morning."

Cyrielle's face brightened a bit. She was anxious for any news, no matter how troubling. It was the uncertainty, the not knowing, that was the hardest to bear.

"Oh, please, let's look at them now," she implored.

He was only too glad to comply. He took one paper at a time and spread it out on his desk and began to read to her all about the fall of Paris to the Nazis. Cyrielle hung on his every word, but all the while her head spun with concern for her beloved papa.

"I tried and tried to get through to your father today, but of course it was useless. I sent telegrams to several of my friends asking them for information. I hope they were received. We won't know anything for a few days yet."

"I'm going to keep my fingers crossed," she said, realizing that Omer was doing all he could to help. "And I'm going to be praying more than I ever have in my entire life. It's so hard, not knowing whether any of my letters have been received or not. He never mentions them when he writes to me."

"It is hard, my darling. Hard for everyone. We'll all be praying," he added. "That's about the best we can do for now. Until we know more and are able to make arrangements to get your father out of danger. For now, why don't we have some dinner? I'll see if the houseman can repair the radio while we're eating. Maybe the reception will be better later in the evening."

Cyrielle's normally voracious appetite had disappeared. She merely sat staring across the table at Omer. All she wanted was to find out if her father was in danger, if he had escaped harm during the fateful day, and if he was making plans to leave the city. She hoped he no longer clung to the thought that the war would not touch him. He would be one of the last Parisians to abandon hope.

"Cheer up, Cyrielle," Omer urged, as they sat close to each other in the library after their meal, glaring at the useless piece of equipment. The dial had been repaired, but the reception was worse than ever. It seemed they would have to wait until morning for further bulletins.

During the first few weeks following the occupation, news reports were confused and oftentimes misleading. What was reported in the morning papers was changed or denied in later editions. The uncertainty was killing Cyrielle, and she lived for the moment when Omer would enter the house with the day's assortment of newspapers.

His efforts to get her father out of the country had proved fruitless. Even making contact was difficult.

"The borders are being strictly monitored," he reported. "Of course, we're going to continue trying, we're going to investigate every possibility, but our chances of succeeding look very slim, I have to admit."

She was silent for a moment, and then said cautiously, "Omer, I've been thinking. What if . . . what if I were to go back to Paris? Just for a short time, of course. Just to make certain that everyone is all right. I wouldn't be suspected, they wouldn't do anything to me. After all, I arrived here without any problem," she continued, blocking the dreadful train trip, the long hours of fear and anxiety from her mind.

Omer looked at her, and saw how serious she was. It was clearly out of the question, he had considered going himself a little earlier, but now it was impossible for anyone to travel without being in grave danger. "Cyrielle, sweetheart, what you're suggesting is just not possible. I'm sorry, but it's become far too dangerous to risk a trip now. I thought of going a week or two ago, but it would have been foolish. No, my love, any attempts we make to get your father out will have to be coordinated from here. Going there, or even attempting to go there, would only be putting everyone in danger. Particularly your father. You must trust me on this, we're doing everything we possibly can, everything in our power."

She remained silent, knowing that any argument she offered would be met with the same response.

"Keep trying" was all she said.

"I'll never give up, my darling," he assured her. "Every day I make more calls, hoping to get a new lead, something to start from. I promise you, I'll never stop trying."

Cyrielle reread the last letter she had received from her father over and over again; so many times had she read it that the edges of the gallery's elegant stationery were frayed. She searched each sentence carefully for hidden clues as to his well-being, but could find none. His tone was upbeat and casual, as if the fact that France was under occupation were the most normal of circumstances. Even though she had heard from Marie-France that life had become practically intolerable, her father seemed to be trying to make light of a horrible existence.

"My darling daughter," he had begun in his fine penmanship,

> *I send you a thousand kisses and wish with all my heart that we could be together at this very moment and that I could be telling you all of this while looking at your lovely face. But for the present time, I'm afraid that it is not to be.*
> *I am well and am carrying on with the small amount of business I am able to pull out of our most faithful clients, but all "luxury" commerce, which ours surely must be, is nearly at a standstill. The Abwehr is everywhere, and one's hands are practically tied with respect to making business deals of any consequence.*
> *Daily life has changed remarkably over the past few weeks. Most of the taxis have disappeared, and the streets are teeming with bicycles, horses, and the latest invention, the "vélo-taxi," an amusing and relatively efficient, I might add, combination of half horse, half car. These are cropping up in greater and greater number. The Métro is shut down from eleven in the morning to three in the afternoon on weekdays, making it generally impossible to travel in any fashion during the day. Every day when it is running,*

the first-class compartments are filled with Wehrmacht soldiers. But by far the most abhorrent event is the daily pa-
rade down the Champs Élysées. Precisely at noon, a Nazi
battalion marches from the Arc de Triomphe to the Place
de la Concorde. They are accompanied by a band playing
"Prussia's Glory." Needless to say, this display sends shopkeepers and passersby alike fleeing from the avenue to
avoid the humiliating scene.

In addition, as if in an effort to deprive us of all our
pleasures, alcohol has been banned three days a week. The
only thing the café owners have left to offer their customers
in quantity is the dreadful "café national" which is a horrible concoction made from acorns and chick-peas. It is a
thin, watery liquid which is meant to replace coffee, but I
think I would prefer a good dose of cough syrup in its
place. Still, I try to meet with some friends at least one
night each week. It is good to keep in touch, and it breaks
the monotony of being alone at night.

I put Jacques on the train for Pau last week to stay
with Nathalie. He will continue his schooling there, as the
programs in the as yet unoccupied part of the country have
not seemed to suffer as much disruption as they have here
in Paris. I feel hopeful that it was a good decision, although I miss him terribly, as I do all of my family. I had a
message from Alexandre last week. I'm told that he is well
and so far has been able to remain away from the combat
area. He is busy working in the communications office. He
hopes to be able to get to Paris for a day or two next week.

I have heard from Omer that the collection arrived
safely, and that he has arranged for storage and safekeeping for the majority of the items. I'm glad you've kept the
wonderful Monet with you, as you well know it was always one of my favorites. Think of us, our beloved family,
each time you look at it, and remember the happier times
when we were all together. Dream and pray the time will
come when we will be together again.

Omer also tells me that you are studying hard and have already mastered the language. Take comfort in knowing that the Turan family genuinely cares about you. I know it must be terribly difficult to be in such a foreign place with a different language, away from your friends, but I want you to make the best of it. Please promise me you will try, for I will be greatly relieved if I receive word that you are happy. I love you with all my heart, and I count the moments until I see you again, my cherished daughter.

With love,
Papa

Cyrielle folded the letter carefully and put it away for safekeeping in the tiny drawer at the top of her secretary. She tried to make herself believe that everything was going to be all right someday soon, but the daily reports in the newspapers told her otherwise. She was troubled the most by the fact that her father was now totally alone in Paris. The situation must have become nearly intolerable for him to send Jacques away. She imagined him ambling about in the large apartment, wandering from room to empty room, with only the housekeepers, Pierre and Martine, for company. Her heart ached with the thought of his loneliness.

Still, she would try to do as her father wished. She wanted so to tell him about Omer, about how much she loved him, and that she wanted to spend her life with him. If only her letters could be delivered. If only she could see her father again . . .

The summer weather set in with a vengeance, making life in Istanbul very unpleasant. Cyrielle refused all of Omer's offers to go on his sailboat on the Bosphorus and out to the Princes Islands in the Sea of Marmara. Semra had gone off for a week with some of her friends, but Cyrielle remained in the big house. Even though it was more pleasant aboard the boat, it was also more remote. As oppressive as the heat was, she refused to leave the house. She wanted to be nearby in case they might hear anything. She wouldn't enjoy being off on a sailing excursion, not knowing how her father was faring. Omer forfeited his trips and stayed in the city with her.

Finally, one evening in late September, the weather broke. A breeze came up and swept across the Bosphorus, offering a little relief to the city's sweltering residents. Omer had called and said that a business meeting would keep him out late. Cyrielle asked to be served outside on the terrace facing the water so she could take advantage of the crisp fresh air. She put on a dress made of the lightest, sheerest cotton and brushed her hair to the top of her head, off her neck and shoulders, then tied it with one of her colorful scarves. Putting on her sandals and a light touch of lipstick, she ran downstairs, anxious to feel the cool wind against her body.

As she had requested, Seta had prepared a light meal consisting only of a salad and the cold yogurt soup made with cucumbers and mint. Cyrielle sat at the candlelit table enjoying the first comfortable weather in weeks. She sipped a glass of white wine slowly.

Ship traffic on the waterway was brisk; boats of all sizes passed in front of the mansion. Many city residents who did not live on the water had taken to going out on their boats nightly to escape the unbearable heat. The water churned and made lapping sounds against the house, since the Bosphorus was only a few yards from her table. Its sound hypnotized her, and she continued to stare into the darkness.

"Cyrielle."

The voice startled her and she jumped in her seat. She hadn't expected anyone, since Omer was not scheduled to return until late.

"Cyrielle, I'm sorry," he apologized. "I didn't mean to frighten you."

The familiar voice calmed her. She had been so lost in her thoughts that she hadn't heard the sound of Omer's footsteps on the ground behind her.

"Hello, darling. I didn't expect you until later. I guess I became so fascinated with the sound of the water that I forgot where I was. It's so nice out here, now that the weather has cooled. Is it always like this in the summer?"

"No, no, this has been a particularly hot, humid period."

Something in his voice caused her concern. It hadn't the usual soothing tone to which she had grown accustomed. She searched his face for clues, and just when she was beginning to panic, he spoke again.

"Cyrielle . . ." he began.

"Omer, are you all right?"

"Yes, I'm fine. But I'm afraid I have some bad news for you."

She sat bolt upright in her chair now, terrible thoughts racing through her mind. Finally, after this excruciating period of waiting, he had received word of her father, and it was not good. She breathed deeply, trying to calm herself, fearing the worst. She seemed unable to get enough oxygen into her lungs and gasped, trying to inhale more air.

"What, what is it? What did you find out?"

Her eyes begged him to tell her the news. Yet, for him, it was the most heart-wrenching duty. He couldn't bear to think of the pain he was going to cause her.

"What is it?" she repeated with an urgency he could no longer ignore.

"I received a telegram today," he began.

"A telegram? About my father? What did it say? Is he okay?"

"No, Cyrielle, it wasn't about your father. It was from your father."

Suddenly she could breathe again. If her father was sending telegrams, then he was all right. He was alive and able to communicate. She allowed herself a brief moment of relief before Omer delivered the unexpected news.

"I'm afraid it's about your brother," he said. "Cyrielle, Alexandre has been killed."

She stared at him, disbelieving. At the same moment she hated him and was thankful for him. She hated him for telling her that her brother was dead. She was grateful that he was there to tell her. He was her best friend, the man she loved so very much.

"I'm so sorry," he continued. "It happened just last week. Outside of Paris. He was returning from seeing your father. Here, you can read the message for yourself."

The telegram was brief. Maurice had seen his eldest son the night before he was killed on his return to the Resistance forces. He would be buried next to many of his countrymen in a cemetery not far from the city. There was nothing about her father—whether he was making any plans to leave, or what conditions in the city were like. It gave no hints, no clues about what was going on.

Cyrielle put the paper down gently on the table and secured it from being carried away by the wind with her empty wineglass. She turned her face back to the sea, totally ignoring Omer's presence.

Alexandre. It seemed as if years had passed since she had last seen him. She remembered him standing in their living room, proud and tall and handsome, so eager to be going off to serve his homeland. Now it just seemed so pointless. What had it all been for? What purpose was served from having a vital young man of twenty-one lose his life in a war that might never be won? She shook her head from side to side, refusing to believe that she would never see him again.

"Cyrielle . . ." came the gentle voice. "I'm so sorry. Is there anything I can do? Is there anything you want?"

She looked up at him, her face now pale and etched with pain. Suddenly she appeared very tired, and the colorful scarf framing her face seemed so inappropriate, like a terrible joke.

His question seemed ridiculous to her. Yes, she wanted to scream, there is something you can do. You can send me home and give me my real life back. A life that I loved, with my mother, my father, and my sister and brothers all together. She wanted to awaken tomorrow and be back in the apartment on their beautiful, familiar street. She wanted to smell the freshly baked croissants the cook always prepared for them on Saturday mornings. Yes, that was what he could do for her. But she managed to still her rage, knowing that all this was not just a bad dream, but the reality of what her life had become. Then she saw the love in his eyes, and knew that he was sharing her pain. She went to him, and released all of the pain and sorrow she was experiencing.

"Oh, my love, I know how it hurts. I lost someone very dear to me once too. It is an indescribable pain. I know, my darling, I know . . ." he said, stroking her and trying his best to calm her and to ease her heartache.

The light shot through the windows of her room and its beams made patterns on the floor. For a moment, she was disoriented, unaware of the time and place. They had stayed outside for hours, in silence and wrapped in each other's arms. The house had been dark when they finally walked through the empty rooms and Omer put her limp body into her bed. Oddly, she had slept soundly. But now, on awakening, her mind was filled once again with the terrible news of last evening. She realized it was all true. She no longer had a big brother. She felt isolated and alone, but at the same time, more grateful than ever for Omer and his love.

CHAPTER

6

*I*N THE MONTHS following her brother's death, Omer did everything in his power to help ease Cyrielle's pain. When he was in town, he came home early every night so that he could be with her. Often they would have a romantic dinner together, and each weekend he planned an excursion to a place he thought she would enjoy.

"I love you more than ever, Omer," she told him one evening after they had returned from dinner with some of his friends.

"And I you," he replied, encircling her with his arms. "Cyrielle, we don't have any definitive news about the war. No one knows for sure when and how it will end. We can't live our whole lives waiting for something to change. Cyrielle, I love you and I want to build a life with you. Marry me. Please say you'll marry me."

"Yes, I will, Omer."

Even though the war did not directly affect Turkey, it had touched everyone's lives, especially Cyrielle's. The last letter she had received from her father was already a month old, and despite their continued efforts to telephone him, or to contact him through friends in Paris, his whereabouts remained unknown. Nathalie and her husband had not heard from him, and they shared the constant worry about him from their home in southwestern France. So, with the weight of so much uncertainty on her shoulders, Cyrielle wanted to have a small, quiet wedding.

"I wouldn't feel right having a huge celebration and not being able to have my family with me," she explained to Omer. "I think it's more appropriate to these difficult times to be a little more restrained. Do you agree?"

"You may have whatever you wish, my darling. If you just want to have my family, that's fine. If you want to include some of your friends from the University, that's all right too. You just let Semra know, and I'm sure everything will be taken care of. Your happiness is all I care about."

With each passing day she loved him more, and she began to count the hours until she would become Mrs. Omer Turan.

"I just wish you liked to swim, then we could go sailing in the south. It would be a truly wonderful honeymoon, I assure you."

"That is something you'll never get me to do. I love looking at the water, but I can't help being terrified of it. To my eyes, it's only for watching and admiring from afar. But if you want to go, I'll be perfectly content to stay on board. I can have a good time just being on the boat."

What he really wanted to do was to take her to Europe—to Paris, or London or Rome. To stay in one of the grand hotels, visit museums, and eat lavishly at the many great restaurants. But the war forbade them from taking the traditional wedding tour he had always dreamed of.

"No, I wouldn't ask you to do that. But I promise you, just as soon as the war is over, we'll go on a grand European tour, and I'll make it up to you."

"All right, my sweet. I can wait. For now I'm happy staying right here."

They were married in a simple civil ceremony in the garden of the Turan house. Cyrielle made a breathtaking bride, and she walked down the grand staircase amidst audible sighs of approval from their guests. Just forty of their friends were in attendance. The elder Turans, pleased that their son had made such a wonderful choice, and an assortment of cousins, aunts and uncles rounded out the group. Besides Semra, Cyrielle's only friend was one of her professors from Robert College. It was a lovely ceremony, understated and appropriate to the world situation.

"I wish that everyone would leave," Omer whispered in her ear as he led her around the dance floor that had been created in the center of the garden.

"Shh . . . someone will hear you and be very offended."

"I don't care, I want to be alone with you. I've waited so long for this night. Can't we announce that it's time for them to go?"

"No, silly, we certainly can't. Look around you, everyone is having a lovely time. Be patient, my love," she told him, feeling a slight bit of anxiety about their impending wedding night. Omer would be her first lover, and she was shy and frightened and excited all at the same time.

She needn't have had a moment of worry. After the last guest had departed, Omer led her up the stairs toward their room. His gentle touch and patient gaze made her relax and welcome the experience that lay ahead.

"Come, my darling, I have something to show you," he said, leading her across the room. Omer's bedroom was twice the size of the one Cyrielle had been living in since her arrival in Istanbul. It was located at the corner of the house, giving it windows on two sides instead of only one. The view out to the Bosphorus was the same as hers, but the side windows gave out onto the city in the distance. He led her to a sitting area directly opposite the large bed. Once there he stopped and, holding her shoulders lightly, said, "Look up. I have a wedding present for you."

When she saw the painting which hung above the fireplace, she was so taken aback she could only gasp with excitement. There on the wall, in a frame identical to the one in her own collection, was another of the extraordinary grain-stack paintings. But this one, instead of capturing the look of the fields at dawn, depicted them at dusk. Instead of the morning mist as it was clearing, one could see the evening falling as the fog rolled in and covered the tall piles of grain, evidence of a hard day's work in the fields. In the morning work the stacks appeared to be the lightest, softest shades of pink, but in this magnificent early-evening scene they were bright balls of fire—vibrant red and orange—soon to be calmed by the covering of dense wet fog that actually seemed to move as one looked at the picture.

"Oh, Omer, it's extraordinary. Really it is. What a lovely, lovely present. Thank you." She kissed him sweetly.

Seeing how pleased she was with it, he said, "I'm so glad you like it. I found it for you during my last trip to Switzerland. Getting it here was more difficult than arranging transport of your father's entire collection."

Cyrielle refused to be reminded of the war just now. She would not allow anything to spoil their first night together.

"Well, whatever trouble it was, I want you to know that I love you even more for being so thoughtful. It means so much to me."

"It was no trouble at all. I would gladly do it again," he replied, sincerity and honesty evident in his every word. "Well, how does it feel to be Mrs. Turan?"

"Like a dream come true." She went to him. Now she wanted to give herself to him, to love him as his wife.

He pulled her to him and kissed her firmly on the mouth, his tongue finding hers, flicking it lightly, teasing her until she thought her legs would no longer hold her. As he had longed to do all evening, he removed the beautiful dress. The sight of her lovely French lingerie excited him beyond his wildest fantasies, and his heartbeat quickened as he looked at her.

"Oh, my Cyrielle, you are so beautiful, every part of you is so beautiful. I want to look at you, touch you, and caress every inch of you."

At his intimate words she lowered her head, uncertain how to respond. She excused herself and walked over to her dressing room, where Melek had arranged all her perfumes and toiletries just as they had been in the other room. Only this dressing room and bath were nearly twice as large as the other one had been. Its walls had been lacquered with a feminine peach color, and delicate crystal sconces lit the space. The far wall was mirrored, with two movable panels that swung out to provide a three-way view. A pastel-hued carpet in tones of pale orange and soft turquoise-blue covered the floor, giving a feeling of luxury and softness. A lovely dressing table with an inlaid top sat in one corner, where Melek had carefully arranged her silver-handled brushes and combs. Cyrielle stepped out of her stockings and slip, removed her lacy panties, released the clasp of her bra, and stepped into the gown that she had chosen for her wedding night. She pulled the thin straps up over her breasts, letting the rest of the elegant white silk fall to the floor, then walked toward the mirror to check her appearance. The lace bodice of the gown ended just a touch above her nipples, and through the sheerness of the white fabric the darker areolae were visible. She smoothed the fabric down over her hips as she turned sideways to the mirror. The gown was fitted to her tiny waist and her slim hips. Her stomach was almost completely flat, there was only the slightest healthy mound between her hip bones. The narrow straps crisscrossed in the back; they were secured at either side just above her buttocks. Below her knees, the gown flared out gently, creating soft flutes of fabric at her feet. Her appraisal complete, she turned to her dressing table, released her hair from its position on top of her head and brushed it into place around her face, then loosely tied it with a white satin ribbon. The end of the thick ponytail reached down to where the fabric of the gown began.

She removed all traces of her light makeup and then lifted the atomizer filled with her favorite perfume. Just as she was about to spray she hesitated, remembering Omer's comment that he adored her own natural scent, so she returned the bottle to its place on the table. Then she went back into the bedroom to give herself to her new husband.

Omer was waiting for her in bed, and when he saw her his breath caught in anticipation. As she walked slowly toward him, the fabric of the gown moved gracefully about her legs, outlining the exquisite contours of her body in a most seductive way. He turned back the covers and opened his arms to her.

As she joined him in bed, Cyrielle's anxiety returned. Her entire body stiffened, and she froze at Omer's touch. All of a sudden she felt the age difference between them, nearly fourteen years, more acutely than ever before. She knew that he must be experienced, and she feared that he might expect too much from her. She had never before known such intimacy with a man, but never before had she been so desirous of it. Her staunch confidence of the days and weeks before this moment flew out the window.

"Cyrielle, my love, please relax. I wouldn't hurt you for the world." He stroked her face gently, arranged her hair delicately on the pillow. She began to soften, to trust him as her husband. "You are so beautiful, every part of you is so lovely. I want to know all of you, to hold you, to pleasure you, to love you," he said, as carefully her hand covered his. Tentatively she guided him down across the tips of her breasts. She urged him to touch the flatness of her stomach, and at last, because she could no longer hold back the desire to have him stroke her, the softness of her round, swollen mound.

Just as tentatively, he reached down and drew the fabric of her gown up over her head. She lifted herself up and allowed him to remove it. He dropped it with a whispery sigh to the floor. She lay back down and again took his hand, this time placing it on her nakedness. She allowed his fingers and tongue to caress her, and slowly her response grew to a frenzy. As the movements of his quivering tongue relentlessly flicked against her, teasing her, baiting her, he awakened in her a feeling she had never known before. She was overpowered with emotion. She melted completely, shed her inhibitions, and experienced the joy of lovemaking for the first time. She clung to him tightly as he rocked her back and forth in his arms. She felt pleased yet frightened by her own powerful response.

He calmed her, stroking her head as he told her, "Yes, my darling, that's what's meant to happen. Exactly what's meant to be."

When she looked into his eyes, she saw that they were moist with tears. He could not contain his happiness at pleasing her so thoroughly.

They rested for a moment, entwined in each other's arms. Cyrielle's confidence was buoyed, and she was anxious to learn the secrets of her new husband. She reached over and touched him, running her fingers along the soft down of his chest. She traced a line up and down, back and forth, teasing him beyond his power to withstand it. This time he covered her hand with his, and led her to his hardness. She caressed the hugeness of him, delighted and curious and timid all at once. He helped her, showing her the motions that excited him the most, but her touch alone was enough to drive him wild. As her hands continued their virgin exploration, his breath quickened, and he reached down and capped her fingers.

"I can't stand it much longer, you're driving me crazy," he whispered. "I must have you soon. I want you more than anything in the world."

"I'm ready for you, my love," she urged him, surprised at her sudden ability to communicate with him in such intimate terms. She placed his fingers inside her, to show him that she was moist and swollen, fully prepared for him. She guided his enormous shaft slowly into her, rising up to meet his hardness. He was cautious, not wanting to hurt her, but she assured him it was not painful.

"I want to take all of you, my darling, please, it's fine, I promise. Come inside me fully, I need to feel the entire length of you."

He exploded inside her quickly, his anticipation so great that he could no longer contain himself. She held him to her, savoring the heat of his fluid as it poured into her.

With his passion spent, and Cyrielle still savoring the wondrous joy of her first orgasm, he wrapped his arms heavily about her, and they spent their first night together as man and wife.

When she awoke in the morning, the first thing she saw was the glorious Monet. She rolled over into Omer's arms, and felt with all her heart that all would soon be right in the world.

CHAPTER

7

MAURICE LAZARE could no longer bear it. Life in Paris had become intolerable. He was unable to do any work; every transaction he proposed was blocked or simply failed to go through for some mysterious reason. Most of his treasures now sat in a warehouse in Istanbul, anyway, so he really had very little inventory remaining in the gallery. Acquiring artwork was the last thing on people's minds, everyone was trying to unload whatever they still owned. And it broke his heart that he no longer had the resources necessary to buy back the art of loyal patrons who were now attempting to flee the city. Where the next meal was coming from and how they would survive the war had become the first priority.

He made his decision late one night, as he sat at an outdoor café sharing a watered-down coffee with those few friends who still remained in their beloved city.

"Well, I'm leaving tomorrow," he announced. "I'm going to Pau. I want to be with my son and my daughter and her husband during the rest of this horrible war. At least they're in the countryside. It will be peaceful and quiet. Surely it can't be as oppressive as it is here." In addition to the sour mood of the city, it had been one of the hottest summers on record. Even now, during the last week in October, the men sat in short-sleeved shirts, without jackets.

"It's the only choice left," one friend said.

"I wish I had a family to go to," lamented another.

"We'll miss you, Maurice. God be with you," added a third.

They were all sad to see him go, but they agreed it was a wise choice. Their friend was no longer the strong man they had known for so long. Maurice's spirit seemed to have died when he sent Cyrielle off to Istanbul. Then his whole being seemed to have withered with the death of Alexandre. His very will to live shriveled and died, leaving only the shell of a once brilliant, vital human being. They would feel a large void with him gone, but they wished him well.

The conversation then turned to a lighter subject as they fantasized about the reunions they would all have when the war finally ended.

Maurice pulled the large wooden door shut on the apartment where he had lived with his family for over twenty years. He bid farewell to Pierre and Martine, the couple who had lived there with him, and who had been nannies to his children as well as superb cooks and housekeepers. Having done that, he set out for the train station with only a few of his belongings packed neatly in one small valise, similar to the one his daughter had taken over a year earlier. In his other hand he carried a briefcase filled with papers and important documents. He walked slowly, feasting on the sights of his treasured city. The buildings of the Louvre, Notre-Dame, Sacré Coeur—so far they had survived the most devastating war the world had ever seen. When he would see them again, even if they were spared, he could not imagine. Everything delighted him except for the imprint that reminded him who was in control of Paris. No matter how many times he passed them, his eyes were always offended to see the street signs that had been erected by the Germans. They seemed to have sprung up overnight, every street corner had been changed.

As he passed through the Place de la Concorde he stopped briefly to look at the massive Corinthian columns lining the elegant facade of the Hotel Crillon. Many had called this square the most beautiful in the world. He silently prayed that it, like the rest of Paris, would by some miracle be saved from destruction.

The train was crowded and noisy. As with everything else, the Germans had claimed the railways as their own. He placed his hat on the rack above his place, took his neatly folded newspapers from his attaché case, and settled into his seat for the long journey south. Reading over the din of the soldiers was impossible. He refolded his papers and watched the Wehrmacht troops with growing hatred as they marched through the cars. As they traveled farther and farther away from his city, his thoughts became darker and darker. He was relieved when the announcement was made signaling their stop in Toulouse. He would disembark there. Before the train schedules had been changed, he used to take the train all the way to Pau. But now trains ran infrequently, so it would be necessary to drive from there.

Jacques, Nathalie, and her husband Etienne were waiting for him when he arrived at the station. When the sound of his daughter's voice rang in his ears, he smiled for the first time since leaving Paris. At that moment he was certain he had made the right decision.

They all piled into the small station wagon and took the road in a westward direction toward the town of Pau. The sweet scent of olive trees brought back memories of other journeys, and for a few moments Maurice was unable to control the tears that fell from his eyes and rolled slowly down his cheeks. He wiped the tears away as they sped along. It was a relief to be in a part of his country that, as yet, remained unoccupied by the Nazis. Even though he could feel their presence not far away, the fact that he did not have to look at their contemptuous faces as they patrolled the streets lifted his spirits.

Two hours later they had passed through the town of Pau. Etienne turned off the paved road onto the rocky entryway that indicated they were on the Lazare property. The Lazares were one of the oldest names in this delightful part of the country. Their country château, Montbrun, sat atop a small hill in the middle of hundreds of acres of land. Built in the late eighteenth century by Maurice's great-great-grandfather, it was an imposing three-storied limestone structure. The house was redolent of history and stability, of leisurely afternoon walks and late-night chats by the fireplace. Every summer the family would leave their homes in Paris and travel with the children to spend long, sun-filled days in the château. It was always a treat for the children, for they would be surrounded by their brothers and sisters, cousins and aunts and uncles. Inevitably, each year there would be a new addition, and the baby was the recipient of much attention, fussing, and ultimate spoiling, which the parents would work all the following year to undo. The children had their own wing in the house, totally separate and away from the part used by the adults. The thick stone walls kept the noise from penetrating to the other side. From June through September, it was a free-for-all—one continual pillow fight and slumber party. For days after their return to the city in the fall, the children would sulk and pout, impatient for summer to roll around again. Maurice had spent every summer of his young life in this haven. He remembered only happy times here, and he was glad to be returning again. After he had married Dominique, they had not come too often to Montbrun, preferring instead to go to their house in Provence, and after her death, it had been too painful for him to return, so he had stayed away. Until this very day.

The crunching sound of the gravel on the driveway ceased as the car came to a halt in front of the inviting, stately home. "Welcome home, Papa," Nathalie said, putting her arm around her father. Jacques walked on his other side, carrying the valise.

"*Merci, ma petite.* Yes, it feels good to be here again," he agreed. They entered the house together, silent with their thoughts of better days, but happy to be surrounded by fond memories of the past.

As expected, life in the countryside had retained more of a normalcy than in the city. At the family home with his daughter and son, Maurice spent leisurely days playing with the dogs and talking long walks around the property. Occasionally they would drive toward town and pay a visit to the château of Henri IV and the Musée des

Beaux Arts. On the way back Maurice would pull the car over on the Boulevard des Pyrénées for a look across the valley at the vineyards of the Juraçon and the base of the great Pyrénées, only twelve miles in the distance.

His favorite pastime was to wander into the village and sit for a spell surrounded by a few old farmers. He liked to study their tanned, lined faces, a testament to the hard life in the fields. They always wore their *bleu de travail,* the blue overalls that are the trademark of the workmen in the southwest. Most of their conversation centered around the harvesting of the many crops grown in the area. Their talk was accompanied by the faint sound of the harvesters as they stripped the fields of their crops. Farming in the southwest was hard work, as first the maize ripens, then the wheat, then the sunflowers. The work was long and arduous; often the farmers and their crews, now greatly reduced because most of the men had gone off to serve in the Resistance, worked through the night, with car headlights strapped to their tractors. Maurice enjoyed the talks, for they were such a welcome change from the depressing subject of war. Sometimes he would even play a game or two of boules. Thus, with the sounds of children laughing in the distance, he was able, for a few moments each day, to forget the terrible state the world was in, and the horrors that raged all around them.

At night the family would enjoy a hearty meal composed of the fruits of their own labors on the property—they raised ducks, pigeons, and chickens, all their own vegetables, and enough wine for their needs. For bread they bartered with the local baker with wheat from their harvest. After eating Maurice would sit outside and write long letters to Cyrielle.

By some miracle, several more of Maurice's letters made it to Istanbul. As Cyrielle sat downstairs in the small room, her legs curled up underneath her, reading them over and over again, her spirits began to lift.

"He says here that Nathalie and Etienne have decided to try and start a family. Oh, Omer, isn't it wonderful? She loves children, and has always wanted a little girl. I hope she gets her wish. I would adore having a little niece to buy things for." Her face glowed as she dreamed of better days.

"Yes, Cyrielle, it is good news," he agreed, even though he thought it unconscionable to bring a child into the world right now, particularly in war-torn France. "Your father seems to have made the right decision by leaving Paris. It's important for him to be with his family."

Her eyes became wide, and she sat up straight in her chair. "Maybe I can go back to France for a visit now," she said. "Yes, why not? It seems as if everything is better now. Perhaps the Germans will be driven out of the country soon. Oh, it would make me so happy to go home. I'm going to write my father this very moment and suggest it. I'm sure he'll agree with me."

Omer looked at her, unable to respond, unable either to squash her enthusiasm or to encourage her hopeless wish. In fact, things were worse than ever. He had received another letter from Maurice just the past week, a private letter intended for his eyes only, in which Maurice had told him the real story. He wrote he was certain the Germans had no intention of giving up Paris without a full-fledged struggle, and he predicted that the liberation of Paris was going to be a bloody battle. He had heard that conditions in the city were terrible and were worsening daily, and there seemed very little hope of an armistice in the near future. Once again he implored Omer to take good care of his daughter—"until our future is decided in one manner or another," read the ominous closing.

There was absolutely no possibility of Cyrielle's returning home right now. But he couldn't bring himself to tell her that; it would wipe the smile off her face and strip her of the only thing that gave her hope—the dream of being reunited with her family.

"Yes, I think you should write to him, Cyrielle, but I wouldn't count on going back just yet. There is still a war going on all around. Perhaps soon . . ."

"Oh, I hope so," she said, refusing to abandon her dreams. "Yes, I'll write tonight."

Maurice's letters continued to arrive, and with each one Cyrielle's dream of returning to France was nurtured. In the meantime, she dedicated herself to being the perfect wife to Omer.

She rose early each morning with him, and they shared breakfast on the terrace. Almost every day, after her classes were over, she made plans to be with Serma or one of the other women she had met at the Turan house. They were all glad to spend time with the charming Cyrielle, and were pleased to see that she was trying so hard to assimilate into Turkish society. They visited all the monuments several times, from the Topkapı to the Dolambahçe Palace, where Cyrielle's knowledge of French furnishings came in handy. For a change she played guide and was able to tell her friends a thing or two about the elegant palace whose 285 rooms contained some of the finest examples of furniture in the Empire style.

All of this touring awakened a desire in her to learn even more about Turkish history, and she became hungrier than ever for knowledge. She wanted to know everything about the exotic culture and customs of the Turkish people. In addition to her language classes and full load of art courses, she added a history class.

Each morning the driver took her through the winding streets of Arnavutköy to the college. It was located at the top of the highest hill in that district, and from her classroom she had an imposing view of the most beautiful part of the Bosphorus. Never had she enjoyed learning so much, and the teachers all adored the beautiful young Frenchwoman who embraced her studies with such enthusiasm. She became a true student of the country.

The reign of Atatürk fascinated her, and she wished that she had been in the country during his time. He had died only three years earlier, but, as Omer had said, the country was still reeling from his unprecedented effect on the lives of the people.

She loved discussing politics with the guests they now entertained in the evenings. Their house became a meeting place for the leaders of industry and business, government officials, and foreign visitors. Cyrielle's impeccable French style, a charming combination of elegant good taste and just the right amount of whimsy, touched every part of their life. Flowers graced every table, the silver was polished as never before, and the house sparkled with her gracious hospitality. No detail escaped her eye as she transformed a lovely house into a warm, inviting home. Soon she became an important hostess in the world of Istanbul's elite society. She used every opportunity to improve her command of the Turkish language. Omer beamed each night when she descended the stairs to greet her guests. He loved her more every day, and each time they entertained he became prouder of her than before.

"I'm so pleased with your progress," he told her one night after all the guests had left. "Not only are you a veritable expert on current affairs in the country, but your Turkish is almost without accent."

She laughed at his comments. "Oh, I may know a bit about the goings-on in the government, but I'm a dead giveaway as a foreigner. Even in the vegetable markets they still give me funny looks when they hear me speak."

"Are you going to take the opinion of a vegetable vendor over that of our friends?"

"Let me master the man in the street, and then I'll be able to take on the world," she laughed, but she said it in Omer's language, in nearly perfect form. His smile told her he was clearly impressed.

"Cyrielle, you look so lovely tonight," he said, kissing her and nuzzling her cheek.

"Omer," she began, "I had a conversation with the Spanish ambassador tonight. What do you think he said my family's chances are of crossing the border into Spain?"

The last letter they had received from Maurice, over a month ago now, had mentioned in cryptic language that they all might be planning an escape through the southern border. She prayed every night they would be successful. If only they could get to Spain! She wanted the next postmark to be from a country other than France, from a safe haven where they could wait out the rest of the war.

Even Turkey was feeling the pressure. The German conquest of Greece and the Greek islands in the Mediterranean had isolated the country. War had come to Turkey on all sides; she sat alone, a neutral country almost surrounded by mighty antagonists.

It was becoming increasingly difficult, but Omer continued to be optimistic. "I don't really know, darling. I've heard that many have managed to cross, but the borders are tightening up now and I'm not certain how closely they are being watched. Your father has good connections, and I am confident that if there is a way out, he will find it. You know I'll help in any way I can. Let's just hope for the best. I'm sure we'll hear something soon."

"I hope," she whispered, a phrase she seemed to use more and more often these days, in whatever language she spoke.

CHAPTER

8

CYRIELLE, you've got to slow down. You'll be having the baby right at school, in the middle of a class, if you don't watch out," Semra cautioned her sister-in-law.

Cyrielle laughed and said, "Why in the world would I want to slow down? I've never felt better in my life. Besides, the first one is always late, and the doctor says it will be at least another two weeks. If not longer," she said, patting her ample belly.

"Omer certainly isn't taking any chances. He's canceled all of his meetings, and made everyone travel here from Ankara. He wouldn't miss being here with you for anything."

"I know. I don't know which of us is more excited. He hasn't been out of town for months, and he's probably a bit stir-crazy, but he's holding up well, putting up a strong front. Hasn't he been terrific?"

"I think so, and I think it's so good of you to let me stay on with you. I promise that as soon as this lousy war ends, I'll be going back to Europe. But every day I'm grateful to you for not kicking me out."

"Kick you out? Are you mad? I wouldn't think of it." And she meant every word. Cyrielle loved having Semra in the house. It was certainly spacious enough; on some days they would go until dinnertime without seeing one another. Semra was busy with her own life, and she was never a bother. Nor was there ever any question that Cyrielle was the mistress of the household. Omer's sister was careful never to involve herself in matters that were Cyrielle's business, and Cyrielle adored her even more for her sensitivity and caring attitude. She hoped that someday soon Semra would find a husband of her own, one as delicious and kind as Omer. Until that day, she had a home with them, and she was more than welcome to stay as long as she pleased.

Semra's prediction came very close to the truth. During her history class the following week, Cyrielle went into labor. By the time Murat had been dispatched to take her to the hospital, little Alexandre Turan, who was to be named after her dear brother, was well on his way into the world.

"Murat, please, could you drive a little faster," she pleaded from the back seat, knowing that her time was very near.

"I'm sorry, Cyrielle *hanım,* the roads are very bumpy, and I didn't want to make you any more uncomfortable. I'll speed up," he said, his voice shaking with fear that the baby would be delivered in the car.

"Yes, thank you," she said between the close contractions. "Please, do hurry."

Omer was by her side when she opened her eyes, and immediately the nurse entered bearing the newborn.

"Oh, my love, I couldn't be happier," said the proud father. "A son. A beautiful, wonderful son."

Secretly, Cyrielle was doubly delighted. Of course she would have been happy with any baby, as long as he or she was healthy. But she knew how important it was to Omer to have a son. How blessed she was to have been able to produce one the first time around.

Alexandre Turan, at once nicknamed Zeki, was a strapping, rambunctious youngster whose main goal in life seemed to be eating and tiring out all those around him. He would cry out from his crib at 6 A.M., and from that moment on there was no rest for his nanny, his doting Aunt Semra, his mother, or anyone else who happened to be in the vicinity.

Omer's parents arrived and added to the outpouring of affection for their new grandson. In a society that put such enormous pressure on the firstborn's being a son, each time Cyrielle looked at the little boy she again thanked her lucky stars.

Omer was the only one who could keep up with him. He adored the child, and it was clear to everyone that both he and Cyrielle were born to be parents. They adapted themselves to their new roles without a backward glance at the life they had led until then.

"I want a whole brood of them," Cyrielle announced one night after they had finally been able to put Zeki to sleep. It was well past midnight, and both of them should have been exhausted by the toddler, but his curiosity and interest in the world around him only seemed to energize them.

"No time like the present to start," Omer concurred, taking her in his arms and kissing her with a passion that continued to grow daily.

"Really?"

"I wouldn't joke about something like that," he said in his most serious tone. Then he covered her mouth with his, and in the quiet of their house, with their young son sleeping peacefully upstairs in a nursery filled with toys, they made love on the floor of Cyrielle's favorite room, the small, intimate corner room that faced out onto the Bosphorus. The windows were thrown open, and as they devoured each other their moans and cries of ecstasy mixed with the sound of the waves lapping against the house.

"I hope this takes," Cyrielle whispered as they lay entwined in each other's arms. "Oh, Omer, I'd love to have another baby."

"Let's make certain, let's not leave anything to chance," he suggested, guiding her hand to him.

Overjoyed by his eagerness and desire for her, she held him gently, stroking and caressing him until once again he was ready.

"You're insatiable," she cried out as they made love for the second time in less than an hour.

Teasing, he said, "Just trying to keep my wife happy. It is no small task being married to such a demanding woman."

So anxious was she to tell him the good news that she instructed Murat to drive to the headquarters of Turan Holding straight from the doctor's office. It was rare for her to visit Omer there, she had only come when she was invited to attend a party or some other company function. Never had she arrived in the middle of the afternoon, and at first her sudden appearance concerned him.

The secretary announced her, and seconds later he came bounding out of his office.

"Cyrielle, are you all right? Is anything the matter?"

"No, no, my darling. I didn't mean to alarm you. There's nothing wrong at all. Everything is fine. I just have something to tell you, that's all. And I couldn't wait until tonight. I thought you would want to know right away."

Relieved that all was well, he guided her into the privacy of his office and then asked, "Something that couldn't even wait until I got home tonight?"

"Well, I suppose it could, but it's not every day you find out you're going to be a father again."

He stopped dead in his tracks, then turned and picked her up in his arms, twirling her in the air. "Oh, my love, how wonderful! Did you just find out?"

"Yes, I'm coming from the doctor now. I'm convinced it was the night in the little room. Don't you agree?"

"I've told you so often, your every wish is my command. Of course it was that night," he concurred, laughing with happiness. He didn't care when it was, so delirious was he with excitement about another child. But of course, he thought, it could have been any night before or after that one, for their passion for each other was so great they rarely went to sleep without first making love.

Turan Holding was prospering, new factories were opening practically each month, new divisions were being added almost daily. Between Omer and his father, they now had their hands immersed in most of the major industries in the country. They controlled manufacturing plants for textiles, automobile parts, canned food, and Omer's newest venture, the mining of chromium ore. Their surpluses were in great demand by both sides, but Omer adamantly refused to supply Germany with any of their products, regardless of the high prices they were prepared to pay. Their real estate holdings, both in the major cities such as Istanbul, Ankara and Izmir, as well as in smaller towns throughout the country, were growing almost as rapidly. They were also speculating about the future growth of the southern coastline of Turkey, about the resort area it might someday become, so every so often they picked up a parcel of land along the Turkish portion of the Mediterranean, an area they referred to as the Akdeniz, or "Pure Waters."

Everything in which they were involved seemed to be profitable; even the most competitive and well-entrenched businesses were no match for the marketing skills of the Turans' well-educated and aggressive staff.

Omer spent his every spare minute with Cyrielle and his new son. He adored the child, and he had to tear himself away from Zeki each morning when it was time to leave for the office, always looking forward to being with him again that night.

The only dark cloud that hung over their lives was the fate of Cyrielle's family. Once or twice they had had the good fortune of getting through by telephone to the house in Pau, but the connection was always bombarded with static, and it usually went dead long before the conversation was finished. Maurice was delighted, of course, to hear about his new grandson. He promised that they would all be together soon. But his letters had stopped arriving altogether, and Cyrielle feared that the worst had happened. Somehow she kept her hopes up, and, against all odds, her faith remained unwavering.

Anyway, she had her own problems to worry about. Unlike her first pregnancy, which had been a breeze, this one was debilitating. Her entire body was heavy and swollen, her bones ached, and her skin bore the blotchy mark of pregnancy. As a result she was constantly tired and irritable. She stopped going to school entirely, and, following the doctor's strict orders, stayed home to rest.

"Will this ever be over?" she complained to Semra one sweltering afternoon.

"Three more weeks, my dear. This has been something, hasn't it? I guess it's just one of those things in life over which you have absolutely no control. Such a contrast to the first one. You made it seem like a piece of cake. Just three more weeks, though."

"That sounds like an eternity to me. It's the same as if you told me that it would be another three years. Even a day seems like forever. I can't understand it. Carrying Zeki was so easy," she groaned, shifting her enormous bulk around in a futile attempt to get comfortable.

The mystery was solved when she delivered a pair of twins the following month.

"Another baby?" she asked in an exhausted voice when the doctor told her to keep pushing long after he had held up a screaming baby girl. "Surely you must be joking?"

"Not at all, Mrs. Turan. I don't know how we missed it. Sometimes these things are a last-minute surprise."

" 'Surprise' is an understatement," she uttered. Minutes later the second of the twins, a robust baby boy, entered the world.

"A pair!" Omer cried, when she was wheeled back to her room from the recovery area. "Bookends! And they're beautiful. Oh, darling, you have really outdone yourself this time."

She was still in shock, unable to believe the news of their double blessing. Two would no doubt be a handful, but they were fortunate to have enough help and space. They had redesigned the third floor to accommodate Zeki and his nanny and the new baby, now they would have to add another two rooms—one for the surprise baby and the additional nanny they would require.

They named the little girl Yasemin and the "bonus" baby, as they came to call him, Ali.

"The atmosphere of this house has certainly changed dramatically over the past two years," Semra commented as they sat among the toys and playthings and the toddlers crawled around them, squealing and giggling. The twins were inseparable, and their older brother had already learned the fine art of teasing them until they cried in unison.

"It's alive now, filled with all these beautiful young children. You have made such a wonderful difference in all of our lives, Cyrielle. I hope you're happy."

"Yes, I am. I feel I'm the most fortunate woman alive. I have a husband who adores me and who is a great father to his children, three healthy children, a beautiful house in which to raise them, plenty of help, and I have a wonderful friend in you. What more could I ask for?"

They both knew the answer to that question, but refused to discuss it right then. It was a topic better left untouched. They operated on the no-news-is-good-news theory, still waiting every day for word about the fate of the Lazares.

"Everything will be fine, Cyrielle, have faith."

Their thoughts were interrupted by the crying of Ali. Zeki had his baby brother pinned to the floor and was holding his hands behind his back. Yasemin sat quietly on the floor next to them, oblivious to all the commotion going on around her, her mind captivated by a new toy. The younger boy cried out for his mother, his usual ally in time of need.

"Thank heavens for these kids," Cyrielle said. "They provide all the distraction I need. They tire me out so much that I have very little time left to think about anything else."

She put up a good front, but late at night, when her darlings were safely tucked in their beds and the house took on a deafening quiet, she often wondered if her precious children would ever see their grandfather and aunt and uncles, or if they would be deprived of the love and attention her own family would shower on them.

9

*I*HAVE to go back," Maurice said resolutely. "I walked out of the apartment as if I was only going for a short vacation. But now it's been over two years. The most important thing is to take care of Pierre and Martine. I must make some arrangements for them, and for the apartment. So many loose ends are left. And I will not endanger you or Etienne or Jacques. Especially you, right now, with the baby due in just a few months. It's out of the question. So stop insisting that you must come with me. I will be fine. I'll go up tomorrow on the train, spend the week with Pierre and Martine, get them squared away, and I'll be back on Monday. There's nothing to worry about. It will be just fine."

"No, Papa, I will not let you go alone. Etienne and I have discussed it, and since you persist in going, he is willing to go too. The doctor has given me permission to travel. All three of us will come with you. We'll help with whatever you need done, and we'll all come back together. You should not stay so long, anyway. I'm sure that with all of us pitching in, we can get everything accomplished in two or three days at the most."

"No, Nathalie, you are not going. You will take me to the train and pick me up. And that is that. Now let's have some dinner, shall we?" Maurice said, closing the subject for the time being.

In the end, Nathalie prevailed. This time the four of them—Jacques came too—drove the long distance from Pau to Paris. Nathalie knew that part of the reason for her father's return was to bring some of the things he most loved from the apartment. If they had the car with them, it would be so much easier to transport the fragile items—the papers and drawings he wanted to have near him. He would never be able to manage with them on the train, and she realized how important they were to him, these things that still remained in the apartment. Things too precious to part with forever. Personal mementos, favorite books, photographs; mementos of his rich, full life with Dominique.

It was a long drive. The roadways were peppered with soldiers at roadblocks asking to see their papers and demanding to know why they were traveling. With each stop Maurice's hatred grew. When would this horrible war end? Word had it that the Allies were very close to Paris. He prayed that they would succeed in their attempt to liberate the city. Soon. Before everything he had ever treasured was destroyed.

They arrived late at night. The streets were empty. Paris seemed like a city deserted, left by its own inhabitants and now occupied by foreign beings. It was almost twelve, curfew time. A strictly enforced curfew, one not to be taken lightly, challenged or disregarded. Only a fool would try the patience of the German soldiers. Since its inception, virtually all of Paris nightlife had shut down. Theaters were open from three in the afternoon until dusk, at least enabling their patrons to enjoy a show and then to return home without fear of being rounded up by the police. Montand and Piaf sang before dark at the Moulin Rouge. Parisians loved their nightlife, and they refused simply to lie down and die. They were determined to make the best of a horrible situation. But still the Lazares risked spending the night at the headquarters of the Military Police if they did not get to their familiar street and inside the apartment soon.

Jacques drove the car expertly through the darkened streets. Etienne had shared the driving with him on the long drive north, but Jacques was more familiar with the Paris streets, so they had switched just before entering the city limits. As they neared the rue de Rivoli, he turned right onto a one-way street and found himself going in the wrong direction.

"It wasn't enough to change all the signs, they've even changed the directions of the streets," he complained, panic creeping into his voice, aware that time was of the essence. Now he was confused and disoriented, uncertain which way to go.

Maurice was of little help, since he had rarely driven himself through the maze of streets.

"Just turn around quickly, son," he urged. "Take the next street over. Hurry, it's getting very late and we shouldn't be out much longer."

Jacques reoriented himself and found the Faubourg St. Honoré without further problem. But the wrong turn had cost them precious time. It was almost twelve-thirty when he pulled the car under the porte cochere of their apartment building.

"Stay in the car," Maurice commanded. He jumped out from his side of the car and fumbled in the darkness for the buzzer. He had sent word to Pierre that they would arrive today; surely the loyal employee, who was really more like a family member, would be up waiting at the door for them. He counted up six flights, only to discover that their floor was dark. It seemed as if they waited interminably for any sign of life within the building. Maurice stepped toward the curb. He tilted his head back and strained his eyes against the darkness, watching, waiting for the light to come on. He felt his heart pounding in his chest. Finally a dim light appeared and he saw Pierre's face peek timidly out from behind the lace curtain of their bedroom. He appeared sleepy and disoriented. Clearly the news had not reached him in time.

"It's me, Pierre. Maurice. I'm here with Etienne and Nathalie, and Jacques," he whispered as loudly as he could without waking the entire neighborhood. He was frightened now, his heart raced even faster, he wanted to be upstairs in the safety of his apartment. It was late, and he had been warned that if he was going to return to the city, he must be inside before curfew. Perspiration dripped down the back of his neck, and his shirt stuck to his clammy skin even though the night air was cool.

Pierre recognized the beloved voice immediately and waved his hand, signaling that he was coming down at once. Maurice breathed a deep sigh of relief and walked back to the car where the others waited patiently.

His hand gripped the door handle just as the powerful, blinding headlights of the van rounded the corner. Terror struck his heart. In that split second as the van moved toward them, he worried not for himself, but for his son and daughter and her husband.

The van picked up speed as its lights rested on their car, a sitting duck in the driveway. Its engine roared, and the vehicle lunged forward. It pulled up behind the car, blocking its path, and thwarting any thought of a last-ditch escape, and in that very moment Maurice knew his destiny had been determined.

"Out!" screamed the officer's harsh voice. "Out! Get out of the car now!"

"No," Maurice cried in return. "Stay in the car, Nathalie. Pierre is coming. Stay in the car!" he implored, but his screams were silenced with a sharp blow from the officer's baton. He collapsed into the gutter, hitting his head on the curb as he fell. Quickly two more soldiers were at his side, propping him up and leading him into the back of the van. Blood trickled from the cut on his forehead, down through the thickness of his eyebrows, but he was unable to wipe it away. His arms had been handcuffed behind his back. Two others descended from the truck and were leading Nathalie, Etienne and Jacques from the car.

It was even darker in the back of the truck than it had been in the streets. Already several others sat on the wooden benches, sedate looks of resignation on their broken faces. Maurice, Jacques, Nathalie and her husband joined the others rounded up that night. As the van pulled out of the street he had once called home and into the darkened night, Maurice heard Pierre's futile cries slowly fade away.

Eight of them—the four members of his family and four strangers with whom they were now joined—spent the remainder of the night jammed together in the back of the van. In the morning Maurice, Jacques and Etienne became inmates in Fresnes Prison. Nathalie was shipped to Romainville with the other women. There they would wait until the buses arrived to take them on the journey to Auschwitz or Dachau. Ironically, they were the same yellow Parisian city buses that many of the prisoners had used to go back and forth to work.

Back in the apartment on the Faubourg St. Honoré, Pierre tried to comfort Martine. She cried in his arms for the fate of her employer and his children, whom she loved as her own. There was no doubt that, unless a miracle occurred, they would never see the Lazares again. Frantically Pierre sat dialing the number of the château in the south, over and over again, hoping for a connection. Then he wrote a letter to Istanbul, fearing that the chances of its being received were slim. But knowing the Lazares' fate was sealed, he had to tell someone.

CHAPTER

10

MONTHS PASSED without any word from the Lazares, and Cyrielle felt certain that they had been taken away, removed from France, and sentenced to a hard life in a work camp, or, most terrifying, to their deaths at the hands of the Nazis.

She tried to block the horrible images from her mind, taking all her pleasure in life from her children. Zeki was a terror, and clearly the pride of his father's existence. He was almost four and had just begun nursery school. He was a striking young boy, large for his age, with a mane of thick, wavy black hair, and his father's rich olive skin tone. But the eyes were like Cyrielle's—sparkling, charming and winsome. When he cocked his head in a certain direction and asked for another piece of candy, or a second helping of Seta's luscious desserts, even the most devoted disciplinarian could not refuse. He was learning three languages—his native Turkish, his mother's French, and a smattering of English that he picked up from playing with his friends at the American school.

Ali and Yasemin, although twins, were as different as day and night. Ali was a quiet, studious youngster who took pleasure from sitting peacefully in the garden. He was a finicky eater who often sat picking at his food, and who, as a result, was a thin, often sickly child, a frequent target for colds and sore throats. Yasemin, on the other hand, was a female version of the wily Zeki. She raced about nonstop from the moment she awakened, bouncing from one activity to the next. She wouldn't sit still even for the briefest moment. Despite the eighteen-month difference, she was a physical and intellectual match for her older sibling. But even as she dashed about looking for trouble, she was always conscious of Ali. She cared for him, sharing her toys and making certain she was by his side if he got into any scrapes with the mischievous Zeki. Even though she played tricks on Zeki, hiding his favorite toy or teasing him mercilessly, she didn't have a mean bone in her body. She was caring and loving, and concerned about those around her. Physically, Yasemin was a miniature version of her beautiful mother. Her long raven hair hung in sweet curls down her back, and her expressive eyes worked their magic on all who met her. Her smile could convey a hundred different emotions, and during the course of any given day these could range from coyness to unbridled happiness to outright flirtation. She charmed her nanny into letting her stay up later than she was supposed to, and she conned the cooks into preparing all the foods that she especially liked. Her giggles filled the halls, and she shrieked with laughter when anything struck her as funny. Even at her young age, she had learned a great deal about the power of her feminine charms. She had her father wrapped about her little finger. When she heard the car pull into the driveway at night, she would drop whatever she was doing and race out into the garden to greet him. Zeki would be right on her heels, and Ali would trail farther behind.

"Baba, Babacığım" they would scream in unison, their staccato voices music to their mother's ears.

Omer would no sooner be out of the car than they would be upon him. He would bend down and sweep all three of them into his outstretched arms while they continued to screech with delight. Each of them would receive a kiss on both cheeks, and then the entire brood would march forward into the house. For the next half hour Omer was theirs. His entire attention was devoted to the youngsters. They would sit on the floor surrounding him, each of them vying for his affection.

"Take turns," he would plead above the racket, "please. Now, Zeki, you go first. Let's hear about your day."

"No, *Baba*. Me first," protested Yasemin.

"No, no, tonight we're going by age. Then beauty," he would rule, wanting to please all of them all the time.

Yasemin acquiesced and would at last sit quietly until it was her turn to speak.

It was evident to anyone who saw them together, Omer on the floor with his tie loosened, his shirt sleeves rolled up after a long day, entranced by their childish gobbledygook, that he loved these children more than his own life.

Cyrielle would stand in the doorway to the living room with her hands on her hips, observing the nightly frolicking. Watching her beloved husband as he listened to the children's tales made her heart swell with longing for him. He was truly a remarkable man, and she was blessed to have him in her life. She could not imagine an existence without him.

Seta came out and called the children in to dinner. Reluctantly they pulled themselves away from their beloved Baba and filed into the kitchen.

"Hurry, now," she said, "your parents have to get ready for this evening. Come along now. Zeki, stop teasing your sister!"

They were having guests for dinner, and there was just enough time for Cyrielle and Omer to have their evening drink together in the library before they went upstairs to dress. Cyrielle kissed her husband, and with her arm around his waist they walked into the library.

"Oh, what a long, draining day!" Omer said, throwing his briefcase on the desk and heading for the chesterfield.

The houseman entered, and they gave him orders for their drinks, a vodka for Omer and a glass of sherry for Cyrielle.

"Right away, Omer, *efendi bey,*" the man said.

Something in Omer's voice had concerned Cyrielle immediately. The way he spoke, his gesture of putting his things on his desk, something was amiss. It was very subtle, but there it was, a trace of unhappiness that only her keen sense of awareness about Omer could detect.

"Darling, what is it? You sound as if it's been more than just a difficult day."

He looked at her and couldn't resist smiling. She knew, and she had known at once, that there was more to his words than merely a comment about his day. Most of his days were long, filled with meetings and questions and an endless stream of telephone calls, but he never complained, for he loved his work.

"Oh, you smart cookie," he said, pulling her over to him and kissing her hair. He loved its sweet fresh scent, and already he felt better. "You're right, something is terribly wrong, and I'm afraid there's nothing I can do about it."

"Not possible. You're my hero, and you can fix anything. I count on you."

He sighed, and then said, "I wish that were the case here. But it's not."

The houseman returned with their drinks and tiny dishes filled with nuts and olives. Cyrielle took them from him and sent him out of the room.

"Go on, darling. What are you talking about?"

"You know that a couple of years ago Turkey signed a commercial pact with Germany to provide them with a quantity of chrome ore in exchange for some things that we can use. It's a decision I have never been in favor of, but there was nothing I could do to prevent it from happening. You know that Turan Holding and the Bora family own most of the mines that produce this ore. Ever since we started buying them they have produced big revenues for us, they've become very important to us. The only other countries that produce any great quantities of the stuff are Cuba, which has already declared war against Germany; Russia, which is obviously out of the question; Southern Rhodesia, which is controlled by Britain; and a small amount from South Africa. So Turkey is really the only place they can look to for the amount they need."

"What do they do with it?" Cyrielle asked, not wanting to interrupt, but curious about this mineral with which she was totally un-familiar.

"Mostly they make piston heads for engines. Engines to run their tanks. Chrome plating is very resistant to heat, which makes it a good choice for locomotives or anything that has to endure a great deal of friction. The Boras have always been more than willing to sell their supply. They don't seem to mind that they will be profiteering from the war, that they are aiding in the Nazis' efforts to destroy so many lives."

"Omer, you can't control what the Boras do. They must make their own decisions."

"Yes, but now I'm being pressured to either sell our supply, or turn the mines over to the Boras so that they can in turn sell the ore."

"Who is pushing, the government or the Boras?"

"Both, but a strong lobby is coming from the Boras. They are accusing us of being unpatriotic, and they are trying to force the government to make us sell our mines to them. At a greatly reduced price, I might add." He sighed again, deeply troubled by the situation. "But it's not the price I'm concerned about. It's the whole idea of it, the principle of the deal. I've never been able to come to terms with it. I could never abide by it. Especially because of you, my darling. Here we are, still not knowing about the fate of your family, and yet we might be forced to sell Germany something that will only help them in their cause to annihilate . . ." He stopped, the look on Cy-rielle's face told him that he was reopening the wounds, bringing the constant worry she tried so hard to control back to the front of her mind.

"Oh, darling, I'm sorry. I just don't know what to do. I can't reason with the Boras. They've been our arch enemies for as long as I can remember, and now this . . . it's just too much. I've always thought that Erol Bora would sell his mother if the price was right, and this is just about as close to that as he can get."

The houseman knocked and told them that their guests were expected in less than half an hour. Cyrielle thanked him, waved him out of the doorway, and returned her attention to Omer.

"Sell them the mines, darling. Forget about them. I know it is completely against your will, but it is better than having the sale of the minerals on your head. Let the Boras do what they feel is best, or what they feel they must do to make money. You are above that, and Turan Holding will survive and prosper. And most important, you will have a clear heart. Someday they will be sorry for doing it, someday in the future. Until then, you must do what is right for you."

"I know, darling. I feel better just talking with you about it. You're right, as you always are. I will sell them. But one day, just as you said . . ."

Talk that evening centered on the only subject that filled their minds —the war. Their guests ate heartily, and as always enjoyed the beauty of the art-filled Turan home and the warm hospitality of their host and hostess. Cyrielle caught Omer's eye during the course of the evening, and although he still appeared concerned, she knew their conversation had done much to ease his mind.

CHAPTER

11

*A*S THE WINTER of 1947 approached, Cyrielle was again nearing full term. The war had been over for nearly two years, and still no word had been received as to the whereabouts of her family. After the devastating news of their capture in Paris had finally reached them, no amount of questioning and searching had brought them any answers. Omer, frustrated by the lack of information, had made one trip to Paris, but his use of all the diplomatic channels he could muster hadn't shed any light on their disappearance. No papers had been recovered, no record of them existed outside of France. It was as if, on that night now so long ago, they had simply vanished into thin air. Slowly the atrocities of Hitler's regime were being uncovered, but the full scale of its horrors would not be known for years to come. In the meantime Omer and his father used every connection they could think of to try and get information.

Cyrielle never gave up hope. She prayed that somehow they had escaped harm. She refused to let go of that thought until there was definitive proof to the contrary.

Omer began traveling to Europe, establishing more businesses and joint ventures with firms trying to recover from the war's devastation. Occasionally a new client was unable to pay; all some people had left was their clothes, and, if they had been fortunate, a few valuables that they had not been forced to forfeit. Some had been able to keep paintings and artwork that by more good fortune had escaped the greedy eyes of the Nazis. It was thanks to a few people like this that Omer was able to continue building his impressive collection. He would often make deals that would take a painting or piece of sculpture as barter for badly needed goods or services. Each time Cyrielle saw a new painting arrive, she felt blessed that the Lazare collection had made it safely out of France.

"When is my little sister coming, Maman? When? I hope it's soon," Yasemin asked, breaking Cyrielle's thoughts. Yasemin patted her mother's swollen tummy and then ran her hand gently across it, trying to feel the movement of a tiny foot or hand. She moved her own small hand back and forth across the taut surface, using the lightest, most delicate touch, as her mother had instructed her.

"Yes, it will be soon, I promise, Yasemin," Cyrielle assured the child. It was a cold, miserable day, and Cyrielle was feeling especially heavy and uncomfortable. She lay on the divan in the little room, her back supported by masses of pillows. "What makes you so sure it's going to be a girl? It could just as easily be a baby boy, you know. We can't be certain until the moment he or she is born."

"Oh, I know it's a girl," the precocious child insisted. "Besides, I don't want another brother, a yucky boy. I want someone to play with, just like Zeki has Ali to play with. What would we do with a boy, anyway? They just cause trouble. And they stink," she added as an afterthought.

"Oh, come on now, they don't stink," her mother said, stifling an urge to laugh. "Little boys are wonderful, and you'll come to love them more and more as you grow older." But under the surface, Cyrielle sensed a potential problem and decided to address it right at that very moment. If she could nip the child's attitude in the bud before it became a real issue, everyone would be better off, particularly Yasemin. She raised herself up, carefully balancing on her elbows. This position signaled that they were about to have a serious mother-and-daughter discussion. The child kept her hand firmly on her mother's stomach just in case the new angle prompted the baby to move about.

"Yasemin, you must listen to me very carefully," she began. "We don't know what kind of baby we are going to have, whether it's going to be a boy or a girl. Even the doctor doesn't know yet. It doesn't really matter. What is important is that, whatever it is, we love him or her equally. Part of the mystery of life is the not knowing until the very second when a baby is born what it is going to be. It is one of the many wonderful surprises that happens to us in life. Having a baby brother would be just as wonderful as having a baby sister. It doesn't matter. As long as he or she is healthy and has all his or her fingers and toes. Do you understand?"

The look on her daughter's face told Cyrielle that she hadn't reached her at all. Yasemin had no interest whatsoever in a baby brother. She wanted the baby to be a girl, and that was the end of it. Her stubbornness was a characteristic she shared with her father, and once she was set on something, all the discussion in the world wouldn't change her mind.

Yasemin pulled her hand away from her mother's stomach as if it had burned her, not wanting to continue touching it if there was the slightest chance that a yucky boy lurked inside.

"Yasemin," her mother repeated, stroking the child's tangled hair away from her beautiful face. She had been practicing her newly learned ballet movements and then had gone to look at something in the garden, and her cheeks were flushed and her nose smudged with dirt. But she was a beautiful mess. Cyrielle leaned over and kissed her on the forehead. "Do you understand what I'm saying to you?"

The little girl contorted her face, which told her mother she had understood exactly what she said, but that she did not agree with her. Yasemin was an extremely bright child, partly because her mother and father spent so much time with her. She was mature beyond her years. So Cyrielle knew perfectly well that the child had understood her completely. Yet the fact that she was spoiled got in the way. As she continued her facial antics, Cyrielle had to hold back her laughter.

"Yes, Maman, I understand, but I don't care. I only want a baby sister. I don't want it to be a boy." She pulled another funny face. "We already have too many boys." She shook her head back in a defiant gesture, sending her long hair flying over her shoulder. "But I know it's going to be a girl."

Yasemin spoke her words with such assurance that Cyrielle decided she would handle the situation when and if it came to pass and another male was added to their family. She looked at the little girl's messy face and saw so many complexities—she had the glorious looks of her mother and maternal grandmother coupled with the shrewd character and volatile temper of her father. Her precious daughter was a mixture of two cultures that represented two very different views of life. She knew both she and Omer spoiled her mercilessly, and she hoped that the arrival of a new baby, regardless of its sex, would help to curb a potential problem before it got completely out of hand.

Yasemin's predictions came true when the Turans were blessed with another baby girl. They named her Nevin, a word from ancient Turkish that meant "something new." Cyrielle and Omer found it pretty and feminine, the same way they had felt about Yasemin. For all their children they had chosen names that were easy to pronounce, so that if they decided to go abroad to study or live, they would not be targets of cruel jokes by their peers, or needless misunderstandings.

Cyrielle loved being a new mother again, and as she sat in the wheelchair clutching the newborn to her as Omer wheeled her out from the hospital, she felt that indeed she was the luckiest woman in the world.

CHAPTER

12

I'LL SEE YOU in ten days," Omer promised as he kissed his wife good-bye one more time, stroked her cheek gently, and then closed the door firmly on the Bentley. He tapped lightly on the hood, a signal to Murat that they should be on their way. Cyrielle sat in the front seat with Nevin on her lap. In the back, the children pressed their faces to the glass; Zeki flattened his tongue on the window and Yasemin pushed her nose tightly against the pane, making her normally beautiful face take on the appearance of a pig. She giggled wildly, convinced that it was the funniest thing in the world. Ali sat quietly coloring in a new book. Omer could barely see Semra, sandwiched between these wild animals, little lovable monsters, as she, too, waved good-bye.

"Have fun," he yelled as the big iron gates swung open and the driver pulled the car out into the busy street. Its underbody scraped on the pavement, so laden down it was with luggage, equipment and miscellaneous paraphernalia for the trip.

"You too, my darling. Give my best regards to Paris. Try to find out something, anything . . ." Cyrielle said wistfully, a trace of hope that refused to die still evident in her voice. "Don't work too hard." But even as she said the words she knew he would work like a madman all week, rushing from appointment to appointment. The business trips he planned followed a grueling schedule filled with breakfasts and lunches and dinners stacked with back-to-back meetings. He would do all of that and then rush like a crazy person, with only seconds to spare, to catch the plane home to Istanbul. From there he would take the same series of flights they would be on today.

"I'll bet he's glad to be rid of us for a while," Cyrielle said to Semra as the car approached the Istanbul airport and the children cheered with excitement. They were on their way to Athens. From there they would transfer to another, smaller plane that would fly them to Piraeus, where they would be met by the captain and crew of the Turan yacht. They would pile all the luggage in the cars and take the short ride to the dock. At last, after hours of traveling, they would board the boat, their home for the next four weeks. They would swim and snorkel (all except Cyrielle), see their friends, and explore some of the beautiful Greek islands. During the war the Germans had occupied the area, and now that Greece was free again, the Turans were anxious to visit.

It was the beginning of the *bayram,* the Muslim holidays that occurred twice every year. Luckily, many of them fell during the summer months. They were major holy days, and a few of the families of means headed for the warm climate and relaxing atmosphere of the waters belonging to their neighbors to the southwest. There they could remain on their boats, relax, and rendezvous with their friends in the evenings, when they pulled in to the small port where they had decided to dock for the night. At the season's peak, when everyone was there, boats bearing the Union Jack, the French tricolor, and the Italian stripes were docked so closely together that one could walk from yacht to yacht, from party to party. It was paradise for parents, for the children could come and go as they pleased, and there was never a worry about their whereabouts or safety. In years past, because of her tremendous fear of the water and her inability to swim, Cyrielle had declined all invitations to mix with this interesting crowd, preferring to stay at home in Istanbul in the summers. But now that the children were older, they had their own friends who would all be there with their families during the warm months. They would also meet children from other countries, and they would have a chance to practice their French with someone other than their parents. Cyrielle felt she would be denying the children one of the great pleasures and rituals of growing up if she continued to refuse to go with them. So she had at last agreed, and now, when they were finally on the luxurious boat, all settled in, she wondered why she had been so stubborn before.

"It's quite lovely, isn't it?" Semra asked her one afternoon, four days after they had left Piraeus.

"Heavenly," agreed Cyrielle. "There are plenty of places to sit which are cool and out of the sun, and it is a pleasure not having to run after the children all day. I've been a fool for fighting it for so long."

The Turan yacht was one of the most spectacular in Turkey. It was a three-masted fore-and-aft schooner that had been built in 1929. Under full sail it was one of the most graceful ships in the entire region. It was completely black, constructed of ebony wood. Mustafa Turan had purchased it from an Englishman in the early thirties. He had christened her *Meltem,* after the gentle winds that were such a pleasant feature of the southern waters. The elder Turan had traveled with her from Southampton to Turkey, and every summer since then she had sailed around Istanbul and the Princes Islands. In recent years, when the community of artists and writers had become more adventuresome, he had sailed with her to the Greek islands and to the newly developing southern coastline of Turkey, around the tiny, as yet unspoiled village of Bodrum. The *Meltem* always carried a variety of passengers—family, friends, cognoscenti of the art world, and business associates. Her six spacious cabins were luxurious by any standards, they had been renovated over the years and were outfitted with the most modern conveniences. She was a floating paradise, and Cyrielle was enjoying every minute of their trip. The captain, a seasoned English sailor named Ivy, and his crew, six young men who were under his strict tutelage, had been with the Turan family for years. Mustafa had bought Ivy a small house in Istanbul where the ship was docked in the winter, and he had made certain that his family was well cared for all year round. Ivy returned the kindness by working doubly hard to ensure that all who sailed with him had a safe, enjoyable, and highly memorable experience. He was an excellent cook, and so eager was he to impress Cyrielle that every night he worked at the side of the regular cook and they would prepare a feast—usually a fish caught that very day, served with local vegetables and potatoes. Once, for dessert, he had even managed to make some ice cream. This extravagance had won the hearts of Zeki, Ali, and Yasemin, and from then on the adults were guaranteed smooth sailing. The children obeyed him whenever he spoke, and Zeki even showed an interest in learning the fundamentals of sailing. Of course Ivy was only too happy to comply.

With the children occupied, Cyrielle's days were carefree and peaceful. The long hours of sunshine were filled with beautiful sights —the whitewashed villages of the islands, the windows of the homes and tiny shops lined with brilliant red flowers, made even more vibrant in contrast to the clear turquoise waters of the Mediterranean. Still, she could hardly wait for her dear husband to join them.

When Sunday finally arrived, she was missing him more than ever. With a child's wide-eyed excitement she watched as Ivy and one of his crew piled into the small dinghy to row to shore and pick up the waiting Omer. She could see him standing on the narrow, rickety pier in the distance, still dressed, as she knew he would be, in his elegant English suit. He had loosened his tie and rolled up his sleeves, and to Cyrielle he looked sexier and more attractive than ever. She waited motionless on the front deck as the crewmen loaded his luggage and then held the boat steady for him to climb aboard. The late-afternoon sun still felt hot on her face, and she went to stand under the protection of the canvas deck while they rowed in with their precious cargo.

The children crowded around the ladder as the boat neared, screeching and yelling all at once.

"Settle down, everyone, you'll have a chance to tell *Babacığım* about the trip. Now move back and give him a chance to get on board," she urged.

But her words fell on deaf ears, so thrilled were they to see their father. They crowded in closer, and as his shoes hit the deck, the children overcame him, each wanting to be the first in his arms.

"Hold on, you little beasts, wait a minute, please, now calm down," he begged. But they charged him, pulling at his sleeves, vying for the affection of their wonderful father.

He gave up. Dropping his briefcase, he opened his arms to all of them. Yasemin and Zeki pushed their way through, squeezing out little Ali and the toddler Nevin in the process.

Cyrielle, with Semra at her side, stood watching this scene just as she did every night at home in Istanbul. Her heart soared with happiness as she saw the love and caring Omer felt for his children. When he had finally calmed them and turned his eyes on her, her expression told him of her adoration. Later she would show him just how much she had missed him.

"Welcome aboard," she said as he turned to her and took her in his arms.

"Oh, it's so wonderful to be here," he responded, with a powerful embrace that told her more than words ever could.

He turned back to the boys as they continued to unload the packages he had brought. There was a present for each of the children, a tin of French pâté for Semra, and a large hat box.

"Careful with that," he cautioned the boy who held the round box by its silk cord. "Be very careful. I would like it taken below and stored in my cabin immediately," he directed. "Now, before you do anything else, please." The boy tightened his grip on the large lavender-colored parcel and headed below at once. Both Cyrielle and Semra watched it disappear, their curiosity mounting. But Omer showed no interest in addressing their quizzical looks, and he turned his attention back to the children. They seemed delighted with their gifts—a deluxe snorkeling mask for Zeki, a new toy car for Ali, an adorable stuffed lion for Nevin, and a lovely new doll with a hand-painted porcelain face, dressed in a lacy French pinafore, for Yasemin.

"Something for everyone except my lovely wife," he said, voicing what had passed through Cyrielle's mind for a brief second. "Well, you'll just have to wait for yours," he teased. "Perhaps this evening."

Ivy and the cook worked all afternoon, and by the time the sun fell behind the horizon line and evening set, they had prepared a dinner of incomparable delights. Fresh fish, new boiled potatoes, a salad made from the day's just-picked ingredients, all complemented by a crisp white wine that Omer had carried from France.

After dinner, with the children all put to bed and Semra in her cabin reading, Cyrielle and Omer sat side by side on the banquettes that lined the front deck. A cool breeze washed over them and provided the only movement in the still night. Visible in the distance were the lights of a solitary ship. Beyond that, all was dark. Not even the sliver of a moon lit the black waters. He put his arm around her and pulled her close to him as they sat sharing the intimacy of the darkness surrounding them.

Finally she asked what she had been wanting to know since the moment he had come on board. "Omer, did you learn anything?"

He had known that she would ask him that question the moment they were alone, and he had prepared his response. "No, no, I didn't," he lied, knowing that he could not break her heart right then. He did not have the strength, and he was selfish enough not to want to ruin their next few hours of reunion. He had missed her terribly; telling her right then, right that minute, wouldn't change anything. So he uttered the false words he had vowed to stand by. For a time, anyway. "I'm sorry, darling."

She looked at him quizzically for a moment, and then seemed to accept this, for not knowing anything was still better than learning an awful truth. At least, with no word, there was still a glimmer of hope remaining.

"Was your trip a success?"

Leaning over and taking the big lavender box from his side and offering it to her, he said, "I'll let you be the judge of that."

She had not noticed the box beside him, and she smiled broadly at the sight of it. "I was really talking about business, you know."

"I know what you meant; but business is unimportant, compared with making you happy."

His words were sincere, and as she looked at him she felt a love stronger than she had ever known could exist. She leaned across the bulky package and kissed him. The elegant printing indicated it was from the best milliner in Paris, a store she knew well, since her mother had been one of their best customers. No one had ever looked better in a hat than Dominique Lazare. Her most famous photograph, one that had quickly become a classic after it appeared on the pages of French *Vogue*, showed her in a simple silk day dress and wearing a hat from that very shop. What a strange turn of fate for her daughter to be sitting in the middle of the Mediterranean sea with a box from Madame Allard's on her lap, Cyrielle mused.

She lifted the lid carefully, then removed the lilac-patterned tissue paper that surrounded the treasure within. She reached in and pulled it out gently. "Oh, Omer," she cried, delight in her voice, "it's so beautiful!" She twirled the straw sun hat about her hand as she examined the bouquet of summer flowers attached at the back. Although they were hand-constructed of the finest silk, she could almost smell the refreshing scent of lavender, jasmine, and orange blossom —a Provençal bouquet from the fields of southern France. "Oh, it's lovely, really. How in the world, with your busy schedule, did you ever find time to shop for it?" The boutique was all the way over on the Left Bank, on a tiny, difficult-to-find street, miles from where all of Omer's business meetings took place.

"For you, my love, I can always find the time," he told her. "It's charming, isn't it? I hoped you'd like it."

"You're the best. I love it! Oh, I want to put it on right this minute."

"Here, let me help you," he offered, taking the delicate present from her.

She released her hair from atop her head and ran it through her fingers quickly, trying to put it into place. Omer waited patiently.

"Okay," she said, lowering her head so he could place it on her crown.

"There it is, you'll have to play with it now, adjust it a bit, to get it just right."

She reached up and fiddled with the brim, but without a mirror it was hard to determine if she was moving it in the right direction. She stopped, lowered her hands, and smiled at him.

"How does it look?"

"It should sit a little bit lower on your head, I think, and maybe a touch forward."

She raised her hands for another go-around, began moving it around once more. She tried to pull it lower once or twice, but it wasn't working. Exasperated, she lowered her arms. "There's something in the brim, something blocking it; maybe Madame left a ticket or a pin in it. Something is definitely in there."

"Take if off and have a look," he replied, seemingly undisturbed by her frustration.

Reaching back up, she removed the hat and turned it upside down in her lap. With one hand she ran her fingers under the grosgrain ribbon lining the inside band. Suddenly she hit the obstacle and her fingers stopped. "Here it is, whatever it is," she said. She pulled the hat up closer to her so she could get a better look at what was preventing her from donning the wonderful present. "What is it? What could it be?" She held the band even closer and finally turned up the entire width of ribbon. "Oh, oh, my," she exclaimed, as the mystery was finally revealed.

From beneath the band she slowly extracted a breathtaking bracelet. She loosened it from the threads that had been sewn carefully around it so that it would remain hidden inside until she discovered it. Once it was disengaged, she held it up. It was a diamond bracelet, four rows wide, and breaking up the gleaming rows of white lightning were two large sapphires and two equally large rubies. They were perfectly positioned along the length of the bracelet: first a sapphire, next a ruby, then another sapphire, then another ruby.

"Two rubies—one for Yasemin and one for Nevin, and the two sapphires are for Zeki and Ali," he said in a gentle voice. "Do you like it?"

"Are you kidding?" she squealed. "It's beautiful! No wonder you were so concerned about it as it came off the dinghy. I would have hated to have it fall to the bottom of the sea. Oh, Omer, it is really special. I'm thrilled. Thank you so very much."

He looked at her with all the love he had in his soul. In a day, or in a week from now, he knew he would have to break her heart, be forced to tell her the devastating news he had discovered in Paris. He would give anything in the world, do anything for her, if he could avoid doing that. But he also knew that nothing could happen which would make the terrible truth go away, so he froze the memory of her joyous face in his mind. He would recall it later when he finally had to tell her.

"You're welcome, my sweet, I'm glad you like it. Here, let me put it on for you." He fastened the exquisite bauble around her wrist. It accentuated her slender fingers and delicate hands.

"I love it, and I love you, darling."

His arms curled around her and they sat kissing like high school lovers for the longest time.

"I missed you," he said when they finally pulled their mouths apart for a brief moment.

"And I missed you so much," she answered.

"Come with me," he whispered. He led her to the front of the boat and told her to remain there, then he went and dragged the cushions from the banquettes back to her. He beckoned her to sit down next to him on this makeshift bed.

He slowly began unbuttoning the tiny pearl fastenings on the bodice of her dress. "Omer . . ." she began to protest, but he silenced her.

"Shh . . . the children are all fast asleep, Semra is in her cabin, and the captain and crew are also sound asleep. They have a long day ahead of them tomorrow. Besides, they wouldn't dare come up knowing that we're here. So just relax, my darling. I want to make love to you under the open sky."

Slowly, as he kissed her, her trepidations fell away and were replaced by an overwhelming passion for her husband.

He freed her breasts from the constraints of her dress, and when they were naked before him, he took one in each hand, caressing them like the precious objects they were. He held them lightly at first, and then, as his hardness grew, he placed his mouth over her swollen nipples, gently rolling them between his lips. Cyrielle's head fell back as she was overcome with a warm sensation that ran from the tips of her breasts to the very core of her being. He finished undressing her, and then stood to undress himself as she lay naked, without the usual protection of the bedcovers and the confines of their bedroom. She felt exposed and open to him, and the thought of what they were doing excited her even more. As he came to lie next to her, she arched her back up to meet him. Sliding his hand beneath the small of her back, he brought himself down upon her. Her legs opened and her thighs wrapped around him, and she accepted his hardness eagerly. Her soft moans were silenced by the gentle flapping of the sails above their heads. They melted into each other, and she held on to him tightly as their rhythm increased.

"Oh, this is how I want it to be always, my darling," he whispered, inhaling the sweet scent of her and feeling the moistness of her skin.

"Yes, love, it will be. Always."

She moaned softly the entire time he possessed her. His eyes became wild, anxious and urgent, and when she knew from his movements that his climax had begun, she covered his mouth with her hand to silence his screams as he exploded into her.

"I love you, my beauty, my Cyrielle," he said, stroking her face and holding her tightly against him.

She cradled him until she felt his breathing return to normal. They lay entwined in each other's arms, savoring their intimacy. But as always when they made love, Omer was not content to rest until Cyrielle too had been pleasured. Just as she began to doze off she felt the light touch of Omer's fingertips as he reached down and parted her thighs.

"Umm . . ." she moaned, raising her body to greet his fingers. He spread her swollen lips and felt the wetness that always awaited him. She continued to groan softly as he probed her most private parts and found the magic spot that always brought her such ecstasy. By the time she could no longer bear it he was again ready for her, and he mounted her with the same intensity of desire he had shown the first time. Only now he could relax and let her build her own pleasure, which she did more quickly than he expected. Her sighs grew until he heard the distinct sounds of abandonment that he had known since the very first night of their marriage.

"Now, darling, now, oh, I adore the way you make me feel," she said as she wound her orgasm to a conclusion against his hardness. "Yes, yes . . ."

"I know, angel. I always know how to make you happy."

She collapsed on top of him, yet still clung to him with her last ounce of strength. He held her close, waiting for her now gentle moans to subside.

Her strength renewed, she smiled down at him and pulled away, wanting to feel the cool breeze flow over her warm, moist skin. The bracelet was the only thing she wore, and she stretched her arm out to its full length, admiring it in the weak light from the cabin below.

"It looks like the tricolor. A very lavish, expensive version of the tricolor," she said. "I love that flag. Oh, France, I can't wait to return for a visit."

When she was cool again she turned on her side, away from him, and molded her body into the contours of his. Her back was against his chest, her buttocks pressed into his belly, their legs forming an identical curve. He wrapped his arms about her and they remained side by side, the only sound now the soft rippling of the tied sails. Minutes passed in silence, but he could tell from her breathing that she was still awake.

"They're gone, Cyrielle; gone forever."

He felt her stiffen with understanding, and yet she remained with her back to him. He continued, uttering the hardest words of his entire life.

"Your father, Jacques, Nathalie, and Etienne . . . all of them are gone . . ." At the mention of each beloved name, those who had meant everything to her, her entire body reacted, jerked forward as if shot through with a powerful dose of electricity. He tightened his hold on her and rocked her back and forth. She remained silent, and then slowly her head began to move from side to side, to shake in denial, her mouth opened, and from the depths of her soul came a scream of pain. This time he covered her mouth with his hands, but she fought him with an enormous strength, biting his palm, and reaching up with her own hand to pull his away. He held her firmly, chanting whatever words of comfort he could find.

"Cyrielle, Cyrielle, I'm so sorry . . . I know what this is doing to you. The pain. If there was any way to spare you . . . Cyrielle, oh, my love, my precious . . ."

A voice from below startled them, asking if everything was all right. Omer assured Ivy not to worry, to stay below. The prospect of waking her children and having to face them now seemed to silence Cyrielle, and at last her body went limp and she turned to her husband and accepted his embrace in silence.

After her tears had subsided, she lifted her reddened face to his. "Why now? Why did you choose such a moment, after you had made love to me like this, to tell me?"

"Because I wanted you to know how strong my love for you is, my darling. I wanted you to remember my touch, my passion, and my love for you. I wanted that to be fresh in your mind when I told you this terrible news. It is so important for you to know how much you mean to me, and how your world is now here with me, and with your children. It is a terrible, terrible thing to lose your entire family like this, but I want you to know that I am here for you, to comfort you, to protect you, and to care for you. You will always have me, and your children. We will never replace the family you have lost, but we will love you and treasure you. That is why I chose to tell you now. I hope you will try to understand. Telling you was the most difficult thing I have ever done."

"Oh, Omer," she sighed, her emotions torn and confused, her thoughts racing through her mind. "Yes, yes, I understand. And I love you even more for it."

They stayed up the rest of the night, as Omer slowly revealed the horrible details he had been able to uncover about the extermination of the Lazares. As painful as it was for him to tell and as difficult as it was for her to hear, she insisted on knowing everything. Wrapped in light blankets, they talked until the sun rose over the waters and she finally succumbed to an exhausted sleep. Her arms were crossed over her breasts, the tricolor bracelet glistening in the morning light.

CHAPTER

13

CYRIELLE adjusted slowly to her new realities. Learning at last the fate of her father, brother, sister and brother-in-law, the only family she had in the world, should have made it easier to accept, but like all death, the finality of the news was devastating. Even today, nearly five years after Omer had broken the news to her, her memories of them were as clear and vivid as the day she had packed for Istanbul. It had been over a decade, yet it seemed like yesterday.

The days were easy to get through, for the children kept her busy from early morning until well past dinner. After school, Zeki was off to sports practice, Ali to his piano lessons, Yasemin to a swimming meet, and Nevin was constantly on the go with her own set of friends. The daylight hours passed quickly, as the doors slammed constantly, with cars pulling in and out of the driveway, depositing or picking up a steady stream of children. Cyrielle had given up most of her studies, but she still took a class now and then, because she loved it and because someday, when the children were older, she was determined to go back to school.

The nights were a different story. In the quiet house, Cyrielle often lay motionless in her bed, reliving over and over again the fate of her beloved family. She would drift off into a fitful sleep, only to be awakened suddenly, sometimes by the perspiration that drenched her, or, more often, by the return of the horrible nightmare. Omer would reach out for her and take her in his arms, holding her and comforting her until the bad dream had passed. She welcomed the first sign of daylight as it came through the long windows, and would leap out of bed, eager to escape her nocturnal hauntings.

Through all this Serma was a source of strength for Cyrielle. She continued to live with them, having delayed her plan to return to Europe, and Cyrielle welcomed her presence in the large house more than ever before. She had a wonderful manner and was never in the way. She stayed completely out of all domestic discussions and arguments and never tried to discipline the children or play the part of a mother to them. She always followed a path of noninterference. If she was asked, she would gladly volunteer her opinion, but otherwise she stayed out of Omer and Cyrielle's private life and the lives of their children. There was no doubt that she loved them all dearly, but she knew her place and that was the main reason the relationship between all of them had prospered.

Her home and her children were the core of Cyrielle's existence. While Omer continued his rigorous travel schedule, building and trading companies, and making Turan Holding an even more formidable entity, she was content to throw her entire energy into the raising of the four Turan heirs. What fascinated her most was the distinctive personalities of the children. As they grew up, their own traits became evident, and she marveled at the differences between them.

Zeki, a strapping teenager, was a physical copy of his handsome father. Strong-shouldered, with well-developed muscles as a result of his keen interest in sports of all kinds, he also possessed Omer's competitive, tenacious spirit. He had his father's features—broad forehead, dark skin, and a mass of dark curly hair, but the deep brooding eyes were like his mother's. If he wasn't on the tennis court, he could probably be found on the soccer field or the basketball court, or pursuing any of a number of other athletic activities. All of this was at the expense of his grades, and even though it worried his mother tremendously, his father claimed it was not a problem. Someday he would be taking over the helm of Turan Holding, so he didn't really have to concentrate too much on his academics.

He'll have the company, and I'll teach him everything he needs to know," Omer insisted.

"But he still needs a proper education. What would you have done without your schooling in England? That has helped you both in business and in life, even more than you realize, I think," she countered.

"It taught me to speak perfect French so that I could seduce the girl of my dreams," he shot back, pulling her to him and kissing her. She smiled at him, but did not give up on her argument. At every opportunity, she insisted that Zeki become more serious about his schoolwork.

Omer did spend a great deal of time with the boy, taking him on tours of the factories, and, when it was appropriate, to an occasional business meeting. Zeki became the focus of Omer's existence. Everything he did—his work, his travels, his leisure time—was based around the boy. He spoiled him beyond measure: the best sports equipment, a new boat when he turned thirteen, outings and excursions with his friends—everything Zeki ever mentioned and all things Omer thought his first son should have, he got. It was clear that Zeki was his favorite of the boys. Cyrielle tried to understand why this was so. At first she felt it was simply because he was the eldest, and the firstborn, which gave him a special place in his father's heart. But Ali, only two years younger, was a delightful child as well. He was not as strongly built, for he had no interest in sports, and his coloring was lighter than that of his father. His features were softer and his hair lighter, bleaching out to a golden color in the summer sun. His face was sweet and kind, and his eyes were less intense than those of his older brother. Ali was an avid student, often staying late in the library and taking more courses than the normal load. Cyrielle sometimes wondered if Zeki even knew the location of the library. Ali's true love, even at his young age, was the piano. He begged to have extra lessons and Cyrielle readily agreed, over Omer's protests that he should be developing other skills as well. Ali was quiet and studious, and a joy to have around.

Of the girls, Yasemin was the one who most resembled her

mother. Even more than Cyrielle she looked like the grandmother she only knew from pictures. She had the same fine features, the identical flowing hair, and the same long-waisted, long-legged figure. If she kept growing at the same rate, she would soon be nearly as statuesque as Dominique Lazare had been. Her looks were Cyrielle's, but her spirit was her father's. Zeki loved to compete in sports, but Yasemin loved to win. She wasn't especially skilled athletically, but sheer determination and tenaciousness gave her an advantage over most of her opponents. She would practice longer and try harder than any of her teammates, making her a valuable asset to any group sport. In individual activities, like tennis, her endurance, from such extensive practice, was stronger than that of others. She was possessed of a competitive spirit the likes of which neither of her parents had ever seen. It was the same with her academically. Not extraordinarily gifted, she would study longer, ask more questions, and delve deeper into problems than her classmates. When exam time rolled around she was better prepared and more knowledgeable than anyone in her class. In this old-fashioned manner, based on hard work, determination and patience, she would eventually secure her position as valedictorian of her graduating class. She was fiercely protective of her twin brother, getting into constant scrapes with those who sometimes took advantage of the seemingly weaker child.

Nevin was the most passive, the sweetest of the children. From her earliest days, even as a toddler, she had been quiet and content, and happy with whatever situation she found herself in. While her older sister ran rampant, exploring and satiating a bottomless curiosity, she sat peacefully playing with her dolls or whatever was at hand. She was an average student, concerned only with learning the minimum, doing her best and not making any waves. She was an attractive girl, pretty in a soft, approachable way. Unlike her sister, who was clearly destined to be a great beauty in the tradition of her mother and grandmother, Nevin's personality fit her looks. Quiet and unassuming.

Cyrielle loved them all equally, and even though she felt that Omer showed favoritism toward the older boy, she was willing to overlook it because he was such a good father to all of them. The children were her life, they gave her what she had missed, a family to call her own. She could not imagine a life without them. She adored them all and their own special traits, the traits that made them individuals. She loved them more than life itself.

As they grew older and needed the attention and tutelage of their mother less and less, Cyrielle did not want to keep them back in any way. She learned to let go, to let them find their own way in the world. With all their various activities, the drivers were kept busy nonstop, and it was a rare occasion when they were all at home for a meal together.

With so much time on her hands, Cyrielle again began her studies. By now she had become a bona fide expert in Iznik porcelains, and each semester she taught a class at the college. She enjoyed doing this; it made her feel as if she was making an important contribution, but still she yearned to do more.

She awoke one morning knowing what it was she was destined to do. She was overcome with a feeling of purpose, of resolution, and now that she knew what it was, she set about researching and planning before she took the idea to Omer. Finally she was prepared and ready for the next move.

Picking a night when they were alone to tell him of her brainstorm, she entered the library a few minutes after he had returned home.

"Hello, darling," she greeted him.

He rose from his desk where he always went right away to review the day's mail.

"How are you?" he said, going to her and kissing her lightly on both cheeks, then hugging her to him. He never tired of seeing her glorious face, and even after the longest, most grueling day imaginable, her presence would renew his energy. At thirty-three, Cyrielle was more beautiful than ever. The sleek model look she had possessed in her twenties had matured and settled into a more refined, more sophisticated appearance that was even more appealing to him. Her figure, after having borne four children, was almost as trim and firm as it had always been. Her hips had filled out, she had lost the narrow silhouette that could easily wear any skirt or dress created, and her breasts were fuller and rounder, but to Omer's eyes, and to those of most other men, she remained a great beauty. She dressed in a classic tailored manner, asking her dressmaker to copy the latest Parisian fashions, or ordering them and having Omer bring them back from his trips. She knew what looked best on her, and she was always impeccably turned out. This evening she wore the simplest black skirt, perfectly cut, its pleats falling in knife-sharp precision down its front. This was topped by a creamy silk blouse with a stock tie that she had wrapped around her neck twice, making an elegant collar of the luxurious fabric. The only jewelry she wore was a strand of perfectly matched pearls, her mother's pearls, which she had been given on her eighteenth birthday. Her long hair was pulled back into a neat chignon that framed her face. At night she released the pins holding her hair and shook it loose, then brushed it with her silver brush. Omer always thought that was the moment when she looked the most beautiful, when his desire for her was the strongest, and he was always disappointed if he came into the room a minute too late and missed this daily ritual. He was thinking of that moment now as he looked at the woman he adored.

"Would you like a drink?" He already had his, and he put his glass down and went to the bar to get one for her.

"Yes, just a sherry, I think. Thank you."

Once settled in the chairs they took naturally, she asked, "How was your day? Busy?"

"No more so than usual. All's quiet on the Bora front, so that always makes it more peaceful." The Boras were another of Turkey's oldest, most important, families. For generations they had traded exclusively in the manufacture of clothing. Then, during the war, they had become involved in the mining of chrome ore. Now, all of a sudden, within the last two years, ever since the eldest of their three sons had taken control of the business, they seemed to be overlapping turfs with the Turans. And not in the most professional or honest ways. Dirty deals had been discovered by both Mustafa and Omer, and it drove Omer wild to have the companies he and his father had worked so hard to build, and to run with integrity, being sideswiped by unscrupulous business tactics.

Cyrielle was pleased to hear there was no crisis there; the matter she had come to discuss was far too important to her to have him distracted in any way. She was hoping he would embrace it as she had over the past few weeks, and would give her his total support. She crossed her long legs and turned to him, anxious to present her idea.

"Omer, I've been thinking . . ."

"Always dangerous," he teased.

She smiled that winning smile of hers, but then her expression turned serious. "Omer, now that the children are older, they have so many of their own interests. Zeki is constantly off practicing his sports, Yasemin is doing a thousand different things, Nevin is busy with her friends, and Ali spends every spare minute he can at the piano. Tonight is a perfect example. Zeki is staying late at school and will be eating dinner at a friend's house; Yasemin is on an overnight school trip; Nevin is upstairs studying, having eaten an early dinner with Ali, who is practicing his piano. So, you see, they really have their own lives now."

"Yes, I'm aware of all that."

"Well, I've a lot more time on my hands now and I have decided that I would like to do something. Something important both for myself and for Turkey. The country has been so good to me, I've found a wonderful life here, and I've come up with an idea. I think it's very good, for many reasons."

"I'm listening."

"Darling, I want to build a museum." She didn't stop to analyze the look on his face. She had to continue, lay out all her thoughts and plans, and then they could discuss it at length. "I want to open a museum, a museum dedicated to my . . . my family. To my father, and my sister, and my brothers." Each time she said the words out loud the pain was renewed, but along with the pain, upon hearing her words, her commitment to her idea increased. "I want to find a wonderful site, up on a hill somewhere, yes, I think that would be best. And then build the most wonderful building, designed beautifully, designed to highlight and to flatter all of the wonderful works of art within. The work of a lifetime of collecting, of loving things beautiful and precious, all the important paintings and sculptures and drawings my father amassed in his lifetime. I want to dedicate it to him, and to my entire family, and to all of those whose lives were taken from them. It would help me so much. Omer, I would feel so happy, knowing that I have done something in their memory. I know it won't change a thing that has happened, but it will help me, as well as others, to remember what atrocities man can inflict upon his fellow man."

Omer sat listening to her as she presented her idea. He heard the excitement in her voice build, the enthusiasm and devotion grow with each sentence. It was contagious, and when she had finally finished he smiled back at her, loving her more than ever for her intelligence, thoughtfulness, and strong sense of family. Of course he would miss all of the wondrous paintings that now graced the walls of their home, but the collection belonged to Cyrielle, it was hers and hers alone, and she was free to do with it as she chose. And she had obviously chosen to share it with the world. His thoughts also dwelt on the social and business aspects of doing such a thing. It would certainly be perceived as a wonderful philanthropic gesture, one that would only increase their already prominent stature in society.

"Cyrielle, I love your idea, and I support your reasons. I think they are all very valid."

"Oh, Omer, I'm thrilled! I had hoped so much that you would feel this way."

"I do, I truly do. I think it will be good for you in so many ways. I'll have the head of the real estate division start pulling together a list of properties that might be available to us. When we finally decide on a sight, then you can choose which architect you would like to design the building. You'll handle all of the curatorial duties, of course?"

"Yes, I know the collection better than anyone, don't you agree?"

"Of course you do. Well, it seems you're all set to start then. I'll get my men working on it tomorrow morning."

She beamed.

"But right now," he continued, "I'm starving. Let's have a celebratory dinner."

"I've already thought of that. Seta has prepared some of your favorite things. I was going to tell her to hold them back if you didn't approve of my idea, but as it is, since you've been so supportive, you can have all of them. Second helpings even, since you've been so wonderful."

He put his arm around her narrow waist and led her out of the library toward the dining room. She pressed herself close to him, once again feeling that she was the most fortunate woman in the world.

CHAPTER

14

THE MUSEUM took six years to build, once they had finally decided on a site. It was an idyllic spot at the very top of one of Istanbul's many hills. Because it was such a prime location, one of the sultans had claimed it for his own and built a magnificent house for himself and his family there. The grand old mansion, called a *köşk,* still stood, and the first time Cyrielle had been driven up the overgrown road that led to it and laid eyes on it she knew it was the place for her museum.

Virtually untouched since the eighteenth century, it retained all of its original detailing and woodworking, which Cyrielle had incorporated into the renovation plans. Some of her advisers had suggested demolishing the house and starting over, but she would not hear of it. Cyrielle had always loved these historic hillside homes, for unlike the *yalıs* that lined the road beneath them and which were open to the sea, the *köşks* were usually surrounded by thick forests. This one was surrounded by pine trees, and the fresh scent of evergreen enveloped the air around the house.

The architect had replaced the multi-paned windows with long sheets of glass, so from every gallery there was an extraordinary view of the city's imperial skyline, as well as of the activity on the Bosphorus. From the main exhibition room one could see out across the water to the Asian side, and from one end of the city to the other. At the far room there was a smaller space which was to be used for traveling exhibits. Through another large expanse of glass the min-

arets of the Topkapı Palace were visible, as well as the great palace
of the Osmanlı Sultans, and the magnificent dome of the Hagia Sophia, the building that had originally been built as the cathedral of
Constantinople. It was once the center of the religious life of the
Byzantine Empire, and even though it was now a museum, it still
stood as a symbol of the ancient city whose heart it had been for so
long. Clearly discernible on most days were the six elegant minarets
of the imposing Blue Mosque. Looking down to the Golden Horn
and out to the point where its waters joined the Bosphorus and
flowed into the Marmara Sea, stood the Maiden's Tower. Visitors
could easily count all but one of the city's seven hills. Each was easily
recognizable by at least one distinct monument or building: on the
first were the seraglio and St. Sophia, along with the magnificent
Hippodrome; on the second, the column of Constantine and the
mosque of Nuruosmaniye; the third held the War Office; the fourth,
the most magnificent mosque of all, that of Sultan Süleyman; Sultan
Selim's mosque was situated atop the fifth; on the sixth was the
mysterious Tekfur Palace whose history no one had been able to
determine; and finally, on the seventh hill, was the Psamatia Quarter.
Below and to the right one could see the elaborate lacy patterns of
the imposing gates that guarded the entrance to the Dolmabahçe
Palace. At nightfall the twinkling lights of the *yalıs,* all the distance
from Bebek to Büyükdere, were distinguishable along the waterfront.
It was easy to spot the Turan family home by first locating the distinctive fishing pier at İstinye.

In order to accommodate the extensive collection, Cyrielle had
added one small building to the existing structure. Executed in basi-
cally the same style as the main building, it was less decorative in
feeling, and it provided the larger expanses of wall space that were
required by some of the paintings. Cyrielle hadn't wanted anything
to compete or to conflict with the original structure, and all who saw
the final results agreed that she had been considerate and sensitive to
history in the design of the new building. Plans were drawn up for
future buildings also. Someday she hoped there would be a wing
dedicated to each of the Turan children, and another spacious gallery
devoted to the Iznik porcelains she loved so much.

Cyrielle supervised every detail of the construction. She chose every element herself, from the door handles and the all-important lighting scheme to the complex security system. At the opening party the new museum was pronounced an instant success. The generosity of her gesture, coupled with her personal reasons for creating the museum, were appreciated and respected by the entire community. Omer lavished upon her the credit that was her due, telling everyone that she had done all of it single-handedly. She had worked alone, unassisted, and she had poured her heart and soul into realizing her vision. He was prouder of her than ever before. To show his unrelenting support, he established a foundation for her whose sole purpose was to fund new acquisitions for the museum. He was her first contributor, donating a substantial sum of money that would allow her to compete at auction for new works. Women, even Cyrielle's closest, most intimate friends, looked at her with a new respect, and gossip buzzed about what a progressive husband Omer Turan had turned out to be. It was unusual for a woman to act so independently, even rarer for those who did to be given credit for their efforts, and it set a wonderful precedent for other women who longed to do something on their own.

Each time Cyrielle walked along the halls surrounded by art that had hung in her home in Paris, or in her father's gallery, she was filled with wonderful memories of the past and renewed hope for the future.

The only thing that marred the official opening of the Lazare-Turan Museum was the country's increasingly turbulent political situation. In April of 1960, students at the University of Istanbul protested the efforts by the existing government to establish a totalitarian regime. The government, concerned by this outbreak, excercised total control over the press and the newspapers. They often made arrests without proper, or even the slightest, cause. Once they got wind of the rumblings at the schools, the government authorized brutal police action. After several bloody events the military took control of the country, and tanks rolled through the streets of Istanbul as a visible reminder that the government was no longer in power. Violence was at last brought under control, and whatever spotty riots did break out after that were usually small and poorly organized, and were immediately squelched. A curfew was enforced throughout the country, and anyone caught out late at night was severely punished. All this turmoil produced a great deal of uncertainty in people's minds. The city was strangely quiet, although the very future of the country hung in the balance. The threat of a civil uprising had been minimized, but Cyrielle had a haunting sense of déjà vu. It was too much like Paris just before the occupation, and it made her nervous and upset.

Omer noticed his wife's edginess and made a suggestion he thought she might like.

"I know you've promised the girls a trip to Paris," he began.

"Yes, I did. It was originally to be for Yasemin's graduation, then we talked about going this year so that I could look at the new paintings which will be at auction in May. There are truly wonderful things coming up, and I had hoped to get some bids in. With all the money the foundation has raised, it appears that a few of them will be within our reach. But now, with all the problems, I don't think there will be any chance of that happening," she sighed, wondering when the curfew and the restrictions would be lifted and they would once again be free to travel. It was horrible and oppressive to live under such conditions.

"Oh, I don't know about that. I think we could arrange something . . ."

He saw her face brighten and was pleased he had brought up the subject of the trip.

"Really, darling? If you could, if there was any way possible, it would be wonderful. Really. And the girls would be so happy, I know they would. Maybe if we're lucky we'll have a chance at one or two of the new paintings also."

"Then it's set. You arrange the girl's schedules at school and let me know when it would be best for you to go. I suppose the auction dates will really dictate when it must be. Let me know tomorrow, and I'll make the arrangements. I only wish I could get away and go with you."

Cyrielle couldn't contain her joy. She went to him and hugged him, then covered his face with kisses. "You're the most wonderful husband in the world. But don't take my word for it, all the women are saying so," she added, referring to the recent spate of gossip.

As the chauffeur navigated the limousine through the busy streets on their route to the hotel, Cyrielle's entire body shook uncontrollably. In an effort to arrest the erratic spasms she clasped her hands tightly together and focused all her concentration on them. She squeezed her fingers against each other until they hurt. Neither Yasemin nor Nevin noticed that the color had completely drained from their mother's face and that she sat absolutely still in the center of the back seat, staring straight ahead. Both girls were so excited to finally be in Paris that they were oblivious to everything else. They practically leaned out the car window, craning their necks in order to get a better view. They squealed with delight each time they spotted a famous monument.

"Those are the buildings of the Louvre," Nevin pointed out, "and over there is Notre-Dame."

"Yes, and on the other side of the Seine is the Left Bank. That's where the Sorbonne is," Yasemin added, looking wistfully in the direction of the great university.

The driver turned down the rue Castiglione and circled the car around the magnificent obelisk in the center of the Place Vendôme. He came to a stop at the entrance to the Ritz. As if from nowhere, the doorman appeared at once, greeting the ladies and offering his hand to help them out of the enormous car. The girls spoke to him in perfect French. Except for a few of their parents' friends and an occasional French family they had met while sailing, he was the first real Frenchman with whom they had spoken. Until now, most of their conversations had been either with Cyrielle or in the classroom.

Now that they were here, they were anxious to practice with the natives.

The Ritz was as beautiful as Cyrielle remembered from the days when, as a little girl, she had come with her mother and father and brothers and sister every Sunday afternoon to have lunch in the grill room, the room they now called L'Espadon. The only differences she noticed now were that the enormous Baccarat chandeliers in the salons seemed to sparkle a little more brightly, and the seams of the porters' uniforms seemed even crisper than she recalled. The furnishings were a touch more elegant and refined, and the hundred-plus vitrines that lined the long gallery between the Place Vendôme entrance and the rue Cambon wing were filled with a wider assortment of luxurious merchandise from the best Parisian boutiques. Not a trace remained of the ugly fact that high-ranking German officers had occupied the hotel during their time in Paris. It was as if that part of the hotel's history had been scrubbed from its slate by the corps of efficient housekeepers.

They were escorted to a lovely two-bedroom suite on the fifth floor. The girls quickly claimed their beds and Nevin said she couldn't wait to take a bath in the luxurious marble tub. As the floor maids helped them unpack, there was a knock at the door, and a big bouquet of summer flowers, accompanied by champagne and fruits, was delivered, compliments of the hotel manager, with a card wishing them an enjoyable stay.

"Can we drink the champagne, Maman?" Yasemin asked, testing the waters to see just how far they could go, now that they were out of Omer's sight.

Cyrielle smiled. "Of course we can. It's for us, isn't it? But not right now. Let's put it on ice and chill it, then we can have it tonight before we go out to dinner."

That seemed to appease the girls momentarily, but the second the unpacking was done and they had investigated the views from each of the elegantly draped windows, they were ready to go out and begin their exploration of a city they had dreamed about visiting for so long.

"I have a terrific idea," Cyrielle said, wanting more than anything to be alone for a few minutes in order to adjust to the fact that she was once again in her homeland. "Why don't the two of you go down and have some tea and sandwiches? There is a lovely room on the main floor; we walked past it on our way to the elevators. They serve teas from all over the world, and the tastiest pastries and tiny snacks; I'm sure you'll be able to find something that appeals to you. Go on down now," she urged them, "and order whatever you like. I'll join you in a little while, and then we'll go out and start doing the town."

They loved this idea, and she sent them off with kisses and a hug. Satisfied that they were well on their way, she softly closed the door behind them, thankful for the few moments alone.

She walked to the open window where Yasemin and Nevin had stood only minutes earlier. Her eyes were drawn at once to the grand avenue of the Faubourg St. Honoré. In the distance she could barely make out the top of the apartment building where she had lived. Everything was at once so familiar and yet so foreign. She no longer felt like a young Frenchwoman but rather like a woman who had been dealt a terrible blow by the Fates, which had placed her in circumstances way beyond her control. But the angels had smiled on her, and had gifted her with Omer. Now memories flooded her mind, memories of a happy, carefree time. She had so many delightful recollections of this hotel. . . . Lazy Sunday afternoons when her mother would dress her and Nathalie in their best outfits, and put little gentlemen's suits on Alexandre and Jacques. Together they would take the ten-minute stroll from their house in two groups of three: the men ahead, with Maurice in the middle, flanked by his two handsome sons; and the women following in the same formation, with Cyrielle and Nathalie holding Dominique's hands. Cyrielle would never forget how the head of every single person in the restaurant would turn as they were led to their regular table in the corner of the room. For a moment she wished she had never returned to Paris. It had been a horrible idea. She must have been crazy even to think of coming here. Then the looks of sheer joy on the faces of her two daughters flashed into her mind, and her strength was renewed. They were so looking forward to the visit. She owed it to them to show them a good time, and to try her hardest to have one herself. Still, as she stood looking across the rooftops of Paris, she knew that today she would not be able to walk in front of the building at number 132. No, not today. Maybe tomorrow, when she was feeling stronger . . . after she had had a chance to adjust to the idea of being home at last. Maybe.

When she joined the girls downstairs they were well into a large assortment of both sandwiches and cookies, but their choice of beverage was Coca-Cola instead of tea. They had charmed the waiters and already seemed to know several of them by name.

"We love it here, Maman," they said in unison. "Everyone's so nice, and just like you said, they do have the best pastries."

"Yes, I remember," Cyrielle said, looking around the charming room and finding that almost nothing had been altered in the inviting surroundings. She took a seat on the small sofa next to Yasemin and ordered a tea for herself. "Well, are you two interested in seeing Paris, or are you simply going to eat the whole time?"

The girls giggled. "No, no, we're ready," they insisted, gobbling up the last of the sandwiches and sipping the remainder of their Cokes noisily.

That afternoon they must have walked at least ten miles, for Cyrielle's feet were swollen and aching by the time they pushed their way wearily through the revolving door of the hotel. Their adventure had been made deliberately longer because she had purposefully led them in a route that carefully avoided the Faubourg St. Honoré. Anyway, it was a glorious late-spring day, and they were happy to be seeing the sights close up on foot. They visited the Madelaine, the Opera House, and the grand old department stores on the Boulevard Haussmann. The girls were overwhelmed with the enormous selection of merchandise at the Galleries Lafayette and Samaritaine. Not once that afternoon were they tempted to take the car that would remain at their disposal throughout the trip.

It was an exciting time to be in Paris. The year before, Charles de Gaulle had been installed as President, and now he was busy setting up the Fifth Republic. The European Common Market was just over a year old, but already its positive effects were being felt. Industry was booming and France was alive and healthy again, in stark contrast to the way Cyrielle had left it.

Cyrielle marveled at the activity in the streets. By the end of the war, France had lost one out of every two hundred of its 1940 population, among them her beloved brother Alexandre. But now, only two decades later, there was clearly a renewed energy and a strong sense of recovery everywhere she looked. New shops and restaurants had popped up on every corner. The women were all dressed in pretty, colorful outfits, a reflection of the lively, upbeat spirit that gripped the city. Cyrielle promised herself she would find the time to buy a few of the attractive new things.

<hr/>

They kept to a rigorous schedule throughout the trip, and even though ten days had sounded like an eternity before they left, now that the trip was nearing the end, they all wished they had at least another week in the beautiful city. Cyrielle had tried to contact some of her old friends, but met with little success. There were no telephone listings—most of them, she assumed, had either married or moved away. But she had been successful at the auction houses, picking up another Picasso, and a very special Giacometti for the garden. They had shopped until they each required another suitcase in which to carry all the new things home. Tomorrow they would return to Istanbul.

"Well, ladies," Cyrielle said, as she looked at the two girls in their recently purchased outfits. They had gone on a mad shopping spree, buying the latest fashions in everything from shoes, to hats, to swimming suits. The girls had put on their new favorite costumes in preparation for their last night out. "It's our last evening in Paris. What shall we do?" Cyrielle had taken them to all the best restaurants, they had gone to Maxim's, the Tour d'Argent and to Lasserre. At each place, not only was the meal delicious, but they had so charmed the maître d' that they had been treated like royalty as well.

The decision was unanimous. They wanted to go to one of the famous bistros, preferably on the Left Bank, maybe even one in the active student quarter. Cyrielle thought for a moment and then decided where they would go.

"We're going to La Procope," she directed the driver. "It's reported to be the oldest bistro in Paris, but I was never sure if that was the truth. Anyway, it's plenty old, and plenty popular," she informed her excited daughters.

They were seated upstairs in the always crowded restaurant. The tables were practically touching, and strangers squeezed together into tight quarters, and the noise level was ear-shattering. But the atmosphere was unique, and Cyrielle knew the girls would enjoy it. The restaurant had always attracted a tourist crowd, but it also remained the bistro of choice for many Parisians who lived in the bordering arrondissements. Once again, her daughters captivated the waiter, and, amidst the din and the frenetic pace, he patiently explained the menu. Yasemin opted for the house specialty of *boudin blanc,* the delicious sausages, while her less adventurous sister stayed with a classic steak served with pommes frites. The meals arrived, and the three of them were silent as they enjoyed the hearty food.

"Good choice, Maman," Yasemin complimented her mother. Nevin, too busy eating to speak, merely nodded her agreement.

Cyrielle only sensed something was wrong when she noticed Yasemin had put her knife and fork down on her plate and stopped eating. The look on her face told Cyrielle that something had happened. She looked confused and uncomfortable.

"Yasemin, darling, what's the matter? Are you ill?"

"No," she answered quietly.

"Well, what is it then?"

Without turning her head, Yasemin shifted her eyes to her left slightly, and then back toward her mother. "It's that man, Maman.

The one over there. He keeps staring at me. He's been doing it since we sat down, and I'm tired of it. He's making me feel funny and I want him to stop."

Cyrielle tried to appear casual as she turned around in the direction of the man. He was seated two tables down and he looked away when her eyes met his. The place opposite him was vacant; perhaps, she thought, his dinner companion had gone to make a telephone call or to visit the ladies' room. He was an elderly man, in his late seventies at least, Cyrielle guessed. He looked sweet and vaguely familiar, but when he looked away she soon decided that he was merely an old man who still enjoyed looking at beautiful girls. It was harmless, she figured, although she wished he would pick someone other than her young daughter at whom to stare.

"Try not to pay any attention to him, Yasemin. I know it's difficult, but I think it's merely a compliment. He thinks you're very pretty."

"Well, I don't think it's a very nice thing to do," Yasemin answered, "and it's not just that *he* thinks I'm pretty, because his wife has also been staring at me. Oh, no, here she comes now, and I know they're both going to look at me in that funny way."

Cyrielle turned to see a petite gray-haired woman, about the same age as the man, returning to the table. She was simply dressed, not expensively, but with an inimitable French style. She clutched her tiny bag to her side as she walked slowly toward the table. As she passed their table she stopped suddenly and turned toward Cyrielle as if pulled by a magnetic force that she was totally unable to control.

"Cyrielle?" she said. It was barely a whisper, and Cyrielle only recognized what she had said by the formation of her delicate lips. "Cyrielle Lazare," she said again, only this time it was not a question. She spoke a bit louder and with more certainty in her voice.

Cyrielle put down her knife and fork and looked into the woman's wrinkled face. Deep lines etched her forehead and the area around her mouth. She had lived long, but the tender eyes remained, eyes that had loved and cared for and protected Cyrielle and her brothers and sister from the day of their birth.

"Martine. Martine, it can't be!" Cyrielle cried, her eyes never leaving the woman's. But even as she said it she knew it was true. She dropped her napkin and rose slowly from her chair, not knowing if her feet would hold her. But her strength came, and she went forward to embrace her. "Martine," she cried repeatedly into the woman's arms like the young girl she had been the last time they saw each other.

Pierre watched the reunion from their table until he could no longer hold back his own emotions. Tears streamed down his weathered cheeks as he stepped forward to greet his long-lost Cyrielle, whom he had loved like a daughter. The three of them held each other in the middle of the restaurant, not caring about the people or the world around them.

Yasemin and her sister sat observing this scene not knowing what to make of it all, and unable to comprehend the depth of emotion the three people felt for each other.

"I just knew it had to be you," Pierre said. "At first I told Martine that I had seen a ghost, that Dominique was sitting at the table to our right. Of course she didn't believe me, she thinks I've gone completely dotty in my old age, but then she looked for herself and she too had the same reaction. Yes, I just knew it had to be you and your two daughters. Oh, we're so happy to see you. It's like a beautiful dream come true."

They all joined one table and talked for a while longer. But Cyrielle had many more things she wanted to ask them about. She had so many questions about her father, her brothers and sister. Martine and Pierre were the only people who might have any information to share with her about what had happened on that terrible night. Suddenly she wanted desperately to be alone with them. She put the girls in the car and directed the driver to deliver them safely back to the Ritz, and then she gave him the address of Pierre and Martine's apartment and told him to come back and wait for her there.

"I'll be back later. Stay in the room and try to go to bed early and get some sleep. We have a long day tomorrow. I love you," she said as she shut the door and signaled the car to move away.

Pierre and Martine lived nearby, and occasionally, as a special treat, since their funds were limited, they went to La Procope for dinner as they had tonight. Cyrielle thought about how much of life was really determined by chance and by luck alone. What other reason could there have been for them all to end up at the same restaurant that night, seated two tables away from each other?

Their apartment was tiny but charming, and Cyrielle immediately recognized many of the things that had been in the Lazare apartment on the Faubourg. The rug they used in their living room had once graced the dining room of the Lazares' apartment. Many of the books and knickknacks were her family's.

"Cyrielle, please, sit down," Martine urged. "This must be shocking for you. After the Nazis . . . after they took your father and brother and sister and her husband away that night, we had to move. They came back and told us we had twenty-four hours to get out. We took everything we could carry, thinking that, of course, we would save it for your father after the war. He did give us one painting before he left for Pau, and because we had no money, we were forced to sell it so we could move into this apartment. That's all we had, our lives had always been with you and your family. We had saved very little money. So that is why everything is here. Over the years we wrote so many letters, but never a response—you must not have received them. Still, we prayed that one day we would find you and give it back to you. Now that you're here, we want you to have it. . . ."

"Martine, please," Cyrielle begged. She looked at these two dear people, these two lovely, honest, caring people who had been just as much responsible for her upbringing as Maurice and Dominique themselves. She loved them, and now, after all these years and all that had happened, they were still acting like employees. She had no interest in anything in the apartment. All she wanted to know was what had become of her family.

"Martine, Pierre, I do not want any of these things. That's all they are to me . . . things. I don't want anything from you, all of this belongs to you now. What I want to know is what happened to my father, and my brother and sister. That's all I care about. Do you know anything?"

Martine's nerves couldn't hold out any longer, and she began to cry. She turned toward Pierre, her husband of some sixty years. He had always served as her strength, and now he would have to do so again.

"Pierre, please, you must tell her. Tell her everything you know."

The old man got up and walked toward Cyrielle. He came forward slowly, a bit unsteady as he took a chair next to her. He reached out for her hands and held them in his. She wrapped her fingers around his palms and could feel the fragile bones beneath the loose skin. His rheumy eyes, red from crying and exhausted by the emotional reunion, looked into hers.

"Cyrielle, I'm sorry," he began, and for the next hour he retold the story of that fateful night. "That's all we know. That's all we saw. But as the police van sped away, we never dreamed it would be the last time we'd ever see them."

Cyrielle pulled her hands back from his and raised them to her eyes. She had waited so long to hear the details that Omer's sources could never have known. Twenty long years. Still, it came as a shock, a horrible shock.

They talked for a little while longer. Pierre remained in the small chair next to her, and Martine stayed in the rocking chair that had been a permanent fixture in the children's nursery. Cyrielle could see from their faces that the evening had tired them terribly, and even though she wanted to stay, she knew she had to go. Her daughters would wonder what had kept her for so long. She said her good-byes, promising to keep in touch now that she knew where they were. Tears once again wetted her cheeks as she looked back from the car at their loving faces.

"The Ritz, madame?" asked the driver.

"No . . . no. Take me to Number 132 Faubourg St. Honoré, please."

"Very well."

He opened the door for her and she climbed out of the limousine slowly.

"You may go now. I'll walk back to the hotel from here. Thank you. Good night."

"Good night, madame."

He drove off and she was alone, standing in front of the house where she had spent the first eighteen years of her life. Barely a day had passed when she hadn't thought of this beautiful building and the memories it held within. How many times had she and Nathalie leaned precariously out the window, craning their necks in hopes that they would be able to spot their father as he came walking down the street on his way home from work? How many times had Maurice sat in the car, waiting patiently for her and her mother to come downstairs so they could go for a drive in the countryside? When she closed her eyes for a moment she could see all of them—the entire Lazare family—Nathalie and she dressed in their most special outfits, with black patent leather shoes and short white socks trimmed with lace, Alexandre and Jacques in suits that fit their growing bodies as best they could—all of them leaving the apartment for their weekly Sunday lunch at the Ritz.

Now at last she had the courage to face the reality of what had happened here. Here, in this very driveway where she now stood, her family was rounded up like so many animals and sent to their death in a concentration camp far from their home. But at least now she knew. Now that she knew the reality she could accept it. She would never forget them, but now they could live peacefully in her memory. In her memory and in her museum. She felt certain that her father would have been happy with her choice of memorial. Now she could go forward with her life, holding the past dear, and treasuring the future that lay ahead.

CHAPTER

15

*T*HE HOUSE was very quiet after Yasemin left for college the following September. Because of her exceptional academic record, she had been accepted at every university to which she had applied. Even though she had once had her heart set on the Sorbonne, she had ended up choosing Radcliffe because she thought the experience of studying in the States was important. It was clear to all that her older brother was destined to take over the helm of Turan Holding, but she wanted somehow to be a part of it, and having a strong background in economics would help her to compete in a world that still belonged almost entirely to men.

Cyrielle's heart ached as she watched her daughter board the plane that would take her far from home, to another world that was totally foreign to her. Before she was even gone she missed her terribly. But she wanted the world for her daughter, she wanted her to be able to explore, to learn and to travel, to do all the things Cyrielle had never had the chance to do. So she held back her tears at the airport, saving them for the privacy of her room.

Yasemin's frequent letters home indicated that she was happy, studying hard, making new friends, and adjusting beautifully, as they had all known she would. Cyrielle comforted herself with the thought that her other three children still remained close by, even though they too were gone more and more.

Ali spent most of his time at the academy. His years of tedious practice at the piano were paying off, and his talents were finally being recognized. He toured all over Turkey, and this year he would be off to Europe to perform.

Nevin had fallen in love with a boy she had met at a wedding the previous spring. He was the son of another of Turkey's important families. Sedat was pleasant and charming, and was very fond of Cyrielle's younger daughter. Nevin wanted nothing more than to have a home and family, and even though she was still a very young girl, Cyrielle and Omer had decided that they would be pleased should she choose to marry the boy. He was not overly ambitious, but he would be a good father to their children, and because of their backgrounds they were ensured of a comfortable life-style.

Zeki had grown up to be a handsome, virile young man and was considered to be one of Istanbul's most eligible bachelors. He was at the top of everyone's invitation list, and there was rarely a night when he did not have one party or another to attend. So far he had not shown an interest in any particular girl, much preferring to play the field, which was wide open for him. His father made certain that he had very little time for a real relationship. Omer insisted that he continue to travel with him, visiting factories and offices all over the country and in Europe. Unlike when Zeki had been a small boy, these trips were all business and were singularly devoted to the cause of grooming the young man one day to take Omer's place at the head of the enormous conglomerate. Zeki did not share his sister's academic bent, but he was learning the rules of the game directly from his father, who gave him the benefit of his own formal training as well as all that he had learned on the job and from his own father as well. Mustafa had retired years earlier, but he still enjoyed dabbling in special projects, and a large acquisition or major decision was never made without his consent. He also had a particular fondness for Cyrielle's museum. It was he who each year managed to raise the most money to support the foundation.

It was on one of those fund-raisers that Cyrielle was now working. The museum party was the last event of the spring social season; in fact, since the museum had opened, it traditionally heralded the start of the summer. Held at the end of May, it was a grand gala, a formal evening of dining and dancing under a spacious tent constructed in the beautiful gardens surrounding the museum property.

This was the gala's third year. As word had spread about the importance of the event, it had become a must for those in, or those aspiring to break into, Istanbul society, so each year brought an increased demand for tickets. As Cyrielle sat in the small room facing the Bosphorus, which had become her unofficial office at home, she struggled with the seating plans and the final menu approval. It was a Saturday afternoon, especially warm for so early in the year, and the late-day sun streamed in through the open windows. A brisk breeze had kicked up over the Bosphorus, and she had to secure all of her many stacks of papers with books or other heavy objects.

Occasionally she glanced up and looked out the window. The *Meltem* was anchored about one hundred yards from the house. She and the children would be going south in a few weeks, and before they sailed Omer wanted to check the work that Ivy and his men had completed over the winter. He and Zeki had been out on the grand old boat since early morning, and every so often, if her timing was right, she could catch a glimpse of one or the other scurrying back and forth when she took a momentary break from her struggle with the tables for ten.

At the last glance the deck had been empty, so she continued her quest for a seating plan that would please everyone involved. She realized that with all the difficult personalities involved, it was a hopeless, thankless task, but she had to try.

She was happy that day. Her life was going along smoothly, she had a husband who adored her even more than on the day they had married, she had four lovely children, each special in a different way, and she loved them all dearly. Yasemin, whom she missed terribly, would be home the following week, just in time to attend the party. All of the Turan children would be there, as well as their grandparents and Aunt Semra. Besides being a wonderful event for the museum, it would be a chance for them all to spend some time together. And that was when Cyrielle felt the most satisfied, the most at peace with herself and the world around her. So the table plans could be looked at in perspective; they were only a small, inconsequential complication in an otherwise wonderful, satisfying existence.

Her lovely thoughts were interrupted by the sound of two heavy objects colliding. It was a heavy, almost thunderous noise, the thick thudlike sound of a slow-moving object ramming into a stationary wall. At first she ignored it, thinking that it was probably only a routine noise from one of the many boats outside her window. But when she heard the first cry for help, she jumped up from her writing table and ran outside to the terrace. Seta and one of the gardeners had also heard the noise and were already at the edge of the terrace, straining to see what had happened. A smaller motorboat, trying to navigate the narrow passage between the *Meltem* and another boat nearby, had miscalculated the distance as well as the power of the current, and had rammed directly into the *Meltem*'s stern. The smaller vessel, made into an accordion by the bulk of the large yacht, had capsized, spilling its passengers into the churning, turbulent waters. The front of the boat was sinking quickly into the dark mass, the only part still visible was the propeller, its blades shooting up and out of the water like the fierce jaws of a hungry animal. Out for a pleasurable afternoon of boating, not one of the passengers had a life jacket on, and they were bobbing around in the water thrashing their arms and trying to make themselves heard above the crashing waves. She could hear the desperate screams of those whose lungs were not already filling with water. The crew of the *Meltem* frantically untied their own dinghy and ropes. They had prepared for such an emergency, but now as it faced them, even the most seasoned of the men shook with fear. Cyrielle could hear Ivy's strong, steady voice calling orders to his crew. They worked at a pace that did not seem possible, arms flailing about, yet somehow synchronized as they released the ropes securing the small boat and prepared to rescue those below.

"Seta, go get me the binoculars from the garage. Hurry now, run!" Cyrielle cried to her, panic in her every word. She stood as close to the edge of the terrace as she could get without falling in.

"Yes, Cyrielle *hanım*," she replied, tearing her eyes away and dashing toward the house.

Cyrielle yelled for the gardener to go inside and telephone the police, so they could dispatch the coast guard in case a fire should break out. He too obeyed his mistress at once, running off at a fast clip, leaving Cyrielle alone and helpless as she observed the scene before her. She grew more and more fraught with fear, for since this horrible collision had occurred she had not seen a glimpse of either Omer or Zeki.

Her panic grew as she awaited Seta's return. Finally the woman appeared with the binoculars. Cyrielle pointed the glasses out to the dark waters, turning the lenses quickly into focus. All she could see were eight or ten heads, she couldn't make an exact count as they were being thrashed about by the rough tide. Occasionally an arm or leg would shoot up through the surface.

"Fevzi, did you reach the police?" she shouted at the gardener. Through the window she could see he was still on the phone. "Tell them to hurry, it's an emergency!" she yelled, not recognizing her own voice. "Now! They have to come right now!"

Holding the binoculars up again, she could see that the crew had hurled ropes overboard, but the current was so strong they were immediately swept out of reach of the desperate people. Ivy and his men were still trying to lower the dinghy from the front of the boat. She was so beside herself that it seemed as if things were moving in slow motion. She was unfamiliar with the power of water and its effects on heavy objects; she had no way of judging the force of the turbulent current. She moved her head about, holding the glasses with white knuckles, searching desperately for a sign of Omer and Zeki. Turning back to the waters once more, she spotted Zeki. He was in the water, grappling with one of the hysterical passengers, trying to get him to relax so he could tow him to the waiting dinghy, which had at last been lowered into the water near the bow of the *Meltem*. She watched with apprehension, her breath quickening and her heart pounding, as he successfully took three of the passengers to the safety of the small boat. She yelled out to him to get to safety himself, but her cries could not be heard so far away. Several of the passengers were able to swim to the protection of the dinghy themselves, but many of the women and children were still in danger of losing their lives. Two of the young crewmen joined Zeki, but they were not nearly such powerful swimmers as her son, and they were pathetically slow to reach the people in trouble. She could hear her son attempting to yell instructions to the boys, but even his strong voice was drowned out by the crashing of the waves. He had been in the cold, rough waters for what seemed like hours now, and she wanted him to complete his heroic rescue efforts and get back on board. But he continued to go back, finally pulling all but one of the passengers to safety. She saw the crew who were in the dinghy hoist the second-to-last person aboard, and then Zeki turned back once more for the last remaining passenger. She followed his determined strokes down the side of the boat, her eyes glued to his every movement. Her temples pounded as she locked her eyes on him; she was out of her mind with worry. She prayed for him to get the last person quickly in his firm grip and return to the dinghy.

Just as he neared the end of the capsized boat, which bobbed up and down in the water like a child's toy, an enormous wave hit with such force that the giant steel blades of the propeller were driven forward. Cyrielle watched in horror as the enormous flat metal blade came down directly on Zeki's head. When the wave subsided, there was no sign of him. Her darling boy, her beloved Zeki had disappeared beneath the surface of the water. She waited, frozen in time, for him to reappear. She clutched the glasses, jamming them against her eyes and never feeling the pain, but there was nothing except the flat, eerily calm surface of the water where he had been only seconds before. The desperate scream of the man who still remained in the water reached her ears, and her own scream, from deep within her soul, joined his. She held the glasses away from her face and continually called out her son's name, but nothing emerged from the dark abyss.

Suddenly she sensed movement from above, and up on deck, Omer appeared. "Omer, Omer," she cried out, "help Zeki. Zeki, he's there," she screamed, pointing into the waters. She did not know that he had been on the other side of the boat, making certain that other boat traffic did not come too near and cause additional backlash and even higher waves than they already had to deal with. Cyrielle watched him as he pulled his shirt over his head and dived into the waters. Ivy was already in, diving repeatedly near the propeller, searching for her dear son. Cyrielle could no longer stand by, a helpless observer from the water's edge. From her vantage point at the end of the terrace she had been the only one to see the exact spot where he had disappeared. Maybe . . . maybe if she could get there, she could help. She threw the binoculars on the ground next to her, ripped off her light sweater and tossed her shoes toward the house, then climbed down the ladder into the churning sea. It was so cold, so new and terrifying, but she did not hesitate as she jumped in. Every moment counted, every second was critical. She started out, but her desperate paddling was ineffective against the powerful current; she would make one outward stretch and then was pushed back several feet by the force of the water. She tired easily, never before had she experienced the incredible force of the water, but an inner strength pushed her on. She had to try and save her son. She took in the salty water, it filled her mouth and her nose, and she gagged as she fought the strong current. She was determined to get to the boat. She had to save her son. Her heart pounded in her chest until she was certain it would explode. As she approached, exhausted and drained, Omer spotted her.

"Cyrielle, no. . ." he cried. "No, stay where you are. I'm coming for you." Ivy and Omer swam forward to her. Omer grabbed her under her arms and forced her back across his chest. He swam with her in the direction of the dinghy, but with every iota of her remaining energy she fought him all the way. "Zeki, Zeki," she screamed, "my Zeki."

"Okay, Cyrielle, calm down, it's all right."

"No, I saw him, I saw him," she wailed with her last ounce of strength. They reached the side of the rubber boat where another crew member waited, and then Omer pushed her to safety.

They stayed on board late into the night while rescue crews searched the difficult waters for Zeki's body. Cyrielle sat shivering in a deck chair, her shoulders wrapped in a blanket. She refused all offers of tea or a drink. She stared out over the side of the boat into the dark waters at the very spot where her son had vanished. Searchlights lit the surrounding areas, as men in wet suits with tanks on their backs looked for her son.

Just before dawn a cry went up, signaling to the other rescue men that one of the teams had located something. Cyrielle stood, and went to the side of the boat. Omer stood by her side as their firstborn son was pulled from the freezing waters. He had been under water for almost twelve hours, and the effects of it on his young body were too painful for her to watch. She turned her head to Omer's chest, and he held her tightly. When the body had been removed they remained standing there, holding each other, for a long time. Omer's tears mixed with hers, and they clung to each other for support. Finally Ivy came and put his hand on Omer's shoulder. He led them away slowly to a boat that would take them back to the house so that they could continue to grieve privately.

On the evening that had originally been reserved for the museum gala, the Turan family instead held a memorial service for their eldest son. The house was filled; outside, young men tried their best to keep the traffic jamming the entrance to the mansion under control. Many who would have been at the museum, friends and business associates alike, came bearing trays of food and to pay their respects to Cyrielle and Omer. Zeki's classmates and teammates from all the sports he had played were there as well, most of them experiencing for the very first time the pain of burying one of their peers.

Cyrielle observed the gathering in her house from her position in the small room where she had been working when the accident had occurred. At first when people had begun arriving she had stood by Omer's side at the front door, welcoming them and thanking them for their support and comfort in their time of need. But she had tired quickly, excused herself, and had gone directly to the chair where she now sat.

She had lost her baby, her firstborn, the son whom she had loved so and who had meant everything to his father. He was the boy on whom Omer had pinned his hopes, his dreams, and his desire for the continuation of an empire he had worked so hard to create. Now those dreams were shattered, and Cyrielle did not know where either of them would find the strength to carry on. Nevin and Ali, along with Semra, had sat by her bedside for the last few days, taking turns, so that when the sedative wore off and she awakened, she would not be alone. They had held off telling Yasemin until she had finished her exams, and when she did receive word of her brother's death she left school at once and flew to Istanbul to be with her family. She too had joined in the vigil, and it was only late yesterday afternoon that Cyrielle had first been strong enough to get out of bed.

It was hard enough to deal with the sudden, horrifying death of the promising young man, but a final cruel blow was struck when they learned that the boat that had struck the *Meltem,* because of the pilot's desire to take a shortcut instead of going around the ship, was owned by the Bora family. The passengers on board the ship were business associates of theirs, in fact they had been in Istanbul trying to negotiate the purchase of a factory on which Omer was also bidding. They had arranged for the families to go on a tour of the Bosphorus that afternoon. So in the final ironic twist, Zeki Turan had given his life to save the lives of some of his father's harshest opponents. Of course, the Boras had put rivalry aside and had sent their deepest regrets about the accident, but all their sympathy would do nothing to bring back the son who had meant the world to them.

As Cyrielle sat in her chair, receiving the condolences from all those who had come, she smiled vacantly and nodded her head in gratitude. But her thoughts were a million miles away, and her head ached with such pain that she was uncertain if she would be able to make it through the long afternoon.

CHAPTER

16

As the turans tried to piece their lives back together again, each member of the family dealt with his or her grief in a different way. Ali went about his own life, trying to lessen the pain by throwing himself into his music. Nevin and Sedat made plans to marry the following spring. Yasemin stayed for the summer months. When her friends were able to convince her to take a break from her mother's side, she spent some time in the south, sailing and enjoying the casual atmosphere of the rapidly growing resort towns on the Turkish coastline. As the shrewd Turans had predicted, much of the tourism that had once belonged exclusively to Greece was now being taken over by Turkey, as people from all over the country, as well as Europe, discovered the beauty of the unspoiled shoreline, the magnificence of the ruins, and the gracious hospitality of the people who inhabited the small, remote villages along the Aegean.

Back in Istanbul, Yasemin spent some time working in one of the offices of Turan Holding. She loved being there, she saw the company as her future, and she didn't mind doing even the most menial job as long as she learned something about the business operations. Proving herself this way, she slowly earned the respect and admiration of those in important positions in the company. As much as possible, she tried to be near her father. Omer was spending more time than ever before at the office; it was his own way of dealing with the enormous loss of the boy he had counted on for so much. Yasemin quietly tried to show him that she wanted to become involved in the business, but so far she had had little success.

"If you want to be helpful to me, stay at home with your mother. She is the one who really needs you right now. She's lonesome, and each day, instead of getting better and learning to live with her grief, she seems to become even more withdrawn. Semra has been away so much lately, she was usually the one who was able to help her the most. So now I need you. Go and be with her, Yasemin, there will be plenty of time later for you to learn the business. Right now you're needed at home. Please, go to her and see what you can do."

The look on his face was so compelling that she could not refuse his request. "All right, Baba, I'll go, and I'll try my best to see what I can do. But as you said, she seems more distant than ever. Maybe she just needs some time alone, time to work things out on her own. Everyone has to adjust to the situation at their own pace. But I'll try. And then when she's fine again, I want to come back and work with you. You know how much I want to be a part of the company. And now that Zeki. . ."

But Omer waved his hands, signaling that it was too soon even to mention the enormous void Zeki's death had created in the company. Too soon to suggest that maybe it was Yasemin who could step in, fill the void, learn the ropes, and someday be an important factor in Turan Holding. No, not yet; it was forbidden territory just now. She took the warning and held her thoughts to herself.

"Go, Yasemin, be with your mother. And tell me if you think there is anything we can do to help her." Omer had felt his wife slipping away from him slowly, in some ways unnoticeable until it was too late to change it. He missed their conversations, their discussions and debates, he missed having his home filled with amusing, interesting people. He longed for the closeness of her, and for the strength she had always been for him. Most of all, he missed her bright shining smile, the radiant eyes, and the outpouring of love she had showered on him. He missed all those things terribly, and he wanted them back, and he was willing to try anything to succeed.

At home on the Bosphorus, Cyrielle's days passed with a painful slowness. Right after Zeki's death she had embarked on the ambitious project of adding a new wing to the museum, a wing to honor her son. She spoke passionately about it; it would be a sleek, modern addition that would be a tribute to his youth and strength. It would be constructed of the finest, sturdiest materials, marble and granite that would represent Zeki's stability, his honesty, courage, and bravery. Inside, it would house a formidable collection of the beautiful Iznik porcelains that his mother loved so much. The porcelains would represent the gentle side of Zeki's personality, the caring and love he had always shown his family. The porcelains would also stand for the fragility of human life as well as the strength and determination of the human spirit.

Omer supported Cyrielle's efforts one hundred percent. As during the construction of the main buildings, he had assigned his top architects to the project. Every tradesman and resource was made available to Cyrielle. Plans were drawn up, models made, the porcelains brought out from the safety of the storage area where they had been kept over the years as Cyrielle's collection grew. They were identified, labeled, numbered, and made ready for their new home. Samples of marble and granite were flown in from around the world. All the stops were pulled out for this important project.

By the end of July, the team working on the addition was ready to begin presentations. Cyrielle scheduled meetings with the architects and engineers. They arrived at the house, were led into the small room overlooking the sea, and would enthusiastically present their work for her reaction and hoped-for approval. It was a project of such importance, and so fortunate did they feel to have been selected to work on it, that they were most anxious for her response, and eager to accept any suggestions and make any changes she might want. At first these meetings went smoothly. Cyrielle was in control, and decisions were made, additions and modifications planned; everything seemed to be going forward on schedule.

By summer's end, Cyrielle's concentration had vanished into thin air. She continued to schedule meetings, but then she would forget about them and would not even be at the house when the people arrived. Contractors sent over cost estimates and schedules that required her immediate attention; the packages would remain on her desk, unopened. Her mind refused to focus, and she would sit for hours staring at the papers in front of her, unable to make even the smallest decision. Before she had always been so confident, so decisive; she had sailed through the entire design process fueled by her own vision, never once hesitating or changing her mind once she had made it up. Now even the tiniest detail, the choice of moldings or typeface for placards became an overwhelming obstacle. Her mind would go blurry on her, her eyes would cloud over and she simply could not concentrate, not on even the simplest matter. She responded to all of this by fleeing the room and going straight upstairs to the safety of her bed. There she would take three or four of the tranquilizers left over from the prescription the doctor had given her right after Zeki's death.

It was there, in her bed, that Omer found her one evening when he returned home early. At first he thought she was only napping for a bit, so that she would be rested for their guests, but when he shook her gently and she did not awaken immediately, he sensed that she might have taken a drug.

"Cyrielle, wake up," he said softly, not wanting to frighten her.

"Ummm, ummm," she sighed, and turned over in the bed. She still wore her day clothes, yet they were wrinkled and did not match, typical of the outfits she put together these days. Her hair was stringy as it lay on the pillow, she had once again missed her weekly appointment. Never before had he known that to happen. These days she no longer seemed to care about her appearance, which had always been a point of pride for her.

"Cyrielle, wake up. It's seven o'clock. We have guests coming in less than an hour. Seta told me you haven't even informed her how many we will be. Cyrielle, wake up, please."

She groaned again, and then turned back over and opened her eyes. It took her a few seconds to focus on him, and finally she appeared awake.

"Cyrielle, what about our guests? They'll be arriving shortly. Do you feel all right?"

"Guests?" she asked dazedly. "Guests? Who's coming?"

He held back his exasperation with her. Over the past few weeks she had forgotten several important things: a dinner date with visiting business people; to send the driver to pick up Ali at the airport when he returned from Europe; to send a wedding present to the daughter of one of their friends, as she had promised. He had overlooked all of these things, reasoning that she was just tired from the pressure of trying to get the new wing underway. But now as he looked at her in her disheveled state, he knew it was more than that. He reminded himself that before this she had raised three—no, four—children, he painfully remembered; she had run an impeccable household; and had been a glamorous, charming hostess all at the same time. A fear gripped him seeing her like this, his heart ached for her. Suddenly he knew she was in deeper trouble than he had previously suspected.

Omer quickly got on the phone and was fortunately able to reach everyone who was expected at their house that evening. He gave some alibi that he was certain sounded very unlikely, a thinly veiled excuse for what everyone else must have already figured out. He had been blind to her needs, so wrapped up in his work and his own escape from the reality of Zeki's death. As he completed the last call he was thankful that at least he had been able to contact everyone before they rang the front-door bell.

By the time he returned to their bedroom, Cyrielle had returned to a state of deep slumber. First he scoured the room for the drugs she had obviously taken. He searched her lingerie drawers and the small shelves in her French writing desk. He ransacked the medicine chest in her bathroom, but came up with only the usual assortment of vitamins and cold remedies. She had hidden the evidence very well, hoping, he was certain, never to be caught in this state. But now that he had seen it firsthand, he made a plan that he hoped would help to get her back on the right track. They had not been away together since several months before the tragic accident, and so he organized a trip for them that weekend.

As they drove south toward Iznik, the place she had always loved so much, he prayed that a change of scenery, and a couple of days spent alone, without the pressures of the house and the phone constantly ringing, would be just the right kind of medicine for her.

He glanced over at her and remembered the beautiful young girl he had first taken to this wonderful spot so many years earlier. He remembered the colorful scarf she had worn, and her concern about her bare shoulders. It was the first time he had been honest enough with himself to admit how he really felt about her. It had been a magical, tender time, one that he had treasured ever since. Now he only saw a part of the woman he had married; the physical beauty was still there, but it was hidden beneath a shroud, a mask of deep pain and grief. This weekend he would try to free her from the weight of that mask.

They checked into the same little inn they had stayed at on their first visit. Little had changed. The proprietors, a man and his wife, were still behind the desk when they entered. They welcomed the Turans with open arms. They were grateful to them, for over the years the generous sums they had paid the couple for some pieces of porcelain that Cyrielle had wanted for her collection had made their lives more comfortable than they could ever have imagined.

They escorted Omer and Cyrielle to the largest room in the hotel. Fresh flowers graced every surface, and a basket of fruit, picked that morning from the trees outside their window, sat on the small table in front of the sofa. They were honored to have such important people as guests under their roof, and had done their best to make the plain, modest room as lovely and inviting as possible.

Cyrielle managed to be gracious to the couple, then claimed a terrible headache and begged to take a nap before dinner. Even though he was disappointed, having hoped they would go out and take a walk through the small town, he urged her to do so, saying he would go out by himself and allow her to rest.

The wife and daughter of the pension had worked hard to prepare a wonderful meal for them. Omer and Cyrielle sat on the terrace, which had only five tables, just enough to seat the guests and, if they were not completely booked, also a few of the townspeople who might have a special event to celebrate.

The wife served them carefully, and then returned to their table often to make certain that they had everything they desired. Although

Cyrielle barely touched her meal, Omer assured the woman they were very happy, and that the food reminded him of his grandmother's cooking.

Once back in their room, Cyrielle undressed, put on her night-gown, and climbed between the freshly laundered sheets. By the time Omer came out of the bathroom, she had turned onto her side and appeared to be sleeping.

He got in beside her and positioned himself against her. Trying to ignore the shiver he felt when he rubbed his naked body against the soft fabric of her nightdress, he wrapped his arms around her, venturing inside her gown and gently stroking her breasts. She didn't respond, and remained motionless as he explored and stroked, hoping to elicit a small sigh of pleasure from her. His own desire was evident, and even though he felt he was unwelcome, he could not help wanting her so. He continued his play, and each light touch of her nipples made him ever more ready for her. Softly he placed his hand on her shoulder and urged her to turn to him, and when she did he saw a look that frightened him. It was not one of passion or of disdain, it was completely blank. Nothing he had done had moved her, had reached her. His advances had not even been acknowledged; she remained unfeeling.

His desire for her drove him forward; he was hoping that he could renew the feelings they had once shared. He ventured down slowly, leaving his hand on the fabric of the gown. This was some-thing that in years past had made her wild with desire. He would stroke her on top of the fabric, all the while holding her hands at her sides or behind her back. He would stroke her and stroke her, at the same time rubbing his urgency against her. Soon her movements against his hand would quicken, and she would tear her own hands free. At that moment, when he knew she was ready, he would release her. She would raise her gown, and then find either his hands or his hardness, and would beg him with her eyes and her moans to satisfy the yearning he had created in her. He prayed now that he would get the same response from her, the same passionate response; that he would feel her wetness seep through the front of her silk gown, and that they could recapture the feelings that had meant the world to him. But despite his efforts she remained motionless. Her hips did not arch up to meet his hand, she did not open her legs to greet him, and the fabric of her nightdress remained dry.

He sat up next to her, his head on his hand. "Cyrielle, what is it? What's the matter?"

She turned to him. Her eyes seemed to want to say something to him, but she remained silent. She looked away and stared into the night.

"It's been ages since we made love, Cyrielle. I can't even remember the last time I held you, and made you happy, and felt myself explode into you. I need that, and I need it from you."

He turned her face back to him with his hand. "Cyrielle, talk to me. I need to know what is wrong. Tell me. I want to help you."

She tried to speak, to pour out the torrent of trapped feelings. Feelings of desire, feelings of pity, but, most strongly, the feeling that she had failed him. She had been unable to save her son, to rescue their son. Maybe if she had called the police herself, maybe if she had been an able swimmer, maybe. . . . She ran through all the maybes, the endless stream of ifs that roamed constantly through her mind, day and night, like soldiers on the march to conquer. But they never seemed to reach their destination, and there were never any answers. These thoughts drained her of all her powers—physical and mental. The smallest task was an enormous event. She had no feelings left, nothing to give to the man who lay beside her, the man who was so loving, so giving, and somehow so pathetic in his attempts to help her.

Her silence was tormenting him. "Cyrielle, if you cannot tell me, then I think we had better get you some help. Find someone in whom you can confide. Please. Don't you agree? Cyrielle, I miss you. I want you back. I want my wife, my lover . . . back." Then he broke down and his tears fell heavily, tears of frustration, of fear and of love for the woman he could no longer reach.

She held out her arms to comfort him. But there was no intimacy in her embrace. It was not the caress of a lover; it was the embrace of a mother for a son. Her lost son.

17

BY THE TIME Yasemin left for her second year at Radcliffe, work on the new wing of the museum had ceased completely. Her efforts to cheer her mother up, to comfort her and to bring her back to the way she had been before Zeki's death, had been fruitless. The night before she was due to leave, she had gone to her father to tell him that she wanted to stay in Istanbul. He had looked at her with sadness in his eyes, but when he spoke he dismissed her idea completely.

"Yasemin, it wouldn't do you any good to stay now. Your mother needs medical care, and we're going to provide the best we can. So far, she hasn't agreed to even seeing a doctor, but in time I hope we can get her to at least go to see someone. In the meantime, I want you to return to school, and not to worry about her. She's going to be fine, it's just a matter of time."

Omer had taken her in his arms and hugged her tightly. Still, she had left frustrated and worried, and she had not been able to spend nearly as much time as she had wished at Turan Holding. She promised to come back home for Nevin's wedding, which was a little more than six months away. On the day she left, Cyrielle had been too tired to go to the airport. Yasemin thought it was more than that, she felt her mother just wasn't strong enough to face her leaving. Even though Cyrielle had not returned to her old self, she had come to count on Yasemin to be at home with her during the long, arduous days. She couldn't face her departure. So, with tears in her eyes, and only her father and sister to say good-bye to her, Yasemin boarded the plane for Boston.

Despite her deep concerns for her mother, now that she was back at school it was time for Yasemin to focus, to devote herself to some serious studying. Especially if she was committed to becoming the son her father had lost. Besides, she reasoned, there was nothing she could do from such an enormous distance. She promised herself that she would write more often and try to increase from one to two the number of letters she sent home each week. She put her worries aside and marched on with her own life.

She missed her family and the luxury of living at home in Istanbul. The dorms at Radcliffe took some adjusting to; their sparse, functional furnishings were rather grim compared to the comfort of the big bed and deep, ample bathtub she enjoyed in the grand house on the Bosphorus.

Because she had such a distance to travel, she had arrived at school a day earlier than everyone else. The campus was still deserted, and she was anxious for her friends to return. Her first days back after a trip home were always rough, and especially this time; she needed her friends close by to help ease the homesickness and the pain of her brother's death.

And, for the first time in her life, she was struggling with her studies. Last semester she had had the hardest time with her calculus course, and she knew she would get a low mark, or possibly even a failing grade, in this year's course if she did not get to work. It was unavoidable; the class was required in order to graduate. She had to pass.

"Maybe I need some tutoring," she said to her roommate Christine one night after they had shared the events of the time they had spent apart. They sat Indian-style in their nightgowns, perched atop their beds. Both were attempting to do some late-night studying, although Yasemin suspected that Christine was writing to her boyfriend back home. "Do you think that might help?"

"Maybe. . ." Christine answered, lost in her own thoughts and not appearing to pay much attention to her roommate.

Yasemin returned to her struggle over the basics of calculus. Every few minutes she would crumple up another piece of paper in frustration, then pitch the paper ball into the wastebasket near her desk below.

"Two points," Christine congratulated her for making the shot. "Do you want me to ask Eric to help you?"

Yasemin glanced up from her book. "Eric who?"

Christine gave her an exasperated look. "Eric who? I can't believe you. Who's the smartest guy, not to mention one of the best-looking, in all of Cambridge?"

"Okay, I know now. You mean Eric Grayton or Gresson, or whatever his name is? The one with the great green eyes and sexy smile framed by the irresistible beard?"

"Grayson, Eric Grayson, that's exactly who I mean. Now, do you or do you not want me to ask him to help you?"

"He won't want to tutor me. He's busy, he's president of all those clubs, and he's on the tennis team. He's way too busy to help me out."

"Last time, Yaz, yes or no? I know I can get him to spend some time with you, at least enough to get you through this exam. Now, what do you say?"

"I'd love it, yes, please ask him. He could really save my life on this one."

"Yasemin? You want me to help Yasemin study for the calculus exam?"

"Yes, Eric, she's really having a hard time. She needs help. Can you do it?"

Eric Grayson wondered what deity he had pleased to be granted such a wonderful opportunity. Yasemin Turan was, to his eyes, and to many others besides, the most beautiful girl at Radcliffe. She was also one of the smartest. Even in a school such as Radcliffe, known for its brainy students, she was a clear head above many of the others.

He had heard that she spoke three languages, and he had seen what a mean backhand she had on the courts. She was charming and fun, and loved to go places, but she always seemed to be with a whole group of friends. Maybe, just maybe, if he could help her with her exam, she might go out with him. It would be a dream come true.

"Well, yes, I guess I can," he answered, fearing that if he seemed too eager, Christine would pull the plug on the entire deal.

"You *guess* you can? What kind of an answer is that?" asked the girl who had become like a sister to him since they had first met during Christine's orientation week her freshman year. "I know for a fact that you, Eric Grayson, have had a crush on my roommate from the moment you laid eyes on her. I'm just offering you a chance to get to know her, as well as to help her out. So what's your answer?"

He couldn't fool his good friend. "Yes, yes, of course I'll do it. When do I start?"

"Tonight's as good a time as any. I'll tell her to meet you around eight. Where is the best place?"

He wanted to tell her to send Yasemin right to his apartment, but she knew him too well and had already read his mind. "No, Eric, not at your apartment. Try to play this straight for a minute, will you? How about at the entrance to Lamont Library? Then you can decide from there where you should go."

"Sounds great," he beamed. "And, Christine, thanks."

For once in his life, Eric Grayson was early, and he was standing in front of the enormous carved wooden doors of the library when he spotted Yasemin coming across the yard. She walked briskly, that was just one of the many things he liked about her. She seemed always to be active and in motion, constantly on the move. She exuded energy. Her beautiful hair blew softly in the crisp fall breeze, and even from a fair distance he could feel the intensity of her deep brown eyes. The thought of sitting close to her and looking into those beautiful, expressive eyes as he explained the basics of differential calculus was almost more than he could bear. As she approached, he remembered his friend's warning.

"It's so nice of you to help me," she said, offering her hand, before he even had a chance to see if he still had his voice.

"It's . . . it's nothing." He did have a voice. That was a good sign.

They picked a table toward the back of the library where they could talk quietly and not disturb any of the other students.

It seemed they had only been there for minutes rather than almost four hours when the announcement came over the speaker that the library was closing.

"Do you want to meet again tomorrow?" he offered as they gathered up their books and papers.

"You wouldn't mind?"

Those eyes. That smile. "No, not at all, my pleasure. I think it's going to take a few sessions until you're really ready for the exam. Let's stay with it until you feel like you can at least pass it."

"I don't want to just pass," she said, displaying the competitive spirit he had heard she possessed. "I want to get an A."

"In that case, we'll just have to work harder and more often until you completely understand," he said, pleased with the notion of spending more time with her.

In the four weeks before finals, Yasemin and Eric were rarely apart. They spent every night studying, and on weekends they would make dates early on Saturday morning which lasted until late Sunday night. She got the calculus down pat, but she also got something she hadn't bargained for. She was certain she was falling in love with Eric Grayson.

"I don't understand why he has to go away this weekend," she complained to Susan, her other close friend, one night.

"Sounds to me as if you're going to miss him. I thought you said you were only friends. *Friends* don't get so upset when their *friends* go away for the weekend."

"Unless, of course, they're more than friends," Christine chimed in from the other side of the room, knowing full well how Eric felt about Yasemin, but still uncertain about Yasemin's romantic feelings for him. Eric called Christine at least three times a week to see if Yasemin had been forthcoming with any news.

"Well, I do like him," Yasemin admitted, "yes, I like him very much, and I wish he were staying in Boston this weekend instead of going off to look at some silly buildings in Chicago."

"He has to do it, you know that. If he's going to be a great architect, that's what he's going to do a lot of—look at buildings, study buildings, materials, cornices, facades . . . all of the things we mortals never even think about. But I think it's the most romantic thing, don't you, Yasemin? I am convinced that all architects are born romantics."

Yasemin smiled at the two of them. Yes, she also found architecture romantic, but she liked even more the idea of a full-blown romance with Eric. She couldn't wait until he returned to Boston. The next forty-eight hours seemed an eternity to her.

Sunday night she refused to budge from her room on the theory that if she did the phone would immediately ring and she would miss his call. She refused all offers to join a group of friends at her favorite Chinese restaurant.

"Are you sick or something?" asked one of the girls.

"No, I just don't feel like going."

"This is a first, Yasemin refusing a chance for an egg roll and orange beef. Whoever it is, it must be serious!" There was kind laughter all around and then they had gone, leaving her alone with the clock in the hallway.

She waited until just past midnight before changing into her tried-and-true flannel gown. It was like an old friend, and even though it had seen better days she couldn't bear to part with it. As she pulled the tattered garment over her head, she heard the welcome ring of the hall phone.

"I've got it," yelled one of the girls who happened to be walking by at that very moment.

Yasemin stood frozen, not breathing. She listened as the girl said "Wait a second" before she heard her own name being called.

"Coming!" she screamed, afraid that the girl would not hear her and would replace the phone before she could get to it.

She dashed from her room as if on fire and screeched to a halt right in front of the phone.

"Hello."

"Hello, stranger. Boy, did I miss you . . . and the calculus equations, of course."

"I hope it was in that order."

"You bet it was. What are you doing?"

She looked down at her torn and faded nightgown. "I'm dressed for a party," she joked.

"Great, so am I. I just got in, but I'm starving. What do you say to a sandwich or something?"

"I'd love it. Will you also tell me all about your trip? About all of the Chicago treasures?"

"Of course. I'll meet you outside the dorm in fifteen minutes."

"Can't wait."

That night their relationship changed from friendship to what Yasemin had secretly hoped for, and to what Eric had always wanted.

"I missed you," he said again as they sat sharing a typical student's dinner of pizza and Coke.

"Me too," she admitted aloud for the very first time.

They walked outside into the cool evening. Fall was in full force now, winter only the first frost away, and some students still lingered either in the streets or on the stoops of the old town houses that lined the Cambridge streets, trying to take advantage of the last bit of weather that permitted them to be outdoors without gloves and mufflers. Windows were thrown open and a variety of music, ranging from classical to the latest rock 'n' roll, blared out from the students' quarters.

"Come with me," he urged. "You've never seen my apartment." Last semester, Eric had moved, along with two other would-be architects, to an apartment just off campus. Yasemin was curious to see where and how he lived, but she wasn't certain that now was exactly the right time to go there.

She didn't answer right away, but as they walked farther away from all the activity, Eric reached over and put his arm around her. She responded immediately by moving closer to him. His arm felt strong and protective. It was a warm, welcome feeling.

"Come with me," he asked again.

She smiled her answer to him and he led her in the direction of his apartment.

The lights were on at the parlor floor when they walked up the narrow steps to his house. It was charming, a typical brownstone that was so unique, and so unlike the small houses in Turkey. She never tired of looking at their intricate detailing, they were one of the things about Cambridge she had grown to love.

They climbed the two flights of stairs. The apartment was empty and she was secretly pleased to find that his two housemates were not at home. He gave her a full tour, and she commented that it was surprisingly neat and clean for three bachelors. Eric put on some music and then led her to the sofa in the sparsely furnished living room. Books were stacked in piles all around, two architectural models from a recent competition covered the crate that served as a coffee table, and photos of a recent tennis tournament against Princeton were leaning up against the mantel.

Eric sat with his arm around her, and she felt the closeness of him. He smelled fresh—a trace of lemon aftershave and shampoo. He must have showered quickly before he came to meet me, she thought. She inhaled deeply, wanting more of his masculine scent, but before she had a chance to exhale, Eric leaned over and covered her mouth with his. At first she was hesitant and uncertain how to return his kiss, but her hands found their way easily to embrace his face, and her lips eagerly parted for him.

He held her gently, kissing her on her forehead, nose, cheeks, and ears. But soon his lips found their way back to hers, and they explored each other's mouths endlessly, as only first time lovers can do.

"Yasemin . . . Yasemin . . ." he whispered when at last his mouth was separated from hers. "You don't know how long I've wanted to do this."

"Me too," she admitted.

They remained on the sofa for what seemed like hours. Their kisses became more insistent, an honest reflection of their feelings for each other. Soon Eric's hands found their way to her neck and to the very tips of her firm breasts. As his fingertips rubbed her nipples ever so lightly, she became even more excited, and she decided at that very moment that she wanted to make love to him.

"Eric, yes, please, I like that," she said, and she cupped his face in her hands and looked into his eyes as she said it so that he would not for one minute doubt that she really meant it.

But suddenly she sensed his discomfort, his hesitancy, and despite the fact that she wanted him to make love to her right there, she knew that something was wrong. He pulled away from her and tried to act as if everything were all right. He held her hands tightly and tried to control his breathing.

"Eric, what's wrong? Is something the matter?"

He merely shook his head, unwilling or unable to respond. Finally he spoke. "A walk, that's what we need. I'll walk you back to the dorm, all right? It's getting late, and I've got an eight-o'clock." She knew that something was wrong, but she was uncertain if she should push him, for she feared that he would be unable to explain his emotions to her right then.

"Good idea," she agreed, feeling confused and uncomfortable, but not knowing what else to do.

They walked back to the dorm in silence, their arms wrapped tightly about each other's waists. Yasemin never wanted to let him go, and she hoped that he felt the same.

"I'm so glad you're back," she told him once again as they approached the steps to her dorm.

"Me too," he said, pulling her close to him and kissing the top of her head.

"See you tomorrow night?" he asked, more a wish than a question.

"Can't wait," she said for the second time that night, but this time it was laced with more emotion that she had ever felt before.

"Good night, sleep tight," he said, squeezing her hand one last time and then gently letting go.

Yasemin, her thoughts warm and wonderful and filled with anticipation, climbed into her bed. She closed her eyes and saw Eric's face, she breathed the fresh scent of it, and felt his beard with her fingertips. She brushed aside any doubts or concerns she had about the evening; they would talk about it tomorrow night and everything would be fine. With that in mind, a peaceful, contented sleep came almost immediately. The next sound she heard was someone gently calling her name. She woke up with a start, convinced that her wonderful dreams had caused her to oversleep and to miss her eight-o'clock class. But the room was still dark, and it was only one of the other girls trying to awaken her.

"What, what is it?" she said, realizing that the dorm was still quiet and the room pitch-dark.

"Yasemin, it's the telephone. It's for you."

"What time is it?" she asked, rubbing the sleep from her eyes and at the same time swinging her legs out of bed.

"Four-thirty," the girl replied. "It must be something important at this ridiculous hour."

Suddenly she panicked. Who could possibly be calling her at such a time?

She ran toward the receiver which still swung back and forth from its metal cord.

Before she spoke she heard the crackling sound of the long-distance connection. "Hello, hello, it's Yasemin. Who is it?" she asked, unable to mask the concern in her voice.

"Yasemin, Yasemin, is it you?" came the familiar voice.

All kinds of terrible thoughts sped through her mind. Her father. Her sister. Ali. Aunt Semra. The news about Zeki had come exactly this way, except at a reasonable hour, if that kind of news was ever delivered at what one would consider a reasonable hour. By the time the response traveled back, she was certain one of them had been injured, or worse.

"Yes, it's me, Maman. What's the matter? What is it? Is it Father? Tell me."

"No, no, Yasemin, nothing's wrong. Everyone is fine here. Your father is fine. He's in Ankara for the week. No, everyone is well. Nevin, Ali, Semra," she reeled off the list of family members.

Yasemin breathed a temporary sigh of relief. But it was short-lived, for she knew that there was a problem just as serious as an injury or death, a problem deeper and more mysterious, that had been the cause of this call.

"Maman, I'm glad everyone is fine. I was so concerned. Do you realize what time it is here?" She hoped that her mother had simply made a common mistake, reversing the time difference, and thinking that it was a perfectly reasonable hour for her to be calling. But her mother, the mother she had always known up until these last few weeks, was the most precise, buttoned-up person, and it would be highly unlikely for her to make such a mistake.

"Oh, I know, darling, it must be very late. But I was worried about you, and I wanted to make certain that you were all right." Lately Cyrielle had been beside herself with concern for her remaining children. It was not unusual for her to get up from her bed and walk the halls to Ali's and Nevin's rooms. Just as she had done when they were tiny infants, she would enter their bedrooms and stand next to their beds, listening for the sounds of their breathing. Last week she had been hovering over Ali's bed when he had suddenly awakened. At first he had been frightened, and then concerned about his mother's odd behavior. Now her anxiety about Yasemin had become so overwhelming she could not keep herself from picking up the phone and dialing the international operator. Of course, she knew exactly what time it was in Boston, and she knew she would be waking her daughter from a deep sleep, but she could not hold herself back. She had to hear her voice, or she was convinced she would go mad with worry. She was possessed with apprehension and fear, and it was difficult for her even to allow Ali and Nevin to leave the house.

Yasemin sensed the worry and sincere concern in her mother's voice. Nevin had told her in a letter the week before that her mother had been acting strangely, becoming overprotective and excited even by the most normal of events.

"Maman, I'm fine, everything is just fine here. I'm studying hard and looking forward to being home soon. You take care, will you? I promise I'll be home soon."

"All right, darling, all right," Cyrielle replied, lacking her usual spirit and enthusiasm. "You take care of yourself, please. Be careful. I can't wait for you to be home again."

"Soon, Maman, soon. Good night now."

"Good night."

Long after she had hung up the phone, she was haunted by her mother's empty voice; she had detected a change that not even the static on the telephone lines could conceal.

Yasemin passed her math exam with flying colors. She was thrilled to pass a class which, just a short time ago, she had feared she was destined to fail. She was pleased with her grades for the semester, but her greatest joy was derived from her growing relationship with Eric. They were virtually inseparable now. Each day she thanked Christine for urging her to get help. Not only would she keep her place on the Dean's List, but in the process she had gotten much more than she had bargained for.

CHAPTER

18

YASEMIN STOOD in the small space that served as a kitchen in Eric's apartment. It was their custom now to eat together in the evenings after their classes were through for the day and Eric had finished working out at the gym or playing basketball with his friends. On the nights when they were free early, they would stop at the grocery store on the corner and then carry the makings of their meal home and prepare their dinner side by side in the tiny but efficiently planned space. On the nights when Eric was late—sometimes he didn't get back to the apartment until after nine—Yasemin would do all the necessary shopping and cooking, and have dinner ready to be put on the table when he arrived.

Sometimes, if all his roommates were out, they skipped dinner completely, and instead ended up kissing and cuddling in front of the fireplace. Often the bags of groceries would still be on the kitchen counter the next morning, waiting to be unpacked. It seemed to Yasemin that Eric was now more relaxed and confident about their intimacy. Even though they had never really discussed it, she too felt better and more relaxed, and had abandoned the idea that maybe there was something wrong with her. She had decided that when the time came, they would finally make love, and even though she was as anxious as ever, she was willing to wait until it was right.

But tonight they were starving, and she too had been late, so she stood now, working at double speed to get everything ready. She proceeded very methodically, not wanting to waste a single motion.

She removed a head of lettuce, two good-sized tomatoes, and a cucumber from the salad bin in the refrigerator, washed them, drained and dried them. Then she began tearing the leaves and putting them into the bowl. She sliced the tomatoes, peeled the cucumbers, and added them as well. Next she made a simple dressing of fresh lemon and olive oil. She did all of this while Eric busied himself preparing the hamburgers for the grill. Yasemin glanced over at him and watched him forming equally-sized patties between his hands. Watching him as he continued his preparations made her all the more upset about leaving him when she went back to Istanbul for her sister's wedding.

"Yaz, don't look so sad, you look as if you've lost your best friend," he said, brushing her cheek with a kiss.

"You are my best friend. It's just that I don't want to leave you, not even for a couple of weeks," she complained.

Eric couldn't stand to see her upset. When she was troubled or unhappy she frowned, which created a deep line between her eyebrows. That line had appeared now, and she looked so forlorn he had to go to her. He washed his hands of the meat and dried them on the towel that hung by the sink, thinking how nice it was to have her touch in his house. Before Yasemin had started spending time there, he would have been looking all over the house for a paper towel on which to dry his dripping hands. Now everything seemed to be in place, comfortable and fun, and he was always filled with anticipation, anxious to see her again. Suddenly the thought of her going away saddened him as well.

He went to her and put his arms around her, holding her close to him. "Oh, Yaz, don't be sad, we'll work around it," he assured her. "If worse comes to worse, I will arrive in Istanbul and rescue you myself. I'll fight off all those other Turks, and bring you back safely with me." He nuzzled his face against her neck and tickled her until she begged him to stop.

At his words, a light blinked on in Yasemin's head. Of course, why hadn't she thought of it before? Yes, of course. As usual, Eric had just the right idea. She pulled back from his embrace and placed her hands squarely on his shoulders.

"You, Eric Grayson, are a veritable genius. You've just solved the problem. I don't know why I didn't think of it earlier myself. But then, it doesn't really matter, as long as we figured it out in time. Yes, there is only one answer."

"And what might that be?"

"It's evident, of course. You'll come to Istanbul with me. It will be lots of fun. Besides, it's spring break, and I won't have to worry about you being loose in the streets. You can meet all my friends, and I'll take you around on a grand Cook's tour of the city. Istanbul is an architect's paradise. Maybe we can even get away and go to the south for a few days. Sailing. Fresh fish. Snorkeling. Maybe even some topless sunbathers . . ." she tempted him. "Oh, Eric, say you'll come. Please?"

The look on his face told of his hesitation. In theory it sounded like a great plan, but he wasn't at all certain it would work.

"Eric, what's the matter? Don't you want to come?" Once again the crease in her forehead returned and the look he could not bear to see crossed her face.

"Of course I'd love to come, it sounds wonderful, but. . . "

"But what?"

"But I just don't think it's a good idea."

"Why not?"

"Yasemin, after what you've told me about your mother, I'm fairly certain she would not be interested in having another guest, another burden, especially not during such an important time—like her daughter's wedding, for example. It sounds like she's having enough trouble coping with all of the pressures of that right now. No, I'm sorry, Yaz, but I don't think now is the time for me to go with you."

"You are the one who suggested it in the first place," she countered, her emotions jumbled and her mind reeling.

"I was really only joking, Yaz, I'm sorry. I shouldn't have said it."

"But you did, and now you've really upset me. I don't know why you think it's such a terrible idea."

"I just told you, for all that and more. I think the timing is not good at all. In fact, I think it's just plain lousy."

"When would it be good, do you think?"

He hesitated, wanting to pick his words carefully, so they would not be misinterpreted or taken literally again. "I don't really know, Yaz, but just not right now. Perhaps a little later." He reached out for her again but she refused his arms.

"Like when? I've already told everyone all about you," she said. She had told her mother, and her sister, as well as Aunt Semra.

"Yasemin, please," he began, and this time when he came to her she welcomed his arms.

"Eric, do you really care about me?"

He held her closer against his chest. "Of course I do, Yaz, I love you. I've told you that so many times."

"Then you'll come with me. Please say you'll come."

He sighed and shook his head. What had started out as a simple problem of a couple of weeks had all of a sudden turned into a major test of his affection for her. Despite his reservations, Yasemin was very persuasive, and it was obviously important to her.

"All right, I'll go."

"Hurrah!" she squealed. She danced around the room like a delighted child. The deep line disappeared and the smile he loved so very much covered her beautiful face. Still, they ate their hamburgers in silence, their minds churning privately with thoughts of the first major confrontation of their relationship and the consequences it would bring.

No one had ever fallen harder under the spell of Istanbul than did Eric Grayson. From the moment Yasemin pointed to the minarets of the Topkapi Palace from the window of the airplane as they made their final approach, he was smitten with the exotic architecture and rich cultural history of the city.

Semra met them at the airport. Yasemin was disappointed not to see her mother waiting at the gate, and her concern increased immediately. But Semra was as charming and gracious as always, assuring her that Cyrielle was just too frantic with all the wedding plans. As the driver slowly maneuvered the car through the jammed streets of Istanbul, the three of them talked of other things; they laughed and joked. Semra was friendly and hospitable, despite the enormous pressure she was under with the last-minute preparations for Nevin's wedding, for it was she who actually had to bear the responsibility for every detail. If she had spoken the truth, she would have told her niece that at this very second her mother was home in her bed, hiding from the reality around her. Cyrielle had been virtually useless in planning the event. Despite all of this, she made Eric feel welcome and pleased that he had come.

"Now, Yasemin," she said, "Ali has offered to take Eric around for the next few days. I know it would be more fun if you were able to do it, but there are so many festivities planned, I don't think you'll have the time. We've got lunch at the Pensoys tomorrow, and a tea for some of Nevin's old schoolmates at the Embassy on Wednesday. Of course they're all wild to see you."

Yasemin made a face that suggested she was not at all pleased with the plans. But even though she looked upset, she couldn't wait to see old friends again whom she had missed. She had expected a plethora of activities, and in fact she was delighted that Nevin was being feted so extensively; mostly she just wanted to let Eric know she really was disappointed that she would not be able to spend much time with him.

"Nevin will give you the complete schedule, it's grown to such proportions, I cannot tell you. I can no longer keep track of it in my head. How it got so out of hand is beyond me. Thank heavens for Lale, the new secretary, she has been such a help. She's terribly organized about these things."

"You'll like Ali," Yasemin told Eric, "he's a terrific tour guide. You'll get to see everything you want to, and he knows all about practically every building in Istanbul. What he doesn't know, my

Aunt Semra surely does. But it seems she is a bit tied up," she said, referring to the extra pressure her aunt was forced to bear.

"Your father is in Ankara and will not return until Wednesday night," Semra said.

It was only Saturday. Yasemin was sorry that her father would not be able to meet Eric for a few days, and that she would not be able to see him until then. There were so many things she wanted to talk to him about, especially her summer job at Turan Holding.

"Wonderful!" Eric commented as he walked down the long gallery admiring the paintings that lined the walls in the Turan house. There must have been twenty of them, each one a treasure. "I especially like the Matisse drawings. They are very special."

"Yes, they are," Cyrielle agreed, "and not only from an artistic standpoint. If you look at the simplicity of the lines and what he was able to achieve, how he was able to communicate with just a few perfectly executed strokes, it is really extraordinary. But they're also very precious to me because my father gave them to me just before I left Paris." She looked fondly at the drawings. "I remember it as if it was only yesterday."

"Your life has been fascinating, Mrs. Turan. Yasemin has told me quite a bit about it, and I must say I admire your courage and fortitude. You've made such changes in your life, crossing over from one culture to another—very different—one. It must have been hard, yet at the same time challenging."

She smiled at the handsome young man. Cyrielle was trying her hardest to be charming and to welcome her daughter's friend into their home. But it was difficult for her, her attention span was so limited these days, and it was nearly impossible for her to concentrate on any one thing for more than a few minutes at a time. She often sat for what she later realized was hours, unaware of the passage of time, and unable to account for her thoughts during those lost hours. She would have the driver take her into the city, only to forget what she had gone for once they arrived. She knew perfectly well that she could never have pulled off the wedding without Semra's help. Her sister-in-law had done it all: taking charge of the guest list, making the arrangements for the food, going with Nevin for her fittings—all of the things Cyrielle just wasn't up to. She longed to participate, she wanted so to help, but the dark cloud hung over her, it followed her every move, making it impossible to function as she once had.

"Yes," she finally replied, "it has certainly been a challenge. I think you'll probably have a better idea about that after you've spent a few days in our home. Let's talk again at the end of your stay."

"I'll look forward to that," he said.

She left him in the hallway and returned to her room.

Ali and Eric headed out early the next morning, and for the next few days it seemed to Yasemin that she only saw him in the evening when they met downstairs on their way to yet another party.

"I miss you," she said, taking his arm and kissing his cheek as they walked toward the waiting car.

"Me, too," he said, "but I must admit, I'm having a terrific time. Ali and I have been all over this city. What a wonderful place! It's exactly what you said it was, a feast for architects, that's for sure."

"Yes, Sinan was quite a guy," she said, referring to one of the empire's most prolific and marvelous architects. In the sixteenth century he was the chief architect of Sultan Suleyman, and it was he who built the great mosque, the Suleymaniye, as well as many other baths, bridges, and buildings that represent the finest examples of Ottoman architecture. "How would you like to have a client like the sultans? It would be pretty terrific, wouldn't it?"

Nevan and Sedat were a handsome couple, and seeing them together Yasemin believed that her sister was truly in love with him.

"I'm so happy," Nevin told her, "I'm really ready to settle down. I want to have lots of kids, so I figure that now's as good a time as any to start."

Yasemin was happy for her and hoped that she was making the right decision. She too wanted a family, but right now she was having such fun at school, she couldn't even think of it. Of course, if Eric asked her to marry him, well then, she might think differently. *If* he asked . . .

The wedding was a great success, a lovely affair planned down to the most minute detail, and befitting of the daughter of one of Turkey's most powerful men. As Nevin appeared at the top of the elaborate staircase and began her descent, the guests stood in awe. The young girl made a beautiful bride, and as she met her groom at the landing and joined her hand with his, there was no doubt about the love they felt for each other. Yasemin took Eric's hand in hers, and she squeezed it a bit tighter as the couple was pronounced man and wife. She looked into his eyes and prayed that he shared her feelings. Someday she hoped they would be making exactly the same promise to each other.

After the ceremony and dinner, Ali and some of his friends decided to go out on the town. She overheard their conversation, and it sounded as if Eric really wanted to go along with them. She was anxious to be with him, they had seen each other so seldom during the last week, and just as she was about to go to his side to ask him to stay with her, she thought better of it. Tomorrow afternoon they would leave, and on the long flight home she would have his undivided attention. Better to let him go out tonight and enjoy himself. He and Ali got along famously, and she didn't want to deprive him of some more time with her sweet brother.

Besides, it would give her a chance to be with her mother and aunt. They had been so busy it seemed they hadn't had a minute to spend alone together. So the four boys—Ali, Eric, and two of Ali's friends—went off into the night, and Yasemin ordered some tea from Seta and went in search of her mother.

She found her in the first place she looked, sitting by herself in the little room of which she was so fond. Omer had remained outside, doing what he loved best, talking and chatting with a few of his old friends. It was tough enough adjusting to life without his beloved son, but in addition to that heavy emotional burden he had been under immense pressure recently. The Boras had renewed their attack on Turan Holdings; only this time in a more blatant and devious manner than ever before. Most of his time these days was spent trying to keep track of their activities, and either to outbid or outfox them. In addition to all of that, his mind was never free from worry about Cyrielle, and about her health and well-being. He had watched with a heavy heart as his sister had to plan his daughter's wedding, so incapable was his wife of handling anything these days. It distressed him more than he had let on, and he was just thankful for Semra's wonderful spirit. So he was pleased for a purely social opportunity, a chance to unwind and relax, and, for a few brief moments, to forget totally about the problems at hand.

Cyrielle smiled when she saw her eldest daughter peek in, and beckoned her to come and sit by her side on the comfortable divan.

"Lovely, wasn't it?"

"Yes, Mother, it was a wonderful party, and Nevin seems happy and so very much in love," Yasemin said, as she sat down next to Cyrielle.

"I really like Sedat. He will be a wonderful husband to her, and a good father for their children. And thank heavens for Semra. She really did it all, you know. Somehow I just couldn't find the energy for all of the details. It has been hard for me, you know, since . . ." Her voice trailed off, and her gaze seemed to search for something a million miles in the distance. But Yasemin was so anxious to talk with her, and to hear her thoughts and ideas, just as they had always done in the past, that she refused to dwell on the tragedy they had all shared, and changed the subject at once.

"What do you think of Eric, Maman?"

Yasemin watched her mother's expression in anticipation, but it remained passive, unfeeling.

Cyrielle finally managed a smile and took her daughter's hand in hers. "He's a wonderful young man, very kind and very caring. I think he feels a great deal for you. And he certainly seems to have hit it off with Ali very well," she added. She wanted to say so much more, to probe, to question, and to find out exactly how Yasemin felt about the charming young man. But suddenly, as always just when she wanted to talk, to communicate, her strength left her and she was drained of all her energy. She sat silently, unable to move or to continue the conversation. She wondered if the new medication the doctor had prescribed was responsible for this hopeless feeling. She made a mental note, which would most likely be forgotten, to call him and check with him in the morning.

Yasemin stared back at her mother, wanting so much to share the things she was certain she would want to hear. But Cyrielle's face told her of her sudden weariness, and she knew there was no point in trying to continue the conversation. Her heart was heavy, she missed her mother's vitality and love. Before she left she would have to speak with her father and see what he was doing to help her.

Cyrielle excused herself and left the room. She was hunched over, her perfect posture gone, her feet dragging as if she were years older than she really was. Yasemin kissed her good-night and returned to her place on the sofa. She looked out at the dark waters and allowed herself to dream—wonderful thoughts about Eric, and about all the things she would have told her mother, if only she had been able to hear her.

Comforted by her thoughts, Yasemin fell asleep on the lush sofa, and when she awoke the light was just coming up over Bosphorus. On her way upstairs she looked out into the courtyard, but Ali's bright-red MG sports car was not there. A late night, for certain. Eric would sleep all the way to Frankfurt, the first stop on their long trip home.

She savored her big bed, knowing that the day after tomorrow would find her back in the skinny cots that served as beds in the dorm.

The house was still calm when she rose and dressed for break-fast. Seta had brewed some potent coffee, whose scent permeated the entire house. Ali and Eric would most likely be good candidates for a strong dose of it, she thought, remembering their late night. Down-stairs, she found only Semra, who was off to visit a friend in the hospital. Her mother had gone out also, having promised to return before lunch.

There was no sign of either her brother or boyfriend.

"They didn't come in until very late," Yasemin told her aunt.

"I'm sure they had a wonderful time. He's such a sweet boy, and he seems to find Ali a long-lost friend."

"Yes. I just hope they get up soon. I wanted to stop by and say good-bye to Father on the way to the airport. We'll have to be packed and ready to go by early afternoon."

"Send Erol up for the two of them if you don't see the whites, or, I should say, the reds of their eyes, fairly soon. I'll be back shortly," Semra said, kissing her favorite niece on both cheeks, grab-bing her sweater, and heading out to the waiting car.

Yasemin read the morning papers, and just as she was about to glance up once more at the clock, Ali entered. He was still in his robe, and he ambled across the kitchen as if blind, using the countertops as guidance. He found the largest cup available, poured the steaming brew, then slowly made his way back to the table where his sister sat.

"Some night," she said.

"Very late," he agreed, shaking his head at the first sip of coffee, "very late indeed."

"Did you have fun?"

"Yes, everyone seemed to."

His voice signaled something strange, alerting Yasemin. Anyone else would have overlooked it, but to his twin it was an unmistakable sign that something was amiss.

"Where did you go?"

"Oh, just around."

"That's specific, Ali," she said sarcastically. "What do you mean, around?"

"Just to a few places, that's all." He drained his cup.

Ali stood, returned to the coffeepot, and refilled his cup. Seta had gone out for errands, and he cut two pieces of bread from the fresh loaf that sat on the counter.

"Do you want some feta cheese and jam with that?" asked his sister.

At the mention of cheese, Ali pulled a horrible face. "No, no, I think that this morning dry is best."

"Lots of drinks, huh? I thought you had had quite a bit of champagne even before you went out. Did Eric drink a lot? He usually doesn't, but he seemed to be having such a good time. And since there is no sign of him yet . . . "

"Yes, Eric had a little to drink. I'm sure he'll be up soon. You have to leave in a few hours anyway, don't you?" Ali's tone was brusque, and when Yasemin said Eric's name she detected a reaction, and not a positive one as she had seen during the past few days.

"Ali, what's the matter?"

He seemed stunned to hear that she had sensed his uneasiness. For a moment he was unable to respond.

"Ali, I asked you a question. Now what is it? Is Eric all right?"

"I'm sure he's just fine, Yaz. I'm sure."

"No, you're not, now don't lie to me. You're being very evasive. I thought that you and Eric were getting along famously. And you've been so good to him, taking him all around while I've been off lunching and celebrating. I was just going to tell you how much I appreciate it, and thank you. But now I know that something is wrong. Something must have happened. Now tell me what it is."

"Nothing, Yaz, everything is fine. We just went out, went to a couple of places for a drink. That's all."

"No, that's not all," she insisted, concern and worry marking her expression. "Now tell me; I don't want to have to ask you again. Please."

He had hoped somehow to get through the morning, get Yasemin and Eric on the plane back to the States, and forget about the horrible experience the previous night. But seeing his sister's beautiful face, and loving her the way he did, he knew that he would be forced to tell her. Forced to hurt her, which was the last thing he ever wanted to do. But he had to, for the truth would come out sooner or later, but sooner was certainly better than later in this case. This kind of deception could go on for years, maybe forever, and later the pain would only be more excruciating than it could be at that moment. He was sorry that he had to be the one to tell her, and even sorrier that after he had done so she would not have her mother to turn to. She would need a woman's ear, a woman's sympathy and understanding. But he knew very well that Cyrielle was incapable of dealing with her own emotions right now, much less those of her children. Thank heavens for Semra, he thought. Once again, she would be called to the forefront to serve as the rock of strength for her brother's children.

His sister's voice broke his thoughts. "Ali," Yasemin insisted, "I'm waiting."

"Yaz, something happened last night, and I've been up ever since we came home, worrying about how to tell you."

She sat in stony silence, not wanting to interrupt him.

"But I have to tell you, and when you hear it you must promise me not to be angry with me for doing so, and you must also try not to be angry with Eric. I know that it will hurt you, and for that I am sorry."

She could remain silent no longer. "Ali, please, what is it?"

He looked down at his half-eaten toast. Even the sight of the dry bread turned his stomach now that he was imminently faced with the task of breaking the news to his sister.

"Yasemin, Eric is a homosexual."

She looked at him, dumbfounded, and then began to giggle.

"Ali, are you kidding? You've got to be joking. Of course he's not a homosexual. It must have been in your dreams. You had more to drink than I even imagined. Just because you . . ." And then she stopped short, never wanting to hurt her brother. She had known about his sexual persuasion for a long time; once they had even discussed it. She couldn't care less about his homosexuality, she only wanted him to be happy and to have a good life. So far, he had managed to juggle the fine line in a society that frowned deeply on such things, and had carved out a satisfactory life which he lived mostly in private.

He stared back at her, annoyed that she would make light of his revelation.

"Yaz, I'm sorry, but it's not a joke, and I'm not kidding. Nor have I lost my mind. Please, you've got to believe me."

"How did you come to such an outrageous conclusion? I've never heard of such a thing. Why, I've been fooling around with Eric for quite some time now. Don't you think I'd know?"

"I'm not ruling out the possibility that he might be bisexual, but if I had to bet money on it, I would say that he is completely drawn toward men, he just hasn't yet come to terms with it. And trying to have a real relationship with you was one of his efforts to see if he was or wasn't. But I'm telling you he is, and your relationship just won't work."

"I still don't understand how you came to this conclusion," she insisted, a little less secure in her fervent position of a moment ago. While Ali was speaking her mind raced back, retracing their relationship. Suddenly things that she had overlooked: his hesitancy during their first kisses; his unwillingness to make love, which she had always told herself was due to his sweet old-fashioned consideration; his original refusal to come with her to Istanbul . . . now everything came painfully into focus, and she wanted to turn her eyes away from the clearer picture she now saw.

"It's not important how I decided. I'm just telling you that I know for sure. Yaz, I'm your brother, and I wouldn't hurt you for the world. I love you, and telling you this has been one of the hardest things I've ever had to do."

She heard every word he said, and she believed him. But still, she had to know it all. "Tell me," she pleaded. "Nothing you can say now will shock me."

His eyes implored her, but he knew she would be relentless until he told her. "I saw him. He left the bar where we were drinking with a friend of mine. It was getting late, and they had been gone a long time. I was ready to go home, so I went to look for him." He paused to regain his strength. "And I found him, I found him with my friend. They were having an experience that one could only describe as a homosexual encounter."

As the last words left his mouth, the sound of Eric clearing his throat came from behind them. They both turned at the same time, and the look they saw on his face told them that Eric had been standing in the doorway of the kitchen long enough to realize the essence of the conversation between the twins.

Eric's eyes traveled from Yasemin to Ali and back to Yasemin. She locked her eyes on him, still not believing, but knowing full well her brother would never lie to her. Her heart pounded as she tried to absorb the shock and the pain of the horrid revelation. When she found her legs, and was certain they would carry her, she pushed back her chair and ran from the room, out of the house and onto the terrace.

She remained there, staring at the boats as they passed, until Ali came out to remind her that in order to make their plane they would have to leave within the hour. She nodded, showing she understood, and without a word went to her bedroom where she packed, bathed and dressed, and then came downstairs to begin the long trip back to school. She was exhausted, her emotions ranging from anger to understanding, from rage to sympathy. But in her very soul she felt used, wounded. She had lost more than a boyfriend, a supposed first love; she had lost her own sense of self. She would begin to put her life back together with a deflated ego, and a lack of trust in her own judgment. Worse yet, she had no one with whom to discuss this painful, devastating event.

CHAPTER

19

YASEMIN SAT in silence next to Eric, praying that the hours would pass quickly and she could finally have some time alone, to think and to sort things out. The dry air in the plane was suffocating her, her throat felt like parchment. She got up from her seat numerous times and walked up and down the aisles, seeking escape. Eric only looked at her, helpless to speak, to explain, or to ask forgiveness. They were the same eyes she had gazed into during the most intimate moments, eyes that had excited her and pleased her, but now she only saw the eyes of a traitor, one whose actions had cut to her very core, who had confused and betrayed her. Wearied by the wordless exchange, she fell asleep for an hour or two, but when she awakened his eyes were still on her.

She remembered a conversation, the only one, that she and Ali once had had about his sexuality. He explained to her in the clearest of terms that regardless of whether or not his life-style was looked upon by the rest of the world as right or wrong, the urges and the desires still existed. They were real, he said, as real as any passion that existed between a man and a woman. At times these urges could even be uncontrollable, times when the heat of the moment over-ruled the senses. As in the case of Eric and one of Ali's friends last night, Yasemin thought. Recalling those things, she wanted to feel empathetic toward Eric, to discuss it with him, and to tell him everything would be all right. But instead she felt only revulsion. It was too soon, and the blow to her ego and her pride was too fresh.

Perhaps someday they could discuss it, even be friends. She wasn't certain when, but right now that day seemed to be in the distant future.

As they had traveled, they parted in silence at the Boston airport. Yasemin refused his offers of both a taxi as well as a kiss on the cheek. She carried her luggage to the taxi line, waited her turn, then threw her bags in and drove off without a backward glance.

When asked about her trip by Susan and Christine, she said that it was fine, but that the relationship with Eric was a thing of the past. The look she gave told them in no uncertain terms that no further explanation would be forthcoming and this would have to suffice until such time when she was willing to tell more.

Yasemin was anxious to get on with her life and to put the painful experience with Eric in the past where it belonged. She increased her course load, taking more hours than most of the students. She was eager to finish her studies and to return to Istanbul and begin work at Turan Holding. Her father had promised her a position in the textile division, a rapidly growing and profitable piece of the business, which with Yasemin's skills could become a very important part of their organization. She had realized during that last visit how difficult things were for Omer without Zeki around. He had banked on him, and his enjoyment of his work had been greatly enhanced by having the young man around to teach and to instill in him the business skills he had worked his entire life to learn. Now that Zeki was gone, she felt that a light had gone out in her father's spirit, and she was determined to be the one who would rekindle it. It was going to be an uphill battle, she knew. Women still only held supporting positions in most of the major companies; they had to work harder and prove themselves to be more capable than any man in exactly the same situation. But she was willing to devote herself to the company, she knew she could do it, and she wanted it to be her future. She was lonely and homesick, she missed her family and the familiarity and comfort of the life she had always known. Now that Eric was out of the picture, her only goal was to finish school and to get back home.

Ali wrote regularly. In his letters he tried to make sense of what had happened, and in doing so to lessen Yasemin's pain. She wrote back and told him she was fine. What concerned her more was her mother's health, and the latest events at Turan Holding. On the business front he was not of much help; he had carved out his own little world in which he lived, and it had very little to do with the family business. Concerning Cyrielle, he was much more insightful. He spent a great deal of time with her, he was patient and loving, and he understood what she was going through. He also realized that as the only remaining son, he now had to pick up some of the responsibility that had fallen to Zeki. He and Zeki had loved each other, but they had not been particularly close. They had very little in common. Zeki had had his sports and his girlfriends, his interest in the business, and his tight, devoted relationship with their father. Ali, on the other hand, had always had his music. And he had always been closer to Cyrielle than to Omer, to the extent that he opened up and shared his feelings at all. He knew, as did everyone in the family, that he was neither interested in nor capable of taking Zeki's place, either in his father's heart or at the head of the corporate board. He made no excuses for this; he was a happy individual, content with the life he had created. He convinced both his mother and father that Yasemin was the one to count on, she would be the sibling who possessed the drive and tenaciousness to carry on the family legacy. Cyrielle knew this was true; Omer was a tougher sell. Turan Holding employed women as secretaries and assistants; none held administrative or decision-making positions.

"That will change, Baba," Ali asserted. "You'll see. When Yasemin gets home you can train her just as you did Zeki. She will surprise you, I know."

His father remained unconvinced. "I know she's as smart as a whip, but I just don't know if a woman can handle all the pressures of the job, the late hours, the continual travel. It would be hard on any woman, especially if she wants to have a husband and family."

"She'll manage," Cyrielle commented. "I think Ali's right. She's a very special person, and she is devoted to the idea of heading Turan. Just give her a chance, Omer. She'll do us all proud."

Omer was so pleased to hear Cyrielle voice an opinion, especially one so strongly felt, that he did not dare crush her enthusiasm by continuing to voice his doubts. He had come to treasure small things in her like this—taking part in a conversation, a willingness to go out to dinner with friends, a desire to attend a concert—all were signs that she was getting better, that each day she was learning to deal with her grief. Soon, he prayed, soon he might have his lovely Cyrielle back.

Nevin was a born wife, and soon she would be a mother, a role that everyone was certain she would play with equal success. She and Sedat moved into their house in Bebek, a section of Istanbul whose rolling hills were peppered with charming old wooden houses and verdant slopes lined with groves of umbrella pines and cypresses. Sedat accepted Omer's offer of a position at Turan Holding, thereby securing a solid future for himself and the family on the way. Sedat was a steady, hard worker who adapted easily to his new surroundings, and he did a good job. He lacked, however, the fire and ambition of a potential candidate to take over the business, and Omer soon turned his short-lived hopes away from the young man.

Semra concentrated her talents on a cause that she felt was very important to the future of the country—improving the plight of its women. She had always been a progressive thinker, and having lived abroad and seen firsthand the greater difference in equality between the sexes in European countries, she knew that Turkey had a long way to go. Over the last few years, because she had become so involved with her brother's family, and had ended up staying with

Cyrielle, she had postponed becoming involved in a major way. Now she began with a vengeance, traveling the country, visiting the inhabitants of the isolated east, urging women to exercise their right to vote, and advocating the end of the ancient practice of permitting Turkish men to take a second wife. She fought to put into practice the equality that Atatürk had granted women forty years earlier. In a separate agenda, she hoped that her absence would do Cyrielle some good; without Semra's daily presence, she would be forced to be more independent, and perhaps she would return to being her old self.

Yasemin graduated a year ahead of schedule. She packed her bags for the last time and bid her dear friends good-bye. They made all the promises that girls who have shared three years in such close quarters make, and Yasemin vowed that once she was settled in at Turan Holding, she would invite them to come to Istanbul for a visit. Amid tears and laughter she waved one last time and headed east, back to a culture and society she longed to be a part of once again.

I TOLD YOU we could do it, *Babacığım,*" Yasemin said, delighted at the way her latest new venture was turning out. "I just knew there was an opportunity for us in that market." The market was the States, and the product was textiles; luxurious, lush cotton towels, blankets and sheets, all produced at three of the older Turan factories, which Omer had considered selling only last year. But before he had the chance, his ambitious daughter had had an inspiration, one that was proving to be very profitable.

"I'm proud of you, Yasemin. You know I was dead set against this idea, and you really pushed me to try it. It cost us a great deal of money to get those factories up and working again, but you've turned it around nicely, brilliantly, in fact. The production is large enough now to command its own management, and at the board meeting next Friday I'm going to recommend that we appoint you president of the division. How does that sound?"

"Oh, *Baba,* do you really mean it?" she said, thrilled at the prospect of having her own little company to run and to build. She knew the board-meeting approval was only a formality. Who was going to veto a recommendation made by the boss for his daughter, especially since she had already proven herself to be such a capable businesswoman?

Omer smiled back at her, pleased by her reaction, and also genuinely delighted by what she had been able to accomplish. When she returned from school anxious to work, he had deliberately given her the most lowly of positions, just a step up from a job in the mail room. He had hoped that she would soon tire of it, and would consider using her talents at home, first as a wife and then a mother. But she had surprised him, she had stuck with it, making the most of a boring situation.

Then she had looked around, asked questions, and studied the company thoroughly. She had come up with a business plan for those old factories in Bursa, a city to the south of Istanbul that had always been known for its production of textiles. The old buildings had sat vacant for years, unused and in need of repair. Yasemin proposed a simple yet valuable idea that would put them to good use. Since she had been in the States, she knew the market well. She had a good feel about what would sell as an export line. She proposed revising the sizes and styles and the thickness of the towels, the weight, sizes and patterns of the sheets, and then revamping and updating the entire color palette so that the goods would appeal to the coveted American market. She was certain that those marketing and design ideas, coupled with a thorough overhaul of the financial operation, were guaranteed to produce good results.

She had come to her father fully prepared; in fact, he had to admit, more prepared than many of his highly paid senior managers usually were. The proposal was so complete and well thought out— she hadn't missed a single detail—that he was compelled to give her the chance she asked for. He had had confidence in her, but she had astonished him with the success she had made of her project. She had practically moved to the small town of Bursa. There she had recruited the workers, trained them, and made allies of them. She had instilled such loyalty in them that they worked overtime, both nights and weekends, happy to be involved in such an exciting new venture. She had made them feel that they were part of a team, with the result that they really cared about the product they were making. A further result was a substantial increase in revenues for Turan Holding.

"Of course I mean it, so you had better get working on your expansion plans. We'll need to look at them at the budget meeting next month. But right now, young lady, it's late. It's already after four, and your mother will have both our necks if we're late. We're due at the museum at eight. So get going, my little dynamo. I'll see you at home later."

"Thank you, *Baba*," she said, gathering up her papers. "I'm leaving right now. I asked Murat to come for me, my car is in the garage today. I'll send him back for you right away. I know how important this event is for Mother. I wouldn't be late for anything."

"Good, get going then, I'll see you later." He kissed her and sent her off with an affectionate pat.

The gardens were in full bloom, and the museum looked glorious, even though the new wing still remained unfinished. The guests were willing to overlook that because they were so pleased to be back for the lovely gala.

It was a perfect spring night. The air was cooled by a gentle breeze, and bright stars blanketed the dark sky. Yasemin rode to the party with her mother in the Bentley, the skirt of Cyrielle's festive evening dress taking up the full width of the seat.

"Maman, you look wonderful. I love that dress. Especially the color. Red has always been one of your best colors." Cyrielle did look glamorous in her red silk gown. The tricolor bracelet glistened on her wrist, and the diamond earrings Omer had given her for her birthday lit up her entire face.

"Thank you, darling," Cyrielle said, in a tone of voice that had improved dramatically over the past few months. She still wasn't back to her old self, but all those around her felt she was making some improvements. She had felt well enough to plan, with Semra's help, this year's gala. They all hoped this was the sign they had been waiting for, a sure signal that soon she would return to being the Cyrielle they had once known. "You certainly look lovely too. It's amazing, you can work so hard all day, and then rush home, and in just a little over an hour you've transformed yourself into the most beautiful young woman."

"Oh, it's nothing, Maman, just those great genes you shared with me, that's all. Besides, look what you do. All I have to worry about is the office, but you run the house and the museum, plan every detail of these events, and take care of *Baba,* which in itself is a full-time job."

Cyrielle smiled with pride at her lovely daughter. Looking at her she saw her own mother—the delicate nose and perfectly formed lips, the exquisite hair, the intense eyes—all of Dominique's startling features she saw on her own daughter. Yasemin's dress, a green silk slip that accentuated her long, slim figure, had once belonged to Cyrielle. Yasemin loved it so much that she had begged Cyrielle to give it to her. She had agreed with pleasure, and had also given her the matched strand of pearls that had once belonged to her grandmother. She knew that her daughter's simple elegance and perfect posture, which conveyed her strong sense of self-confidence, would make her by far the most attractive young woman in the room tonight. All the other young women would pale in comparison with the composed, sophisticated Yasemin. She had that magical power, that same magnetic quality which Cyrielle remembered from her own mother, a power that caused her entrance into a room to become an event, stopping conversations in mid-sentence as both men and women felt compelled to turn in her direction.

"In any case, you look lovely," Cyrielle insisted, "and I'm so very proud of you and the way things are going. Your father is just beside himself with happiness. He told me about the plans for your promotion. You've made all the difference in the world to him."

I wish I had been able to do the same with you, Yasemin wanted to say, but she held back her words. At least her mother was going out again, and maybe tonight would be the start to recapturing her old life.

The crowd sparkled, the women had donned their very best ensembles for the great event. Many had made a special trip to Paris to shop for just the right dress, and not since the last gala had Istanbul's high society been out together in such force. The guests mingled and chatted, the men smoked their cigars and chatted in groups, while the women critically assessed each other's jewelry and gowns.

Yasemin took a glass of champagne from the silver tray carried by one of the many uniformed waiters and went in search of her sister. But Nevin was nowhere to be found, and as she wandered the long hall of the main gallery in hopes of spotting her, she felt many pairs of eyes on her as she passed. She would never be used to the stares, and she prayed that Nevin would appear soon so she could stop her endless searching. She smiled at familiar faces and stopped several times to greet friends of her parents, and one or two old friends of her own. The crowd was mostly older, with the exception of several young married couples and a few foreigners, most of whom she did not know. Since she had returned from school, she had not rekindled her old school friendships; instead she had devoted most of her attention to work. As she had promised, she kept in touch with Susan and Christine, but the rest of her efforts, and nearly all of her time, was spent on her projects at Turan Holding.

As she continued her walk, past the Picassos and Braques, one pair of eyes stayed with her, and somehow sensing the powerful stare against her back, she turned to find out who was being so overt. She rounded the new Rodin sculpture and stopped short only millimeters from the face of the intruder. She was prepared to confront him and demand to know how he could be so rude, when she was greeted by the widest smile she had ever seen.

"I was wondering how long it would take before you turned around."

"I wanted to stop you before you drilled a hole through my dress," she countered.

He smiled again, revealing perfectly straight white teeth. He was tall, with strong, broad shoulders, which were accentuated by his beautifully tailored dinner jacket. Instead of a plain black silk bow tie, the type worn by ninety-nine percent of the men, his was a deep forest green, the same green, she noticed as she took her time, looking at him the way he had been studying her for the last few minutes, as his mesmerizing eyes. She was drawn to his eyes, his handsome face, and extraordinary smile. She wanted to be angry with him, to scold him for flirting so openly with her, but instead she just smiled back, anxious to meet this intriguing stranger.

"I'm sorry," he said, "I've been away for a long time. I have forgotten how exotic Turkish women can be. Plus I like the way you walk. It's very seductive."

"It wasn't meant to be," she replied, suddenly self-conscious in the tight-fitting dress. She hadn't thought of herself in those terms lately; ever since Eric there had been no one in her life, and until that moment she had liked it just that way. She had been so busy working, she had not even had time to think about anything else, but somehow all of that was changing right before her eyes.

"Well, intentional or not, it was. And I'm pleased to tell you that you are even more beautiful from the front than from the back."

This total stranger was so flirtatious, so forward, but for some reason it was not offensive to her at all. On the contrary, she liked being complimented in this way. Standing in a group of three hundred or so people discussing the way she walked, while most of the other guests were chatting on about the weather or some other mundane subject, made their conversation even more intimate.

She smiled at him, unable to respond to his comment. "Where have you been locked away that you have forgotten how women walk?"

"It's not that I've forgotten, I said I have forgotten how wonderful Turkish women can be. You know, they have that certain *je ne sais quoi* about them—whatever it is, it can be very, very attractive. I missed all that in England. It must have something to do with the gruesome weather."

"England?"

"Yes, studying. And after I finished I decided to stay for another year. Don't quite know why now, I'm bloody happy to be back here, as they would say. Especially if I can meet a pretty woman like you . . ."

"You're awfully forward. Do you always talk to people you've just met like this?"

"Only if I find them extremely attractive. And you are without a doubt the most attractive woman I have seen in a very long time. Can I get you another glass of champagne?" he offered, noticing that hers was empty.

"No, no, thank you," she said. She was afraid that if he left he might be trapped in the crowd. She didn't want to risk it.

Nevin's voice came from behind her, and all at once she wished her sister had never spotted her.

"Where have you been?" Nevin asked.

"Looking all over for you, that's where," Yasemin replied.

"Well, I'm glad I found you, Mother needs both of us right now, for some photographs or something. Come, everyone is waiting for us."

Yasemin turned back to the enchanting stranger, whose eyes still had not left her. "I . . . I have to go now. It's been nice talking with you. . . . I don't even know your name. . . ." she began, and before he could answer she felt Nevin pulling on her arm.

"Yasemin, now, we've got to run."

"I'll catch up with you later," he said, his smile dimming ever so slightly.

"All right," she said, reluctantly being dragged away by her younger sibling.

He still stood staring at her as she was led away. He had heard so much about Omer Turan's eldest daughter, but it was always in relation to her work at Turan Holding. He had been told she was a crackerjack businesswoman, a superb negotiator, and probably a formidable opponent. He never dreamed that she might be beautiful as well.

"Fraternizing with the enemy, huh? It's a good thing Baba didn't see you, or he'd yank that promotion right out from under you. Really, Yasemin, I'm surprised at you!"

Yasemin stopped in her tracks and turned back to look in the stranger's direction. "What are you talking about? I don't even know his name. But he sure is gorgeous."

"He may be gorgeous, but forget about it. And don't kid me, everyone knows who he is."

"Nevin, I'm not kidding. Remember, I've been away for a long time. Now stop keeping me in suspense. Who is the dark stranger?"

"I can't believe you don't know. He's the youngest of the three sons, and you're right, he is handsome. Became a real playboy when he was in Paris and London, I hear. But forget about him, Yaz. If his name was anything other than Bora, it would be all right. But it isn't," Nevin said firmly, once again pulling at her sister's bare arm. "Now come on."

"Bora," Yasemin repeated. "You mean he's the brother of Timur and Tayfun? What's his name?"

"It doesn't matter, Yaz, forget about it. If Baba knew you spent even one minute with him, he'd have your neck."

"Oh, come on, Nevin, he's the one who's not even involved in the business, isn't that so? I heard somewhere that he came back here and started his own firm."

"That's true; he's gone back to their original business, which, as you know very well, is the production of clothing. But it doesn't matter, he's still a part of that family, and from what I've heard from Sedat and Baba, they're out to get us."

"They may be, but it doesn't mean that the younger one, whatever his name is, is also a bad guy. Really, Nevin, I think you're overreacting. It was a harmless conversation, and it really had nothing to do with business, I can assure you."

"It may not have, but I don't think it matters. Just stay away from him, the whole family is trouble, and I'm sure that includes him."

As they approached the area where the photo session was taking place, Yasemin glanced back in his direction once more, but the charismatic, intriguing stranger had moved away from where they were standing, and she couldn't see him through the crowd.

For the rest of the evening Yasemin's time was not her own. She was seated at a center table surrounded by business associates, and every time she tried to make her escape, her mother or father or grandfather was at her side, dragging her around to introduce her to one person or another. By the time she was ready to leave, most of the guests had already departed. She searched the room carefully, knowing all the time that she should take her sister's wise advice and forget completely about ever meeting the handsome young man whose first name she still didn't know. The Bora family was nothing but trouble; with each move they made they were becoming more and more competitive with Turan Holding. Competition was healthy, but the Boras' business tactics continued to be questionable and their motives were clear: they wanted to be the biggest and the strongest company, and they would stop at nothing to achieve their goals. Then, of course, there had been the horrible mess about the chromium shipments during World War II. And furthermore, Cyrielle still blamed the Boras in part for Zeki's death. Of course Yasemin realized that the capsized boat could have belonged to any number of families, or to any company or country, for that matter, but her mother would never be convinced that it wasn't some horrible force of fate that had, in fact, made the boat belong to the Boras.

It was late when she arrived at her office the next day. She had gone to the Hilton Hotel in Taksim for a breakfast meeting with some people who were interested in importing the goods she was producing in the Bursa factories. It had been a great success, and she left the meeting with an order twice as large as any they had ever had before.

She practically floated into her office. "Leyla," she said to her secretary as she breezed past her desk, "please call my father and tell him that I must see him the very first moment he is free. It's urgent."

"Yes, Yasemin," the girl answered, trying to stifle her giggles.

Yasemin stopped, wondering whatever was the matter with her. Leyla was usually a quiet, composed young woman who kept very much to herself. But now the girl was possessed by laughter, and when Yasemin looked quizzically at her, she could only point toward the closed door of her boss's office.

Yasemin opened the door and knew at once what had caused Leyla's outburst. Crowded into the tiny office were at least two hundred tulips. They were all arranged beautifully in simple glass containers; their stems were long and elegant, their blooms the most vibrant shade of yellow. They were like a strong ray of sunshine illuminating the entire office. Vases covered the surface of her desk, the shelf by the window, and the overflow had been placed around the floor. Yasemin threw her papers and her prized orders down on the small sofa and made her way slowly through the maze of flowers in search of a card. She looked carefully on all the vases, and when she finally reached the second to last, she found the small white envelope. "Good morning, beautiful stranger" was the message. She flopped down on her chair, the card still in her hand. Even though he had not introduced himself, it was apparent that he knew who she was. Even so, she had never expected such an extraordinary gesture. She was stunned, and torn by her emotions. She knew what a commotion she would cause even by becoming friendly with a member of the Bora family. But his handsome face had been foremost in her dreams last night, and she had found herself thinking about him as she waited patiently in the heavy Istanbul traffic on the drive back from the hotel that morning. For the moment, however, she decided to make every effort to push all thoughts of him from her mind and concentrate on business. She buzzed Leyla to find out when she would be able to see her father.

Just as Leyla was picking up the intercom, Yasemin looked up and saw her father standing in her doorway.

"My, my," he said, observing the floral display, "I think someone is interested in you. Either that, or they have made a terrible mistake at the florist's and sent all the arrangements to the same address. Yasemin, this is quite something."

"Yes, I was shocked too," she admitted, wanting to move on from the subject of the flowers to the topic of the successful morning meeting. A moment longer on the flowers and the question about whom they were from was certain to come up. "Baba, I was just on my way to you when I saw the flowers. I wanted to share the good news. Look at the orders I got this morning from the English company," she began, going over to the sofa and searching for the confirmation papers. "Look here, there are orders for the next six months. It's more business than we've ever had before. I hope the production staff can keep up with it."

Omer flipped through the orders. He looked up at his daughter's beaming face and shared her happiness. "Yasemin, this is wonderful. You're really becoming quite an entrepreneur. I'm so proud of you, I could send you flowers; but under the circumstances I don't really think it would be appropriate."

She laughed and went to his side to hug him. "You're right about that. I think I'll have Leyla distribute these around the offices. From the looks of it, everyone could have their own vase. I'll have to leave for Bursa tonight anyway; I want to tell them the good news myself. It would be a shame if the flowers were not enjoyed. I'll send them around this afternoon."

"That's a sweet idea, Yasemin. Well, I've got to be off, I'm late for another meeting. I'll see you at home tonight. And congratulations, my little one, both on your new business and your new friend."

"Thanks, *Babacığım*."

Yasemin, still stunned, sat at her desk surrounded by the sea of yellow blossoms. She breathed a sigh of relief that her father had gone without asking who had made this extraordinary gesture. Even if he had asked, the only way she could have described him was as the youngest son of his arch enemy.

It had been quite a morning. She was quite certain of how to handle the new orders; how to deal with her new admirer was something else entirely.

CHAPTER

21

Y OU CAN'T avoid me forever," said the voice, which, ever since the moment she had first heard it, had been reverberating over and over again in her mind.

She had worked late, and by this hour most of the cars in the parking lot were gone. Somehow he had known which one was hers, and when he spoke to her she looked up and saw him leaning against the side of her car. He too had come from his office. He had removed his jacket and rolled up the sleeves on his light-blue dress shirt. His tie was loosened and he looked weary, but underneath the exhaustion his face brightened when he saw her. He looked even more attractive to her now than he had in his elegant dinner jacket. She had held that picture of him in her mind, and by this morning she had convinced herself that he just couldn't have been as handsome as she was picturing him, it was only her mind playing tricks on her. Now she knew how wrong she had been, for he looked even better than she had remembered. She had not responded to the tulips, or to the roses the following week, or to the mixed bouquets that had arrived the past Monday. It would have taken only one phone call to find out his name, his office number and any other information she had wanted, but she had kept herself from picking up the phone, thus trying to purge him from her memory.

"I thought that maybe you didn't like either roses or tulips, so I tried the mixed flowers. But when I still didn't hear, I thought I had better come and see what I am doing wrong. Will you have dinner with me?"

"I . . . I don't even know your name," she replied, unable to think of a better response, since she was still so surprised at seeing him, and even more afraid that if she did not say something, anything, she would agree to have dinner with him at that very moment. Doing so would be dangerous at best, lethal at worst.

He smiled. "Yes, I had considered changing my name, since I was certain that if you knew it you would never go out with me. But I'm afraid that I have very strong family ties, and I don't think they would take to that very kindly. Since you already know my last name, you might as well know that my first name is Osman."

Now was her chance, and she tried to take advantage of the delicate subject he had broached. "Well, I'm afraid it's just those strong family ties, on both our parts, that will prevent us from having dinner together, and from being friends. You know everything that has happened between our families; some of it is about business, but more importantly it is about my brother's tragic death. I'm sorry, but those are the undeniable facts."

"Yes, Yasemin, I know the history. But I don't understand how you can judge, and even blame, one member of the family for things that really have nothing to do with them. I was out of the country when your brother was killed. What makes it even worse is that it was a horrible accident which could easily have been avoided. Zeki was very brave to do what he did. He died a hero, but that was his nature. I liked him very much. He was a classmate of mine in grade school. We played on some of the same teams together. I was saddened when I heard about his senseless death, but not at all surprised at his courage. As for whatever is going on between our families, I don't even know all the details. I run my own company, and I sometimes go for weeks without seeing my father or brothers, except at family events. So you see, I have had nothing to do with any of the deals that have happened recently. I don't even know about that end of the business. And I certainly didn't have anything to do with the decisions they made during the war. Still, I don't think that two people should be kept from being friends, or lovers, because of circumstances beyond their control. I'm very attracted to you, Yasemin. I think you're beautiful and charming, and from everything I have heard, you are one hell of a businesswoman. I want to get to know you. Please have dinner with me. Besides, I'm running out of different kinds of flowers to send. What do you say?"

She melted. Everything she had thought and convinced herself of during the last few weeks crumbled, and she allowed her thoughts to be replaced by his seemingly logical explanation. On the business side, she found it hard to believe that the Boras had segregated their business dealings to the extent that Osman was not involved at all in the other side of the company. The majority of companies that were controlled by large families were operated in much the same manner as a family; even though the individuals had various responsibilities, they all voted on the major issues, and most of the time everyone knew what everyone else was doing. But it wasn't right, she knew, to blame him for what had happened to her brother. He hadn't been in control of the boat; it hadn't been he who had made the decision to take the shortcut that put the lives of his passengers in danger. And as for the war dealings, it was true, they had both been mere children at the time. In that split second she decided to trust him and to believe what he said.

Her expression told him her answer, and she put her papers in her car, kept her sweater, and climbed into the seat of his small black two-seater sports car.

"Thank you for at least giving me the chance to get to know you. I hope you won't be disappointed," he said, pulling the car out into the traffic.

Osman was decisive. He didn't ask her where she wanted to go for dinner, but instead he drove directly down to the pier where they took a waiting boat across the Bosphorus. The tiny fish restaurant on the Asian side of the city had only ten tables, and a reservation, even for those with clout, could sometimes take up to two weeks. For a moment she worried that someone might see them together, and she was happy as she glanced around at the diners to find there was no one whom she recognized. Yasemin was impressed as the owner led them to a table right at the water's edge. Evidently Osman had felt confident that his invitation would be accepted.

No sooner were they seated than a small fishing boat pulled up next to their table. The ragged old fisherman, the lines of his deeply tanned face illuminated by his kerosene lantern, smiled up at them. In the bottom of his boat he had carefully displayed his daily catch, from which they would choose their meal.

Osman smiled over at her. "Make your selection, pretty lady. I think I'm going to have the *lüfer*," he said, pointing.

"Mmmm, they all look so good. How did you know I liked fish so much?"

"A lucky guess."

"I'll take one of the *levrek*," she decided.

The man nodded, giving their selection his approval, and then he held up Osman's bluefish and Yasemin's sea bass and passed them to the waiter, who whisked them away to the kitchen.

"Can't get much fresher than that," Yasemin commented, pleased with his choice of restaurant. "I bet you couldn't eat like this in London."

"That's the understatement of the century. In fact, I prefer not to dwell on the English food, particularly when I'm about to have a delicious meal like this. Simple grilled fish with a good *çoban salata*, and a nice bottle of cold white wine."

At that the waiter appeared once more, to uncork and pour the bottle of wine Osman had brought with them on the boat.

"Here's to you and your wonderful good judgment in having dinner with me," he toasted. Then he smiled that magical, wonderful smile, and she knew her dreams were not exaggerated—he was devastatingly handsome.

They spent the evening discussing everything but business. Even without mentioning it, talk of their work seemed to be a forbidden topic. They discovered they shared a great deal in common: both of them had left Istanbul right after graduating secondary school to study abroad; both had decided to come back home afterward; and both had had unsuccessful first love affairs that had ended painfully. Yasemin found herself opening up to him, but she stopped short of telling him everything about Eric. Osman denied his reputation as a veritable playboy during his years in Europe.

"If I had run around as much as the press claimed I did, and still maintained my top scores, as I really did do, then I would have had to have been some kind of superman," he protested.

"You may very well be," she commented, thinking that he certainly was a special man, caring and romantic, but also strong and decisive and driven. Yes, perhaps even a superman.

By the time they left, the little restaurant was deserted, and the boat traffic on the Bosphorus was almost at a standstill. Osman drove her back to her car, and when they said good night she found herself wishing that the evening could go on and on.

As if reading her thoughts, he said, "I don't want to leave you. I want to stay and talk with you all night."

"The parking lot is not a very good place to stay all night," she responded.

"Nor very romantic," he added, again voicing her most private thoughts. "How about this weekend? We could go sailing. Would you like that?"

Deeper and deeper into trouble she fell, as she readily agreed to spending the two days of the next weekend on his boat.

"I'll be by to pick you up at ten on Saturday morning. How does that sound?"

The thought of him pulling up to the Turan house in his boat terrified her. Her mother and father, maybe even Ali, would be at home, and there was no way she could get into his boat without their knowing who he was. "No, no," she said, perhaps a little too forcefully, "I'll come to the dock. Where do you keep the boat?"

"Still afraid of letting anyone see you are with me, right, Yasemin?" He seemed hurt, and she felt bad that her reaction had been so evident. "You should have seen yourself tonight at the restaurant. The look on your face changed from despair to overwhelming relief once you were certain there was no one there who knew you. I wished I'd had a camera. And I can't imagine what you would have done if there had been someone; it was very clear that we got off the boat together. There is nothing else there but the restaurant."

She was embarrassed to learn that her concerns had been so evident. But concerns they were, and they were very real. "I'm sorry, really I am. It's just that . . . well . . . you mentioned all the problems yourself earlier tonight."

"Yes, but maybe we can overcome them. I don't find them as insurmountable as you do. Oh, well, time will tell on that front. I'm just glad you agreed to have dinner with me. I had a wonderful time, Yasemin," he said, kissing her lightly on each cheek. "Good night."

She drove out of the lot, and he followed her until she put her blinker on, indicating that she was about to turn into the imposing gates of the Turan mansion.

They ended up sailing from morning till night that weekend. Osman owned a racing boat—long and narrow, and built for speed. Yasemin stood at the bow as the boat smacked down against the waters, her hair blown back by the wind. He taught her how to steer it, and she loved its agility and swiftness as it raced across the Bosphorus. They visited some people on other boats, friends of his, not hers, for even though she recognized many of the other boats, she hesitated to go visiting her own friends. The growing rivalry between the two families was well known, and there would be too many questions to answer, too many questions that she had not yet had the time to answer for herself.

So they avoided being seen together; not only on the water, but around town as well. At first she didn't mind, for she loved being alone with Osman. He was all the company she needed. They could talk for hours, about any subject in the world. What she liked most about him was his determination, his clear-cut goals. He had decided long ago how he was going to live his life; it would be exactly as he saw it, unhampered by the conventions imposed upon him by his family. He loved his family dearly, he was committed to his mother and father, as well as to his two brothers. But he was going to lead his own life. So far he had been able to do just that.

Yasemin found that this characteristic carried over into his personal relationships as well. Osman was a man who knew what he wanted. The first night they made love, the first time she had ever made love with anyone, was the most wonderful experience of her life.

They had gone to dinner at a small restaurant, and then dancing in one of the late-night clubs. Yasemin loved the music, and they spent all their time on the dance floor, totally absorbed in each other.

They left the club late and went to Osman's apartment on the waterfront. Yasemin was hot and tired from dancing, and she went immediately to the terrace for some cooler air.

Osman joined her shortly, approaching her from behind and wrapping his arms about her waist. She shivered as he touched her, and her head fell backward as she warmed to his sweet kisses.

"You are wonderful, Yasemin," Osman whispered. "Never in a million years did I think I would ever meet someone whom I could love as much as I love you."

His kisses continued, all along the nape of her neck, up under her heavy dark hair, around her ears to her cheeks. He drank in her scent in long, deep breaths, wanting to memorize the sweetness of her soft perfume. She pressed her head back against him and sighed softly as his lips explored the sensitive area around her temple.

She longed to feel his lips on hers and turned slowly to face him. Lifting her eyes to him, she wordlessly conveyed her needs. She knew that tonight she would give him a special gift, one that she would give willingly and selflessly, for she was certain Osman was the only man she would ever love. Their lips parted and their tongues met. They teased one another mercilessly as their desire for each other grew. They stood locked in a lover's embrace, kissing long and passionately as the cool breeze brushed over them.

"Come inside before you catch a cold, my little executive. We can't have you getting sick on us," he said, leading her into the house.

It was a simple home, a true bachelor's abode, with but few masculine furnishings, mostly leather pieces, and sparse accessories. He traveled so much he was rarely around to pay much attention to his surroundings. Still it was pleasant, and Yasemin always enjoyed the time they spent there.

Osman held her hand and guided her toward the bedroom. She didn't hesitate, for she felt the same desire as he. Tonight, she knew for certain, she wanted him to make love to her. He placed her at the foot of the bed and proceeded to undress her slowly and carefully, his fingers savoring every moment while his anticipation grew. He felt his own lust hardening until it became painful to endure, but he held himself back from rushing the beautiful event. With trembling fingers he undid the delicate buttons on her blouse and brushed aside the soft fabric. He released her breasts from her lacy bra, and, without breaking his gaze into her eyes, he used the lightest touch imaginable as he grazed his fingertips across her nipples.

"Beautiful, you are so beautiful," he said, stroking her and fondling her lovely nipples before lowering his mouth to caress them. Yasemin reached down and held her breasts out to him, making them ready for his lips.

"Yes, feed me, darling, I want to taste you, envelop you, every part of you."

He cupped her breasts in his hands, running his tongue furiously back and forth over her swollen nipples, alternating his mouth from one to the other until she cried out for him to stop.

He looked at her, and with a sly smile on his face asked, "You don't really mean it, do you?"

She returned the grin. "No, I don't, not at all . . ." she said, trying to catch her breath.

"Good. Then I'll never stop. Ever. I want to taste every inch of you, because everywhere I look you are so beautiful." He returned to the joy before him.

He continued undressing her, unzipping her skirt and removing her panties with the same cautious, tender manner he had shown earlier. Only when she was naked against his white sheets did he leave her side and begin to remove his own clothes.

"Yasemin, you are the most wonderful woman," he told her, and she answered with her eyes, full of longing and anticipation for what lay ahead. "You're not frightened, are you, love? You know I'll be gentle with you. I love you. I wouldn't hurt you for the world."

She nodded slowly, loving him even more for expressing his concern for her. "I'm not afraid. I want you so very much," she whispered.

He undressed slowly, and as he revealed his hardness to her he watched Yasemin's anticipation grow. Her eyes widened when she saw him for the first time, and her expression confirmed the intimacy she was anxious to share with him.

He went to lie by her side, and she opened her arms to him. Feeling his naked body next to hers for the first time was a magical sensation she loved at once, and she wrapped her long legs about him in an effort to meld into him, to be as close to him as possible. For a brief moment she was surprised by her actions, for never before had she felt so drawn to a man, never before had she felt such an overwhelming need to become one with anyone.

He continued his gentle caresses, stroking her as softly as he had at first on the terrace, but as they became acquainted with each other's bodies, the growing urgency of his kisses conveyed his desire for her. He pressed himself up against her, and she could feel the entire length of him while he throbbed with passion. He held her for what seemed like hours, petting her and telling her of his need for her, and all the while he felt that his own explosion was imminent. He was at the threshold of his power to contain himself, but he was determined not to allow his own pleasure to come before hers.

Looking directly into his eyes, she sighed, "I'm ready for you; please fill me now."

"Are you sure, love?" he asked, knowing that once he began to enter her, he would relinquish all control.

"Yes, I've never been more certain about anything," she said, reaching down to guide him into her.

When he took her there was no hesitation, he did so with a fierce determination that made her want him even more. With each thrust his need to climax became more frenetic, and as he reached the pinnacle of his orgasm the expression on his face became twisted and forceful, a reflection of the enormous release he felt. She held him tightly as he rocked into her, draining himself and savoring the intensity of the moment. Try as she might, the images of Eric's uncertainty flashed through her mind, but they only served to make her more conscious of Osman's all-consuming passion. Now her self-doubt had vanished, and at last she felt like a woman who was desired as well as desirous—a woman who had the power to love and be loved.

Osman's breathing returned to normal, and he smiled down at her with an expression she had never seen before. His eyes, now peaceful and serene, looked into hers with all the adoration and happiness he felt.

"I love you so, Yasemin. You make me very happy. And now I want to do the same for you."

He lay facing her, and once again began his tireless exploration of her body. At his urging, she relaxed her arms by her side and opened her thighs to his touch. Gently he placed his hand on the triangle between her legs, calming her swollen lips which had taken the hugeness of a man for the very first time. She welcomed the comforting touch, for although she had beckoned him inside, it had still been painful for her to accept all of him. Once he relaxed her, she arched up to him and guided his probing fingers into her wetness. Once more she was momentarily stunned by her ability to communicate so intimately, but her embarrassment subsided quickly as she was overcome by the pleasurable sensation of his rotating motions. As he lowered his head, kissing the length of her throat, brushing her nipples with his tongue, tracing the flatness of her belly, and finally coming to rest between her legs, she did not hesitate to open herself to him completely. As his tongue flicked wildly on her outer lips, she begged him to explore her further, and she eagerly wrapped her legs around his head in order to allow him total freedom with her.

She moaned, at first softly, and then, as she ground herself into his face, a sound emerged from the very depth of her, a sound that was so foreign to her that at first she did not recognize it as her own.

He held her tightly, his head buried in her, until the spasms of her orgasm had finished racking her body. Only then did he return to her side, kissing her forehead, nose, cheeks, and finally returning to the eager softness of her lips.

She had no words left, her passion spent, her weakened arms were all she could offer him.

When he was ready, she allowed him to take her once more, but this time she opened herself to him with wanton abandon. His spell over her was intoxicating, and from that night on she became a virtual, but willing, slave to him.

"Love you, love you, love you," she cried into his arms, as she felt him pouring into her again. His strong embrace told her he echoed her emotions.

The next day, despite the perfection of the previous night, her concerns still lingered, and she turned to the person she felt would give her the most honest, forthright opinion about the tough situation she now found herself in.

"Ali, have dinner with me," she said to her brother one morning.

"Sure, Yaz, what time?"

"Early, and not here," she answered, knowing that they would not have the privacy they needed at the house, and also remembering she had promised to meet Osman later that evening.

His look told her he understood that a discussion of some importance was in the cards, and he readily agreed to meet her at the restaurant she suggested.

"Ali, I'm in love with him. He's the most wonderful, caring, generous soul I've ever met. I adore him, and he's a red-blooded heterosexual; I'm sure of it this time," she added, now that she could finally make light of the unfortunate incident with Eric.

"Well, that's the good news," Ali agreed, "but I must admit, that may be the only thing you will have going for you when you announce this to Mother and Father. He certainly doesn't have many other characteristics they are going to appreciate. Yaz, he is the son of Erol Bora, the man father hates the most in the whole world. Mother has convinced herself that if it hadn't been for the Boras,

Zeki would be alive today. So I'd say you don't really have much chance of getting their blessing."

Yasemin sat with her chin in her hands, her meal untouched in front of her. She sighed, not surprised by Ali's honest assessment of the situation. "Oh, if only I hadn't worn that dress to the gala," she joked, shaking her head, but internally tormented by her love for Osman. "So, Ali, that's just great. You've stated all the facts. Don't you think I know everything you've said is true? You sound like a recorded message of myself. But what you haven't told me is what you think I should do."

"Oh, you want the whole thing," he teased, "first the facts, and then how to deal with them. It might take another dinner, Yaz; that's a lot to ask for all in one evening."

"Stop teasing, you monster. This is important, perhaps the most important thing I've ever had to deal with. And now you're making a joke out of it. Now come on, try and be serious."

"Okay, listen up. I'll tell you exactly what I think you should do. You're in love with Osman, right?"

"Yes, I already told you that."

"Okay, take it easy. Are you prepared to marry him? No, don't answer that. Do you want to marry him?"

"Yes."

"Has he asked you?"

"No."

"Well, then, until he does you have no reason to worry."

"Ali," she cried, "stop it. I'm beginning to think that you were the wrong person to ask about this."

"All right, all right. I'll tell you exactly what I think you should do. If you love him, and he makes you happy, and you've decided that you would like to spend the rest of your life with him, then that's exactly what you must do. Go to Mother and Father, tell them what you've decided, and then they will have to either accept your decision and learn to live with it, or they will tell you they do not approve. Other than that, there is not much they can do. You are an adult, and even in a society which is supposedly very strict, and very controlling, there is simply nothing they can do if you should decide to marry him, and if you decide to stick with your decision. They may tell you that they will disown you, and all of that, but even if they do, which I doubt they will, in time they will come around. Neither Mother nor Father will risk losing you and your love over something like this. If you look at what I have done, and the decisions I've made, your problem pales in comparison. I know that's not easy to believe right now, since I've already gone through all the pain and anguish, but believe me, everything will turn out for the best. When they first realized what I was, you would have thought it was the end of the world. For a time they were confused, I think *Baba* even hated me for a while, but eventually they both became more accepting, more understanding. It may take some time, and you'll have to be prepared for that, but it will be all right in the end. On the other hand, who knows? Maybe their reaction won't be nearly as violent as I've predicted, and everyone will ride off into the sunset, happily ever after. The only way you're going to know for sure is if you tell them. But the person you should talk to first is of course Osman."

Yasemin sat across the table from her brother, listening to his every word. She too had come to the same conclusion weeks earlier, but still it felt good to have it confirmed by someone she respected and trusted.

"You're right," she said. Her appetite suddenly returned, and she picked up her fork and began eating.

When they returned to the Turan home, Ali stopped her at the top of the stairs.

"I love you, Yaz, and whatever you decide, you know I'll be standing right by your side, if you need any help. You just let me know."

"Thanks, Ali," she said, kissing him good night and heading upstairs to her bedroom.

"Osman, I'm tired of not being able to go out anywhere, to see my friends, and go anyplace we choose, because of these family problems," she said the next night. She had chosen to force the issue and was prepared to accept whatever he had to say, even if it was going to be very painful for her to endure.

They sat side by side in the restaurant, and he was not at all surprised by what she was saying. He too had felt the constraints on their relationship, and he resented that they were having to pay the price of a family dispute with which they had nothing to do. Everything that had happened between the Turans and the Boras—the chrome deals, the dirty business play, the horrible boating accident—all those unfortunate events had been totally out of their control. He would fight to his death to have the woman who sat before him, and now was as good a time as any to solve the problem as best he could.

"You're right, Yasemin, and I suppose there is only one thing we can do about it."

"And what might that be?"

"Get married, of course."

She had been ready to walk away or to accept a proposal, but now that it was on the table, she couldn't contain her emotions. "Are you sure? Are you certain you want to marry me?" With tears brimming in her eyes, she went into his open arms.

"You're the best thing that ever happened to me," he said, hugging her and trying to calm her so they would not become the focus of attention for the entire restaurant.

"Everything will be fine," he assured her, stroking her hair and holding her to him. "Of course I want to marry you, silly girl. I just hope you'll have me. I love you, Yasemin, and that love is strong enough to overcome any problems we are faced with. And even though we might have to make some tough decisions, I know we'll be able to handle it. I refuse to let our lives be ruled just because of our last names. You'll see, everything is going to be wonderful."

The conversation could have gone either way, and as she wiped the tears of happiness from her eyes she wasn't certain what she would have done if it had not worked out like this. "Yes, yes, I know it will be," she answered, anxious to leave the restaurant and go back to his apartment to celebrate their momentous decision.

_M_AKING HER DECISION was the easy part. Sharing her news with her mother and father was an entirely different thing. She had tested the waters with Nevin, making her promise not to breathe a word of her plans to either Cyrielle or Omer. Her reaction had been exactly what Yasemin had predicted; she admonished her for ever getting involved with Osman in the first place.

"Oh, Yasemin," she said, "how could you do a thing like this? Do you know what this will do to Mother?"

"Don't try to make me feel guilty, Nevin. Mother is ill and I have always believed that the only way she will ever get better is through proper medical treatment. We all know how hard _Baba_ has tried to get her help. We've had this discussion many times, the first time before I went back to Radcliffe. I didn't want to go, but even then he told me that my staying wouldn't affect things one way or another. When he was able to get her some help, they confirmed what we've all known for a very long time, that she suffers from clinical depression. But she refused to accept the diagnosis, and brushed off all suggestions that she take the new drugs they are using as only a ploy that would make her even sicker. No, Nevin, she needs more help than either of us can give, but she first has to want to help herself. The most difficult thing to accept is that some days she acts perfectly normal, just like her old self. When she has a good day, I start to believe, I want to believe, that she is getting better. But then the next day, or the day after, she is back to wearing that vapid, empty expression. It's so hard, so hard for all of us. But what I have done will not make her any better or any worse.

"And as for your other question, I just couldn't help myself. I fell in love with Osman. I'm unwilling to admit that it was a crime. I felt that way about him from the moment I met him. Just be thankful you fell in love with someone who was acceptable to our family, otherwise it could have been you who had to go through this. It's painful, let me tell you, I've had to make some tough decisions, and it hasn't been easy; in fact, the hardest part is still to come. I'd like your support if that is at all possible."

"Yasemin, I still don't understand how you could have allowed this to happen," she continued to harp.

"Well, damn it, I did, and it did, and that's it. Now, I've taken you into my confidence, and I've shared my feelings with you, hoping that I could make you see my point. But apparently I've failed. So I'd appreciate it if you could simply keep your promise to keep your Goody-Two-Shoes mouth shut until I've had a chance to tell Mother and Father. After that you can take sides against me, if you still feel as you do."

"Oh, Yasemin, I didn't mean . . ."

But her sister was too angry, too upset to hear her weak words. If Nevin couldn't stand by her and support her decision, she didn't need to spend a moment longer with her. Yasemin had left Nevin's house in an angry state, and she hadn't heard from her sister, even though a week had passed.

Semra had been out of town, so she would hear the news at dinner that night, at the same time she told her parents.

When she announced her decision, the stunned faces that surrounded her remained motionless and quiet for what seemed a very long time. Semra was the first to speak.

"Yasemin, I find this news disturbing, yet in another way under-standable. You know how we feel about the Bora family and all the

horrible things that have happened to us as a result of their careless-
ness and devious business tactics. Now you announce that you are in
love with, and are planning to marry, one of these people. Of course
that is difficult to swallow, but what I think is important, and what
we all have to realize, is that the conflicts and arguments we have
with them have nothing at all to do with you and Osman."

"Semra, it was never my intention to hurt anyone, I hope that
you know that and believe it. I thank you for your understanding. It
just happened; I suppose it is one of the strange coincidences in life. I
want your blessing, it is important to me, you must realize that. But
as I said, I am willing to go forward with my plans even without it, if
I am forced to."

Cyrielle began to cry softly, and she held her dinner napkin up
across her mouth. She made a high-pitched, muffled noise, a sound
like an animal in the forest. Then, with one sudden motion, she
pushed her chair out from under her and ran out of the room.

Omer looked pained as he spoke, but his reaction was indicative
of his true character. His first and foremost concern was for his
daughter. Yet Yasemin was still stunned when she heard his words.

"Yasemin, if we had chosen a hundred young men as candidates
for you to marry, Osman Bora would certainly not have been on the
list. But now that all this has happened, and you have made your
feelings very clear to us, I think it would be best if we all tried to
adjust to the idea of having him in the family. As for the business
aspect, I understand that Osman is not involved in any of the other
Bora dealings. He sticks strictly to the garment business. I have never
had any occasion to deal with him, but from all I have heard he is the
most upstanding, honest member of the family. But I don't want to
have any misunderstanding. The Bora family has pulled some pretty
fast tricks over the last few years. They have on two occasions cost
us quite a good deal of money. As long as I am at the helm of Turan
Holding, I will continue to fight them, and all that they stand for.
That includes Osman should he ever decide to become involved in
the other businesses and conduct himself in the low manner of the
rest of his family. I abhor that kind of behavior, and I will fight to the

death to crush it. But as long as he stays out of the other dealings, I don't think we will have any problems. We will most likely, however, not have a warm and genial relationship with the rest of the family just because you are going to marry this young man. I can't see us being close with them, as we are with Nevin's in-laws, for example.

"Yasemin, your happiness is the most important thing in the world to me, and if this choice is going to make you happy, then I will support it one hundred percent. You know your mother and I love you very much, and your joy is all we care about."

Yasemin's eyes filled with tears of love for her wonderful, generous father. "Thank you, *Babacığım,* for your support, and for feeling the way you do. Osman does make me happy, and I love him very much. I know we will be able to overcome these problems, and your confidence is exactly what we will need to start off in the right direction. Thank you."

Semra did exactly what Yasemin knew she would. She supported her brother.

"You know how I love to plan weddings, Yasemin, so if there's anything I can do to help, you need only ask. And I'll spend a little time with your mother. She'll come around, you'll see."

"I hope so. Oh, Aunt Semra, thank you, thank you for everything. You always seem to be here when we need you, you always have been. And I'm going to take you up on your offer. I want a big wedding, a grand, formal event! I want all of our friends to come. I don't want anyone to think that we have anything to hide. And, Aunt Semra, I want a henna night. I know Nevin didn't have one, but I think it's one of the most wonderful parts of the ceremony. I want to have my friends Susan and Christine here too. They would love it!"

Semra and Omer smiled across the table at her. The enthusiasm had broken through her voice as she spoke, and she was clearly a young woman in love, terribly and hopelessly in love with the man of her dreams. They were both pleased to hear the lightness in her voice, to see in her face the joy of a new beginning with a man whom she obviously adored.

CHAPTER

23

*Y*OU WILL MAKE *such a beautiful bride, the most beautiful bride." She couldn't place the voice, but the words were what was important.*

The women had all come to the Turan mansion to take a glass of sweet tea. They sat upright, their backs supported by the many pillows that lined the divans, in the small room at the front of the house where they always gathered. It was the most intimate space in the otherwise formal and imposing seaside villa, a room of manageable proportions, decorated with colorful kilims and bright, inviting fabrics printed with traditional Turkish patterns, perfect for an afternoon gathering.

The guests had arranged their long, full skirts gently around their legs, shifting and wiggling until they were comfortable and ready to settle in for a few hours of gossip and chatter.

Yasemin and Nevin were on the floor in front of the women with their gangly legs tucked beneath them. The women stroked their long ebony hair, which reached halfway down their backs. Yasemin's thick tresses were neatly pulled back and secured with a barrette, while her sister's curly mop hung unrestrained in a delicate, feminine manner.

"Oh, Yasemin, what a lucky man who will have you as his wife," said a close friend of her mother's. "You will have beautiful children with lovely black hair and big bright eyes, just like yours," she continued, all the while toying with Yasemin's luxurious mane of hair.

Half awake, yet wanting to prolong the pleasant remembrance for as long as possible, Yasemin pulled the covers up tightly around her and turned over in the big bed. At the same instant her mother's voice broke through her semi-conscious state.

"Yasemin, you can't *possibly* still be in bed!" Cyrielle cried, more of a statement than a question. "Yasemin, really, it's terrible, lounging around like this. Christine and Susan were up at the break of day, anxious to go out for another round of sightseeing. They had breakfast out on the terrace with me. I wanted to wake you, but they insisted that the bride should be allowed to sleep on her next-to-last day of life as a single girl. We really expected that you would be up shortly. We waited and waited, and finally I sent them off with Murat. He's taking them back to Hagia Sophia and the Topkapi Palace, and if they have time afterward they'll go on to the Covered Bazaar. Christine can't seem to get her fill of it, she's totally enamored by the beauty of the city. She's fallen totally under the spell of Istanbul."

Yasemin turned over slowly and peered out over the top of the comforter at her mother. The dream vanished, and she was no longer a little girl but a young bride on the threshold of a new life.

"Yasemin, please, darling, you must get up. You've got a big day ahead of you. You've lots to do. It will be time for your henna night to begin before you know it. Now, up . . . let's go," she urged, walking across the large room to the windows. "Come on, up!" she repeated, pulling back the lace-patterned white cotton curtains and swinging open the long windows that faced out to the Bosphorus. The warm mid-morning breeze drifted in softly, its scent a startling, refreshing mixture of the salt air and the flowers in the garden below.

Yasemin pulled on her robe and walked toward the open windows. The cool breeze met her warm skin, awakening her senses to the outside world. Activity on the busy waterway was brisk. Tankers and cruise ships plodded by, and a smattering of private yachts snaked their courses bravely around them. One day long ago she had been sitting in the room below and had counted over three hundred ships that passed in front of her house. She had tried to note the nationality of each one, and if she couldn't recognize one she would quickly draw the flag it displayed—later she would look it up in her encyclopedia. Then they had begun to pass too quickly and she had been unable to keep up. It was a game she had mastered over the years, and now as she surveyed the water traffic she could easily name all of the nations represented.

The Bosphorus would always be an enigma to her. She could never look at it without thinking of Zeki. It was a deceptive body of water, one that looked like a river, but smelled like a sea. For nineteen miles it ran north and east to the Black Sea, toward Turkey's old enemy, Russia.

She squinted her eyes as she looked across the shimmering sea to the Asian side of the city. She thought of the life she had led in her parent's home, which was a mixture of the two cultures. She hoisted herself up into the wide windowsill and looked to her left. There stood the house that had been purchased by her family as a wedding gift for Yasemin and her new husband. It was another *yalı*, a large wooden structure not nearly as grand as the one she had grown up in, but still quite sizable.

She sat staring at the building that symbolized the beginning of her new life. Her new home that the day after tomorrow she would move into with her new husband, a man whom she deeply loved, to a life filled with passion, and caring and dreams of the future.

Yasemin was startled by Cyrielle's gentle touch on the back of her neck. She turned quickly to look at her. She reached out to her mother's arms, and they cradled each other.

"Maman, you have been wonderful. I know it has been terribly hard for you to accept what I am doing, and I want you to know how much I appreciate all you have done. It's going to be a lovely wedding, and you have helped so much."

Cyrielle looked at her daughter. Yasemin's words were only partially true, she had been able to help with a few of the details, but once again Semra had been the strength of the family. The thought of Yasemin marrying Osman Bora still troubled her greatly, but she had tried with all her will to pull herself together and to be helpful. She wanted to be a part of the wonderful celebration, for she had always regretted that because of the war she had never had a big wedding, a grand festive event. But even after the passage of time since Zeki's death she was still not completely her old self, the self she longed to be. Perhaps, she hoped, if she could accept and welcome Osman into her family, somehow the pain would lessen, and she could get on with her life.

"You know it has been difficult for me, Yasemin, but I treasure your happiness, just as your father does. I just hope that all of this will turn out all right. The feud between the families goes on, and just because everyone has thrown aside their own desires for a few weeks in order to allow you and Osman to have a joyous occasion does not mean that the old wounds have healed or that the fight is over. Not by any means. I just pray that your love will survive whatever the future may bring."

"Maman, everything is going to be all right, you'll see." Yasemin looked imploringly at her mother, begging her to trust her, but hoping most of all that soon she would be well again.

The rest of the day was a blur. Yasemin asked for tea and toast to be brought to her room, and by the time she had showered leisurely and changed into a bathing suit, it was well past noon.

The main floor was a frenzy of activity as caterers gathered in the kitchen, flower arrangers scurried throughout the house carrying enormous bouquets, and the usual bevy of housekeepers, chauffeurs, and maids traversed the shiny marble floors. Seta supervised all of this with the skill of a seasoned commander. Yasemin's presence was barely noticed as she walked through the house and out to the pool to take a swim.

The weather was perfect, the kind of clear summer day that

blessed Istanbul from early June straight through September. The days were endless, with daylight stretching well into the late evening. The mid-eighty-degree weather may have been too hot for many of the city's inhabitants, indeed most of their crowd had shipped their boats to the south and had fled the city. They were only obliged to return before the middle of September for the important event of a Turan-Bora marriage. It was going to be *the* event of the summer, and no one graced with an invitation would be staying away.

Yasemin found the strong rays of the late-afternoon sun both soothing and relaxing. She swam her usual forty laps in the refreshing water and then immediately sought the comfort of one of the terry-covered chaises that lined the surrounding deck. Lost in her own private thoughts about her future, she was still there when her guests returned from their adventures late in the afternoon.

Susan's laughter rang out and Yasemin looked up to see her old college friends laden down with packages, a result of the day's sightseeing and shopping activities. She couldn't help but smile at the sight of the Americans, so totally foreign did they look with their long, streaky blond hair and cerulean eyes. The two of them could have been sisters they looked so much alike, but Christine had been blessed with the finer features and the exquisite body that had driven every boy in Cambridge to distraction. Their typical American outfits gave them away: Susan in jeans and a T-shirt; Christine in a tailored, too-short skirt. They must have caused quite a commotion in the bazaar, Yasemin thought. She could just envision them being trailed throughout the mazelike building by gaggles of leering Turks.

"Couldn't tell that you two are from out of town!" Yasemin yelled out. "I thought you were sightseeing and doing all of the culturally invigorating things Istanbul has to offer. Maman told me that she had given Murat instructions to take you back to the Topkapi Palace. Looks to me as if you went directly from the mosque to the boutiques."

Susan's giggling continued, but Christine was quick to rationalize their actions.

"It's all part of the culture," she insisted, "you know, the clothes, the new styles. Don't you think these things will look great back home?" Soon all the bags were plunked down on the empty chaise longues, and before Yasemin knew it a full blown fashion show was in progress. They had bought shirts, and bathing suits, and wonderful summer sandals made and sold in the bazaar.

"And how do you like these for winter?" Susan asked, holding up brightly colored hand-knitted knee-high socks with gloves to match. Each finger and toe was a different vibrant color; one purple, one pink, one orange, one red and one yellow completed the crazy pattern. They were the traditional kind that had been worn in Turkish villages for ages. Of course they were considered too silly for the cosmopolitan Istanbulis, but Yasemin had always found them charming. "They're just like the ones you used to wear in the dorm when we first met you, remember?" Susan asked, smiling at the thought of their friendship and the girl whom they had grown to love so much.

It seemed like so long ago when the three of them had been a trio on campus. Walking together across the common, they had made heads turn, the two stunning blondes and the dark, exotic Yasemin with her almond-shaped, nearly black eyes and equally dark hair. They were a contrast in looks, but at heart they were as close as sisters.

The three of them were still sitting there, chatting away endlessly, oblivious to the passing of time, when they were joined by Cyrielle and Nevin.

"What are you all doing out here? Do you have any idea what time it is?" said Cyrielle. "It's nearly six o'clock. We're due to leave for the *hamam* in just over an hour."

"Hello, Susan and Christine," Nevin said. She was sweet and caring, and attractive in the same exotic way as her older sister. But there the similarities ended. Their personalities, each charming in its own special way, were as different as the two shores of Istanbul. Nevin had been content to stay in the family fold and to do exactly what was expected of her. Educated at a fine private school in Istanbul, she had then, immediately following graduation, fallen in love with and married a man of whom her family heartily approved. Now she was the mother of a wonderful little boy. What she did not possess was the razor-sharp intelligence and fiery spirit of her sister. What appeared to Yasemin to be complacence and settling for something less than what she could be had kept Nevin and Yasemin from enjoying the closeness that Yasemin shared with the two girls who sat with her by the pool. For this she felt a sharp sadness, but also a hope that perhaps the distance between them would be lessened now that her own life-style was going to change so dramatically. They would certainly have more in common—a house and servants to keep, a husband to care for, and most likely a family to raise. The opportunity to become closer to her only sister was one of the many positive things Yasemin hoped would come out of the impending wedding.

"Well, we'd better get moving then," Yasemin agreed, standing up and kissing both her sister and mother in greeting. "Come on, let's get going and get these two initiated into the ritual at hand. You've never experienced anything like this before," she said, with an enthusiasm and cheerfulness that the girls had always seen in their pal. They looked a bit bewildered. "Not to worry, we'll take you right through every step of it," she assured them. "It's really quite a lovely experience. And I guarantee you'll never again attend one as beautiful as this is going to be! Let the celebration of the henna night begin!" Linking her arms through theirs, she marched them quickly into the house and up the stairs to her mother's dressing room.

"Come this way," she said, "we're stopping in here first for a minute. We've got a little surprise for you two."

❦

The henna night. The three girls had spoken about it earlier, or rather, Yasemin had explained it at great length to the uninitiated. They had sat outside under the enormous white umbrellas, shortly after their arrival at the Turans' house, eating a traditional Turkish lunch and reviewing the schedule of events for the wedding.

The henna night. The name alone was so exotic, it conjured up all sorts of mysterious and veiled intrigues.

"The henna night is one of the most important celebrations in the Muslim religion," Yasemin had told them. "It's not only for weddings, but for any type of event that we want to bless with good luck. In the case of weddings, the henna night is always held on a Wednesday so that the actual ceremony can take place on Thursday, the eve of the most holy religious day. The traditional henna night takes place in a *hamam*, one of the old Turkish baths. In Istanbul today there are still over one hundred Ottoman *hamams* in use, and we'll go to one of the most famous. It's called the Cağaloğlu. It's also one of the largest ones, with separate sections for men and women. Of course, our event will only be for women, Osman and his friends will have their own version of a bachelor's party tonight at his parents' home, complete with belly dancers and singing.

"The Cağaloğlu bath was built in the mid-eighteenth century by Sultan Mahmud the First. Its revenues were used to support the library in the Hagia Sophia. The *hamam* itself is a very interesting building, and I'll explain more about it when we actually get there. My Aunt Semra is really the one who should take you around for a complete tour. She's an expert on the architecture of the baths and she will know the answer to any questions you might have. It's important to remember that in the olden days, when, if you can believe it, women were even more sequestered than they are today, the *hamam* was just about the only place where they could meet and talk freely and openly. Even now a visit to the hamam is the focal point of many women's social lives in the city. It is also, for many of the poorer people, the only place for them to bathe."

This explanation had whetted the girls' appetites and they were anxious for the event to take place.

Cyrielle's large dressing room was lit by its crystal sconces centered on the carved panels of the peach-colored walls. It was the epitome of femininity, and Yasemin's mother fit her surroundings perfectly.

"I hope you like the dresses we've had made for you," Nevin said, reaching up and removing one of the four dresses that hung on golden hooks on one side of the room. She handed the magenta-colored one to Susan and then returned for the bright purple garment that had been ordered for Christine. "It was so hard to decide which colors would look best on you two," she said, watching as the girls held the dresses up under their chins. "There aren't too many Turkish women with your fair coloring."

From the smiles on their faces, the colors were perfect and the dresses were a great success. Even Susan, who was content to wear her usual uniform of jeans and a T-shirt to even the fanciest of parties and who was totally uninterested in clothes, wore the look of an excited little girl.

"They're beautiful!" exclaimed Christine. "Look at the exquisite embroidery work. It must have taken years to make this intricate pattern. And this luscious silk. Is this really for me? Surely it's just for tonight, just to wear to the celebration, not for keeps."

"Of course it's *for keeps,* as you say," replied Cyrielle. "We wanted you to have a reminder of this wonderful event that you were so kind to travel all this way for."

"Thank you, thank you so much, Mrs. Turan," the two said in unison.

"Really it is Nevin whom you must thank," Cyrielle said graciously. "It was she who chose the colors."

Nevin was smiling widely, happy that she had been able to do something to endear herself to Yasemin's friends. They were so very nice and fun to be around, yet so totally different in their views on life. They believed that women should have the same rights as men, both in the boardroom and the bedroom! Neither of them had married yet; they had gone on to graduate school and were concentrating on their careers first. It was a concept so foreign to Nevin's way of thinking that she was at the same time fascinated and frustrated. She felt they were terribly sophisticated and worldly, just as her sister.

"These dresses are made to wear on occasions like tonight," she explained. "They're called *bindallı*, which means 'a thousand branches.' If you study the embroidery pattern carefully, you'll see that it appears to branch out from a main spot, or tree, if you will," she said, holding the sleeve of one of the dresses and tracing the delicate pattern with her fingers.

"I guess it's sort of like a tree-of-life dress," Yasemin added, anxious to make a comparison to something that she knew would be familiar to their friends.

"Well, they're absolutely terrific, and wildly romantic!" proclaimed Christine, twirling around in front of the large, ornately framed mirror. "I can't wait to put it on."

"You'll have your chance very soon," Yasemin said. "Why don't you take your dresses, go back to your rooms, and be ready to leave for the hamam in about an hour. Don't forget, wear the top of the dress pulled down low around your shoulders, that's what the elastic is for, and belt it tightly. The pants are the same style as the ones you bought today, harem pants called *şalvar;* they're supposed to be full in the leg and fit snugly around the ankles." Yasemin demonstrated by slipping on the pants of her own outfit holding her bright-red dress up under her chin. The embroidery on her dress was even more spectacular than theirs. It had been in the Turan family for over one hundred years and had originally belonged to her great-grandmother, who had been blessedly tall. Its embroidery was stitched with the thinnest threads spun from real gold.

"What about shoes?" Christine asked in a panic.

"Those sandals you bought today will be perfect. That's all you'll need. The dresses will look sensational on you, I know."

Yasemin was pleased with her friends' reaction to the dresses. Nevin had been so concerned, worrying that they might not like them. At first Yasemin had protested, saying that they might feel uncomfortable wearing such a traditional, costumelike garment, but Nevin had insisted. Now Yasemin was glad she had. Every woman at the hamam tonight would be dressed in her most spectacular *bindallı*. Some of them would also wear a *beşibirlik,* the dramatic necklace that was rimmed with gold coins. Many would cover their heads with a scarf. Yasemin, as the honored bride, would be expected to do so also. She was pleased that her friends would be sharing in the tradition by wearing their new dresses. It made her feel even more happy about an event she was looking forward to with such anticipation.

"Thanks, Nevin," she said to her sister before she left the room. "They really love the dresses. It was a wonderful thing to do."

"You're welcome. I'm glad they liked them so much. Oh, Yasemin, I'm sorry I've been so awful these last few months. My reaction to your news about Osman was very selfish. I was only thinking about Mother, I suppose. But now I've realized that she is really trying to adjust to the idea of your marriage. Please forgive me. I want to be your friend, and I hope we'll be closer now that you are going to be a wife as well."

Yasemin went to her sister and hugged her tightly. "You're right, Nevin, I hope we'll be a lot closer now too. I forgive you. I'm going to need your help now, you know. All these domestic duties are brand-new to me. I don't know a saucepan from an omelet pan," she joked.

"And you won't have to," Nevin responded. "Believe me, you'll be so busy you'll never even see the inside of your kitchen."

"Thank heavens for small favors," Yasemin replied. As she walked down the corridor with her elegant heirloom *bindallı* draped over her arm, she was truly thankful to have her sister's support in her new life.

The hamam was an exotic place indeed. Both Susan and Christine loved being there and were hungry to know more about the tradition and customs of the age-old ritual that was about to take place. As they strolled slowly around the ancient building, clothed in their festive dresses, they felt as if they too were a part of the history.

Between greeting old childhood acquaintances and her many newly acquired relatives from Osman's side of the family, Yasemin found a minute to corral her aunt so that she could answer questions for the curious visitors.

"I told them you are our resident expert in Ottoman architecture and that you might show them around."

"I'd be delighted," said Semra. "It will be a test to see how much I remember. It's been a long while since I've been called upon for a grand tour. I'll do my best."

Yasemin smiled at her modesty. She knew it wasn't true at all, for Semra was constantly playing hostess to her many friends from Europe, giving them tours of all of Istanbul's important buildings. From her extensive travels, she knew many interesting, vital people from all over the world.

"You're in good hands, I assure you. Don't let her fool you for a minute. She knows everything about this place. I'll bet you can't come up with a question she doesn't know the answer to," Yasemin predicted as she excused herself and went back to join the others.

"This way, please," Semra urged her eager charges. "Follow me and enter the world of the Turkish bath. Not as exotic as the harem, I admit, but far more refreshing, and not nearly as oppressive," she added in her typical straightforward manner.

Susan and Christine followed dutifully, their eyes opening wide in awe as they ventured on.

"This room is called the *camekan,* what the ancient Romans called the apodyterium," Semra said. The girls' eyes widened even more as they stood in the center of a magnificent room constructed of white marble. "It is the largest of the three main rooms, and it's almost always designed as a square room covered with a dome. A fountain is usually found in the center of the room. This is the area where the bathers undress and leave their clothes. It is also where they return to after they have finished. So, for lack of a more elegant phrase, it is the reception room."

They then toured the tepidarium, the intermediate room, and anteroom to the main baths. "The purpose of this room is to keep the cold air out on one side and the hot air in on the other," she explained.

"And finally there is the *hararet,* or the steam room," Semra said as they approached an imposing entryway. "This was called the caldarium in the time of the Romans." She swung open the large doors and the girls could almost feel the rush of steam wafting toward them. Of course it was purely a product of their heightened imagination, for the steam had been shut off earlier in the afternoon so that Yasemin's henna night could take place in this magical marble space. The *hararet* was by far the most elaborate part of the *hamam.* It was a vast square room constructed totally of white marble and covered by a dome.

"This is really the heart of the room," Semra said, leading them over to the large marble platform in the center. "This is the bellystone. It is heated from below and bathers lie on it, on their bellies, of course. Here they are massaged thoroughly before they shower at one of the wall fountains which line the sides of the hararet."

"How luxurious!" Christine exclaimed. "I could use a massage right now after all the walking and stair climbing we've been doing. I'd love to visit when the baths are being used."

"Yes, you really should come when the baths are in operation, and when it is daylight outside. The light filters down through the little glass windows up there in the dome. The room is immersed in a thick steam. It is quite magical."

Now the only source of light was the flickering of hundreds of votive candles that had been placed around the edge of the square. The room had a haunting, mysterious quality.

Just as Semra finished speaking they heard the sound of voices. The tall doors swung open once more and the women began to enter. Yasemin was led in first, flanked by her mother on one side and Nevin on the other. She wore a diaphanous veil about her face. Nevin carried a small silver tray on which sat two handkerchieves, one with its ends tied up with a red ribbon. Osman's two sisters and mother followed behind. Then came the grandmothers of both the Turan and Bora clan. It was heartwarming to see the mothers of two of Turkey's most powerful men coming together, throwing aside their personal feud for the evening so they could add their own good wishes for the bride.

They led Yasemin to the center of the room and beckoned her to sit upon the marble platform. Nevin placed the tray next to her sister, then she joined hands with two of the other women. Several then formed a circle and they began to sing, swinging their hips gently to the rhythm. The tempo of the songs increased and the dancing became very spirited. The swooshing sounds made by the silk of the *bindallı* dresses and the clanging of the gold coins on the belts and necklaces they wore added another dimension to their chanting. Even though Susan and Christine did not know the songs, the women urged them to participate in the dancing. Soon everyone, even the oldest of the women, was on their feet. Yasemin joined them for the last dance, and when it was over she took her place again on the marble tableau.

Except for Nevin, all the women now took seats on the large kilim pillows that had been scattered around the platform for the celebratory evening.

Once all the attendants were settled, Nevin went forward once more to her sister's side and slowly untied the handkerchief. She revealed the mystery within—the bright orange-red henna—for all to see. Its brilliant hue shone in the hazy candlelight of the hararet. Gently Nevin took Yasemin's right hand and, holding it up, sprinkled a quantity of the powdery substance into her palm. Then she delicately touched each of her sister's fingertips, leaving a bright red mark on each, as if she had just been fingerprinted.

"Usually you ask your closest friend to put the henna in your palm, I mean your closest Muslim friend," Yasemin had quickly corrected herself when she explained the custom to her American friends. "It's not usually done by a member of your family. But the only one I could think of who I wanted was Aunt Semra, and she couldn't do it because it must be done by someone who is married—not by a divorcée or a widow. I don't understand, or agree with this at all, but it is a very strict rule of the ceremony. So that's why Nevin will be the one to wrap my hand."

Susan and Christine now smiled at each other, remembering the explanatory conversation.

The woman who had been introduced to them earlier as Osman's mother rose and walked slowly toward Yasemin. She held something in the palm of her own hand that she now placed in Yasemin's. Only because Susan and Christine had been told so earlier did they know that it was a gold coin, meant to guarantee the newlyweds prosperity in their new life together. With the coin resting safely in her palm, the henna on her fingertips the woman, aided by Nevin, tied the other handkerchief around Yasemin's hand. That hand, containing its several blessings, would remain bound until tomorrow.

Suddenly the women broke into song again, signaling the end of the formal ceremony and the beginning of the party.

Yasemin sat on the still-warm marble platform surveying all that was happening around her.

Someone came toward her with a tray of pastries—*baklava,* the deliciously decadent sweet made of thin leaves of pastry filled with nuts and drenched in honey; the tasty *kadın göbeği,* the "lady's navel," lemon-flavored cakes soaked in syrup; and the *dilber dudağı,* the "belle lips," fried dough dipped in syrup. She sought out her favorite, the *künefe,* shredded wheatlike strands of pastry with cheese inside. As a child growing up, she had loved all of these delicacies. When she was a little girl, she would beg the cooks to make the gooey confections for her, and then she would sneak several more pieces than she was allowed up to her room at night.

The passing around of the desserts signaled the end of the ceremony, and Yasemin and her family and friends said good night to all who had shared the wonderful evening with them.

"What a lovely ceremony," Christine said during the ride home. "It was exactly as you promised, Yaz, unlike anything we'd ever seen before. And your Aunt Semra was terrific. What a dynamo! Just as you said, she knows everything. I'm afraid we exhausted her with our incessant questions."

"She's lovely, isn't she. She's a very special part of my life," Yasemin said.

They reached the entrance to the house. The outer security doors swung open and the guard dogs, the German shepherd and the two enormous *Sivas Kangalls,* began their noisy barking routine. Murat hushed them to silence and swung the car into the interior driveway.

"I'm exhausted, everyone," Yasemin said.

"Not to worry, darling," her mother offered sweetly. "It's late. Go upstairs and have a good night's sleep. Tomorrow you're going to need all your strength. It's such an important day."

Yasemin kissed everyone good night and climbed the stairs to her room, her bandaged hand gliding along the banister, the sound of the golden coins on her necklace echoing softly.

The windows in her room remained open to the sea and the cool evening breeze brushed her skin as she let the *bindallı* and the harem pants slip to the floor. She stepped out of it and walked slowly to her bed.

The light bedcovers enveloped her, and as she fell into a peaceful, fantasy-filled sleep her last vision was of a beautiful bride . . . the most beautiful bride in the world.

CHAPTER

24

*T*HEIR FIRST DAYS together were indeed magical. The morning after the ceremony and celebration at the Turan yalı, they left for a honeymoon in Europe. It was a lovely itinerary. Osman had planned a grand tour of the south of France. Yasemin loved visiting all the quaint little villages she had heard her mother speak about. They stopped along the way, staying at some of the charming resorts and dining at world-class restaurants. The days were wonderful; they sped along the narrow country roads or down the winding Grande Corniche in the convertible that Osman had reserved for them. Yasemin loved the feel of the wind in her hair, and the scent of lavender and jasmine. She felt alive and happy to be there.

The nights were equally wonderful. They would pick a spot that looked interesting to both of them for dinner. Osman loved good food, and they especially enjoyed the variety of seafood available from the waters of the Mediterranean. Even though the south of Turkey provided good fish, there were many more types available in France, and the preparation was always creative and superb. They would deliberate over which wine to have as if it were the most important decision they would ever make. Osman was amusing and considerate and generous. Yasemin loved being with him, and as it had been since their first night together, they never lacked for things to talk about. The emotional spark, the compelling connection that made people choose to live as man and wife, was even more powerful now than it had been during their courtship. They found themselves finishing each other's sentences; laughing at jokes no outsider could possibly understand.

After dinner they would stroll through the village where they were staying, often stopping for a drink at one of the outdoor cafés. Local men played boules and drank pastis late into the night, and sometimes there were roving musicians who came to serenade them with ballads about lovers and their trials and tribulations. Yasemin locked her eyes with Osman's as the musicians sang their songs of love. Inevitably, the game of boules would reach a conclusion, the old men would put on their lightweight jackets and down the remainder of their drinks. The waiters would begin to sweep the area around them. It was time to go home.

Once inside their room, which was usually a charming suite that had all the amenities to encourage coziness and lovemaking, Yasemin would give herself to her husband in ways she had never before dreamed possible. Osman would stroke her hair and gently caress her face. "Yasemin, darling, you are so beautiful," he would say, as he took down the straps of her nightgown and beheld her lovely breasts. "Every part of you is so wondrous. I will never tire of looking at you."

They would make love late into the night; oftentimes they would still be fondling and caressing each other as daylight streamed in through the windows.

As wonderful as the trip had been, she was happy to get back to Istanbul, back to the house her father had bought for them as a wedding present. It was only two blocks from the one in which she had grown up, and although it was not nearly as grand as the Turans', it had a wonderful feeling of space and airiness. The floor plan was nearly identical. The first floor contained a large foyer, and all the rooms branched off from there. There was a large living room, and adjacent to that on one side was a formal dining room that could easily seat twelve, and on the other side, an elegant wood-paneled room that served as a library and study. Off this room, bounded on three sides by water, was Yasemin's favorite space. It was a small area, no more than fifteen feet square, which was where she spent most of her spare time. She decorated it in much the same manner as the room that Cyrielle so loved—with colorful Turkish fabrics and brilliantly patterned kilims. The walls of the room were lined with low banquettes whose tops just bordered the long windows out to the sea. She was happiest in this room and she spent hours there, finishing up work she couldn't get to during the day, and taking care of her social correspondence.

The bedrooms on the second floor also faced out onto the Bosphorus, and the floor-to-ceiling windows allowed the light to filter in with the first break of day. Yasemin busied herself with their decoration, scouring the Covered Bazaar and the antique markets for special rugs and furniture that suited their more casual life-style. Osman was delighted by her pleasure in this; he often surprised her with some new piece that complemented her taste perfectly.

As close as they were in their marriage, they went about their professional lives in a most private manner. Osman went to his office every morning, as did Yasemin. Both of their businesses continued to grow, yet they rarely discussed matters of work when they came home at night. Osman had stayed true to his commitment to run his own firm, and Yasemin continued to head the Turan textile division, which each year became more and more important to the overall profits of Turan Holding. From time to time she heard her father mention the other Boras, but she preferred not knowing about the dealings or the continuing conflict. The most important thing in the world to her was her marriage, and she was willing to go to the ends of the earth to protect the loving, fulfilling relationship in which they both took such joy.

CHAPTER

25

I'T'S REALLY a great idea, Maman. Did you think of it?"

"Well, not all by myself, I admit. Your Uncle Osman had a lot to do with it. So you like it, sport?"

"I think it's the best," the handsome young boy answered enthusiastically. "I can't wait to ski in Switzerland; I hear it's the best there." Kaya, Nevin's son, was only four and a half now, but he had the spirit and competitiveness of a much older boy.

"Kaya, please, everything cannot be the 'best.' Don't you have any other words in your vocabulary to describe the trip?" his mother asked.

"All right, Maman, I will simply adore to go," he said, placing his hands on his hips and swaying back and forth. "That's what Uncle Ali would say."

Nevin and Yasemin looked at each other, shocked by Kaya's impression of their brother. If it was that obvious to a young child, what must the rest of the world be thinking? Yasemin really didn't care, Ali had made a name for himself in the tough, competitive world of concert pianists, and beyond that she was not terribly concerned about what others thought of him. He was successful, happy, and content with the life he had chosen. For that she was thankful.

"All right, Kaya, that's enough," Nevin cut her son's impression short. "Now go and pull out the things you want to take. Not too much, remember; you are only allowed one suitcase, that's all. Your grandfather and uncle will be here to pick us up around eight. So get going."

A few days before, Osman had suggested a ski vacation that would include the entire Turan family—Nevin, Sedat and young Kaya, as well as Cyrielle and Omer. The men all wanted to go skiing, and Osman thought that they should fly to Zurich and then drive down to Klosters. The skiing was superb there, and nearby were several other resorts, such as Davos and Arosa, which offered a full range of slopes, from the beginner bunny hills that Kaya would require, to the more challenging runs to suit Sedat, Osman and Omer. Yasemin hadn't skied for years and wanted to take some lessons, and Osman assured her that all of that could be found at Klosters. But when Yasemin approached Nevin with the idea, her sister came up with a brainstorm, an idea that was even more appealing to her.

"Why not let the boys go off to Switzerland, and you, Maman and I can go to Paris and shop and play for a few days? We haven't been away together for years, not since we were teenagers. Don't you think it would be fun? I'm not too keen on traipsing up and down a mountain all day when we could be shopping and visiting museums. What do you say?"

Yasemin thought it was a brilliant plan, and told her so at once. Especially now that Cyrielle was almost exactly like her old self. It would be such fun—just the three of them off together—just like old times. So the new plans had been made, and the seven of them— Cyrielle, Yasemin and Nevin booked to Paris, and Omer, Osman, Sedat and Kaya to Zurich—were due to depart within hours.

"Kiss your mother good-bye," Sedat told Kaya when they reached the departure gate. "Hurry, Kaya, your mother has to go and catch her flight." But the little boy was too caught up in his admiration of the giant planes.

"Well, I guess you've already lost him to the boys' weekend," Sedat said, taking Nevin in his arms and kissing her for both of them. "Have a wonderful holiday, you deserve it. We'll see you in ten days."

"Have fun, everyone," the women yelled in unison as they rushed toward the gate. Their Air France flight was scheduled to depart a half hour earlier than the one to Zurich.

On this trip Yasemin and Nevin were able to recall their own memories of the Ritz, and for the second time, it did not disappoint them. Yasemin had arranged to have the same suite they had all shared when they first visited together years earlier. The hotel offered the same gracious ambience, and they recognized the faces of many of the staff members. This time, however, it was winter in Paris, just after the celebration of the New Year. A light dusting of snow had blanketed the city the night before, and the buildings looked magical with their shimmering white covering. Even before unpacking, Cyrielle was drawn to the window where she had stood years before after dispatching the girls to have tea.

"Isn't it wonderful to be here, Maman?" asked Nevin, going to stand at her mother's side. "I can't believe it's been so long."

"Neither can I," Cyrielle said as she stood there, her eyes frozen on the rooftop of the building where she had grown up. And yet, it all looked very much the same—unchanged in physical appearance, despite the enormous events that had occurred. The last time they had been there, General de Gaulle had just established his Fifth Republic.

"So much has happened since then, hasn't it?" said Yasemin, coming to join them at the window.

"Yes, and so much for the good," Nevin said. "Well, I'm for some tea, just like before. I wonder if they still have those wonderful sandwiches we ate so many of the last time," she added, wanting to pull everyone away from the view as soon as possible to avoid a shadow of sadness from slipping over their trip.

"You're right," Cyrielle agreed, "let's go down and plan what we'll do with our time here. I know I can't wait to get into Chanel, and Dior, and find out what's really happening in the fashion world.

Of course I've got to save enough time to have a look at the auction houses. And there's a wonderful new show at the Rodin Museum, plus the Matisse exhibit at the Grand Palais—so we'll have to make sure we get over and see both of those."

"All right, Maman, we'll do all those things, but right now let's get started by celebrating our arrival here."

The three Turan women joined arms and went out giggling like schoolgirls down the hallway. Their adventure had begun.

The snow melted the next day. It was replaced by crisp air and clear skies that promised to remain for a good part of their stay. Each morning they dressed in their best outfits, wrapped themselves in their fur coats, and headed out for a day of adventure and fun. Each day they chose another wonderful restaurant where they would spend a good part of the afternoon, discussing the morning and planning the evening's events. Soon their stay was drawing to a close.

"I think I'd like to go back and eat at La Procope again," Nevin said.

Yasemin turned to her, shocked. "What is the matter with you?" she said in a louder voice than she had anticipated. But she was horrified that her sister could be so stupid, and so unaware of Cyrielle's feelings. Perhaps she had been too young to remember everything that occurred that evening so long ago when they had met Pierre and Martine. When Cyrielle had found out what had happened to her family during the war. How could she be so thoughtless? What had come over this usually caring, sensitive sister of hers?

The moment she had spoken, Nevin regretted it. Seeing the look on Yasemin's face told her how cruel she had been. In fact, she had only remembered the good parts, the happiness she had seen in the faces of the two sweet old people when they recognized who the mother and young daughters really were. But now she realized what she had done by bringing up the subject, and she was ashamed.

"Oh, Maman, what a terrible thing to say. Oh, I'm so sorry . . .

I didn't mean to bring up all those terrible memories. How selfish of me . . . I'm terribly, terribly sorry."

Cyrielle had tried to come to terms with that evening long ago. But as shocking as it had been, and as long as it had taken, she had finally learned to live with the pain of her loss. When she thought about it, she only saw the kind faces of Pierre and Martine, and their happiness at seeing her again and meeting her beautiful daughters for the first time. Martine had died shortly after she had sat in their apartment that night, and Pierre had passed away less than a year later. She had been notified because they had instructed in their wills that all items once belonging to the Lazares should be returned to her. Cyrielle had reviewed the list of things with their lawyer; most of the possessions had been simple household articles they had taken from the apartment on the Faubourg St. Honoré. There were the three valuable drawings Maurice had been unwilling to part with, and Cyrielle instructed that they be sent to Istanbul, where they now hung in her museum—one each in honor of her father, her sister, and her brother.

But now she thought that perhaps she would like to go back and eat at La Procope again. Tomorrow was their last day, and it would be fitting to eat there before leaving for Istanbul. Tomorrow they would all fly home, the men from Zurich, and the women from Paris. They would land at the airport just fifteen minutes apart, making for a wonderful reunion, and saving extra trips for the drivers. So tonight would be just a perfect night for celebrating their good stay here. And yes, she would take her daughter's suggestion, and they would go back to a very special place. She smiled in anticipation.

"Nevin, don't worry," she said, trying to calm her visibly upset daughter. "And Yasemin, don't be so rough on your sister. She obviously feels terrible. But she needn't. It think it's a terrific idea. Let's do go there tonight. It would be great fun, I think."

Yasemin was startled by her mother's reaction. She wanted to make sure she wasn't just saying that to make Nevin feel better.

"Are you certain, Maman, you really want to go there? It wouldn't upset you to be there again?"

"Not in the least. We'll ask the concierge to arrange it for us when we get back to the hotel. But now, oh my," she exclaimed, checking her watch and seeing that this discussion had delayed them too long. It was already after three. "It's late. I have an appointment, and it's all the way across town. I've got to leave now."

"Go ahead, Maman," Yasemin urged. "You take the driver with you and have him wait for you there. Nevin and I will walk or take a taxi back. We'll see you at the hotel. Don't be late for our big night out," she said, kissing her mother good-bye quickly and helping her to locate her coat check.

"I'm back, and I was successful. I got the Monet," Cyrielle shouted as she entered the living room of their suite. Yasemin sat at the small desk finishing up an important business call, and Nevin emerged from the bedroom when she heard her mother's voice.

"That's wonderful," they both agreed. "What a nice addition."

"And I'm glad you're back, because I'm starving," Yasemin added. "But you must be tired. Take a little rest, and a hot bath if you want, our reservation is at eight-thirty."

"I think I'll do just that," Cyrielle said, shedding her coat and shoes and heading toward her bedroom. "Don't forget to wake me if I'm still fast asleep at seven-thirty," she called out, pulling the door partly shut behind her.

Yasemin wasn't tired at all, so she settled on the overstuffed sofa with a project she had tried often to finish in Istanbul, but had been constantly interrupted. Now, on the last afternoon of this idyllic vacation, was her chance. Nevin disappeared into the bedroom they shared, and she was left alone in their luxurious living room.

She worked for about an hour and then became restless. It had begun to rain lightly and had turned colder, so she dismissed the idea of a walk. Instead, she decided to watch television. Switching back and forth between channels, she settled on an old American movie starring John Wayne, which had been dubbed in French. Immediately she became involved, more in the humorous translation than in the story itself. She was laughing heartily when the program was interrupted by a special news bulletin.

"We are sorry for the interruption," the newsman said, "but we bring you news of a tragedy this afternoon in Davos, Switzerland. There has been an avalanche of enormous proportions, and many skiers, enjoying the last days of the New Year's holiday, are believed to be either trapped or killed beneath the weight of the sliding snows. The avalanche occurred this afternoon around three o'clock, when the greatest number of skiers were on the slopes. Rescue crews have been dispatched; they have so far pulled fourteen bodies from the site of the disaster. More on this tragedy later as the story develops. Now back to our regular broadcast."

Yasemin sat in stunned silence, seeing nothing but the face of the newscaster as he announced the tragedy. Osman's itinerary called for the men to be in Davos today; she knew that for sure because she had looked at their schedule only an hour earlier to confirm their departure time from Zurich tomorrow.

She ran from the sofa into the darkened bedroom. Nevin was sound asleep under the covers. Yasemin went to her, trying to remain as calm as possible.

"Nevin, wake up; you must wake up now." She shook her sister's shoulder gently, but she was unable to disguise the panic in her voice.

Nevin sat up in a start, for a moment disoriented and uncertain of her surroundings. "What is it, Yasemin? Are you all right?"

"Yes, I'm fine," she managed to say, but she was frightened and unable to control her voice or her quickened breathing. "But, Nevin, there's been a terrible accident in Davos. Many skiers are buried beneath an avalanche. I just heard it on the news. Oh, Nevin, that's where the men are supposed to be today." Her voice broke. "Do you think they're all right?"

Nevin was wide awake now, listening intently and with growing horror to her terrified sister. "Yasemin, take it easy. Slow down. Tell me everything you heard on the news."

Yasemin repeated the sketchy details that were available at the time. "Oh, I'm frantic. Let's call the hotel where they are supposed to be right now, and see if we can find anything out."

"Go ahead, I'll be right out," Nevin said, getting up from the bed and putting on the snow-white toweling robe from the hotel.

The circuits in Davos were all tied up, and despite their frustration there was nothing for them to do but wait. The concierge had put one of the switchboard operators in charge of doing nothing other than trying to get through for them. As the hours passed, and the grisly new details were revealed on the intermittent news broadcasts, their panic grew.

Their dinner reservation long forgotten, and the hotel manager's offering of a room-service meal untouched on the cart in the living room, they sat side by side on the sofa, mother and daughters, waiting for the phone to ring.

At three in the morning they still sat there, petrified that the long hours of uncertainty had sealed the fate of their loved ones, but each trying to be strong for the others. When the harsh ringing of the phone finally cracked the silence, they looked to each other for an instant. Nevin jumped up to answer it.

"I'll get it," she said, her hands already shaking with fear.

She picked up the receiver cautiously, praying with all her might that she would only hear good news.

"Yasemin?" came the voice.

"No, no, it's not Yasemin, it's Nevin. Osman, is that you?"

The silence seemed to go on too long. "Osman, is that you? Are you all right?"

"Yes, yes, I'm fine. Is Yaz there?"

"Of course she's here. We've been trying desperately to reach you, but the lines have been tied up. Is everyone okay? We heard there was a terrible accident."

"Yes, yes, it was terrible. Nevin, please, let me talk with Yasemin."

"Yes, I'll put her on. But first I want to know if everyone is all right. Is Sedat there with you? Are *Baba* and Kaya okay?"

This time the silence was too long, and she knew that something terrible had happened.

"Osman," she yelled into the phone, "what is it?"

Finally the voice came. "It's Sedat, Oh. I'm so sorry to be the one to tell you. He and your father went out on the slopes right after lunch; I stayed down below with Kaya. We were tobogganing in front of the lodge, and then we stopped to watch the skiers as they came down the hill. And then, about an hour later, we heard this terrible noise. Something like an explosion, or a big clap of thunder, but much worse, much more intense and much more frightening. It wasn't until much later that we found out what had happened. Anyone who was up there didn't really have a chance. Your father was one of the lucky ones. He's in pretty bad shape; how bad, we don't know yet. He's in the hospital with the doctors now. But Sedat was crushed to death. Oh, Nevin, they just identified the body a few minutes ago. I called as soon as I found out." Osman was weeping openly now. "I'm so sorry."

Nevin put the phone down and motioned to Yasemin to pick it up. Cyrielle ran out from the bedroom where she had been on the extension. She had heard it all. She stood frozen in the doorway, paralyzed by the news. Yasemin listened to Osman as he repeated the story, then placed the phone back on its receiver. She turned to her sister, took her into her outstretched arms, as the tears flowed down their cheeks.

"He loved his little boy so much," Nevin sobbed. "He wanted nothing more than to be with him, to see him grow up. And now they'll never know each other."

When they finally released each other, they faced Cyrielle. She remained silent, staring into the room, a blank look on her face.

Nevin went toward her, but Cyrielle turned her back to her. The girls watched, stunned by her behavior.

"Maman," Nevin began. "I . . . I . . . ." But Cyrielle started to walk away from her, trying to escape the pain by retreating into the safety of her room.

"Maman," Yasemin yelled. "Maman, Nevin needs you!" she

screamed. "She's a widow now, a widow with a little boy whom she will have to raise without his father. You still have your husband; he may be injured, but he's still alive. Nevin's husband is dead, and she needs you. Don't turn your back on her like you have done in the past." Where the words came from Yasemin would never know, but she was certain that they had to be spoken. The look on her mother's face had been clear; she was sinking, retreating, traveling back down that long, deep road into her depression. And if Yasemin allowed her to go again without trying to stop her, she was afraid she might never return.

Cyrielle turned back to face her daughter, but still she was unable to comfort her now. She walked on, pulling the door behind her, shutting out those who needed her most.

Yasemin calmed Nevin as best she could, then went about the task of arranging for their flight to Zurich in the morning.

That done, she sat on the sofa until the first light of dawn streamed through the windows. She thought there was an injustice in the fact that the rain had once again cleared out and the morning sky was crystal-clear. She mourned for Sedat, and for the little boy who would never know his father's love. She ached too for her sister and the pain she was experiencing, as well as that of her mother whose mental anguish matched any physical agony she could ever know.

CHAPTER

26

CYRIELLE SAT in the chair in her bedroom, paralyzed from the blow they had all just received. She stared straight ahead, unseeing, yet fully aware of her surroundings. Her eyes were dry; the wounds she had were too deep for tears.

Months ago, when she felt she had reached the bottom of the deep hole into which her soul had plunged, she had seriously considered taking her life. Whenever she neared the terrace in front of the house she thought of throwing herself into the churning waters and letting the Bosphorus take her as it had taken her darling Zeki. When she stood looking out from the high ledge in the garden at the museum, she contemplated hurling her empty body down the mountainside. At home she often looked contemplatively at the sleeping pills on which she had come to rely so heavily. But she had taken none of those roads, those cowardly paths to self-destruction. From somewhere an inner strength had surfaced. After all these long years, after days and weeks and months when she felt she hadn't the strength to go on, from someplace deep within her a willpower had surfaced, a willpower that gave her back her desire to go on, to pick up the pieces of her shattered life.

Slowly, day by day, she had begun to near the surface, to pull herself up from the long, dark tunnel into which she had traveled. Every step along the way, Omer had been there for her, and her smallest improvement had given him cause for celebration. Her most painful realization had come when she saw how hard her illness had been on him. But through it all he had remained right by her side, waiting patiently for her to show even the most minuscule signs of recovery. And for such a long time she had been unable to communicate with him on any level. Unable to respond to him in any way.

Their sex life had ceased to exist years ago, and she was certain that he must have turned to other women for comfort and to fulfill his most natural urges. For the longest time, even that thought did not bother her, for she had lost all sense of self-esteem, and with that loss had gone all confidence in herself as a woman. Omer had been very discreet about these dalliances, never embarrassing her, and never flaunting them before her. And he had always been there when she needed him. At the slightest sign that she was improving he would be there to cheer her on, to encourage her and to provide anything she might desire. His devotion to her had been unrelenting, a reflection of the love he felt for her.

So, from deep within, a slow improvement had begun. When the morning light came through her windows, instead of pulling the covers up and hiding from the day, she had begun to get up and dress. Once again she was often able to be downstairs to have breakfast with her husband before he left for work. She began reading the papers every day, and showed an interest in current affairs. She was again able to hold a conversation on her own, and they had accepted dinner invitations for the first time in ages.

She had considered the trip to Paris a real turning point in her recovery process. How she had looked forward to being alone with her daughters again, to getting reacquainted with them and their lives. Once they arrived, things went even more smoothly than she had anticipated. At auction she had bid successfully on several paintings she wanted for the museum. This time she had been attracted to bright, lively canvases that had a joyous feeling to them. Once again she loved the happy, vibrant colors and peaceful scenes of the Impressionist works. Since Zeki's death she had felt compelled to purchase only dark, somber works that bespoke of death and destruction. The museum now had more than its fair share of the intensely troubled works by the Austrian Expressionists Egon Schiele and Oskar Ko-

koschka. Thankfully that period of her collecting had passed, a healthy sign of her own improving sense of self. She felt alive again. She wanted to shop, to buy new clothes, to have her hair styled, to have a facial and a manicure and pedicure. In short, she wanted to feel like a woman again. It was the first step toward being able to be a wife to her devoted husband once more. To be a mother to her children, and to make up for the neglect she had inflicted on them. With the help of both Yasemin and Nevin, she had been able to do all of that.

She sat now, surrounded by her purchases, beautiful, elegant clothes that were befitting the wife of one of the world's most powerful and attractive men. Chanel, Dior, Patou—she had been to them all. Packages of new, lacy lingerie, boxes of shoes, pairs of gloves, and several scarves to add to her collection were all stacked up in the corner, ready to be put in suitcases and carried back to Istanbul. All the accoutrements that showed she was ready to begin her new life.

Now all of her renewed dreams had been shattered by a single phone call. The past few hours had seemed an eternity to her. The not knowing, the uncertainty, had nearly driven her out of her mind. She had been reminded of the long wait she had experienced before she found out about her family in France. Her patience was being sorely tested, and she was failing the test.

Omer. Her wonderful Omer. The only man she had ever loved. She had gone to him a virgin, and he had been the only man she had ever wanted. He had taught her all she had ever known about her own sexuality, her own womanhood. He was her strength, her support, her life. Her dear, darling Omer. She had loved him from the very first moment she had seen him, standing in the doorway of the room that had become her favorite in the large house whose mistress he had made her.

She had embraced his religion and they had raised their children according to their shared beliefs. She had never wanted for anything; all her material desires had been met. Heaven knew he had tried to meet all of her emotional needs. And he had, many times over, until Zeki's death. He had stood by her side during her times of grief, difficult, trying times, and he had never wavered. Now he had been injured, how badly they didn't yet know. She prayed as she never had before that he was not seriously hurt, that he would be well soon, that they could go back to Istanbul and begin again. But something told her he was in terrible pain, and that he might not recover. She tried to force the horrible vision from her mind, but as she sat in the chair, waiting, it crept back in, tormenting her and driving her nearly out of her mind.

Cyrielle heard Yasemin's voice in the distance, talking on the telephone, trying to make plans for them. She wanted to be there with her, she knew she should be by her side, helping her. As their mother, now was the moment when she should be strong, comforting them, and arranging to be by Omer's side as soon as they possibly could get there. But she remained immobile, unable to move from her chair.

Every now and then she could hear the sound of Nevin's crying coming from her room across the suite. She yearned to be with her, to cradle her in her arms, to tell her that everything was going to be all right. But it wasn't going to be all right. Her husband had been killed, and she was a widow now. Left alone to raise a son, and to live a hollow life. Nevin had loved him so, and she would long for him until the day she died. Cyrielle knew this to be true, for all around her were the memories of those she had loved. The faces of her lost family were forever etched in her mind. Her mother, father, brothers, sister, son—she knew it was a pain from which you never recovered. So she remained in her chair until a new day dawned on Paris and the three of them began the journey to Switzerland.

The snowstorm that blanketed Switzerland and Italy made travel by airplane almost impossible. Those flights that did receive clearance to take off were delayed for hours and often couldn't land at their planned destination. They were anxious to get moving. They decided that train was the surest way.

They threw together all of their luggage, hastily packing their new purchases about which they had earlier been so excited, and boarded the train for Zurich. Yasemin, with the help of the concierge at the Ritz, was able to reserve a first-class compartment for them, and they were all thankful to be able to escape the noise and the crowds. Because of all the delays the station was packed, people were pushing and shoving, determined to board trains that were already booked to overflowing. The porter who had been sent along with them hustled through with their belongings, and at last they were situated in the privacy of their own compartment. Yasemin pulled the door tightly shut and breathed a sigh of relief that they were on their way. Cyrielle took one of the seats near the window, and Nevin sat opposite her. Her daughter's face was pale, drawn and fatigued; it appeared as if she had aged a decade since last night. Cyrielle reached out and took her hands in a wordless gesture of sympathy.

Cyrielle refused all offers of food and sent the two younger women off together to have lunch in the dining car. As she sat alone in the compartment, with the chugging, monotonous drone of the wheels turning and propelling them forward, she remembered another trip out of France, the trip that had taken her so far from home to a new life on foreign shores.

Osman and Kaya were on the platform as they pulled into the station. Nevin ran to her son and held him close to her.

"Maman, Maman," he cried. "*Baba*'s gone, and Uncle Osman tells me he's not coming back. And Dede is in the hospital, but they won't let me in to see him. Only Osman can go in, and then only for a minute or two. I know he's lying to me about *Baba*, isn't he, Maman? Tell me he's lying," the confused little boy pleaded.

"Kaya, Kaya, calm down," Nevin said, trying to force back her flow of tears. "Now, take it easy, and try to listen to me. Your uncle would never lie to you. He loves you very much. Just like we all do. Now come along, and I'll explain everything to you once we get to the hotel. Please, Kaya, try to stop crying and I promise we'll talk about it when we get settled at the hotel," she repeated herself, not knowing what to say, or where to find the words that would comfort the young boy, words that would explain to him that which she would never be able to comprehend herself. How could she stand to see the look on his angelic little face when she confirmed to him that he would never see his *baba* again? That his uncle was telling him the truth, and that, as painful as it was, there was nothing she or anyone else could do to change it.

Osman put his arms around his sister-in-law and tried to say words that would lessen her pain. "Nevin, I'm so sorry. But I do keep thinking how blessed we are that Kaya wasn't injured. I know that doesn't bring Sedat back, but it is a miracle that he wasn't hurt."

Nevin tried to manage a smile, but her tears broke through the facade of false strength.

"Nevin, try to get control of yourself. You must, for Kaya," Yasemin whispered, putting her arm around her also. "We'll be with *baba* soon, and you'll feel better then. Come on, the driver has all of the suitcases in the car, and he's waiting for us."

Osman turned his attention to Cyrielle and attempted to break the news about Omer to her in the gentlest way possible. "He's badly hurt, Cyrielle, and since this morning he has gone into a coma. I traveled with him in the ambulance last night, and he was conscious all the way. That's why they felt it was safe to move him from the small facility near the resort. But after we arrived here, and he was taken to the room, he seemed to be very tired, and he slipped away. The specialists were due to come in this morning, in fact they should be there about now. I told them we'd come just as soon as we dropped your things at the hotel."

Her expression did not change when he told her the news. She remained completely passive, and Osman wondered whether or not she had heard him at all.

"I've made all the arrangements for Sedat," Osman explained to Nevin as they rode to the hospital.

"Thank you, Osman, I don't know what we would have done if you hadn't been here. And thank you for taking care of Kaya for me.

I know that must have been the most difficult part. He's so young, and it's so hard for him to understand. Difficult for all of us," she sighed, glancing over in her mother's direction. "I'm still not certain how much of this he comprehends," she continued in a low voice, hoping for some guidance from her mother or sister. Yasemin was the only one to respond, quietly, so that Kaya would not hear from his perch beside the driver.

"He understands that something terrible has happened, but he doesn't realize yet that his father is not coming back forever. Forever is a long time for a young child to understand. But he'll learn to accept it, and so will you, Nevin. The next few days will be a nightmare, particularly with *Babacığım* so sick, but you will find the strength to help Kaya. It's just going to take some time."

The hospital was modern and efficient, equipped with far more up-to-date equipment than the hospitals in Istanbul. Yet its gray hallways, seemingly endless corridors, and overwhelming odor of antiseptic solution were as depressing as any hospital in the world. The click of their heels as they walked toward Omer's room was the only sound that broke the silent atmosphere.

"One at a time," the nurse had warned when they arrived outside Omer's room, "and only for a short while. I would advise staying out until the doctor has had a chance to speak with you. He will be here shortly."

"I will go in for a moment," Cyrielle announced, speaking for only the second or third time since their arrival.

"Are you sure, Maman? Do you want to go alone? Will you be all right?" Yasemin asked.

"Yes, I'm fine."

The four of them sat outside the room on the cold steel bench, waiting for Cyrielle to come out and for the doctor to arrive. It was so quiet they could hear the second hand as it made its way around the face of the electric clock on the wall above their heads.

Cyrielle stood inside the spacious private room, her back pressed against the door. She inhaled deeply, gathering the courage to move closer to the bed where her devoted husband lay. Slowly she moved forward, toward the big oxygen tent that covered Omer like a shroud. The only sound was that of Omer's labored, raspy breathing, made possible by the hideous contraption attached to his nose and mouth. She moved closer, until she was able to peer through the cloudy shield. For a moment she was tempted to turn away, to run from the horrible sight, but she held firmly on to the metal railings of the bed and continued her own deep breathing while she stared into the bed.

"Omer," she whispered. "Omer, my darling. It's me, I'm here now. Omer . . ." The hardest thing was not being able to reach out and take his hand, his strong, powerful hand that had always represented security and stability to her. She stood helpless, unable to touch him or to communicate with him in any way. His harsh breathing continued, and she noticed that one of his legs had been bandaged. His left arm was also covered, whether it was a cast or merely a cloth covering she was unable to tell. She pulled a chair up to the side of the bed and sat staring into her husband's face. Each time the door opened, she asked if the doctor had arrived. Told no, she would wave the intruder away with her hand and turn back to Omer.

As she sat next to him, lulled by the mechanical rhythm of his breathing, her mind began to wander. She returned to her earliest days with Omer, the trip to Iznik, their wedding night and the beautiful Monet he had given her. She thought about the nights they had taken the *Meltem* out on the Bosphorus to have a romantic dinner together, the summers spent in the south, the lovely gifts he had so thoughtfully chosen for her. She thought of the children—her lovely Zeki, the twins who were so very different, but both wonderful in their own way, and her darling Nevin, now a mother and widow, forced to experience such pain at a very young age. Most of her memories were pleasant, filled with love and laughter and joy. The many positive aspects of her life stepped up to the forefront, and the negative aspects took their proper place in the back of her mind. As her thoughts flooded her, she felt as if she were floating, yet her visions were clearer than they had been since that tragic day when

Zeki had drowned. The numbness that had possessed her for so long dissipated and she was left with a concise, potent picture of her life and her future. Suddenly, in a realization as powerful as if she had been shot through with a bolt of lightning, she knew that the worst was over for her. She felt secure and certain about her future, a future that until that very moment she had not cared about. She had lived day by day, seeing and feeling only the minimum of human emotions. Now all of that uncertainty vanished, and she knew, without a doubt, exactly what she had to do, and how she would go about doing it. The realization exhilarated her, and she felt younger and more full of energy than she had in years. She rushed to the bathroom and splashed cold water against her tear-stained face, and then left the room.

The change was evident at once; they all knew from the look on her face that something drastic had occurred behind the heavy wooden door. Yasemin was the first to speak. She jumped up and took her mother's hands. "Maman, did he wake up? Did he speak to you? Tell us, you've been in there for so long; what happened?"

Cyrielle responded by leading her back to the bench where Nevin and Osman waited. She wrapped her arm about her older daughter and kissed her cheek. "No, Yasemin, your father is still in a coma. I talked to him, but I don't know if he heard me. But I do know that he is going to be all right. In time, he's going to be just fine. I know it, I'm certain of it."

All of them were so surprised by the commitment in Cyrielle's voice that they merely sat staring at her. It had been so long since she had spoken in such a forceful manner, and ages since she had sounded so sure of anything.

"Cyrielle, all you all right?" Osman asked, getting up from his seat and motioning for her to sit down.

"Yes, darling, I'm fine, and I don't need to sit down, thank you. Now where is the doctor?"

"He just called, and he will be here in an hour. He's had another emergency, and he's coming the moment he's finished," Yasemin reported.

"All right, then, what we should do now is go and have something to eat. Nevin, you haven't eaten for two days, and I want you to have something now. Even if it's just tea and toast; you must have something. You are going to need every ounce of strength you can muster. Both for yourself and for Kaya. Now up, let's go see if they have anything here that appeals to us. If not, we'll have something sent over from the hotel. They know your father at the Baur au Lac; the general manager always sends him a basket of fruit and a bottle of champagne when he stays there on his business trips, so I'm certain he'll be happy to prepare some things for us. But first let's go see if there's anything decent here."

They looked at each other in amazement. Before them stood a new Cyrielle, or rather, the old Cyrielle who had been missing to them for so long. Once again, suddenly, shockingly so, she was back. She was in control of the situation, she was in command, and everything she was saying made perfect sense. They were all so overwhelmed to see this remarkable change in her that they followed her down the corridor without raising any questions.

CHAPTER
27

*H*OW OLD WERE YOU when you left France, Madame Turan?"

"Eighteen."

"And you never went back until after the war was over?"

"That's right, not until many years later."

"Not until long after you learned that your father and sister and brother had been killed in the camps?"

Cyrielle nodded.

"So you never really grieved properly for your family, you never had a formal burial for them, or finalized their deaths in any way?"

"I built the museum."

"And did that help you?"

"Yes, until . . . until Zeki died, and then the pain began all over again."

"I see. Can you tell me what it was like?"

"At first it was just a mild disorientation. I knew that something terrible had gone wrong. It seemed that my own life, my daily existence, was no longer familiar to me. It was a feeling beyond grief, beyond the pain of having lost the son whom I adored. It was as if my mind was spinning out of control, and I could no longer get ahold of it. Then everyday, normal events became major crises. A rainstorm seemed like the end of the world; it upset me and troubled me greatly, far more than it should have. Everything was blown out of proportion. I found I could no longer concentrate on even the simplest project. I remember one day I was lying in bed paralyzed, unable to move. I truly didn't know how I was going to get up and get myself dressed. It seemed like the biggest, most insurmountable challenge in the world. Then my physical health began to deteriorate, at least in my mind, anyway. A common cold was a sign that I had some terrible disease. I would rush to the doctor at the smallest sign of a problem. That same problem in the past would not have even merited a trip to the pharmacy. I lost my self-confidence. I was constantly afraid. I worried about my children obsessively because I was so concerned that, just like Zeki, they too would be killed or injured."

Cyrielle recounted the months, the years of agony and dire physical pain that had accompanied her mental illness. For hours every day she sat with the doctor, talking and divulging her innermost feelings.

Seeing Omer in the hospital had jarred her back to reality and started her on the road to recovery, but she was knowledgeable enough about her illness to realize that it was only the start. She knew she needed medical help to guide her along to full health.

Once she was certain that Omer was receiving the best medical care available, she went in search of the physician who could help her. She had been extremely lucky when she found Dr. Klauber, a renowned psychiatrist at the clinic where Omer was being treated.

"Madame Turan, what you have been through is called a clinical depression. It is real, it is a disease, and anyone who tells you otherwise is lying. In earlier times it was called melancholia, which was considered nothing more than having a bad day or two. But everything you have described points to a true case of clinical depression. The pain of this illness cannot be described by anyone who has not studied patients such as yourself. But the pain is there, it is unrelenting, and for many people, unfortunately, suicide becomes the only solution. Thankfully, much is now understood about the disease, but many things still remain a mystery. Such as why it begins, and why oftentimes, as in your case, the patient is able to pull himself out before it is too late. Maybe someday we will look back and regard your husband's accident as a blessing. Indeed it could have been the cause of your awareness, and your recognition that you needed help. And that's exactly what you're going to get here.

"Now, the first thing we have to do is to get you off the drugs you've been taking and have become dependent upon. We'll do it with the minimum amount of pain and withdrawal symptoms possible, but it is a critical, indeed a basic, step to recovery from a clinical depression. If you're willing to work with me on that first, then I'm sure we can get somewhere," the kind man had told her.

Dr. Klauber was in his sixties, with a gentle, patient manner and a warm, sympathetic face that communicated the compassion and concern he felt for his patients. He was handsome in a rugged Swiss way, with ruddy cheeks and a shock of silver hair. When he came into the office wearing his white coat he always looked flushed, and Cyrielle sometimes accused him of coming directly from a mountain-climbing expedition.

Dr. Klauber had put Cyrielle in the hospital while they began the process of weaning her body from the pills that had become her best friends. She was in a room near Omer's, and she could visit him, could sit by his bedside for hours at a time.

She told her husband everything—she talked about her days in therapy, her conversations with the doctor and other patients in her group sessions—and even though the only response she received was the measured, labored sound of his breathing, it helped her to hear herself talk. She was going to be fine, and with each passing day she was confident that she was one step closer to recovery.

And she had made remarkable progress. Dr. Klauber released her after only three weeks, saying that all they would do now was continue the sessions, but on an outpatient basis.

Cyrielle moved back into the hotel, where she was committed to remain until Omer was well enough to travel and she could take him home to Istanbul. Unfortunately, the doctors couldn't give her any idea when that might be. Semra, Yasemin, and Ali took turns traveling to Switzerland to see Omer and to keep her company. Depending on their schedules, they would stay for a week or two at a time. Nevin was only able to make the trip one time. Kaya was having terrible, haunting nightmares about the accident, and she didn't feel comfortable leaving him at home or returning him to the scene of his trauma. She counted on her sister to keep her well informed.

"I'm so thrilled with Maman's progress," Yasemin announced to her after her last trip. "She's really doing well. She likes her doctor, and the change in her attitude and outlook is remarkable. She was even questioning me about things at the museum, so I know she's better. Now if *Babacığım* would only recover. It's so hard; the waiting, the not knowing, is the worst part. It seems as if he has been in a coma for such a long time."

"It has been nearly five months," her sister reminded her. Nevin knew exactly to the day how long ago the tragic accident had occurred, for not a moment went by when she did not yearn for her beloved Sedat.

"You're right, but there is nothing more for us to do, just keep praying. We can never, not even for a second, lose hope that he will get well."

Four months later their prayers were answered. As Cyrielle sat in Omer's room during her usual nightly vigil, she sensed a movement under the hideous plastic tent. Even from her position on the other side of the room where she was reading a magazine, she immediately felt a change in the bed where her husband had remained still for such a very long time.

She threw the magazine to the floor and ran to his side.

Inside the tent his hands were moving slowly toward his face. He reached up and tried to pull the tube away from his mouth.

"No, no, don't do that, darling," she cried out, reaching under the offensive plastic shield with one hand, and with the other pressing the nurse call button. "Omer, put your hands down, my sweet. Stop it now. Please," she begged. "Omer, the nurse is coming. Oh, Omer, can you hear me?"

His eyes opened slowly, and then he blinked several times. The brightness blinded him, and she turned the light over his bed off to one side. For a moment he merely stared at her, and in that instant a wave of fear swept through her. What if, after all this time, he could no longer recognize her? What if something had happened to his brain, and he had suffered a memory loss? Just as all these questions were racing through her mind, the edges of his dry, cracked lips curled up into a smile.

"Oh, Omer, darling, you're going to be all right. I'm here with you, and you're going to be fine."

The nurses arrived, and immediately summoned the doctor to come also. By the time he arrived, Omer had been conscious for over half an hour, and in that short time he was already anxious to have the tubes removed from his mouth and nose. He was able to breathe on his own, and even though his first words were raspy, Cyrielle could clearly understand him when he uttered her name. She stood at the end of the bed, out of the way of the doctors, tears of joy running down her cheeks.

Everything was going to be as she had said it would be over nine months ago in the hallway outside this very room. Just as she had been given a second chance at life, Omer was going to have one too. And as he had been there for her, she would be right there for him. He would be well again, and she was going to be by his side every step of the way.

CHAPTER

28

SHE WAS ABLE to take Omer home the following month. He was still seriously ill, his mind often wandered, and he forgot things easily. His left arm had not yet healed to the doctor's satisfaction, and he was unable to walk unassisted. He would require months of arduous physical therapy, but he insisted that he wanted to do it at home, in Istanbul. Cyrielle too thought it would be best if he could recuperate in familiar surroundings, and she made arrangements for one of the members of the clinic's staff to come and stay with them for however long it took to get him on his feet again.

Dr. Klauber released Cyrielle from his care, saying that he had never been more certain in his entire career about the solid, stable condition of a patient.

"Cyrielle, you have done wonders. In a relatively short time you have improved remarkably, and I truly think you are nearly completely recovered. Now go off, take care of your husband, and reclaim your life."

"That's exactly what I intend to do, Doctor. There is nothing more important in the world to me now than seeing that Omer gets his health back. I'm going to devote myself to it. And, I want to be a mother to my children again, to be a part of their lives, to enjoy my grandchildren and watch them as they grow up. Then, of course, there is the museum, and I want that to become something even more special than it is now."

"You're doing just fine, darling," Cyrielle said as Omer made his way slowly down the staircase. He could now make the previously impossible trip once each day. She would stand at the bottom of the grand staircase, urging him along and cheering him every step of the way. It pained her to see him like this, his once sure stride now unsteady and measured, his once powerful frame now hunched over, his physique diminished by lack of exercise. On the rare occasion that it became too difficult for her to watch she would turn her head or make an excuse that she had forgotten to do something, and would rush from the room so that he could not see the anguish etched across her face.

On days when he had the strength, they would have lunch together out on the terrace. Cyrielle would ask Seta to make his favorite things, and they would sit side by side, watching the freighters and yachts as they passed in front of the house.

"I want to go out on the *Meltem* soon," Omer said one afternoon. "I miss her, and I miss being on the water. I hate just sitting here all day, staring at her. I feel so helpless."

"Yes, darling," Cyrielle responded, wanting to change the subject at once. There was no room in her master plan for self-pity. She wouldn't allow it. "Just as soon as the doctors say it's all right, we will go. I promise, my love. Nothing would make me happier."

He would smile his crooked smile, a result of the paralysis on his right side, a paralysis that the doctors had said would be permanent. She would take his hand in hers, pretending that she did not notice his weakness. No one could be more supportive, more caring than Cyrielle was as she nursed him back to health. He was her world, and she would not let up on her relenting dedication to him until he was fully recovered.

The rest of Omer's family also rallied around. Sibel and Mustafa made an occasional trip from Ankara. Mustafa, approaching his ninth decade, but still possessed of his razor-sharp mind, would sit with his son, talking and reminiscing about the olden days. Sibel would head straight for the kitchen where she would help Seta prepare the dishes her beloved Omer had adored as a young boy. Semra was there, as she had always been, right by Cyrielle's side, filling her full of hope and positive thoughts about the future. Nevin spent hours with her father, perched at his bedside, often reading to him from the newspapers. She brought Kaya to see his grandfather, and the sight of the little boy never failed to bring a smile to Omer's face.

Kaya had become the sole focus of his mother's life. Nevin was very involved in activities at the child's school; she served on every committee available, attended every meeting, and volunteered for all the things the other parents always claimed they were too busy to do. This involvement helped her to recover from her immense grief; she needed to keep as occupied as she could. Caring for her father and spending time with him was another diversion that she welcomed.

Ali, too, dedicated himself to helping his father make a complete recovery. He visited the house two or three times each week, often staying to have dinner with his parents. Sometimes he would play a piece from his most recent concert tour on the grand piano in the living room. Omer seemed to enjoy this, he would sit and listen, sometimes moving his head to the rhythm of the music.

But of all his visitors it was Yasemin who brought the biggest, brightest smile to Omer's face. His entire expression changed as if a light had suddenly clicked on inside him. His eyes sparkled with their old vigor, as he held open his arms for her.

"*Babacığım,*" she would cry out with her usual enthusiasm. She would go to him, embracing him with all the love that was in her heart. "*Baba,* you look wonderful today," she would say, rubbing his cheek with her hand.

"I've come to tell you everything, all that's going on," she would say. She would pull up a chair and sit by his side, then proceed to tell him every detail of her work at Turan Holding, sharing with him not only the continuing successes of her now formidable division, but telling him also of the problems and frustrations she was encountering with the additional responsibilities she had assumed since her father's absence. Slowly she had tried to ingratiate herself with the management of the other divisions. Not for a minute did she think she would be able to handle all the companies; she concentrated on the ones related to her own very profitable division, the ones that were mainly manufacturing plants. She had made an effort to spend as much time as possible with their management, trying to keep abreast of the situation. She wanted to help in whatever way she could.

Omer pretended to comprehend, but both Cyrielle and Yasemin knew that it would still be quite some time, perhaps a very long time, before he would once again be able to be a contributing force to the company he had built.

CHAPTER
29

THE BORA FAMILY, Osman's brothers Timur and Tayfun, and their father Erol, wasted no time before they began taking advantage of the fact that Omer Turan was no longer at the helm of his empire. They were very knowledgeable about the management of the company, they had made extensive studies of Turan's top executives, and even though they realized that Yasemin was a talented and skilled manager, they knew there was no way she could run the entire organization single-handedly. Practicing their usual unscrupulous business tactics, they were able to persuade many of Turan's best clients, and even many of their employees and factory workers, that Turan Holding was a company in deep trouble, a company that would soon fall by the wayside. The Boras positioned themselves as the white knights who could slay the dragon and save the day. Unfortunately, by the time Cyrielle heard about all of this, the hole had been dug, and recovering their ground and repairing the damage was going to be a very difficult battle indeed.

The house was peaceful. Cyrielle sat in Omer's library, sorting through the mail that was sent over daily from his office. She flipped through the usual assortment of invoices, magazines, and inter-office memos, dividing them into piles that would later, when he had the energy, be delivered to Omer to glance at.

When she first heard the dogs barking noisily, she thought nothing of it. Oftentimes they were excited by the passing of a stray dog outside the gates, or by an unfamiliar noise coming off the water. But when she heard Murat's voice quieting them, followed by the sound of a car as it passed over the gravel, she went to the front door to see what all the commotion was about. Not expecting anyone, she couldn't imagine who would be disturbing Omer's afternoon nap. He was usually exhausted from his morning session with the therapist, and after he made his daily trip down the stairs and had lunched with Cyrielle, he then went straight up to his room for a two-hour rest. Cyrielle cherished the hours between three and five, she used the time to catch up on her correspondence and management of the household. It was most unusual for anyone to visit during that time, and so her curiosity was aroused.

She opened the front door and immediately recognized the car as belonging to Oktay Demir, Omer's oldest and most loyal employee. Oktay had been Omer's right-hand man when they first started the branch operation in Istanbul. He had stayed on year after year, content to be always in the shadows. He was a dear, sweet man whom Cyrielle had always liked. When his wife died almost a year ago, she made every effort to watch over him, to bring him closer into their family life. But he had refused all offers, preferring to stay at his home. He was a quiet, gentle soul, highly religious, who lived in the same unpretentious house where he had lived all his life, even though his career at Turan Holding had been tremendously successful and he had been generously compensated over the years. Now, as she watched him get out of his car, Cyrielle panicked. Had she made a date with him and then forgotten? Was Omer expecting him, and she had failed to remember? Over the past year she had been organized and composed, just as she had been before her illness. Now she wondered if her memory had failed her again.

"Oktay, *hoş geldiniz!* How nice to see you!" she called out, still baffled as to the reason for his sudden appearance.

The small man looked up when he heard her voice. He turned back and removed a folder from the car. Slowly he walked toward the door of the imposing mansion.

"Cyrielle *hanım*, please forgive me, I've not called, but I was driving home, and I thought maybe I could see you for a moment. . . ."

Cyrielle relaxed, and then once again snapped back to being concerned, for it was most unusual for him just to stop by. Recovering, but still confused, she said, "Of course, of course, Oktay, you know you're always welcome here. We miss seeing you. How have you been?"

"Fine, just fine, Cyrielle. You look especially well, I must say."

"Thank you, I feel good too. Seing how much progress Omer is making keeps me going. He's really doing very well, you know."

"Yes, I've heard, and I'm sorry I haven't been back to visit since the last time. The time passes so quickly, everyone has been so busy at the office, just trying to keep up. It's very different without Omer there. He did the work of eight men. Now the rest of us have to try to stay on top of things."

"I know, it must be very difficult. I hope that someday soon he'll be able to go back. It's his fondest wish, but I'm afraid we still have some time to go before that will be possible, even on a part-time basis. He still tires very easily. In fact, he's having his nap now. I hope whatever you have come to discuss can wait until he wakes up later this afternoon."

"Actually, Cyrielle, I've come to talk with you, not with Omer."

"Oh," she responded, once again catapulted into a state of confusion. "Of course. . . . Well then, please come in."

They went inside together, and she led him into the library. "Let's go in here, Oktay, that way we won't disturb Omer. He sleeps with the windows open, and sometime voices from the terrace awaken him. Now, what can I offer you to drink?" she asked, ringing for the houseman. "Would you like a glass of tea, perhaps?"

"Yes, I will have one, thank you." He looked at Cyrielle and gave her a kind smile. He had always liked her, ever since the day she had married his employer. Over the years she had been very nice to him, always including him in important business dinners, and often inviting him and his wife to go sailing around the Bosphorus in the spring. He had been saddened to see her so ill, and now he was glad that she was her old self again. She was beautiful, and poised, and gracious, and even though in no way did she remind him of his departed wife, she did make him think how nice it was to have a woman's touch in a home. He had been so lonely since his wife died. They had been a quiet couple who had been content to spend almost every minute of their free time together, and now he was like a lost soul. They didn't have any children, so now that she was gone, he was more grateful than ever for his job at Turan Holding. It was the only thing that gave meaning to his life. He had worked for Mustafa and Omer for over thirty years, and he was terrified that soon the company they had built would be in such big trouble that it would be beyond hope. That was why, as he was driving home after spending all day Saturday at the office, he had made the detour and had driven directly to the Turan mansion. He just had to tell Cyrielle, she was his only hope. Maybe she could do something before it was too late.

The houseman appeared in the doorway, and Cyrielle ordered their drinks. "Have you been at the office all day? Would you like something to eat also?" she asked Oktay. She knew he worked incredible hours, and she suspected that since he was now a widower, his meals were not what they should be.

Actually he was starving. He had had a coffee and some bread early in the morning, and then had left directly for the office. He had worked straight through, not stopping for lunch. Now it was almost five, and he still hadn't had anything. But he didn't want to impose, or to try and eat while he was talking to her about this terribly important issue, an issue that would have tremendous impact on both their futures.

"No, no, thank you, Cyrielle, I'm fine," he said.

But he was not convincing. Cyrielle saw through him right away. "We'll have the tea sandwiches, and some pastries also," she said, turning her attention back to Oktay. "Your timing is perfect. He's just finished arranging them, so they would be ready when Omer awakens. Don't worry, he can always prepare more. Now please, sit down and tell me why you've come."

Oktay sat across from Cyrielle in the big leather chair. He placed the folder he had been carrying in his lap. Just as he was about to speak, the houseman reentered, bearing a tray laden down with a tea service and an assortment of little sandwiches made with cheese and meats, as well as pastries and fruit. Despite the gravity of the situation he had come to discuss, Oktay's eyes widened at the appetizing display.

"Help yourself, Oktay, please, I know you must not have eaten all day."

"Thank you, that's very kind," he said, taking a selection from the tray.

Cyrielle served the tea and watched as he tried to nibble gently several of the sandwiches. She smiled to herself; she had known that he was ravenous, and she was glad to see him eating the snack so heartily.

"I was hungry," he finally admitted, wiping his mouth with the linen napkin he had been offered. He drank the last of his tea, and his manner turned solemn.

"Cyrielle, I'm afraid I've come to discuss a very serious matter. I deliberated long and hard about whether or not I should come and burden you with the problem, but after a long time thinking about it, I decided that if I didn't, I would always regret it. So here I am."

Cyrielle leaned forward in anticipation of what he would say next. "Yes, whatever it is, I'm glad you did. I'm glad you are taking me into your confidence. Please go on."

"Cyrielle, Turan Holding is in great trouble. Deep, very grave trouble, I'm sorry to say. Over the past year, since Omer has been ill, there hasn't really been anyone in control. Yes, Mustafa does manage to come in one or two days each month, but as you well know, he's in his late eighties now, eighty-seven, if I remember correctly, and he just can't manage to keep up anymore. Besides, it's a totally different company since he turned it over to Omer. Omer built a giant enterprise. Do you realize we manufacture over five hundred different products? Then there's the real estate business, which is an entire empire unto itself. Of course you probably know all of this already.

I've tried to keep control of as much as I possibly can, but I'm not a manager, I'm a financial man, and that's what I've always done for Omer. Your lovely daughter Yasemin, she is an extraordinary woman. She handles herself skillfully, and she has the business sense and professional knowledge to match any man in our organization. She's trying, we all know she's trying, but she can only do so much. She has more than she can handle on her plate. Pardon me for saying this, but if she were a man, the company might just be able to accept Yasemin's stepping right into her father's shoes. But unfortunately . . .

"Anyway, that's not really the point. I've come to tell you that with some of the things I see going on, we're in a terrible position, a position which threatens the entire company. You see, we've been taken advantage of, and the deals have been dirty. They've really been hitting us hard, especially in the factories. They've gone directly to the workers, and in some cases they've been able to convince them that Omer is never coming back to run the company again, and that Turan Holding is finished. You know how vulnerable the workers are. They need their jobs more than anything else, and they will go with the highest bidder. Oh, it's terrible, Cyrielle, it's almost as if an entire campaign has been launched against us, a campaign destined to destroy us if we don't act fast."

"Who is doing this?" Cyrielle asked, already knowing full well the answer she would get, but needing to hear it anyway.

Oktay sighed. "The Boras, of course. Not so much the father but the two brothers; they're evil, straight from the devil, I say, and they'll stop at nothing to get their way. Just last week, in one of our largest plants, they convinced our workers to change to their factory after they had a meeting with them offering more money and promising job security. They're hurting us, Cyrielle, and hurting us badly. And the terrible thing is, I don't know how to stop them. First we need an additional source of money to top their offers, and keep our people, then we need someone to go out and make them believe in the company again."

"Money and management, the old story," Cyrielle repeated. Her voice was calm, but inside the fire of hatred raged. Her disdain for the family who had caused her so much pain and heartache rose once again to the surface. Ever since she could first remember hearing their name, it had been associated with unhappiness and trouble. During the war it had been their eagerness to sell chromium ore to the Nazis, then the tragic boating episode that resulted in her son's death. Over the years, on and off, they had been involved in devious deals, all of which had been slated to hurt Turan Holding in some way. Sometimes they had been successful, but more often, when Omer was at the helm and in tight control, he had been able to thwart their efforts. But now that he was injured they were coming on strong, and apparently they were making a great deal of progress.

"They've got to be stopped," Oktay reiterated.

"Yes, yes, I agree. Oktay, what does Yasemin know about all of this?"

"Yasemin has done wonders with her business. In fact, she's made such a success of it that it takes up most of her attention and energy just to stay on top of it. She concentrates almost all her work at the factories in Bursa. They love her, and they would do anything for her. Her business is safe. Timur and Tayfun have stayed totally away from her, I'm quite sure because of her marriage to Osman. Otherwise, her division would be fair game too, especially because it's so profitable. But they have left it alone. So, to answer your question, she is not really aware of the problems we are having. Even if she were, there's not much she could do. We need heavy financial commitments and a strong manager who can go out into the factories and make the workers believe in us again. Yasemin has been very successful at doing that, but I'm afraid she might not be able to convince everyone all by herself. Unfortunately, even though she is as capable and intelligent as any man, many of these laborers would not listen to her. I'm sorry about that, it is a regrettable fact of our society, but it's true. Yasemin has worked twice as hard as any man to get where she is, but it's going to take more than her efforts alone to save us."

"All right, Oktay, I think I understand the problems, and I have some ideas about what to do. I'm going to need a little time to get it all together, but I will be in touch with you next week."

"Cyrielle, I feel so much better. I'm certain now that coming here was the right thing to do. I knew you would be able to talk to Omer and find a way to help with this. It's so terribly important for all of us."

"Yes, it is, Oktay, and I'm glad you came. Now let me get to work." She did not add that she had no intention of taking these problems to Omer.

"Yes," he agreed, taking the folder from his lap and handing it to her. "Here are some notes I've made about the different divisions. You'll be able to see clearly just how much trouble the Boras have caused. You will know how serious the situation really is."

"Thank you," she said, taking the folder and putting it on the top of the pile she had been working on. "I'll review it this afternoon and get back to you."

"The sooner the better," he urged, "every day the Boras seem to pop up in another area. I'm telling you, they're out to destroy us, I'm sure of it."

"With all the power I have, we will stop them."

The commitment in her voice was so strong, her will so clear, all he could do was nod his agreement.

THE HEADLIGHTS of the car beamed against the darkness of the museum buildings. The powerful lights cut a streak across the large glass walls, and by the time they pulled up next to the entrance the interior spaces were illuminated, and several men moved quickly through the quiet gallery on their way to investigate the unexpected visitors.

"I suppose I should have called and told the guards we were on our way," Cyrielle said. "That would have been the right thing to do. Now I'm going to upset them. I just wasn't thinking."

"Don't worry; they'll recognize the car and they'll unlock the doors for us. If *we* can't get in, who can?" Semra reasoned.

Cyrielle laughed and looked lovingly at her sister-in-law. Once again, as it had been throughout their long relationship, Cyrielle was so glad that Semra was her dear, trustworthy friend. She turned the ignition off and they got out slowly, wanting the guards to see them and to recognize them, so that they were not mistaken for robbers. As they approached the door, the exterior lights came on, putting them under a bright spotlight.

"It's only me—Mrs. Turan," she assured the guard who was peering out from behind the locked front door.

"Ah, good evening, Mrs. Turan," he said with relief in his voice. He was glad he would not have to put his long-forgotten security skills into action. He was visibly surprised to see her there at such a late hour, but after all, she owned the museum, and he supposed she had the right to visit it whenever she wished. He opened the door and stepped aside to allow them to enter. He locked the door behind them and went to turn on the lights in the galleries.

"You may leave the porcelain gallery, and the modern gallery, dark," Cyrielle advised. "We will only be in the rooms with the Impressionists and the Old Masters. And I'll need two men to help me. Please send them in to find us. I want everything we choose to be wrapped and crated, carefully, of course. You'll be able to have that done for me, won't you? I will be by in the morning to pick them up. Please make certain that everything is waiting for me."

"Very well, I will take care of it," the guard said, backing out of the room and heading toward the central light controls.

When the lights came on Cyrielle and Semra began to walk through the quiet spaces.

"I'm so glad you're here with me," Cyrielle told Semra, "it will be much easier for me to do this."

"Cyrielle, it's the right thing to do. And for all the right reasons," she assured her sister-in-law.

The men joined them, and they walked the halls quickly. The clicking of their heels as they crossed the marble floors was the only sound.

Cyrielle had given tonight's project a great deal of thought, and she knew exactly what she was doing. "We'll take that Picasso, this Miró over here, the Chagall, and that other canvas right there. Yes, that's right, the one numbered 123. Semra, do you think the Kandinsky should go?"

"Yes, why not? He's become very popular lately."

"Okay," she agreed, "that one too, please."

She pointed to three or four more paintings, and the men then carefully removed them from their places on the walls.

"Replacing these will be the hard part," she sighed. "I'll have to have the curator take a look and see what will work best. It took us forever to decide about the arrangement to begin with, I just hope it doesn't mean we'll have to rehang the entire gallery. That means repainting, adjusting the lights—it's a big job."

Semra knew the museum was Cyrielle's most treasured possession. It meant so very much to her, and the paintings in it represented all that was left of her family's heritage. She had conceived the idea, executed it, and nurtured it—it was like another child to her—and now she was going to use some of its wealth to help save her husband and his company. Semra admired the brave woman who had experienced so much tragedy in her life. She knew this was hard for her, but as she watched her she noticed that Cyrielle walked with a firm pace, fully aware that what she was about to do was the only choice left to her if she was to fulfill her own happiness and therefore that of her family.

"I think that should do it," she announced after she had selected a few more paintings. "Except for one last thing. Come," she said, leading the way back toward the museum entrance.

"Oh, no, Cyrielle," Semra protested when she saw where she was headed. "Do you have to?"

"Yes, I must," Cyrielle insisted, "I know this will bring a good deal, and even though I love it more than any of the other works, it is also one of the most valuable. It's all right," she said, mostly to reassure herself as she took the small Rembrandt down from the position it had held since the day the museum had opened. Under the tiny drawing was a brass plaque that dedicated the museum to the Lazare family. The names "Dominique, Maurice, Nathalie, Alexandre, and Jacques" were delicately etched on it. "It's all right . . ." she repeated, pausing for a moment to look at the plaque. "Of all the people who would understand what I am doing, my mother would be the first to give her blessing. I'm certain of it."

"Yes, Cyrielle, I'm sure you're right" was all Semra could say. Her thoughts drifted back to the first time she had seen her, as she came off the plane, clutching her small valise to her side. She had been exhausted and confused and frightened, but she would not release the suitcase from her grip. She had slept with her knees pressed securely up against it on the way in from the airport. Semra would never forget watching her as she unpacked the only thing of value she had brought with her from Paris. Her eyes had teared when she unwrapped it from its safe spot inside her lingerie pouch. Semra could remember the day as if it were yesterday, instead of over thirty years ago.

"Come, let's go home," she heard Cyrielle's anxious voice interrupting her recollections. She had done what she had come to do, and she was ready to return to her house. If Omer awakened and found that she was gone, he would be concerned.

"Coming," Semra responded, following her out of the gallery. They drove home in silence, each of them grateful for the other's strength.

The gallery was as beautiful as she remembered it, even though the last time she was there she had been a small child.

She waited patiently in the private office, a grand, elegantly appointed room that was reserved for the gallery's very best customers. She studied her surroundings, taking in every detail. The walls were lined with a seafoam-green moiré silk that served as the perfect background for both the enormous Rubens and the magnificent Titian, which hung in ornate gilded frames on opposite sides of the room. She sat quietly, perched on the edge of the delicate Louis Quinze banquette, staring at the wondrous works of art.

She had been nervous on the trip to Switzerland, and she was glad to have finally arrived with her precious cargo. She had made rather unconvincing excuses to Omer about having to see Dr. Klauber one more time, just for a checkup. If all went well she would be away for three days at the most, but she was praying it would be only two. Semra assured her that she would be right by her brother's side until the moment Cyrielle returned, but still she was concerned. It was the first time they would be separated since the terrible accident. She told herself there was nothing she could do right now except wait; she was here to do what had to be done.

She busied herself by examining the extraordinary colors and vibrancy of the canvas by one of the greatest painters of the Venetian school. In addition to Titian's skill in using color to produce extremely powerful images, his acumen as a draftsman was well developed also. She studied the fine lines of the nude figures in the picture and for a few moments she was lost in her own private thoughts.

"Sorry to have kept you," she heard a voice from behind her say.

She turned at once to see the handsome face of a young man. No more than thirty at the most, he was dressed in a well-cut suit, with a conservative striped tie and light-blue shirt. She thought immediately of Zeki, for the young man appeared to be about the age he would have been.

"I'm sorry again," he offered, extending his hand to her. "I'm Alain, Henri's grandson."

"Hello, I'm pleased to meet you," she replied, offering her hand in return.

"My grandfather will be with you in a moment. He just sent me in to offer his apologies for having kept you waiting at all."

"It's not a problem. I'm just sitting here enjoying the beauty of this extraordinary painting," she said, pointing her hand in the direction of the Titian.

"Yes, it's magnificent, isn't it? It's a study for *The Sacred and Profane Love,* which hangs in the Villa Borghese in Rome.

"Yes, yes, I know it."

"Of course you would, my grandfather has told me of your background. I've had a chance to look at some of the works, and I must compliment you. It is an extraordinary collection."

"The compliments are due my father," Cyrielle replied. "It was he who possessed the remarkable eye."

"Indeed he did," the young man agreed.

The private door opened again and an old man shuffled slowly across the room. He too was stylishly dressed, and even though his shoulders were no longer straight, and he used the edge of the center table in the room to help him navigate his way around the room, it was evident that he had once been a very elegant man. When he neared Cyrielle he raised his head to her. The lenses of his glasses were extremely thick, but his gentle eyes sparkled from beneath them.

"Cyrielle Lazare, welcome to our gallery," he said.

"It's been a long time," she answered. "A lifetime."

"Yes, indeed it has," he agreed, taking the chair next to the sofa and placing his hands firmly on its arms. "Cyrielle, my, my. You are your mother's daughter, aren't you? The resemblance is remarkable. It makes me think I am in a dream. A very wonderful dream, of times so long ago. You know, your father was going to send you here, to stay with my wife and me. But my wife was very sick just before the war, she died in 1941, and we just felt that we could not take proper care of a young girl. Did he . . . did Maurice ever tell you that?"

"No, no, he never mentioned it to me."

"Well, it's true, and I always regretted not being able to have you come. We could have found a way to take care of you, I'm sure. But instead you went off to Istanbul, and I know now that you have made a life for yourself there. Oh, how things happen in our lives, isn't it strange? And now you're back here, with paintings from your father's collection. You know, we used to work together, in a way. Since our tastes were so similar, we would often recommend each other to our clients. One hand always did the other a good turn."

"That I remember. And I do recall coming here. I was very small, maybe only seven or eight, but I remember this room very clearly. It seemed so enormous to me, and the paintings were the largest I had ever seen outside of a museum."

"Yes, I too remember that visit," he said, drifting off into his own thoughts. He pulled out a starched white handkerchief, took off his glasses and dabbed at the corners of his eyes. "I've been very moved by looking at the paintings you brought, Cyrielle. Some of the works—I never knew what happened to them; I remember them as if it was yesterday. I'm honored that you are bringing them to us to sell for you. Since they have been out of circulation for so long, they will cause a great deal of excitement, and because of that I am certain they will bring very good prices. But are you certain you want to sell them?"

"Yes . . . yes. I . . . I have to."

"If it is a question of a temporary situation, I would be delighted to loan you the money, and merely keep the paintings until all is right again."

"That's very kind of you, but no, I think I would prefer to sell them outright. I don't know when I would ever be able to repay you."

"Very well, then, if that's your decision. We accept the paintings, all of them, for sale here. Would you like us to advance you some money against their projected sales price?"

"That would help me immeasurably," she answered.

"I will be happy to do that. You know, ever since it happened, I have regretted telling your father that I would not be able to care for you. Now I think this might be my chance to make up for that mistake in some small way."

"I thank you, Henri, you will probably never know what this means, but I hope you will believe that it is everything to me. Your kindness is greatly appreciated."

"It is the least I can do, my darling Cyrielle, daughter of my dear friend."

She thanked him one final time, kissed both him and his grandson good-bye, took the enormous check and tucked it safely in her handbag, and directed the driver to take her straight to the airport. She had accomplished all that she had wanted to do in only two days, and she couldn't wait to get home to Istanbul and to Omer. Her heart was heavy, knowing that she would probably never again see the beautiful paintings she had sold, but even deeper in her heart she knew that she had done exactly what she needed to do, for the love of her husband was far greater than any attachment she could ever have for a piece of canvas.

The first part of her quest was over, she had the money Turan Holding would need to get them back on their feet again. The second part of her mission would most probably be the more difficult one, but she was buoyed by what she had been able to accomplish in Switzerland, and as she heard the pilot announce that they were making their final approach to the Istanbul airport, she was very confident about her chances for success.

CHAPTER

31

"M AMAN, I don't think we've had lunch together for over a year!" Yasemin exclaimed as the waiter led them to a table at the far end of the lovely restaurant.

"You're right, I know for a fact I haven't been out more than once or twice since we brought your father home."

"Well, I'm happy we're doing it. I'm tired of having a simit and Coke at my desk. The simit is usually stale, and the Coke flat by the time I get to it. This is really a treat."

The two striking women settled themselves at the table. They were both so beautiful and bore such a strong resemblance to each other, that heads never failed to turn when they entered a room. In the crisp fall weather, Cyrielle had selected a smart tweed suit, which was perfectly fitted on her. She wore only the simplest jewelry, a strand of pearls, and her thick gold wedding band. Yasemin looked equally well-put-together in a beige suit with a feminine silk blouse underneath. She had taken to wearing scarves, just as her mother and grandmother before her, and little by little she was managing to decimate her mother's collection. The men in the restaurant turned to look at them, and many of their friends, or Yasemin's business associates, waved hello.

"I want to hear all about your trip. Tell me how it was," Yasemin began once they were seated.

Of course only Semra knew the true reason for Cyrielle's sudden departure to Switzerland. She hadn't wanted anyone else to know until the deal was done and she had achieved her goal. Now was the time she would be able to tell Yasemin the real story and to approach her with her idea. But first she needed to find out a few things from her daughter.

"Oh, I'll tell you everything a little later. Let's talk about you first. How is Osman?"

Yasemin's face lit up at the mention of her husband. "Oh, Maman, he's wonderful. We really are so very happy. He's been terribly busy, though, I think he's traveling too much. But I guess it's all part of the game. He wants to be successful, and if he has to be away from home during these first years while the business is growing so fast, then I guess that's just the way it has to be. For a while, anyway; then I want him to stay home for a time. Long enough to make a baby, at least."

Cyrielle smiled, pleased to hear her daughter talk about having a child. She knew Yasemin would be a loving, caring mother, and she would love to have another grandchild.

"Making one's half the fun!" Cyrielle commented, and at once even she was surprised at herself.

Yasemin looked at her, shocked to hear her mother say this. She had never heard her speak so openly about such things.

"Maman!"

"Oh, Yasemin, don't be so astounded. I just said that remembering all the fun and love and tenderness between your father and me when we were trying to have all of you. That's all I meant. You must enjoy every day of your life."

"I know that, Maman, that's why I'm so happy that you are healthy again, and that *Babacığım* is doing so well. I think in a very short time he's going to be just fine."

"He'll recover, Yasemin, but he'll never be the man he once was. He has some permanent damage that will never heal. He will never again be able to head Turan Holding. Oh, he'll be able to go to the office and serve in some capacity, but the energy and the sharp skills required to run that empire are gone, I'm afraid. Gone forever. Yasemin, that's the main reason why I wanted to have lunch with you today. I want to talk to you about Turan Holding."

"Yes, Maman, I know there are some problems."

"Yasemin, it's more than that. The company is in grave trouble, very grave. Oktay came to see me last week to tell me what was happening. There are things going on which I'm not sure even you know about. Unfortunately, it's once more about the Boras. They are going all over, to every factory and every plant we have, trying, and in many cases convincing, the workers that Turan Holding is a dying company. They are saying that without your father to head it, it will soon collapse and dry up completely. They have convinced many of our workers that they would be better off if they were working for the Boras instead of for us. Apparently most of this vicious activity is being conducted by Timur and Tayfun, Erol seems to be staying pretty much out of it. I've heard he's slowed down lately too, although I'm certain he's fully aware of what his boys are up to. They have been very effective in this campaign, Yasemin, and it has hurt us badly. My trip to Switzerland had nothing to do with seeing Dr. Klauber. I just used that as an excuse so that I would not upset your father. I went to Switzerland for the sole purpose of raising some cash to help tide Turan Holding over until we can get the situation under control."

"How did you get cash?" Yasemin interrupted.

"I sold some of the paintings from the museum."

"Maman, paintings from the museum?" she repeated, horrified. "Paintings from your father's collection?"

"Yes."

"I can't believe what you're saying. Wasn't there any other choice?" Yasemin felt very bad for her mother. She knew that she treasured the paintings more than anything. "Maman, oh, I'm so sorry. I know how much those things meant to you."

"Yasemin, they mean nothing in comparison to your father and to you, and Nevin, and Ali. And of course Semra. You all are my life. Nothing in the world is more important to me than our family's welfare. I did what I had to do, but I did it for love. I found out a very long time ago that if one does things first for love, then every-thing else will fall into place and it will all turn out for the best. I truly believe that. It's one of the thoughts I clung to when I was trying to recover from that terrible depression."

"You're right, Maman, I should listen to you very carefully."

"Yes, I think you should, and what I'm going to suggest is prob-ably going to sound absurd at first, but I want you to think about it. I am convinced it's an idea that will work."

"Okay, I'm listening. . . ."

"Yasemin, the Boras are clearly out to destroy us. They have left you and your little division alone, but only because you are married to Osman. They will stop at nothing to bring our company, the company your father has worked his entire life to make successful, to its knees. Yasemin, I've given it a great deal of thought, and the only one who can save the company is Osman. He has the intelligence, and the connections, and the energy to turn it around. You've got to convince him that he must take control of Turan Holding. You must."

"But, Maman, he would never do such a thing. He's very happy with his own, very profitable little business. I don't think . . ."

"You don't think what, Yasemin? That he would go up against his own family, even though he must know that what they are doing is wrong, and deceitful and underhanded? That they are lying and cheating their way into our business? Yasemin, think about it, and consider it seriously. Here is a chance for you to really have a life, a wonderful life with your husband, and the family you want. It's an incredible opportunity to bring our business back to what it should be, to secure our position and our future. If I thought you could do it alone I would tell you so, but I think it would be an impossible task for a woman in this country. But with Osman's help and presence, together, you could do it. Think about it, I beg you."

Yasemin sat in stunned silence. How could things have become so bad in such a short time? Even more troubling was her concern at learning the tactics used by Osman's own brothers. How could any-one be so low, so cunning, and so totally amoral?

"I will think about it, Maman. Right now I just don't know what to do. I'm so confused by all of this."

"And you should be. It is a most remarkable, disturbing situation. If your father hadn't been injured and incapacitated as he is, none of this would have happened. He would have been here to protect himself, his company, and his family. But he is unable to, and therefore we must do it for him. Talk to Osman, darling, and tell him about this. Be as convincing as you were with your father and me when you decided that you were going to marry him, no matter what we said. If you can be as sure about what you think he needs to do as you were about your love for him, then I know you will have no problem at all. If you need my help, you only have to let me know. Yasemin, I know that between you and Osman you can make things right with Turan Holding once again. You can defeat the lowly tactics of the Boras, and by doing that you can ensure your future and that of your family. Please listen to me; I found out how important family is the hard way. I lost many precious years during my illness, I missed so much of my children's lives, I was so out of touch that I couldn't feel or see, or be a part of your growing up. I would give anything to have those years back again, to live over the time I have wasted. But I know very well that is impossible, so I now am asking you—for your sake as well as your father's, and for your entire family—convince Osman to come aboard and run Turan Holding."

"I'll try, Maman, really I will." Tears of understanding burned bright in her eyes.

"Wonderful, darling, I just hope it's not too late. Move quickly, will you?"

"I'll talk with him tonight," she promised.

CHAPTER

32

YASEMIN, do you realize what you're asking me to do?"

"Yes, Osman, I do. And I've given it a great deal of thought. I wouldn't ask you if I didn't think it was important, and necessary, and exactly the right thing to do. You must merge your company with Turan Holding, and take the reins of the company over and turn it around. You are the only one who can do it. The workers will believe you, they will trust you, they will know that what you are telling them is the truth, and that what they have been hearing has all been nothing but lies. When you admit that your own family has lied to them, just to further their own selfish interests, they will surely believe you. In addition to that, you will have the power of truth on your side. Plus, thanks to Maman's sacrifice, you now have the capital it will take to put things back into shape. Please, darling, you are the only one who can do it. You have the connections, the intelligence, and the drive to pull it off," she continued, echoing her mother's words. "Please, my love, say you'll do it."

"Yasemin, everything you've said is very flattering, and I admit it makes a great deal of sense. But you must realize that you are asking me to denounce my own family to save yours. A move like this will totally alienate me from even the limited relationship I now have with them. That is something which is very difficult for me to swallow, to live with. Even for the sake of having a wonderful and lucrative future."

"Let me ask you this—do you believe that what they are doing is deceitful, wrong at the least, and evil at worst?"

Osman turned to look at her. She was backing him into a corner into which he did not care to be pushed. He studied her face and read the determination in her eyes. In his heart he knew that his brothers were everything she had said; they would lie and cheat and steal in order to make their fortune. Someone had once said that they would sell their own mother for a profit. He knew about everything they were doing: the meetings with the factory workers, the overbidding on properties just to make certain that Turan Holding did not get ahold of them, the stealing of key employees from the corporate office —all of this and more, many things Yasemin didn't know; he had heard it all, and he was disgusted by it. He had been troubled by it for years, it was exactly what had led him to leave the country and, upon his return, to make the decision to operate his own business. But denouncing them, and going head to head against them in a war that he was certain would only end if he brought them to their knees —that was a big price to pay.

He continued staring at the woman who meant the world to him. The woman with whom he wanted to have children, and with whom he would be happy to spend every day of his life. She brought him joy and love, things that he had never had growing up in a family that was as cold and calculating in their personal dealings as they were in business.

Yasemin's expression was resolute, and a thought went through his mind that sent waves of shock throughout his body. He felt himself actually shiver at the idea. There was no doubt in his mind that if he did not agree to her proposal, a proposal which, he had to admit, made perfect sense, in addition to affording them both a wonderful opportunity . . . no, there was no doubt; she was prepared to leave. And that he was not willing to risk. Once Yasemin had chanced losing the approval of her family in order to marry him. They had been fortunate that Omer Turan was such an understanding, generous man. Everything had turned out just fine, and he had not been punished for the sins of his family. Omer had accepted him, and trusted him, indeed had *entrusted* him with his most precious possession, his daughter. Both he and Cyrielle had opened their hearts and their home to him. He had always known that they genuinely cared about him. Now was his chance to repay them both. Now was his chance to prove his love for Yasemin, as she had proved hers for him in the past.

"Yasemin," he began, "I will take on the challenge of running Turan Holding. But just as you were not willing to marry me without first at least speaking with your parents, I will not make a move like this without first discussing it with my father, and with Timur and Tayfun. But I promise you I will be strong, and committed to what I am going to do. I just want to give them the courtesy of telling them first. For I'm afraid that after I am in place, it will be too late. It will be a fight to the finish, and once I pledge myself to do it, there will be no turning back. It will be up to them to decide if they choose to stop their intolerable practices, or if we have to take measures to stop them ourselves."

Yasemin's smile told him how happy he had made her. She rushed to his side and hugged him with all her might. "Oh, darling. There will be some rough times, but I know in the end we will triumph. As a team how can we possibly lose?"

"I hope you're right," he said. "But I'm still concerned about one thing," he added, pulling her arms down to her sides and looking at her with the most serious expression.

"What's that?"

"How will I be able to keep my hands off you at the office?"

"By keeping them on me all the time when we are at home, my angel," she answered, leading him off toward their bedroom, anxious to pleasure him and to show him all the love she felt for him.

CHAPTER
33

$\mathcal{C}$YRIELLE SAT at her dressing table, preparing for bed. She turned up the lights on the makeup mirror and carefully examined her face. She ran her fingers across the delicate skin under her eyes, tracing the lines that had appeared slowly over the years. On her next birthday, a month from now, she would turn fifty. Already she had lived twelve years longer than her mother. She felt blessed, not only for her health, but for the way everything seemed to be turning out.

Osman and Yasemin had become a formidable team at Turan Holding, and for a couple who previously had vowed never to discuss business between themselves, they were a born twosome. The business prospered, and the threat from the Boras diminished.

Nevin was devoted to her son, and Kaya was becoming a fine young man. Last month her daughter had announced that she was seeing someone, someone who was very special to her, and that perhaps, if all went well, they would have a future together. Cyrielle hoped so.

And Ali. She loved him so. Ali was his own special being, so different and so removed from those around him, yet so talented and charming at the same time. He was happy, he had told her so only last week, he continued his tours each season, and as time went on his interest and enthusiasm in the piano continued to grow. Yes, she was indeed a very lucky woman. She was blessed with the things that were important in life, plus a few more, like wealth and good skin, she decided, grinning.

As she reached up to remove the barrette that held her hair, she caught Omer's reflection in the mirror. At first she was startled, for it had been ages since he had come to her room at night. Since his injury he had insisted on sleeping in the room down the hall, the room she had once occupied when she first arrived from Paris. She watched him, her hand frozen on the clasp of the barrette, as he walked slowly toward her.

"Please continue," he said softly, nearing her.

She removed the tortoise clip from her hair, releasing the cascade of ebony silk down the middle of her back. It touched the lace that edged the top of her ivory gown and she shook it free, sending it over her shoulders.

"I used to love to watch you brush your hair at night," Omer said. "When . . . before, when we were together, I would always be disappointed if I came into the room too late, and you had already finished."

Her eyes met his in the mirror. She put the silver-handled brush down and turned to face him. His expression was unmistakable. Even though it had been ages since she had seen it, it was locked in her mind forever, and despite all the changes in this man whom she loved, she was still unbearably attracted to him, and he could still send shivers up and down her spine with a mere glance in her direction.

He raised his arms out to her, and she stood before him as she had not done for years. He pulled her toward him and caressed her loose hair in his hands. He embraced it carefully, stroking it and moving it gently off her face. He lowered his lips to her long neck, and at his touch she felt her legs weaken. It had been an eternity, she had waited each evening for him to come to her, and each night when he didn't come, the wait had become longer and longer. She ached for him, but he had been unable to meet her needs, to fulfill the desires he had taught her to have. He had once possessed her so completely, and now, for so long, there had been nothing.

She moaned against his chest, and her hands found the sash of his robe. She released it, and continued on hurriedly, her fingers searching for the tie of his pajamas.

"Come, love," he said, leading her toward their bed. "Come, I want you, I need you."

"Oh, please," she said breathlessly.

He put her down slowly on the lush sheets, holding his hand under her head as he lowered her onto the pillow. She pulled him to her, and their kisses were as passionate as they had been on their wedding night. She desired him with a power that was so overwhelming she clung to him, for fear of ever losing him again.

"My darling, I've missed you so," she whispered.

"Cyrielle, it has been far too long. You have been so good to me, and for that I love you more than ever. Oh, you are the world to me."

He covered her mouth with his. Soon he found her breasts, and he fondled them as if he were touching them for the very first time. At first his fingers were tentative, he passed his fingertips over her nipples with the lightness of a feather. But soon she could no longer stand it and pressed her hand over his. He pushed her hand aside and placed his mouth on her firm breasts. He suckled her forcefully and she urged him on, even when it began to hurt her, for it excited her more than it pained her. He passed his mouth from one distended nipple to the other until she begged him to stop.

When his fingers reached the center of her, she was swollen and wet, and ready for him.

"Oh, darling, how I've missed you," he said as he entered her slowly.

She arched her back up to him, and as she felt the full power of him, she could no longer hold herself back. He climaxed a mere second later, and they clung to each other as if to life itself.

When Cyrielle awoke she reached out to touch Omer, just to confirm that what had happened the night before had not been a dream. Indeed, he slept quietly next to her, and when he felt her touch he rolled over and took her in his arms. The only one who was unnerved by the events of the previous evening was Omer's therapist, who was shocked to find his room empty when she went looking for him in the morning. But she chose to be discreet and waited patiently down-stairs until Cyrielle appeared and told her that Omer would be skip-ping his daily treatment.

CHAPTER

34

CYRIELLE ENTERED the breakfast room, and as she passed by Omer, who sat reading the newspaper, she leaned over and kissed his cheek. "I think lovemaking agrees with you, darling. You've never looked better."

"It's a secret cure for many of the world's ills," he said. He folded the paper, placed it by the side of his plate, and pulled her back to him, this time kissing her on the lips.

"Ummm . . ." she said, "what a nice greeting, and what a beautiful day. Summer has finally arrived, I feel it in the air. I hope we can go south before it gets too hot!"

"You've become very spoiled, my love," Omer teased.

"Yes, and I love it. I wouldn't want it any other way. Especially now that you are feeling so much better."

Omer's progress over the past three weeks had been remarkable, and even though she liked to joke about it being directly related to the revival of their sex life, she knew that the passion and love they felt for each other did have a great impact on his overall well-being.

"We're going to head for the south right after your party," Omer continued. "I already spoke with Ivy this morning; he will leave the morning after, and we will meet them in Bodrum the following week. He's planned a whole tour from there; we'll go out to Marmaris, and to Kaş and then to the island of Kekova. We'll be out on the water for about three weeks, then we'll put in for a week or two, probably at Marmaris. I'm anxious to see what the two tigers have bought down there. Whatever it is, I'm certain that they have made a good buy. It's sure to become a huge area for tourism in the future."

"Osman was well advised on those purchases, and I just know you are going to be pleased," Cyrielle replied, referring to the major tracts of land he and Yasemin had committed to last year. "They felt it was the way to go, and I think they were absolutely right."

"I do too, Cyrielle. You certainly raised a little dynamo of a businesswoman. Never in a million years did I believe that what she and Osman have done, and in such a short time, would have been possible."

"Faith, Omer, it's all about having faith." She wanted to move on quickly from the conversation about real estate. He might begin to talk about prices, and to ask about where they had found the money to make such huge purchases. Even now that he was well enough to understand, she had never revealed the real purpose of her trip to Switzerland.

She glanced at her watch, then said, "And I wonder just where the little dynamo is now. She said she would stop by on her way to the office to discuss some last-minute plans for the party. Something about the band. Omer, do you really think we need a band aboard the *Meltem?* I think it might be a bit too much."

He sighed, folding the paper once more. "Cyrielle, of course we need a band. Just three or four pieces, that's enough. I thought we went over all of this before. Even though I can't really kick up a storm yet, I thought it would be very nice to have music. I don't think it would be too good to invite thirty of your friends to celebrate your fiftieth birthday, and then just have them stand around the boat. Yes, I think a band is in order."

"All right, all right, a band it will be. But if she doesn't get here soon, I won't even be around to discuss it with her. I'm due up at the museum for a meeting at eleven. It's already ten-twenty."

"Maybe she had some emergency at the office. It's a wild place up there these days with the two of them at the helm."

Omer was now able to go to the headquarters of Turan Holding for an hour or two each week. His office had remained untouched, even the fresh flowers and magazines were delivered weekly and arranged as they always had been. It was clear that Osman and Yasemin had things under control, and the company was prospering, but he still loved to feel as much a part of it as he possibly could. He had resigned himself to the fact that he could never be in charge again, and between the three of them they had come to an understanding that would benefit all involved.

"No, if something was holding her up, Leyla would have called. I'm really becoming worried, darling. Do you think I should call and find out? I didn't talk to Yasemin yesterday, she was out in the afternoon and I had to leave a message." Even though she considered herself fully recovered, she had still not lost the occasionally overwhelming fear and anxiety sometimes brought on by a completely normal circumstance.

"Cyrielle, it could be the bloody traffic, or any one of a number of things. I would give her another ten minutes, and then, if she hasn't shown up, you can call. Enjoy your breakfast now. She'll be here before you know it."

Seta served the usual selection of *beyaz peynir,* the white cheese Cyrielle loved so much, tomatoes, cucumbers, olives, and fresh bread, with an assortment of jams and honey. She took Omer's advice and began eating and reading the remaining section of the paper. She was absorbed in an article on the diplomatic problems brewing in Cyprus when she heard the sound of her daughter's voice coming from the kitchen.

"No, Seta, nothing to eat, thank you," she heard her say. "Are they still having breakfast?"

Cyrielle put the paper aside as Yasemin entered the room. She was dressed in a simple cotton dress. Her hair was tied back with another of her mother's scarves, and on her feet she wore plain sandals. She looked like a country girl. The only giveaway that she was a successful businesswoman was the attaché case she carried, and the additional stack of papers she held in her arms. Cyrielle took one look at her and knew that something was wrong.

"Yasemin, whatever happened to you? You look awful. You're

pale and you're perspiring," Cyrielle said, rising and walking toward her. "Did you have an accident? And why are you carrying all those things?"

Despite her disheveled look and her obvious discomfort, she smiled at her parents. "No, Maman, I did not have an accident. And I'm carrying all of these things for *Babacığım*, they're some reports he wanted to read," she said, putting them down on a nearby table. "Oh . . ." she moaned as another wave of nausea swept over her. "Oh, will it be like this for long?"

"Like what?" Cyrielle asked, then she studied her daughter as Yasemin held her stomach and tried to quell the awful feeling. Suddenly she knew.

"Oh, Yasemin, are you . . . are you?"

"Yes, I am, Maman. Oh, I'm so excited . . . but this sickness. Every morning. I've missed two meetings this week already because of it. Will it last long?"

But Cyrielle wasn't listening. She knew that the morning sickness would pass, she had had it too, especially when she was carrying the twins. But she was far too excited by the news to dwell on that right now.

She went to Yasemin and hugged her. "Oh, sweetheart, I'm so happy for you. When did you find out? What did Osman say?"

But Yasemin was too sick to respond, and she extracted herself from her mother's embrace and waved her hand as she hurriedly left the room. Cyrielle watched her go, knowing that she would probably prefer to be alone for a few moments, until it passed. She turned to Omer, who sat watching the entire scene from his position at the breakfast table.

"Oh, Omer, isn't is wonderful?"

"Yes, it is. She will be a terrific mother. I know that they have wanted this for a long time." He smiled. "How do you feel about being a grandmother again?"

"Just fine, thank you. And you, Grandfather?"

"Fine too. The only troubling thing is that it seems like it was only yesterday when you drove to the office to tell me that you were pregnant. Remember?"

"I sure do," she answered. "To me, in some ways it seems like yesterday, and in other ways, it seems that an eternity has passed since that afternoon. So many things have happened to us since then, both good and tragic. But when I hear news like this, the good always seems to outweigh the bad."

He smiled and they hugged each other in their happiness as they waited for their daughter to return.

When Yasemin came back to the breakfast room the color had returned to her face, and she said she felt fine again.

Cyrielle asked her the usual battery of questions and Yasemin answered as best she could. "Maman," she insisted, "all of this is very new to me, you know. I just found out yesterday afternoon, and I was only able to tell Osman late last night when he came home from Ankara. I thought I had a virus or something, it never occurred to me that I would get pregnant so quickly. We only decided to start trying last month. Anyway, enough about me. We have loads of things to discuss about your party."

She pulled out a folder marked "Party" from her briefcase. "The band. The food." She shuffled notes and scraps of paper. "Ali says he wants a little time so he can play a piece from his new tour. Those things, and a hundred more. And we have to talk about presents. That's the most fun! Osman and I want to get you a great present. Is there something special you would like?"

Cyrielle looked up at the daughter who had given her such joy, and whom she loved so very much. "Yasemin, you've just given me the most wonderful gift I could ever imagine. Everything in the world pales in comparison to a new life."

Yasemin's eyes filled with tears, and she went to her mother's arms, knowing that truer words had never been spoken.

CHAPTER

35

*I*S THAT RAIN I hear?" Cyrielle asked when she awoke on the morning of her birthday. She raised her head in the direction of the windows and watched as a sheet of water lashed against the windowpanes. "Oh, no, it can't be! It never rains in Istanbul in July."

"Not for very long anyway. It will pass quickly. Don't worry, my darling. I promise that by this evening it will be clear and beautiful for your party."

"From your mouth . . ."

"Yes," he said, "but for now, there's no point in getting up just yet." He turned to her and took her in his arms. He nestled his cheek along her face and down her neck and she responded by moving closer to him.

"I always love the feel of your beard in the morning," she told him. "There's something very seductive about it."

"You think so?"

"Yes, I do."

"I'm glad. Because you are about to be seduced."

She giggled like a schoolgirl as he ran his face along her neck, down across her chest and finally to the tips of her breasts. She pulled his mouth down to her and he took her nipples gently between his lips, kissing and caressing her until her laughter turned to soft moaning.

"Open for me, angel," he urged as he ran his hands between her legs, "I want to make love to you to celebrate the beginning of your next fifty years."

"Oh, it sounds so old," she complained.

"But I will make you feel so young," he assured her, positioning himself between her long legs.

"Yes, yes, I think I would like that."

Omer pleasured her as he always did, and as they reached the pinnacle of their climax, she felt as one with him.

"Oh, Omer, I do love you so."

"And I love you, darling."

They lay still in each other's arms, relishing the intimacy of their life together. Omer held her close, kissing the top of her head over and over again, as if he couldn't get enough of her. "You are delicious," he declared, "and I think we should start the day with a present, don't you?"

"What was that I just had?"

He laughed. "Oh, that? That was standard fare. No, I have something special for you, and I want to give it to you now, while we are alone."

Her expression was a mixture of curiosity and confusion as she watched Omer climb out of bed. His first steps were still tentative, but as he put on his dressing gown and walked toward the mahogany secretary on the other side of the room, he gained confidence. He took a long rectangular box from one of the drawers, put it in the pocket of his silk robe, and returned to her.

He climbed back into bed next to her. "Darling, this is for you. They're to thank you for all you've done for me, all throughout our wonderful marriage, but especially during this past year. I know that it has probably been more difficult for you than for me, but I want you to know that if you hadn't been here with me, by my side, I would never have recovered. Of that I am certain. I love you, my darling," he said, handing her the leather box.

She was speechless, and she covered his hand with hers as she accepted the present. She continued to look at him, into the face she still found so devastatingly handsome. Then, with the enthusiasm of a little girl, she lifted the lid of the box. Inside was a stunning necklace, a necklace that matched the bracelet she had found in the band of a summer hat so long ago. There were four rows of many glistening diamonds, with two sapphires and two rubies inserted at each side. It was glorious and even more special for what it represented. Their children—the girls Yasemin and Nevin, and the boys Ali and the lovely Zeki who, even though he had been gone for years, was in her thoughts every single day.

"Oh, Omer, it's beautiful." She looked up at him with tears of joy rimming her eyes.

"I thought you'd like it and I felt that now was just the right moment to give it to you. I've had it for a long time. I bought it at the same time I bought your bracelet, but somehow, as the years passed, with all that happened to us, it never seemed right to give it to you."

"You never thought I could handle it, did you?" she asked, her expression now one of pure, unadulterated happiness. "Well, you were probably right, for a very long time I couldn't have. But now everything is fine. We've had our share of tragedies, but we've also had a great deal of laughter, and an excess of love. Oh, Omer, thank you. I love you."

"Happy birthday, sweetheart."

They kissed again, and then, with one sure motion, she threw back the covers and sprang from the bed with the eagerness of a young child on Christmas morning. Tonight she would be surrounded by her family and good friends, and she did not want to miss a moment of this special day.

As Omer had promised, during the day a strong, mild wind swept across the Bosphorus and the clouds disappeared. They were replaced by a crisp, clear blue sky free of any trace of pollution or smog. The afternoon temperature was in the low eighties, and as the sun slipped behind the hills, the evening promised to be one of rare beauty.

Semra helped with all the last-minute details, fielding questions and acting as the majordomo. The pace in the house built to a frenzy in the hours just before the guests started to arrive. Caterers dashed from the kitchen to the boat waiting at the front of the house. All the food had been prepared under Seta's discerning nose, and it was then loaded onto the smaller boat and taken out to the *Meltem*. Flowers, liquor, chairs, tables, linens, silver, and the musicians' equipment were all transported in this manner. The *Meltem* was slowly being turned into a beautifully decorated party setting.

"It's going to be a spectacular evening," Semra assured Cyrielle. "But you should try to relax a little. You're as nervous as a bride."

"Well, I am," Cyrielle agreed. "I'm worried about Omer. This is the first big social event he's been a part of since his accident. I just hope it's not too much for him."

"Don't worry, Cyrielle. If you remember, it was his idea to begin with. He was dead set on giving you a big party. I know he's up to it. He looks well, and he has the stamina for it now. I wouldn't have said that a little while ago, but he's doing so well now I just know it's going to be fine. And good for him too, seeing all his old friends. Besides, the doctors would never have allowed it if they didn't think it was all right. They've been very strict with him up until now. They know what they're doing. Now why don't you go upstairs and start to dress. You even have time to lie down for a few minutes if you want. Everything is under control here, go ahead. It's your night, you need to look your very best, my dear sister-in-law. Go upstairs and take your time getting ready."

Cyrielle hugged Semra, feeling much more at ease after their conversation. She heeded her advice and headed upstairs to prepare for her big party.

When she descended the stairs a few hours later, looking her most glamorous, she was surprised to hear laughter coming from the small room at the front of the house. When she went to investigate, she found Omer, Semra, Yasemin and Osman, Nevin and Ali there, all dressed in their evening clothes. Omer had a linen napkin wrapped around a bottle of champagne. He held it in the air as he gently loosened the cork.

"Ah, there you are," he said when he saw her. "You look lovely." He liked the simple silk column dress she had chosen to wear for the occasion. Its color was the sharpest red, similar to, but even more vibrant than the one she had worn to the museum gala years earlier. The bracelet sparkled on her wrist, the matching collar shimmered on her elegant neck. "There's no doubt that you are the birthday girl.

"Actually," he continued, "we were just about to send the troops out looking for you. It's time for us to have some champagne before the rest of the crowd arrives."

"What a good idea," she agreed, coming forward to kiss each of her children and Semra.

Omer filled the tall crystal flutes, and when they had all been served, Yasemin stood to toast her mother.

"Maman," she began, "I've been selected to give the toast. Why, I'm not quite sure, but I guess it's because Nevin and Ali have always thought I would never be at a loss for words." They all laughed. "But tonight I'm going to keep it short. We just want you all to know how much we love you, and how glad we are that you are well again, and that you have helped to make *Babacığım* well again. But more than anything, we're all happy to be together here tonight. You've taught us what family really means, and what is important in life. And for that we will always cherish you."

She raised her glass in toast and then went to kiss her mother. Cyrielle hugged her to her chest, and was soon surrounded by Ali, Nevin, and Osman as well. Cyrielle wiped the tears from her eyes and managed a small thank-you.

"And now for the presents," Yasemin recovered quickly. "Yes, this is from all of us," she announced, taking a small package from its place atop the brightly colored sofa and passing it to her brother. "This is from your children, but credit for the idea goes to Aunt Semra. As always, she helped us out when none of us could come up with any ideas. We hope you'll like it."

Cyrielle accepted the elegantly wrapped parcel from Ali's hand. She untied the ribbon and then pulled the paper away to reveal the small Rembrandt drawing. She had last seen it in the gallery in Switzerland. When she left that day she had been certain that she would never see it again. But now here it was, returned to its rightful owner, where she vowed it would remain forever. She held its frame in her trembling hands and stared down at it, the most beautiful memory of her mother and her own family.

When she had control of her emotions, she looked up at Semra. "How did you ever get it back?"

"Oh, it wasn't easy, I admit. Monsieur Henri had sold it to a man in London, who is now living in New York. We finally tracked him down, and after much discussion, we persuaded him to sell it back to us. It was a lot of correspondence, that's for sure, but I can see by the look on your face that it was well worth it. I can tell you that we were committed to travel to the ends of the earth to find it."

Cyrielle looked at Omer, and in that moment when their eyes met she knew he had found out what she had done to save Turan Holding during its darkest hour. He smiled at her knowingly, and the look in his eyes confirmed to her that she had done exactly the right thing, and just how much he loved her for it.

They heard the sound of Ivy's gruff voice as he pulled the small boat into their dock. He had come to take them out to the waiting *Meltem,* so they would be aboard when their first guests arrived.

"Come, my birthday girl, your ship is waiting." Omer laced one of his arms through Cyrielle's, the other through Semra's, and he led the procession toward the edge of the terrace. Osman, Yasemin, Nevin and Ali linked arms and followed.

Ivy raced the engine and started out across the black waters. From the boat they looked back to watch the outline of the city, made so magical by the many minarets that pierced the clear sky. The silhouette of the Topkapı Palace was visible in the distance. The lights of the *yalıs* along the waterway were illuminated, highlighting the lovely residences. It was an exquisitely beautiful scene, and Cyrielle never tired of looking at this enchanting city, so steeped in history and rich in cultural traditions.

As they neared the grand yacht, anchored and awaiting them just a few hundred yards in front of their house, Omer said to Ivy, "Now, please."

Ivy immediately signaled to his men, who were waiting on deck, and suddenly the entire craft was alight with millions of tiny white lights. They had been strung across each of the three tall mainsails, down the ropes to the bow and back to the stern. Hundreds of strands of lights had been woven in and out, up and down the entire length of the yacht. Every inch of the grand dame was outlined in a band of glistening white dots. They sparkled brilliantly in the darkness, illuminating the ebony waters. The *Meltem* had never looked more graceful; she was a commanding, splendid presence on the water. It was indeed the perfect place to celebrate a memorable birthday.

"Oh, Omer, it's magnificent," Cyrielle exclaimed, holding her husband's hand tightly as she stared with wide-eyed excitement at the beautiful sight. She was thinking of the wonderful future that stretched before her. There was so much time left, and she knew in her heart that she was destined to live every minute of it to the fullest.